Selah

WRITTEN BY JONI D. HAYWORTH

Selah

WRITTEN BY JONI D. HAYWORTH

XULON PRESS

Xulon Press
2301 Lucien Way #415
Maitland, FL 32751
407.339.4217

www.xulonpress.com

Printed in the United States of America

Paperback ISBN-13: 978-1-6322-1663-2
Hard Cover ISBN-13: 978-1-6322-1664-9
Ebook ISBN-13: 978-1-6322-1665-6

Dedication

—

To those who labor, finish the race!

Chapter One

Selah was mad. Sweeping the small courtyard angered her even more. The sound of a broken clay pot startled her. She didn't notice she swept it off its perch while waiting for her husband to come home. *Where was he?* This was the third time this week. He had been gone a full day. The noise of the city different this week. Passover. Pilgrims converging to the city to celebrate. The dust thick from the constant traffic, beggars too had begun to surface, a prosperous time for them as they took advantage of the joyful feast. She longed for the sea. Especially now. Tiberias. The water called to her, worry and anxiousness left at its banks. How many days had she attempted to count the diamonds contained within its embrace, the sun warming her very soul, only the calls of the local fishermen disrupting her tally? She could almost smell the nets as they dried against the rocks, a remnant of small fish clinging to life before a very discerning flock of gulls discovered their hiding place. She missed her mother's cooking; the aroma of lentil soup would draw her away from the soft lapping of waves. There would be fresh bread and honey cakes as a special treat. It was this comfort she longed for. The city had been in an uproar. No one could escape the political climate or the Roman soldiers, the streets filled with their clanging armor and hideous hats. She loved Jerusalem. She had traveled each year with her family and childhood friends the required feast times and marveled at the contrast of her quiet, hillside home. This is where she met Malchus. She was nine, he was twelve. He threw a small pebble at her to get her attention. She threw it back. Eleven years later she found herself sweeping Jerusalem's dust from her courtyard, careful to pick up the clay chards, the last few years a relative blur.

Malchus traveled accompanied by friends to bring her to the place he prepared. The journey was uneventful. A bride should be excited at prospects of beginning a family, settling in a new city, but she wasn't. Malchus and his friends spoke and argued about politics, the Romans, and of course God. He was consumed. They were passionate. She was bored. When they arrived that first late afternoon, the colors of the city were hues of gold and red, the sun smiling on every building. It was breathtaking. The amber glow however didn't benefit the dull colors of her home. Her heart began to race. She wasn't prepared for this. She glanced over her shoulder hoping to see her family following at a safe distance, ensuring her things would be fine. *Let's just turn around and go back,* she would say quite firmly and Malchus would recognize the sensibility of her request. She couldn't breathe. The dust of the city clung to her skin, and filled her eyes and nose. Malchus helped her dismount the donkey she rode upon; her legs numb from both the travel and the unknown. He did his best to give her an encouraging smile searching her face for any sign of approval. He worked hard to secure this home. The location was perfect. He was close to the house of Caiaphas and she would have every convenience Jerusalem offered.

He glanced at her as she collected her belongings and waited to speak. *What did he really know about her?* They had met in this very city during Sukkot. It was the best week of his life. Her family settled to celebrate the feast close to where his built their temporary booth. She was beautiful with shiny, dark chestnut hair and eyes the color of the sea. He wondered about this young girl whose laughter filled his heart. He watched her for two days before he finally had opportunity to get her attention. She was under the shelter of her booth. He shifted his weight thinking about how to approach her. As his feet continued to shuffle, he quickly glanced around for her parents. He uncovered several small rocks. Without hesitation, he tossed one at her. She looked at it in amusement, picked it up and threw it back. He caught it and they both began to laugh. Now, searching the eyes of this carefree girl he fell in love with, she found his hand and simply said, "Shall we go in?" The gate didn't fall off its hinges and he watched her intently as she seemed to study every part of the courtyard. Yes, it needed a woman's touch and he knew it wouldn't be long when it would feel like home. He could feel his heart swell. She looked at the front door, the mezuzah placed where she anticipated. Tradition. She smiled at the familiarity. This was their home. Here they would have their own children. The thought brought a blush to her cheeks, she cast a quick look to see if he noticed. Together they entered into this new life and future, nothing certain and full of wonder.

"You have to go now?" Selah needed him to show her around the city, where to go for grain and perhaps find dyed garments to bring color into the bland stone house.

"Yes, I must, Caiaphas is waiting for me," Malchus responded.

"I know, but couldn't I go along and wait for you to finish?" she asked anxiously.

"I don't know how long I'll be Selah. The zealots are causing great unrest again."

"What does this have to do with you Malchus?"

He brought her face between his hands, "Selah, don't concern yourself about these things. There will be plenty of time for you to get acquainted with the markets and I can arrange for some of the older women to come and take you to purchase our needs."

"I don't want to go with strangers," she cried. "I want to go with you! And if you don't have time, I would rather go by myself. I'll be careful. The markets are just outside our door, only a short walk. Please Malchus, I must be permitted to go on my own. I'll take Balaam with me."

"You named that donkey Balaam?" he laughed now.

"Yes, from a story I was told. The prophet couldn't see or didn't know where he was going and his donkey told him or something like that," she looked quite serious which made him laugh again. "All I know is the donkey kept him out of trouble and my little Balaam will do the same," she eyed him coolly. "Please Malchus, I'll be fine," she assured him.

Caiaphas would be waiting. He needed to go. "Agreed, on one condition," he finally spoke. She leaned in to kiss him, hoping to soften the condition. "Will you make your mother's lentil soup?"

She jumped with excitement. "Yes, and maybe I'll find pomegranates or dates and we'll have a feast tonight!" He couldn't resist her enthusiasm. Her eyes sparkled when she was happy.

"Pomegranates and dates it is!" he whirled her around as he headed towards the door.

Caiaphas was waiting, Malchus saw him through the open window as he made his way through the outer courts. He could hear shouting behind him. He knew the discussions today would be of zealots, tax collectors and the Temple's finances. He understood the zealots. *Why did we want to live peacefully with the Romans?* They were compromising the city and their brutality no one comprehended. They were taxing for everything! The people were becoming restless and it only took one loud voice to cause division.

"Barabbas!" they shouted. One afternoon when leaving the Temple, a roar arose from several blocks away. He ran towards the crowds. Barabbas had been accused of murder and somehow evaded arrest. The cries of his followers drowned out the commands of the soldiers, it was complete chaos. Now as he completed his inspection of Caiaphas' inner room, he heard the name once more.

"Barabbas! This zealot will be the death of us! He and his so-called followers are stirring up the emotions of the people to not pay taxes and it's affecting the Temple. They need to obey the law!" Many fists were pounding the table. He didn't want to enter the room, but it was his duty. He was there at Caiaphas' bidding. Most times he listened with half interest, but lately there had been much conversation. He positioned himself in his usual place, ready to serve. What he didn't enjoy was playing messenger. Caiaphas chose to remain discreet and summoned him often to deliver letters to select members of the Sanhedrin, and one place he prayed he would never return. The home of Pontius Pilate. He thought him a cruel man. He recoiled at the memory of Pilate reading the message from Caiaphas, the low light of the room hiding his scowl. He mumbled to his sentry's and with a whoosh and salute they disappeared into the night, Malchus dismissed with a wave of his hand.

"Malchus! Can't you hear me? Should I shout again?" Caiaphas wasn't angry, Malchus knew him too well; he was impatient.

"Make sure my interior room is well lit and there's water. You may be dismissed for the day."

He practically ran out. *Why would Caiaphas need his room lit for the evening?* His mind raced. Part of him didn't care, but with the rise of Barabbas and taxes increasing, many were disgruntled. And there was the other man who was causing commotion, disrupting at times at the Temple of all places and had followers of his own. Jesus. No one was talking about him. He wasn't inciting violence like Barabbas, but he was causing a stir. When one of the elders mentioned his name, Caiaphas became irate. He never saw such hatred on his face. This Jesus had done nothing to gain this reaction. There were many that called themselves prophets. They never lasted. Someone told Caiaphas Jesus had been baptized in the Jordan River. This didn't provide any response, but when some said they heard a voice from heaven, Caiaphas went pale. He was unsure, was it shock, disbelief that caused him to lose color? He sat waiting. Caiaphas said nothing. He arose, beckoned for him to follow and commanded that this "story", this "fable" never be repeated again within the Temple walls.

Selah and Balaam were having fun. The city began to swell this late morning and she and Balaam took their time through the narrow passageways. Balaam found every piece of dropped food and didn't have to be coaxed once all the way to the open market. The spices were pungent. She smelled a hint of cinnamon, a rarity indeed. She didn't know where to look first. She felt grown up. No more hiding behind her mother's tunic, the aggressive merchants shouting their bargains. Her mother knew how to haggle, she didn't. No time like the present.

"How much for these pomegranates please?" she held her place.

"Beautiful eyes, for you I sell all for just a smile," the toothless grin made her uneasy.

She settled on three. She was amazed at the clamor of the people. She stopped to admire rich, vibrant scarves. Blues and purples, even scarlet danced in the soft breeze.

"How much?" She wouldn't haggle with this woman; she looked all business. The woman eyed her suspiciously and turned suddenly to disappear behind the opening of her tent. Before Selah could decide if she didn't understand her, she reappeared with a beautiful turquoise scarf. She gasped. It was iridescent, strands of silver woven through and the color, it reminded her of the sea.

"I'll take it!" Selah smiled at the woman who seemed to have known she would love it and had reserved it, hidden from everyone else. She felt special.

"It will look beautiful with your eyes, yes?" The woman now smiled, friendship in her greeting.

"I've never seen such a wonderful color. Why it shimmers when you turn it, look!" The woman draped it around her shoulders bringing it close to her face.

"Yes, it matches your eyes." Selah didn't remove it from her shoulders. She paid the woman. The merchant grabbed both her hands and simply said, "Shalom."

"Peace to you as well, thank you," Selah replied. Her fingers couldn't stop touching the soft material. *Would Malchus like it? Would he think I spent too much? Should I hide it waiting for the right opportunity to reveal it? Perhaps I could simply wear it as a veil and nothing else, and surely, he would have no objections.* She giggled to herself. Balaam turned and seemed to know exactly what she was thinking. *Crazy donkey.*

Malchus was waiting for Selah to return. He hoped she was able to navigate the market and avoid contact with any who would do her harm. She was young and naïve. *Her and her donkey!* He couldn't believe she named him Balaam. He laughed out loud. The small room echoed his outburst which made him laugh all the more. He heard the gate open and jumped to his feet. He hadn't laughed like that in months, it put a spring in his step.

Selah was surprised to see him home so early. She was grateful however as he helped her unload Balaam of all her purchases careful not to squash fresh greens neatly tied in small bundles. "I found cinnamon and raisins!" she proclaimed quite proudly.

He started a small fire and she busied herself putting things in order. He watched her closely, amused at the attention she gave to the smallest detail. Their home had a complete transformation. She had made curtains from garments she had outgrown. There were flowers on the table and the fresh herbs she began growing in small clay pots sat like good soldiers on the ledge he carved out on one wall. She was humming now as she cut carrots, celery and leeks to add to the lentils. He checked on Balaam secure behind their sleeping chamber and gazed up to the sky. There alone in the back of his small home with the sky as his witness, he felt a peace he'd never experienced. He looked around nervously for a neighbor's unwanted presence. He began to smell dinner, Selah's sweet voice easily heard as she removed the window covering to let fresh air cool off the house. They sat lounged against pillows and talked about their day. She made him smile while relaying all her haggling for pomegranates and spices and how Balaam ate all the way to the square. She continued describing all she saw and he didn't interrupt her enthusiasm. It had been good for her to get out on her own and discover the city where they first met. Suddenly all her chatter abruptly ended and he saw her watching him.

"What is it?" he asked.

"Nothing Malchus, it just seemed you stopped listening."

"No Selah, I was listening," he brushed her hair back in response.

"I haven't told you about something I bought for myself," she said softly. He waited for her to continue when she jumped up and said, "Don't move Malchus, I would rather show you." With the light of the small lamp, she gingerly stepped back into the room, wearing only her new turquoise scarf.

Pilate was pacing. Caiaphas was never on time. *No wonder this country was so easily conquered, no sense of order.* He was growing weary of these meetings, the same grievances over and over. He thought he'd go mad if he heard the word taxes one more time.

"Prefect, Caiaphas has arrived," his sentry stood motionless awaiting his command.

"Send the High Priest in." Pilate wasn't in the mood for his nonsense and rambling on today. It was always a dilemma. Caiaphas would pontificate about his Temple, what this god of theirs set forth for the people, how they accepted Roman rule, they only wanted to be at peace. Pilate had other words he didn't want to hear today, he had composed a short list; taxes, Barabbas, zealots, prophet, he was giving himself a headache.

"Caiaphas, be brief, I have a busy schedule today," he barked at him as if he were a guard, statuesque among his furnishings.

"I will Prefect. I've come to ask your soldiers to stop this wild man baptizing in the Jordan River."

Pilate stood with his mouth agape, incredulous. "Are you mad? You want me to direct resources of a Roman army to run down some rogue man who is playing in the river? Honestly Caiaphas, I thought I've heard and seen about everything in this city, but your request is ridiculous and has no bearing to Rome." He now had a new word to add to his list, *Caiaphas*.

"Pilate, let me explain our concern. We follow the Law of Moses and this man is confusing our people. He's mad, I tell you, but more and more people are seeking him while he shouts to repent," Caiaphas felt weak repeating the words of John the Baptist. "Why it's blasphemous. I'm High Priest; our law dictates that I make atonement in the Temple every year. I wouldn't ask but our law," he stopped speaking when he saw Pilate shuffling parchments becoming impatient.

"Law? Whose law? Do you not know to this day what law governs your people? Tell me Caiaphas, do you need me to explain my concerns about what you're asking? I will not grant this request. Rome is the law here. I am the law. I don't care about a silly man shouting in a river. You must think Rome is bored here, is that what you and your council suspect, that we came here out of boredom?"

Malchus stood outside waiting, the guards looking at him with disdain. He heard several stories the past year of the behavior of these soldiers. There were about three thousand in the city. How many followers did Barabbas have? Not enough! Rome would send legions. It was better to pay tribute! He didn't look away from their mocking faces. They were servants as he, no different in his mind with the exception of who they served.

Caiaphas hurried past him and he practically ran to catch up. He tried to read his face. *Did the meeting go well?* His steps were hurried and Caiaphas' jaw firm. He attempted to block those who wanted to greet him as he made his way back to the Temple. But no one approached. It was then he followed the gaze of the crowds who were approaching another man. It was silent. There was no shouting, no loud voices, no jostling of the people. Caiaphas stopped abruptly and his eyes on the crowd ran into him.

"Watch yourself, my robes," Caiaphas spoke harshly. "What is it? Who are the people gathered to see?" They both hurried up the steps when a few men shifted from where they were standing giving them a clear view. Jesus. He could only stare. Jesus, the man he recently heard about, this was who John the Baptist claimed was from God or the people said they heard a voice from heaven declaring as much. The Sanhedrin had an emergency meeting that evening after Caiaphas' spies came to his home with their reports.

"Malchus, let us get away from here. I haven't time to listen to yet another madman. But go, find out what he's saying. Is he a follower of Barabbas or does he also hide out in the wilderness making false claims about God? Go!" He was at the top of the stairs before Malchus moved. By the time he made his way towards the gathering of people, Jesus was gone. Caiaphas would have another disappointing report.

Selah walked briskly to the market. She didn't need anything, well, she needed a friend. She hoped to find the woman who clothed her in the color of the sea. She almost skipped as she thought how she might begin their conversation. She began to recognize the pungent spices and to her relief, the woman was there.

"Hello again," the woman smiled and Selah returned the greeting.

"My name is Selah, I'm so happy to see you, I, we, I mean my husband, I mean we, well I just love my new scarf." *Why am I so tongue-tied?* She knew and cast her eyes down a little, a brief smile resting at the corners of her mouth.

"Yes of course I remember, the blue with the silver thread worked through it. I was saving it for myself, but when I saw you, and you have such an unusual eye color, I had to show it to you. I'm glad you and your husband like it. I'm Kezia, it's nice to meet you Selah," she looked around a little nervously, "and this is Mary." Selah said hello, Mary only stared.

"I was just finishing up for the day," Kezia said. "Please, let us sit inside and get out from the heat of the day." Mary followed, still staring.

Once inside and after her eyes adjusted from the bright sunlight, Selah was overwhelmed by the magnificence of all the rich, vibrant material. She let her eyes linger as she gazed from corner to corner. Kezia also had jewelry and bottles of perfume. She could stay inside all day to touch the fabric and let the silk caress her hands. Kezia watched her as she poured her a cup of water.

"Kezia, these are beautiful! I've never been in such a place where one could choose from so many colors. Where did you purchase all this wonderful material? Have they come from the East? My mother told me men traveled here and brought their treasures and it must be true!" Kezia began to respond but Selah was giddy.

"Why look at this one!" She pulled a dark magenta silk robe from the pile closest to where she sat down. She never expected the material to feel so cool to her touch. She briefly held it to her cheek. "Oh, I'm so sorry, I shouldn't have taken such liberty. Who can purchase these garments? They must cost a fortune! Can you tell me, who in this city would buy this magnificent robe?" her eyes were as big as saucers and Kezia enjoyed her queries.

Kezia laughed, "First call me Kezi. Yes, our people cannot afford this type of robe so I sell to the Romans. I charge them triple what I normally would. One way to get our taxes back! One day several soldiers stopped by, and hidden behind the group was Pilate!"

Selah drew closer. "Pilate, the Prefect?"

"Yes, he paced back and forth asking questions. At first, I was uncertain why he was here, and then he saw one of those robes. It shimmered like the sun does right before it sleeps, gold and brilliant and he just pointed and said, "That one" to one of his guards who approached me, asked how much, I gave him the price and he practically threw the money at me. They were gone in a matter of a few seconds. Can you imagine one of my robes on the wife of our oppressor? So, my new friend, where are you from?" Kezi decided they were close in age and her surprise visit this day was welcomed.

"Tiberias," Selah said.

"Tiberias!" Kezi now echoed. "I'm from Magdala, and so is Mary!" Mary remained silent.

"Kezi, we were neighbors! Why some of my family members moved up to Magdala and it's truly not even a day's journey." They embraced warmly feeling like long lost sisters, an ease came over both as they sat and spoke of their childhoods.

"Oh my, whatever time is it? I must get home. Malchus, my husband will no doubt be worried if I'm not there when he arrives."

"Wait, I'll walk with you, it's grown dark," Kezi was concerned for her safety.

"No, I can't ask you to leave your things," Selah protested. "I'll be fine, truly it's not far." As she stepped out of Kezi's tent, she turned, "Look, there's still light."

Selah took both Kezi's hands, "Thank you for a most pleasant afternoon. I'm so happy we've met and can you believe we grew up so close to each other?" She looked at Mary and told her she was happy to have met her. Mary showed no emotion. "We shall see each other soon."

She was a little concerned. The sun seemed to be setting. She picked up her pace. She noticed several men turning to watch her as she made her way through the last of the carts with unsold goods. *Oh no, I haven't prepared for dinner!* She quickly assessed the cart's remains that were in a semi-circle around her. "Sir, pardon me, do you have any small fish?" If Malchus were home, at least she wouldn't come home empty handed.

"No, I've sold all," the man replied.

She turned again, eyes searching, feeling a little panicked and a sense of dread suddenly filled her. She began to walk faster, shadows moving with every step playing tricks on her, faint sounds of the market making it difficult to concentrate. *Were they Roman soldiers?* Her knees felt weak. Run, her heart told her but she couldn't. Footsteps close behind her made her let out a muffled scream.

"Selah, it's me! Where have you been? I've been searching everywhere! The hour is late! Do you know how dangerous it can be for you to walk alone? What must people think? What kind of woman walks alone at night?" His grip on her arm hurt. She remained silent while he continued his tirade.

"Malchus, I'm sorry. The woman I told you about, her name is Kezi and we were talking and I lost track of time," she began as they arrived home.

"You mustn't be out alone again! Especially at night!" He was upset. He was pacing in front of her now. She noticed the oil in the lamp, he had been home for a while before coming to look for her.

"I'm sorry, but you mustn't be angry with me. I was lonely and Kezi, she's from Magdala! We had such a nice time talking today. I feel as if I've known her my whole life! There's also a young girl with her named Mary and she's also from Magdala."

She grabbed his arm, "Malchus, I'm sorry. I won't do this again, that is I'll make sure I'm home before sunset."

He held her close. "Selah, there's much activity that's happening. Caiaphas is certain there will be trouble if he can't convince others to intervene?"

"What are you talking about Malchus? What kind of trouble?"

"It's too much for me to discuss. I can't disclose what I hear but I must ask you, no I'm telling you, don't make me have to look for you again."

"I won't. How many times must I apologize? Are our lives in danger? I don't know where you're at all day or what Caiaphas has you doing. There are rumors he's seen often at Pilate's house. What's he doing there? I don't trust this Caiaphas! Does he tell you Malchus what he's doing, why he's meeting with Pilate?"

He was tired. He couldn't answer any of her questions, not tonight anyway. He was mentally exhausted from his frantic search for her and after arriving safely in their home, he wanted to lie down and sleep. What troubled him the most is he had the same questions. He overheard too much, hushed whispers in corridors, doors and fists slamming in unison. He hadn't taken an interest in all of Caiaphas' dealings, he was only a servant and was reminded more often than he liked by Caiaphas himself. He didn't want her to fear walking home from the market, but there were too many pockets of unstable behavior brewing under the guise of nationalism. Barabbas alone had stirred the hearts of many who had their homes ransacked, their grain taken and their animals collected as surety. John the Baptist, who they said dressed in fur, wore a leather belt and only consumed honey and grasshoppers all the while yelling, 'Repent, for the kingdom is near', Jesus, his name now heard in and around the Temple and it wasn't good, Pilate was a curse word, he shouldn't meditate on these things. His eyes grew heavy. His last thought was the irony of how Caiaphas probably couldn't sleep and perhaps paced the floor mumbling, *Barabbas, John, Jesus, Pilate*.

Selah watched Malchus until he was out of sight. He had fallen asleep last night while she was still asking questions, busying herself with her hands, not looking directly at him. She'd never seen worry behind his eyes. It was early morning and she had hours before he would return and even with the events of the previous evening, she didn't hesitate to throw her favorite worn blanket on Balaam and gather her baskets to shop. She would look for Kezi, let her know she made it safely home, neglecting the part of Malchus and the temporary shadows the city ushered in.

Malchus saw her as she came into the square. A woman walked briskly to her, their greeting warm and sincere. Selah relieved Balaam of her weight and the two women walked side by side as old friends. This must be the woman she mentioned to him, who sold her the scarf. As much as he enjoyed her displaying her new purchase and wanted her to make friends, he didn't know anything about this woman so he stepped out from behind his cover careful to weave his way through the crowds.

"Malchus," he heard his name and saw several of the wealthier patrons of the city approaching him.

"Peace to you Malchus this fine day. Are you here to hear all the latest gossip of the day?" Many chuckles followed. It was no secret he was the eyes and ears of Caiaphas and this well-known fact made most leery of him and reserved in his presence, unless of course they wanted to influence Caiaphas with suggestive ways to earn a few more shekels. Caiaphas would see to it these suggestions were duly noted. He couldn't escape their inquisitiveness and lost sight of Selah. Caiaphas would also be waiting for news, the mood of the people, what they were saying; the smallest detail he wanted to know. He needed ammunition when meeting with Pilate. *Did Pilate want news of disorder to reach the walls of Rome casting negative thoughts on his governing abilities?* Caiaphas thought not. Pilate was a man, and men had both their strengths and weakness. Caiaphas determined to uncover both. It was his only strategy.

Malchus wouldn't tarry. He looked for bright colors among the more subtle ones. *Didn't Selah speak of this woman's vibrant fabrics?* Her eyes danced when she spoke of all the wonderful robes and tunics. The other girl's name was Mary. Common enough he thought. There must be hundreds of Mary's in Jerusalem. He would look for Balaam instead.

"Malchus, my friend, join us, won't you?" He was beckoned over. He couldn't pretend he didn't hear. He decided to take advantage of this meeting hoping to learn all Caiaphas had expressed to him to listen for.

Selah sat comfortably in Kezi's home. It was much larger than hers. She wondered how a woman living alone could have such a home. Kezi observed her looking around politely, not wanting to appear nosy when she spoke.

"Selah, I hope I haven't kept you from your shopping. I know you must prepare for Sabbath."

"No, I have plenty of time," she replied aware of the distance and when the sun would be setting. "Your home is lovely Kezi. You've never spoken of a husband. Was this his home? Were you married?"

"This is my home Selah; I have no husband." She wondered if Malchus heard rumors about her. She liked Selah and needed a friend. The young girl Mary she took in was five years younger. Her family couldn't cope with her instability and she herself had dealt with many trials in her own life. She hoped Malchus wouldn't put two and two together, her name was synonymous with a certain profession and it wasn't flattering. He would never allow Selah to visit her home if he believed the local gossip and busybodies. She made sure Balaam was in the shade and attended to. They ate lunch slowly. A knock on the door interrupted them. Kezi excused herself and Selah heard men talking excitedly.

"Selah, I'm sorry but I must go. Someone, I mean something has come up and I'm needed. Please forgive me," she began clearing the table. Mary appeared out of nowhere and startled Selah. There was something peculiar about her.

"Is everything alright? Do you wish for me to go with you?" Selah was alarmed. *Who were these men?* It must be urgent for her to leave this pleasant lunch.

"No, I must go alone. There's nothing wrong. I just need to meet with someone who's been traveling and, well I must go."

She gathered her things and went to untie Balaam. The men she heard were waiting. She took her time adjusting Balaam's blanket hoping to catch a few words of their conversation. They remained silent. They knew who her husband was. She heard Kezi telling the young girl Mary to stay inside. She came around to bid her friend goodbye while taking one last look at the men who disrupted her lunch. The younger of the two had a warm smile, almost as if to say, '*Hello, we hope to see you again*'. The women embraced and Kezi apologized for having to leave so abruptly. She covered her head and joined the men.

Balaam nudged Selah's back. "Ok donkey, we're going. Yes, I'll be home before dark. Yes, I'll buy you some carrots. Yes, I'll let you walk without me, we'll share the road Balaam, side by side." If it wasn't for Kezi Selah thought, this donkey would be her only friend.

Malchus would be home late ensuring Caiaphas was satisfied of all preparations for the Temple. Selah may never know the whole capacity of his duties as Caiaphas' servant. He never wanted to discuss the day's events. Once he simply said he was the "eyes and ears" for Caiaphas. She thought that strange as Caiaphas himself could see and hear. The idea of Malchus lurking in dark corners eavesdropping on other's conversations made her sick to her stomach. She knew he wasn't the first to do so and wouldn't be the last. She hurriedly picked out fresh greens and purchased a small jar of oil. She had plenty of time to arrive home to begin dinner. She wasn't hungry. Lunch had been filling. She looked over her shoulder hoping to see Kezi or the men who called her away. She wondered about them since she left Kezi's house. She thought of the young girl. Kezi didn't take her along. *Why? Why was everyone so secretive about what they did? Malchus, Kezi.* She felt alone just then.

She wasn't brought up to question others, but Malchus was her husband and there were things she wanted to know. She would start asking. She would start tonight.

A cool breeze lingered in Pilate's room. It was welcomed. He wasn't accustomed to this dry heat. *Who would want to live in this desert?* Claudia was giving orders to the household. They were having a party. He would attempt to excuse himself early. He would have to elude his wife.

"Why do we have to entertain these dreadful people? I'm in command to govern them, not socialize," he almost pouted.

"We need laughter in this house," Claudia responded. "The mood has been most unpleasant. Everyone is suspicious of their neighbor, no one trusts anyone. I can't walk from room to room in my own home without the servants running out pretending they have some special chore they need to complete at that very moment, so we're having a party. You'll stay until the last guest departs, and my husband, you will look cheerful and lastly, no talk of politics."

He pulled her close, his arm around her waist and guided her to the balcony. "Look at this city," he gestured with his hand at the life below them.

She only saw her husband. *What was in his eyes just now? Pity?* Jerusalem wasn't Rome. They accepted this position; they had no choice. They would return one day so until then, they would make the best of their temporary assignment. The only consolation was Jerusalem was part-time. She much preferred their home in Caesarea.

"It's this god of the people that has caused all their problems, this god and his law. What law do they ramble on about? And how can they only have one god? Caiaphas and his council have become a nuisance. I swear Claudia, he's like an annoying mosquito around my ear. I do wish I could swat him away most days. If I hear him complain about taxes one more time, I think I'll jump off this balcony!"

She continued to listen. It was cooling down and so was he. The imported white silk curtains wrapped them in their embrace as they stood watching the sunset, faint calls of the city's inhabitants coming to rest. This was a strange place she thought. She also didn't understand this one god and his ways, this Sabbath where no one was to work or carry items. How could she manage a party with those who followed this god? They didn't even have a name for him. Caesar had been generous to send their own household staff, those familiar with Roman ways. She solicited a few local women, those who didn't care as deeply for this god, and she was grateful as there was much to prepare and everything needed to be perfect. She missed the laughter of her husband. It had been a long time since she heard him genuinely laugh, not the mocking tone when shouting orders or being facetious with tales of Caiaphas and his pathetic council. Try as she might she didn't understand the disgust her husband had for Caiaphas and the people of this country. Yes, a party will do wonders. She knew he would overindulge in all things and she didn't care. She just wanted to hear him laugh.

Herod was having his own party. He had many. The stories of his guests were retold in every setting. Most couldn't believe the events that took place. Some men envied those who had open invitations, others wouldn't be caught dead at his gates. Malchus heard tales of Herod's parties while simply strolling through the city, loud raucous laughter from men who had no morals, gossip laden disbelief from women who blushed all the while providing the smallest detail. They knew the exact jewelry and color veil Herod's wife Herodias wore at each event. They seldom caught a glimpse of her and had to rely on strangers in the market after too much afternoon wine to paint the pictures repeated to friends and neighbors.

One afternoon as Herod's caravan was heading to confer with Pilate, a man began shouting it wasn't lawful for him to be married to his brother's Philip's wife. Herod was incensed, Herodias furious! How dare this madman shout to the Procurator of Judea!

"Stop!" Herodias would give this fool a piece of her mind! Her carriers quickly obeyed and took advantage to lay her litter down to rest. The sun was hot this day and only contributed to her short temper. She pulled the drapes back and gasped. She saw the man they called John the Baptist, unmoved, his gaze as steady as his stance. He looked dirty she thought, wild, untamed standing in his unusual covering. *What was that? Goat hair? Camel? Hideous!* The thought of him inside her litter with her beautiful pillows and hand-carved wooden couch sent a small shudder. She parted the curtains again; he hadn't moved. Now he raised his hand and pointed directly at her, no doubt to anyone who his remarks were directed.

"Repent!" he shouted. "What you do is unlawful! You have married your husband's brother! Fornicator! Adulteress!" His voice echoed against the rocks and shook her soul.

She noticed a few women attempting to peer into her litter, and she abruptly brought her carriers to attention with one word, "Go!"

John stood until her cart was no longer in view. Herodias glanced back several times as he watched her. It unnerved her, but she would never allow anyone to see her moved by such insolence. She sat up, her bangles singing as both arms were raised to adjust her jeweled headdress, the slightest reflection from its stones caught dancing on her litter's interior, the march of her four carriers trance-like, only the midday sun to warm her. Everything else seemed cold. Herod would get an earful this evening. She wouldn't be humiliated. She would have her revenge. She would wait for the perfect opportunity. She was patient. *Fool!* She laid back against her tufted cushions and fell asleep.

Malchus stood at the Essene gate, his entry and exit from Caiaphas' house to his own in the lower portion of the city. Caiaphas didn't want to be bothered today. He waited outside of his house listening. There was strangeness to the silence. Finally voices. When he approached his fellow servants, they were deep in conversation, he hid behind a column.

"They say he performed a miracle! There was a wedding and the master ran out of wine. They say he turned six water pots of stone from water to wine!" the first voice exclaimed.

"I don't believe it," his friend replied.

"And the wine was better than all they drank before!" He was getting excited Malchus thought.

"Impossible I tell you. Someone has told you a tale, a riddle," the friends were not convinced.

"My daughter, she knows the mother of a servant who was in Cana at the wedding, they told her it's true!"

"And this man, who is he?" the friends demanded.

"I only know they said his name was Jesus."

The silence returned. Malchus didn't breathe. His heart seemed to be racing all of a sudden. He stepped out to casually join their conversation but they were gone. He stood now at the gate recalling this story wondering if Caiaphas overheard.

Selah watched Malchus as he slowly walked through the courtyard. He looked peculiar this early evening. It appeared he was talking to himself. He was muttering! He kicked a rock and when his sandal slipped, his toe made contact, he muttered even more.

"Malchus, be careful! Who are you talking to?" Selah greeted him with concern and amusement. She never saw him acting out obvious frustration. She kissed his cheek while looking to see if his toe was swelling as they walked inside. She placed a cup of broth before him and some bread.

"What has you troubled?" she stroked his head, comforting him as she would a child. He responded. His eased his shoulders and let out a deep breath and started talking.

"Selah, you can't believe the story I heard today about Jesus. They said he turned water into wine. And Selah, not just a cup of wine, but six large water pots! Isn't that crazy? Have you ever heard such a thing? This is the same Jesus they said when he was baptized, they heard a voice from heaven!" He took a breath and continued. "But then this one man, I didn't see him, I was hiding."

"Hiding? Why were you hiding?"

"I wasn't hiding, I just happened to come upon them and before I reached them, I overheard this "story telling" and I just stopped. I was hidden from their view by the columns on Caiaphas' porch," he took a bite of bread. Selah thought he practically ripped it to shreds.

"I wanted to jump out and say, "*You fools, water into wine, really?*" especially at the house of Caiaphas. But when I turned the corner they were gone," he seemed angry and before he could say anything else, she placed another piece of bread in front of him and filled his cup with more broth.

"Malchus, why is this upsetting you so much? Who cares what other people say? Like you said, they're just telling stories. Did they have some of this wine made from water?"

If Caiaphas overheard, he knew he would be in a foul mood tomorrow and he'd be commissioned to go and listen to see if anyone else was talking about Jesus. The part he neglected to tell her was that some people, those who heard the voice, said the voice said, *'This is My beloved Son in whom I am well pleased'*. He couldn't repeat these words. It was difficult just to recall them. *Was this God's voice from heaven? He said this to His son?* It made no sense and he didn't want to hear anymore talking for the rest of the evening.

She sat quietly. After a few moments she placed her hand on his arm. "Come husband, let us sleep now. You need rest, you'll feel better in the morning." He allowed her to lead him to their pallets on the floor. They laid in the quiet of the night, he turned on his side. She did as well. They were both wide awake. They were both lost in their own thoughts, and little did they know, they were both thinking about Jesus.

Claudia shone, arrayed in gold and copper. She looked the perfect hostess positioning herself at Pilate's left side. He refused to relinquish his short knife, always at the ready, and she wouldn't complain tonight. He was smiling, being cordial, greeting every guest warmly, eyeing the young wives of his sentries, a little too closely for her liking, but even this she would allow. The servants were finishing the food platters and the order in which they were to be presented. Several young boys were serving wine and she continually checked to ensure everyone had their fill. Stuffed mushrooms with fresh chopped parsley and an assortment of local vegetables and fresh breads would be served at all times. She had procured four cows, six lambs, one deer and had several peacocks brought in as a delicacy most would never taste in their lifetime.

The platters were adorned with fresh herbs and flowers to enhance the fragrance and visual appearance, the servants careful of their placement. Behind opaque curtains musicians performed and she positioned dancers in front for the pleasure of the men. Pilate and a small group had taken notice immediately, their wine spilling from their cups as they raised them in unison cheering on the girls who moved seductively to the songs of the evening. And then she heard it. Her husband was laughing. It was genuine. She caught his eye and he raised his cup in salute. She knew he acknowledged the party a success and it was exactly what he needed. She hadn't eaten but now lingered over honey dipped almonds and figs, pistachios and dates and filled a small bowl of melon and blackberries. The aromas were tantalizing. Pilate arranged for pepper to be brought in and the meat platters were speckled with the spice crushed to release its distinct flavor. There were pears, dried apples and pomegranates flavored with cinnamon, another spice she had requested in abundance. She thought of everything.

The noise level from the intoxicated men became deafening, but she didn't mind. She would retire to her chambers soon. She found herself calculating the number of girls who would continue to dance into the early morning and her eyes once again settled on her husband. She would overlook his transgression. *Hadn't she always?* She lifted her head and Pilate nodded his goodnight. Her aide followed and she undressed while the young girl opened shutters and turned down her bed. As she laid down, she could hear the faint sound of lyres and thought it a perfect lullaby for the close of the evening.

Malchus had a restless night. The steady breathing of Selah somehow unnerved him. He was selfish. *How could she rest when he was so troubled in his thoughts?* He had risen to get a drink of water purposely dropping the cup in hopes of waking her. No matter how he positioned himself, he simply couldn't stop thinking about this man they called Jesus. *Turning water into wine. Who would believe that?* But yet weddings were filled with many people. There would have been a hundred perhaps. And the servants! This was not a one-day event. How many were at the Jordan River that day? Some said it was thunder but he knew it wasn't, which led him down the tortuous path of unrest. He was paid to listen. He heard other stories. He kept them to himself. There were those who whispered, could he be the "one" we've been looking for, the "one" to come? The Messiah? His entire body shook. *No, impossible!* He was beginning to understand the hope behind these recent stories. The people were tired. They were being taken advantage of. They were oppressed under the Roman's, the rich were getting richer, the poor without recourse.

He thought of Caiaphas and the wealth of his family, knowing he had participated in some small way by informing him of those using false weights to benefit him and the treasury. It now made him sick. The people were looking for someone to bring justice and conquer their oppression. It wasn't Barabbas. He knew Caiaphas would be expecting him. The two-mile walk to his house would seem a day's journey today. He grabbed his outer garment, fed Balaam and then vomited into a bucket.

Selah was awake. She watched Malchus dress and heard him attending Balaam. The next sound she heard startled her. He was sick! She jumped up and dressed quickly but by the time she reached the back of their home, he was gone. Balaam was staring at his bucket. Malchus had disposed of its contents and it had been washed. She knew he hadn't slept. All the while he tossed and turned, she pretended to sleep. She didn't want to talk. She bit the inside of her lip when he dropped the cup, partly to stifle her laugh and cover up her own restlessness she didn't want discovered. *Why did these stories have such an impact?* She needed to find someone to share her curiosities, help her understand the politics of Rome and the connection with the Temple, and the governing of both. She thought of Kezi. Perhaps she would have knowledge as a merchant. Surely, she would hear the men discussing such topics. She remembered the two men that came to her house. Malchus would be gone the better part of the day and she went through her tiny home like a whirlwind, sweeping, straightening and measuring out grain to save her a step when she returned to prepare dinner. She hoped Kezi could spend time with her. She had a list of questions. She would start with Kezi herself. What was her story?

"Selah! Please, come in. It's good to see you my friend." Selah breathed easily at Kezi's warm welcome and they settled themselves down on cushions facing each other. She looked around for Mary.

"Selah, what is it? Are you alright?" Kezi leaned closer.

"Yes, I didn't sleep well and either did my husband all because of this story he told me," she hesitated.

"A story?"

"My husband, Malchus, he attends Caiaphas," Selah noticed Kezi nodded as if she already knew this, "and he sees a lot of people. He, well, Caiaphas has requested, I mean part of what he does is listen to what people are saying," she looked for any reaction from her and continued. "He reports to Caiaphas what he hears, you know in the market or outside the Temple. Kezi, you must know how the people feel about the Romans and the burden they've become enforcing taxes."

"Yes Selah, I'm listening."

"Malchus, he doesn't speak to me about these things, I know he can't tell me but I don't understand what's happening? Do you know? What are zealots, and who is Barabbas that's causing so much trouble lately?"

"Go on Selah," Kezi said.

"This man they call John the Baptist, one day he was baptizing this man and people said they heard a voice from heaven," she noticed Kezi didn't seem to be surprised at anything she said. "But wait Kezi, there's more! Yesterday when Malchus came home, he was very agitated and after a while he finally told me this story he overheard. There was a wedding and men were talking about how this man turned water into wine!" She couldn't read Kezi's expression. It made her uncomfortable so she laughed.

"Is that absurd Kezi? Malchus, when he told me, he seemed so upset by it and I couldn't understand why. I mean it's just a story, but he said there would have been a lot of people there and it seemed he struggled with the notion it may be true," she hesitated again. "Kezi, I think he's most upset about this man they call Jesus. Some say he is Messiah," she exhaled. She felt relieved Kezi let her talk without interruption.

Kezi took Selah's hands and looked at her and said, "Selah, do you want to hear another story?" She found Mary and sent her out for an errand so she and Selah could speak freely, and then she sat, eyes direct to keep composed and began.

"When I was a young girl, I went down to the sea all the time. I loved to watch the men come in after fishing all night. I didn't have any brothers and, in a way, it was my make-believe family." Selah nodded and smiled.

"One day, I don't know why, I decided to go home a different way," she hesitated. Selah knew something happened. It was written all over her face.

"A Roman soldier was watching me, he was at the top of the hill I was climbing, and Selah, I never saw a man like that so close. When he looked at me the way he did, I was so scared I couldn't move. I couldn't speak. I knew the men at the shore couldn't see me. I was too far away."

Selah saw the tears forming in her eyes. "Kezi, you don't have to tell me. If you're uncomfortable, please, I don't want you to get upset."

"No, it helps me Selah and it led me to be here, now telling you, my new friend, and it's important to me. The soldier, he was off his horse and had me on the ground, his hand over my mouth before I knew what was happening. He held his hand over my mouth the entire time. When he finished, he simply got back on his horse never looking back and went down the hill. I saw him at the shoreline. I opened my mouth to scream and no sound came. I knew I would bring much shame to my family. I was devastated."

Selah grabbed her hands, "But it wasn't your fault!"

"I know, but I shouldn't have been so far from home alone. No man would want to marry me. I couldn't hide that I lost my virtue."

"I'm so sorry Kezi," Selah cried.

"I stayed in that field all night. I cried. I screamed. I slept. The next morning, I walked back down to the sea and took a bath. I felt so dirty. This animal robbed me of everything!" Kezi took a deep breath and continued. "Without going into detail", and now her eyes were downcast, "I entered into a life of prostitution," she looked directly into Selah's eyes to read her thoughts. *Was she disgusted?* Selah didn't let go of her hands.

"I traveled with the soldiers. They paid me well. I wasn't the only girl, we all had similar stories. We missed our families, but were determined to make as much money we could so we could start over, a new life, somewhere no one knew us. The soldiers who took advantage of us were sent back to Rome. It was lawful for them to pay us, but to rape us was not permitted, even for them. I'd been away for almost seven years. I grew up fast Selah. I wasn't proud of what I was doing. I felt I had no choice. We were staying north of the sea in Caesarea Philippi. Pilate was named as the new Prefect and we heard he would be traveling throughout the province. We were headed to Jerusalem. I knew this would be my home. I began to abstain as much as I could. I had money. There were four other women who said they wanted to stay. We knew there would be opportunity. On the way, we stopped around Cana," Kezi stopped to take a drink and Selah did too.

"We were behind a wedding party, they had been guests in Cana, and there were many servants also traveling back to their homes when we heard a miraculous story!"

Selah held her breath.

"They told us this man turned water into wine! The soldiers were laughing calling this man names but we asked the servants questions when one of them pointed to a man and said, 'There he is, his name is Jesus'. He and his friends stopped and waited for us. We were ashamed, we kept our heads down. I couldn't look at him. I felt his hand, he lifted my chin and said, 'Go and sin no more' and he smiled at me with his eyes. I can't explain it, I may never be able to understand, but I know he didn't look down on me as others had. It felt warm and sincere and I knew I would never sell myself again. He gave me hope. We came to Jerusalem, the five of us started the shop. We had a lot of difficulty Selah, the Romans didn't let us forget our former profession, but we worked hard and eventually gained the respect of our fellow merchants. After several months I've been able to go out on my own. I've been very successful. I'm happy here Selah. This man Jesus, he touched me in a way I never experienced. It was pure, in my heart." She placed both hands over her heart and Selah saw peace and joy in her countenance. She wasn't sure how to respond. Five words had changed her life! *Go and sin no more.* How could one man influence a person's life in an instant?

Kezi studied Selah unsure to continue. She didn't want to jeopardize this new friendship. She swallowed, nervous to tell her more.

"Selah, I wish to travel with Jesus, to follow him."

"What do you mean? Follow him where?"

"I know this is a lot to take in Selah. I believe Jesus is the Messiah," and before Kezi could finish her sentence, Selah jumped up.

"I must go! You're right Kezi, my head is spinning. Wait, are you saying I shall not see you again? No, that can't be, is it Kezi? Where are you going? I must speak to Malchus about these things."

"No Selah, please wait! Don't say anything yet I beg you. There's much to fear. I know your husband. He would repeat all to Caiaphas and right now I'm asking you to wait. I know where your home is Selah. I promise I'll come to speak with you soon."

Selah shook her head from both disbelief of all Malchus told her and now feeling like she was losing a friend. Kezi hugged her and whispered over and over to trust her and not be discouraged. She would know all things soon, because it was written.

"Kezi!" Selah cried. "That's why I came here. What is written? I have no one to teach me. I know we must follow the law, but I know there's more. Please, you must promise to come soon. I have to go now." As they said their goodbyes, neither of them noticed Mary, curled up, hidden behind a pile of garments. She heard the whole story. As the door closed, Kezi wasn't certain if she would ever see Selah again.

Selah tried as hard as she could to process all Kezi told her. *The Messiah? What did she really know?* She thought about the day when the two men came to her house, and now wondered if they too were following Jesus. And Kezi! She had only known Jesus a short time, just a few months and she was going to travel with him. To do what Selah had inquired? *'To preach the good news,'* Kezi explained. She sat now on the floor, her grinding stone outside waiting on her. She didn't feel like preparing dinner. She couldn't reconcile all Kezi told her. She would keep these things buried in her heart. Somehow, she knew Kezi was right for her not to share this with Malchus. She sensed another restless night.

Chapter Two

"We mustn't let this Jesus or anyone else disrupt our ways!" The council was assembled. Caiaphas gave each one his full attention and nod of approval as each spoke about the dangers of heresy. The hall in which they met echoed each remark with a clarity he seized upon.

"He's teaching contrary to our law!"

"He must be stopped!" Caiaphas grew more confident as each member agreed to the other's comments.

"Miracles! The Messiah! What, has Elijah come?"

"Some say this John the Baptist is Elijah come back." A solemn hush fell in the room, Caiaphas was displeased.

"We shall not speak and speculate about such things sacred to the Holy Scriptures when discussing the absolute blasphemous talk of this Jesus. I would rather have the zealot Barabbas inciting the people to rebel against paying taxes than this imposter who they say goes about casting out demons. Bah! It sounds like the work of someone who himself has one."

Malchus positioned himself behind the Temple guards. Caiaphas knew he was near; he didn't need to be seen. Passover was at hand and this made Caiaphas all the more militant concerning Jesus. He was in the area and the number of his followers were growing. The water turning into wine miracle had circulated through every social circle with some even mockingly leaving full water pots outside of their doors hoping they too would be turned to wine. He didn't know what he thought about this. He didn't find it amusing as the soldiers did. He heard them as they played games after their watch finished, laughing, slapping their knees at these ridiculous tales, but the council were not laughing. This was serious to their welfare. They depended on Rome to enforce and assign tax collectors to keep the functions of their lives in order.

The city was crowded. It took days to prepare for Passover. Caiaphas was anxious. Every animal had to be inspected, the accompanied priests assembled for their duties, the Temple readied for all who needed to purchase the required sacrifice. He'd been particular when he chose those who sold doves and would be allowed to change money, the private selection lucrative for him. Malchus heard carts overflowing with cages keeping them from escaping their plight. He tilted his head to tune in every sound. Merchants scrambled to be close to the outer courts for last-minute purchases, no doubt already investing much to the pockets of Caiaphas to secure. The clanging of weights resembled a song, the thud on the tables a constant beat, he found himself tapping his foot to the rhythms of the city. With the constant bird calls and excessive flapping of their wings, he smiled thinking they were applauding the approval of the merchant's overture.

Travelers would be lined up as far as one could see waiting for their turn to provide an offering. He wondered if Caiaphas was calculating the mandatory half shekel tribute tax and what his take would amount to. No one could describe the city during the feasts. The sights, the smells, this he told himself is why people are so faithful to make the journey. The reward of all they would experience lasts a lifetime. It had for him. He grew up learning the history of the land when King David ruled and when his son Solomon built the Temple, and after it was destroyed, Herod swept in as master builder and now he stood in the hall, attendant to Caiaphas, High Priest, Temple guards parting to allow him free reign when Caiaphas conducted his administrations. He sensed a little pride as he looked around and took leave of his previous post. He would hear if Caiaphas called. He trained his ear to detect his voice above all, no matter the location or circumstance. Screams jolted him from his daydreaming, the noise deafening! He heard tables crashing, men cussing and shouting and money falling to the ground. The guards knocked him to the ground as others rushed by, he scooted back out of the main thoroughfare.

"What are you doing? Stop! Guards! Someone, call for Caiaphas! Now!"

He didn't move. He heard a strong voice commanding people to leave, accusing them of turning the Temple into a den of thieves! He was the one turning over tables, doves granted freedom as their cages broke against the stone floor. He made his way towards the calamity. He had a whip! Who was this? How dare he come here and disrupt commerce. Did he not know it was Passover? And then he heard the name that prevented sleep. Jesus. He couldn't look away. Merchants who knew him were shouting to help.

"Malchus, my money!"

"Malchus, my doves!"

"Malchus, don't just stand there, help me recover my coins!" "Malchus!"

The next statement, words that he heard were simply astonishing, *"Take these things away; stop making My Father's house a place of business."* Jesus, his followers close behind him. No one breathed. Caiaphas and the priests gathered to confront him. They asked whose authority he had to do this and to give them a sign. His head was spinning along with his stomach. The words were marvelous. No one knew what he meant. He said, *'Destroy this Temple, and in three days I will raise it up'.* He watched the construction of the Temple his entire life. What was Jesus saying? Coins were scattered everywhere. Merchants weary of what Jesus or the priests would do next, didn't move until Jesus and his followers began walking away.

"Malchus!"

"Malchus!" His name was called from every direction.

People were pushing and shouting as animals darted through overturned tables, he never witnessed a spectacle like this in his life! His breathing was hard. Caiaphas hadn't seen him. Even though several remained calling for him to help, he stood there. He raised his outer garment over his head and slowly descended the steps. He didn't want to go home. He knew his private place of solitude in the valley would be overflowing with people. He thought to himself this Passover would be remembered for a long time. Caiaphas would be seething, even more so at his absence, but at this very moment, he didn't care. He saw Jesus. He turned suddenly and ran home.

Caiaphas could tear out his beard! What a disaster today! Several friends demanded he speak with them immediately. They lost money today. It was a free for all they said. Why didn't he have guards stop this man sooner? They didn't anticipate good outcome. They asked the same question, '*What are you going to do about it, Caiaphas*'? And now he sat, replaying the events of the day in his mind with Malchus nowhere to be found. He gritted his teeth to avoid shouting at no one. He would meet with Pilate. He had to convince him to act. He didn't care how he would accomplish this, not concerned about the well-being of his countrymen, he only had thoughts of himself. His father-in-law would replace him in an instant if he suspected he was losing control. He tapped his fingers on his desk trying to recall the last moment he saw Malchus. He needed information. He summoned his guards. He would send two to his house and request his presence. He sat a little straighter calculating his next move. He had four more days for Passover to end. He would use this time to rehearse his conversation with Pilate and ready himself.

Pilate had a hangover. Claudia's party had horrible timing. It had slipped her mind the Jews would begin traveling to the city to celebrate another of their feasts. Passover. It lasted a bloody week Pilate cursed. Claudia's party had also. Some who journeyed for the occasion found themselves trapped in the city not wanting to depart until everyone went home. There were too many robbers on the roads. Pilate couldn't sacrifice his soldiers to ensure safe passage back to the sea for friends who had embarked from Rome. Fortunately, it was only a few and Claudia insisted they stay through the Passover celebration and after, weeks if needed, so they could rest and then begin their travels with Pilate's sentries leading the way. His head hurt. He couldn't enjoy his balcony, the dust of the city blanketing everything. And the stench of the animals! He felt trapped in his own home.

"Husband, come and sit," Claudia implored him. With a short clap, servants brought in small platters of fruit, Pilate resting in her lap. She began to massage his temples, quite familiar with his headaches. She kept her voice low hoping the solid doors and shutters would drown out the noise of the city. "Did you hear about the commotion today at the Temple?" He arched his eyebrow curious as to the level of gossip in his own home. She smiled down at him. He was calm today in his manner.

"Yes, I heard. They're a strange people."

"It's all the kitchen staff are talking about. This man Jesus has captured all of Jerusalem's attention. I'm surprised your High Priest hasn't come for a visit to complain," she fed him some grapes.

"Don't even speak it! Thankfully he's tied up at his Temple," he opened his mouth for another grape. She was happy to see him relaxed.

"You know they're waiting for their messiah, someone to put an end to Rome's rule. Can this be the man, this Jesus?" She shifted her weight and Pilate adjusted himself bringing her hands back down to resume the massage.

"These people my dear have many myths and stories they've told over many years. Centuries! This is just another man, a rebel with a cause, probably an acquaintance of Barabbas sent to stir things up. Barabbas knows he would be arrested and this Jesus no doubt volunteered to come and wreak havoc today right in the middle of this Passover of theirs."

"I don't know about these things, but I know the servants don't speak about this man as they did Barabbas. They believe he performs miracles."

"Claudia, don't listen to mindless chatter of local kitchen staff. As soon as our guests have gone, they will leave as well and our home will be back to normal. There is unrest, yes, but there's always been unrest. No two countries or governments ever agree on all which concerns the other. You'll always have dissidents, zealots, messiahs, whatever you want to label them to attempt to overthrow the prevailing authority. Put it out of your head. I can see you're thinking too much about these local myths." He wanted to change the subject. He brought her head down to look at him.

"You threw a great party, thank you. Your robe was beautiful and you looked lovely. Do you know how much I appreciate all your efforts?"

"Yes husband. It has done you well to see old friends and enjoy yourself." She wouldn't mention the afterhours of the party when he and his friends were really able to enjoy themselves. Now it was she who had the headache.

Selah couldn't believe how many people were in Jerusalem. Standing in her courtyard she was approached a dozen times with offers from those looking for shelter while here to celebrate. She hoped Malchus would be home soon. She retreated back inside unsure of her next move. She brought Balaam inside too. Malchus would have a fit but she didn't care. If these hordes of people were walking inside her courtyard, what would prevent them from going around back? She'd tell him she was concerned for his safety; that someone might try to take him. Not many had a donkey. He was lying down watching her and she thought she would have a conversation with him while waiting.

"So, Balaam, are you comfortable?" He said nothing.

"Do you like being in the house?" Still no answer.

"What about my friend Kezi, what do you think about her?" Balaam only stared.

"Do you like apples?" she began to giggle now. She pulled up a stool and came closer.

"Is Caiaphas a mean man?" she laughed out loud.

"Do you think I'm pretty?" Balaam shifted his weight.

"I'll take that as a yes," she laughed again.

One last question Balaam, "What do you think about Jesus?"

Balaam jumped, rose to his feet so quickly she fell off her stool. He pawed the ground and resting on her elbows, she waited for him to stop. Without hesitation she grabbed his blanket. She would find Kezi. She had a few hours of sunlight left. She headed towards the Temple hoping Malchus wouldn't see her. Balaam took charge and nudged his way through the people. She began to question this decision and looked for any familiar faces from the market she had come to know. She felt crushed between the crowds. She heard languages she didn't recognize, and every few seconds there was an outburst of activity followed by shouts of excitement, but even with the view from Balaam, she couldn't see what was going on. *This is madness!* It would take hours to weave through this mob of people.

Passover was in four days and the city would grow even more. She couldn't turn Balaam around now, she was stuck, her legs scraped by baskets and children's sticks used for walking and playing. All these people! Hundreds. Thousands, and she didn't recognize one person. Her heart sank. She hadn't slept, her mind busy with questions she never thought she would ponder. Between Malchus and Kezi, she wanted to put the pieces of information from their stories together, but nothing made sense. She bit her lower lip. She couldn't focus, there was no escape from the middle of this clamor and celebrating. Where would Malchus be now? He would be upset to find her and Balaam missing. *God of Abraham help me!* She let the tears flow freely. Balaam stopped, a man standing in front of him blocking his way.

"I know you," he smiled and she bristled at the familiar toothless grin.

"Sir, please, I must try and get through here quickly, if you could just step aside." She didn't look at him. He didn't move. His stare unnerved her and Balaam also.

"You shouldn't be alone here. There's danger for a young girl in the city with all these strangers about. Where are you going?"

A simple question she thought. She saw the swell of the crowds and the complete mayhem she managed to get herself in the middle of and felt ridiculous going nowhere, pressed about in every direction. She began sobbing.

"There, there now, no need for that miss. Ol' Simon will help you. Don't cry. I'll get you out of this mess." He had sincere eyes. She had focused on the missing teeth diverting her eyes from his and hadn't noticed the warmth hidden within. He reminded her of her grandfather.

"Speak up, let me help you get through to where you're going," he held Balaam waiting for her to give him directions.

She felt the tears streaming down. "That's the problem, I don't know."

"Where's your family? Do you have a husband? Are you trying to find them?" Simon asked.

"I'm looking for a friend of mine. She doesn't live too far, but I'm not certain she's there."

"Then why are you trying to go there?" he released his hold on Balaam to throw up his hands in defeat. She sensed another rush of tears.

"Who's your friend?" He needed to keep her talking or he would be there all night with a crying young woman, sitting on a donkey, who kept nudging his satchel, the promise of food enclosed. In between sniffles she finally spoke.

"Her name is Kezia. They call her Kezi. She sells garments in the market."

"I know her!" He clapped his hands. Progress he thought as he smiled to himself.

"I was trying to reach her home. I want to speak to her about," she couldn't finish her sentence. She couldn't speak his name right now. Simon took a hold of Balaam and started pushing through the press of the people.

"Wait! Where are we going?" He couldn't hear and she couldn't risk jumping off of Balaam. She didn't have any reason to trust him but she did. He lived nearby. He maneuvered his way to his home and had Balaam tied up with water and the coveted apples. He offered her the same.

"Now tell me where your friend Kezi lives and why you're trying to reach her today. Why would you risk coming out alone on a day like this, so many people, just to talk to her?"

She sipped her water debating how much she would say. Before she could respond he clapped again as if he just remembered something.

"Did you hear what happened at the Temple today?"

Selah was alarmed. "No! What happened?"

"Oh, it was something, a sight for these old eyes I tell you. This man came into the outer court and," he stopped and looked at her. "You haven't told me your name."

"It's Selah. Please, tell me what happened!"

"This man had a whip and began pushing over tables. Coins were flying everywhere, sheep pens were broken apart, people were yelling, and this man was shouting at those selling doves to get out of there, oh it was crazy! The priests came running, they were running! Men were on the ground grabbing their money, fights were breaking out, and this man, he turned over almost every table. No one came near him the entire time. He went from table to table, scales crashing to the floor and everyone stayed out of his way."

"Oh my!" she placed her hands on her cheeks astonished at his account. *Who would do such a thing? Any why wouldn't anyone stop him?* She wondered if Malchus saw this happen. Surely, he would have. It was getting dark now and her stomach felt queasy with this information and Malchus perhaps in the middle of it.

"Who was this man? Was he arrested?" She was growing impatient as Simon had taken time to light a lamp.

"His name is Jesus."

She fainted.

Simon patted her face with cold water.

"What happened?" she was dizzy.

"Have you eaten today besides the few bites of apple I gave you?" He was concerned. He didn't know anything about this young woman. She was in his home. It was the middle of Passover, he was old, his neighbors curious and Balaam needed to relieve himself.

"Come Selah, let us get you outside for some fresh air. Sit here and let me get you some bread." She could only nod.

"You say this man, this man at the Temple was Jesus? Tell me Simon, do you know anything about him?"

He made her eat a couple of bites of bread and poured a small cup of wine.

"They say he has many who follow him and speaks very wise words even the Pharisees can't deny. There are stories that he performs miracles and his followers say he is from God."

She drained the small cup, "Go on."

"I don't know of such things but today, when he came into the Temple and disrupted everyone's afternoon, he said, *'Don't make my Father's house like the market*, or something like that. It makes an old man like me wonder about such words."

"Simon, my friend Kezi, she knows him and she told me the most wonderful story." She looked at those grandfather eyes to know if she should continue. "My husband, he works at the Temple, actually he's Caiaphas' servant. He also heard these stories and the last time I saw Kezi, I went home thinking of this man and found myself wanting to know more about him. I came out today to find her and ask her questions, I have no one else to speak with."

Simon said, "Wait here Selah. I'll be back in a few minutes." If there was one constant in life, it was the knowledge that people talked, and people would be talking about what happened today. He didn't have to go far. His neighbor provided much information.

"Selah, I think I know where your Kezi and Jesus are." It was the first time this day Selah smiled.

"We need to leave Balaam; he'll be fine here. My house is secure." Simon walked between his rooms as he spoke.

"Wait! What do you mean, we, Simon?"

"I mean you and me Selah. We'll go find your friend Kezi. She's with this Jesus, right? And this is who you seek? You can't travel alone. Not now. Besides I know this city. You'll be safe."

"But where are we going Simon? How do you know where they are?"

"My neighbor. He told me those who were followers of Jesus bought everything he had today. It was right after the commotion at the Temple. He overheard their conversation. They were afraid for their Rabbi, fearing the Pharisees would bring trouble to him. They were headed to the Kidron and are camped there. So, we'll go and start asking every person we see if they know where we can find Jesus."

She was thankful the moon was bright, she felt secure as they walked briskly outside the city's wall. She was surprised how quickly Simon moved over the rocky slopes. Tents were pitched as far as the eye could see. He was several steps in front of her speaking with a man and a woman. He called her to join him.

"Selah, this is Joses, a friend of mine. He invited us to have dinner and I gladly accepted." He leaned in, "You need to eat. We'll find your friend Kezi, it may take us a few hours and we both need nourishment." She nodded in agreement. He told Joses they were looking for a friend of Selah's thought to be with Jesus.

Joses spread his hands wide, "Look at this valley my friend, they could be anywhere." But he said to walk east and so they did.

"Stop!" Simon grabbed her arm. Selah pulled her outer garment tighter around her.

"Look to the right. See that man?" Simon had keen eyes.

"Where?" She only saw shadows.

"Follow me," he whispered.

"Simon."

"Shhh, be quiet. I know that man." He turned again and put his finger to his lips cautioning her to be quiet.

"Who is it Simon?"

"Nicodemas, a Pharisee."

Malchus sat alone in the dark. No Selah. No donkey. No dinner. No feeling. He was shaken by the day's events. He'd seen trouble before. There were men before Barabbas who preyed on the weak and needed a leader, but Jesus, he didn't need anyone. He came through the Temple like he owned the place. This is what disturbed him the most. The merchants, the priests, the Pharisees, the Temple guards, even Caiaphas didn't attempt to stop him. *Why?* Others would have been arrested, man handled and yesterday's news, but not this man. He strode up the steps with purpose. He thought back now at how even his followers huddled together watching in amazement. They, like all who were in attendance, stood motionless until the sound of the last shekel to drop on the ground was heard. He began to whimper. He couldn't rationalize the emotion. Jesus was powerful in his actions and words, which made him begin to tremble as well. Now he rocked back and forth. *He must be in shock!* No matter what he did to block the image of Jesus, whip in hand, doves flying, sheep running, every man and woman shouting, he couldn't dismiss the power he sensed Jesus possessed. He sat in the dark, the earthen floor his only comfort.

Selah shivered. The night had grown cold and she longed for the warmth of a fire, but here she was with Simon, a stranger, crouched down behind bushes hardly breathing to observe a Pharisee named Nicodemas. Simon said he was a leader and thought to be a fair man. Nicodemas wasn't moving. He stood listening. Simon still had his finger to his mouth to "shoos" her. Once Nicodemas began moving,

Simon held her upper arm to ensure she didn't. *Why was he so curious about this man?* She couldn't remain in this position any longer.

"Simon, I want to find my friend Kezi. Are we following this man now?" She was tired, and the thought of Malchus wondering where she was started to burden her.

"I hear others talking." He tried to detect where the voices were coming from. He finally let her stand up, keeping Nicodemas in his sight. The voices were becoming louder. He walked on his tip toes careful as each step brought them closer. He was adamant about staying out of sight. The group became quiet. Nicodemas inched closer and by the sounds of the collective gasps, they knew the people who were gathered were just as surprised to see him. They were close enough to hear, still hidden behind a clump of trees.

"Rabbi," Nicodemas began.

"Rabbi?" Selah squinted her eyes to see who he was talking to. There in the moonlight with the amber glow of the fires, she had her first look at Jesus.

Nicodemas continued, "We know you're a teacher come from God for no man can do these miracles that you do, except God be with him."

"Miracles," Simon repeated.

"Shhh," Selah gave him a quick look. And then she heard him speak.

"Truly, truly, I say to you, except a man be born again, he cannot see the Kingdom of God."

"Born again?" Simon wouldn't stop talking. "What does he mean, born again?"

"I want to run and ask him," she took a few steps forward but he grabbed her arm again. Now she was standing on her tip toes looking at each face. She saw the two men who had come to Kezi's house! She cried within her heart and he realized she recognized someone. She searched for Kezi but couldn't take her eyes off of Jesus.

He spoke again. "Are you a teacher of Israel, and know not these things?" Simon watched Nicodemas' reaction to these words. He said nothing. He looked pensive. Jesus was still speaking. "If I told you earthly things, and you believe not, how shall you believe if I tell you of heavenly things?"

Simon and Selah were whispering, talking over each other, careful not to speak too loudly. They couldn't believe the exchange they happened upon. Jesus and Nicodemas! She wanted to jump up and down! She almost did when she felt a warm hand on her shoulder from behind.

"Kezi!"

The sun was rising as they walked back to the gates of the city. Jerusalem seemed different this morning. Selah was different. Simon couldn't stop grinning and she now loved this toothless smile. It was different too. He was whistling. The night was mesmerizing! She couldn't concentrate, every moment flashing through her mind bringing joy and fear simultaneously. She understood now the peace of his presence Kezi spoke about. She sensed the calm in her soul. She would need someone to explain what Jesus meant when he said, *'You must be born again'*. They discussed it as they traced back their steps.

"Simon, thank you. I'll forever be in your debt for all you've done for me."

"What I have done for you?" He was kicking up his feet dancing down the small hills. "I should be thanking you. I haven't felt this good for years! What an exciting time to be alive! What a Passover this year! What a beautiful morning!" They reached the bottom of the hill to make the final ascent home and he stopped. He searched for privacy among the midst of all who were starting their day and spoke in a low tone.

"Selah, we've seen great things. Nicodemas is a ruler of Israel and yet, this Jesus appeared to rule over him," he scratched his beard before he spoke again. "I've known of Nicodemas a long time. He's knowledgeable in the things of God, but last night, when he listened to the words of Jesus, Nicodemas was the student! I don't understand what was spoken and I will never forget the expression on Nicodemas' face at the words of Jesus, which I've hid in my heart this day, and we need to be careful and not mention this to anyone and I'm sorry to say, especially your husband."

"But Malchus should know. See how we have this joy in our hearts! Everyone should seek Rabbi Jesus and listen to his words. Why would we keep this from anyone?"

"Nicodemas is close to Caiaphas. Remember what his followers told us last night about what happened at the Temple?"

"Oh, my goodness Simon! Malchus! He must be so upset. Oh Simon, what shall I tell him? Where should I tell him I've been all evening? Simon, help me! I can't think. How can I pretend nothing has happened in my heart?" Her joy turned into worry.

He continued to scratch his beard. He knew she didn't want to deceive her husband.

"Let us pray." They walked in silence, a stark contrast to their surroundings. When only a short distance from her home, she turned and hugged him, they had a bond now, connected by something neither could explain.

"Chin up, you'll be fine. Now you know where I live and my door will always be open." He patted Balaam and said, "You too donkey" which made her smile. He saw the uncertainty in her face looking towards the final path of her walk home. *Would Malchus believe her?* They decided to tell him Balaam got loose from her grip and it was impossible to reach him. She knew she couldn't let him get away. She would tell Malchus she was yelling for people to help her and Simon, this merchant she recognized, began chasing Balaam as he headed towards the Temple. She wouldn't have to exaggerate the story when recalling the excited voices and animals running loose and when they were finally able to catch him, and fight their way through the crowds, it was dark. Kezi convinced her she shouldn't travel home the short distance. That was her story. She was exhausted rehearsing it. She didn't want to lie to him. She hoped one day she could tell him what really happened, but after she and Simon spoke, she agreed to keep secret the evening that somehow opened the eyes of her heart. How do you not share with a person the smell of rain or the color of a purple sky? Or watching a butterfly dance among the flowers? But she knew Simon was right. Hadn't Kezi said the same words to her? She took ahold of Balaam and hugged Simon one last time before she faced what she thought could be a very contentious husband. Her legs were heavy with each step. She looked back and he simply nodded his encouragement. When she turned back around, she saw Malchus.

Kezi worried about Selah. She sat smiling as she played the events of last night in her mind. She'd gone home planning to empty her house of all her belongings, some of which she planned to give to neighbors, some she would sell, but she didn't do anything. The sun was setting and she needed to walk quite a distance. She began making her way to the olive groves east of the city. That's when she saw him. Nicodemas. She decided to follow him. He was moving quickly. At one point, he stopped, so she waited. Jesus wasn't far from where they were. *What was he doing? Spying?* They walked further when both she and Nicodemas heard the laughter of the small group, all with raised voices talking excitedly. He found Jesus. He stopped again looking around nervously, deciding if he should continue. Sparks from the fires flew above the canopy of trees and within their light she saw him take the final step. She began to follow once again when she caught a glimpse of two others who were also watching and her heart began to race. She hid as they were and didn't move.

She heard Jesus speaking and longed to know what he spoke to this ruler of Israel. He must have been witness to the commotion at the Temple today. She placed her hand over her mouth to not laugh out loud. It was quite the moment. Everyone was talking about it. The two people now became braver and were edging closer to the group. They were telling each other to be quiet and Kezi could tell now one was a woman. She relaxed a little, not as concerned for her safety.

"What does he mean, born again?" Kezi recognized Selah's voice and her heart leapt! She wanted to run over and embrace her friend but who was with her? Malchus? She waited.

"Simon, I'm trying to listen!" It was a stern command.

Simon, not Malchus. Kezi came out of hiding and laid her hand gently upon Selah. She knew she would startle her. Nothing prepared them for the evening they would share. She led them to the small group of women who were preparing dinner so they could listen without being noticed. Nicodemas disappeared into the night and Simon wanted to follow again but Jesus was here. He was teaching. They had just as many questions as Nicodemas. While most settled for sleep, Simon and Selah kept Kezi awake.

They spoke rapidly, pouring out every thought and question on their minds as they knew this was a privilege, a blessing they happened upon this night. They would need to leave soon, hints of morning already interrupting. Kezi was careful. She was thinking of Malchus. *What on earth would Selah tell Malchus?* She was the one who suggested she tell him she spent the evening at her home. She turned back west and scanned the horizon. Selah was probably home by now and she couldn't help wonder what the future would hold for her. Would she continue her own personal journey of faith and belief or would she relent to Malchus and his understanding of the Scriptures taught each week at the Temple in which he served the High Priest? It was that moment she knew she would stay in Jerusalem. Her heart ached to be with Jesus but Selah needed her more. She prayed Selah would find courage in the days, weeks and months to follow and meditate on the words she heard spoken and that Simon would too. She made them promise they would keep in touch so they could discuss these things openly. *The Kingdom of God was near.* She knew her life was changed. She knew the lives of those around her had been changed. As the women were calling her, she also knew the lives of Simon and Selah were changed. Her last thought was if Nicodemas and Malchus' lives would also.

Selah hadn't left the house in over a week. Malchus was worried at first, but his concern turned to doubt and then anger. He arranged for the neighbors to make sure she had enough water and grain. He would bring home any other needs.

"So Malchus, you would have me as a prisoner in my own home?"

"You may go into the courtyard," he wouldn't look at her.

"The courtyard! So, the women can wonder what crime I've committed that restricts me to this patch of gravel?"

"Selah, we won't have this conversation again. I've inquired about your friend Kezi and there are conflicting reports. I won't discuss this! You failed to tell me the truth and until I regain your trust, I don't want you to leave our home. In fact, I forbid it!"

"Forbid it! Malchus, I won't live like this. You said you were concerned for my safety. I didn't feel safe to come home that evening. You know yourself there were thousands of people here. They were coming into our courtyard! They saw I had no husband at home. What's the difference now? You aren't home and I'm alone."

"The women will watch over you. You're not alone."

"You don't care about me Malchus. That night I was truly frightened! All those strangers asking to sleep in our home, some I couldn't understand their words. And when two men went around back and disturbed Balaam, I thought I would go to Kezi's and at least have company and not be by myself."

His hands were raised, an indication he didn't want to listen, but it didn't stop her.

"I couldn't believe the change in the market! You could hardly move and Malchus, I did want to turn around and come back but I was stuck! People were pushing and shoving and it was so noisy I couldn't think straight."

His hand was on the door. He was late again. He hoped she was almost finished.

"Well then like I told you, someone or something startled Balaam and he just bolted!"

"Selah, I must go."

She ignored him and continued. "It took hours to move through that crowd and retrieve him, I was so mad." He began pacing.

"Of course, later when I found out what happened at the Temple that day."

"What did you say?"

"I think Balaam got frightened when he heard people shouting and some animals, sheep mostly must have got loose, and Malchus, I really was upset that day," she took a deep breath. He was looking past her.

"Malchus, I've been meaning to ask you. Where were you that day?"

"Hmm. What?"

"Were you at the Temple that day when all the commotion took place?"

"What did you say?"

"Malchus, what's the matter with you? I said, were you at the Temple the day Jesus came and caused all that commotion?"

If he told her he was, he knew she would want details. He wasn't ready to share with her how that day challenged him. "Yes Selah, I was there. Now, I'm really late. Caiaphas will have my head! I must go."

He went pale. He was there! He saw Jesus. Something happened and he doesn't want to talk about it. She wouldn't pursue the conversation. But sitting in the quiet, she recounted the past week and was convinced Jesus impacted her husband's life. He hadn't slept. She heard him up earlier each day and he would be gone by the time she arose. That morning he stood before her; she knew he was upset. He genuinely was concerned, and she knew he had every right to be. She was ashamed. She deceived him. They had walked home in silence, his jaw clenched, controlling his temper. He left early that morning before the sun came up, so when they arrived home together, the neighbors had no inkling of anything out of the ordinary. Once that door was secure, it was a different story. He actually took her by the shoulders firmly and said in sharp, clipped words, "Don't ever leave this house again. You're my wife. I had no idea where you were. You were gone all night! Did you even think about me Selah, what I must be going through?" He released his grip and to her surprise pulled her close. She could feel his heart beating. He held her tight and she welcomed his embrace. No other words were spoken that morning. They were both exhausted. They slept soundly all day and through the night.

They celebrated Passover and he never spoke of the night again. Caiaphas kept him occupied those final two days and life returned to normal, with one small exception. She was forbidden to leave. This couldn't last. She felt punished as a child. He would see how ridiculous this was. She would give him a little more time. Shavuot was less than six weeks and surely, she wasn't to be kept prisoner until then, especially during another feast. She was bored out of her mind! Kezi must be wondering what happened and has come to the conclusion he was very angry. *How could she get word to her friend?* The young girl Mary she'd seen from her courtyard and she waved beckoning her to come but she just stood there. Something wasn't right with her. Kezi was taking a big risk allowing her to have free reign in her home and business. Oh, if only she were home, free to go wherever she desired. She missed the sea! She swore she could still smell it in Balaam's blanket now coated with the dust of Jerusalem. Balaam was forbidden to leave too. Malchus punished him as the culprit of their big adventure. He was probably just as bored as she was.

The women were watching her. She smiled and went to the back of the house, untied Balaam and brought him to the front. She saw out of the corner of her eye three of the younger women rise as if they were ready to run to Caiaphas' house and warn Malchus, '*She has her donkey, she's leaving!*' She laughed to herself and walked Balaam around the inside walls of the courtyard. There wasn't anything to do. How many times could she rearrange rocks? She began humming. It helped her think. She and Balaam paraded around the small courtyard several times; the women next door perplexed. She kept humming. Balaam stopped. She had been leading this procession and when she turned to coax him to continue, a big toothless grin greeted her on the other side of the wall.

"Simon!" She couldn't hide her excitement from the watching women. Where was the line of suspicion and hospitality drawn? She didn't care. She hurried to the gate, handed him Balaam and went to get water and cups for them.

"How did you know where I live? How's Kezi? Simon, Malchus has forbidden me to leave! Can you imagine? Oh, Simon, I'm so happy you're here! I've been out of my mind, bored silly."

He sat grinning and Selah stopped chattering. She looked around nervously.

"Simon, Malchus, he was so upset and I understand, but to forbid me to leave!"

"Malchus will settle down. Give him a little more time. Your neighbors no doubt will tell him of my visit. They'll let him know I'm old, harmless, and didn't enter his home. I can stay until he arrives if you think it best. I simply inquired where the house of Malchus was and most everyone knows who he is. I'll tell him I was the one who helped you catch Balaam, hadn't seen you in the market and only came to see if you had taken ill." She smiled at his sensibility.

"I'll let Kezi know upon my return of your circumstances. She's fine. The young girl Mary has gone home. There were several families from Magdala here for Passover and she's traveling with them. She's an emotional one that girl. Kezi looks forward to your next visit. With Mary gone she's been busy."

"Simon, I could help her! That's how I'll get out of this house!" She clapped her hands at the thought.

"Malchus would allow this?"

"I can only ask. Perhaps if they met. We could go one day to her shop and he would see how wonderful she is. He knows she's from Magdala, that she's my only friend I've met since I came here. Oh, Simon, pray he lets me do this! He could check on me at any time. The market's not far from the Temple and just on the other side of the wall from Caiaphas' house. Will you speak to Kezi for me? She doesn't have to pay me. I'll tell Malchus I'm there to help with her garments while Mary's away. Yes, I'll tell him or rather ask him, please can I try this on a temporary basis, just a few hours, I'll have plenty of time to get home and prepare dinner and take care of the house."

He rose to leave. The women were getting on his nerves. "I'll speak to Kezi. She'll be thrilled! You speak to your husband. We have much to discuss, yes?"

She nodded. He brought hope to her this day. She could imagine having lunch every day with him and Kezi where they could speak freely and she could learn and ask questions and talk about the words Jesus spoke. She untied Balaam, smiled and bowed to her guardians and closed the door. Lentil soup for dinner tonight, and skipping inside, she took out her turquoise scarf.

Caiaphas wore out everyone with his non-stop complaining of the events that took place during the week of Passover. Malchus tried to erase them from his mind. The disappearance of Selah had brought him out of the daze he'd been in. He hadn't much thought about that day, he simply got caught up in the moment. If it were not for Caiaphas' constant reminders, he would have forgotten it entirely. At least that's what he told himself. When Selah asked if he was there, he used the excuse he needed to go, hoping she wouldn't bring it up again. And she hadn't. Little fox he thought as he acquiesced to her request to work with Kezi. Cunning she was serving him dinner in that sea colored scarf. Her eyes had sparkled that night. She practically glided around the room. He smiled. *Who is this girl I married?*

She had washed his feet when he arrived home, the house filled with the familiar scent of his favorite soup, the low light seducing him into relaxing his guard. Seeing her so happy he could care less of the women's report of some old man that came to visit. He knew who he was. She told him it was Simon who helped her that day. He realized she probably was truly frightened. He grew up here. She was from a much quieter area and when her family came to celebrate, she was a young girl surrounded by the safety of her family and neighbors. You're fearless when you're a child, but as a young woman, crushed into the crowded city, alone with her silly donkey, he felt ashamed of keeping her prisoner of her own home as she had put it. She would only be gone a few hours, home right after lunch and if he didn't want her to continue, she wouldn't. He didn't have any reason to say no. She could start after the next Sabbath. Yes, his heart had softened and there was peace again in his home.

Selah burst into the tent and Kezi ran to embrace her.

"Oh Kezi, I'm so happy! I can be here now every day! Did Simon speak with you? You did know I was coming? I have much to tell you!"

Kezi laughed at her friend's exuberance. The two women talked for over an hour. Kezi told her Mary went home, she came from a good family, a wealthy family in fact and was certain she would be well cared for.

"Kezi, I have so many questions. I have much to learn. I wish Simon were here so we could talk together. That night I came looking for you, if it wasn't for Simon, I would never have seen Jesus. My heart is full and I can't speak to Malchus. I wasn't completely honest with him you know. He heard stories about Jesus but I don't think he believes them. They must be true! Why would all these people say these things if they were not true? Simon told me Nicodemas is a very wealthy man, one of the richest in the city! Yet when Simon realized it was him that night going to see Jesus, he didn't understand why a man of his means wouldn't just summon him or make arrangements to speak with him in his home. Why sneak out in the middle of the night? I couldn't answer any of his questions. I know he was thinking out loud. Kezi, can you explain any of these things?"

Yes, Kezi thought to herself she could, but at the moment they needed to work. "Perhaps you can come earlier and I'll ask Simon if he would like to meet also and we'll discuss all we know. I'll provide breakfast and it will be our second family, but now we need to sell some clothes!"

Herodias furious this evening as she caught Herod fixated on Salome her daughter. No amount of perfume or seductive promises would turn his head. She wanted to rush to the terrace and see for herself if Salome was innocently walking in the garden or something much more sinister. She expected the latter and knew if confirmed, it would break her heart. She understood the attraction. Her daughter was beautiful and full of desire and even though she thought herself the same, Herod's actions spoke otherwise. She watched him for several minutes and couldn't hold her insecurity any longer.

"Herod, what has you so enraptured you haven't taken notice of my new perfume?" the practiced smile hurt her cheeks.

"Your daughter is entertaining, and quite charming Herodias. Perhaps I have underestimated her ability to distract my court, and she would be better suited in another position." He stopped short as she looked displeased, he had enough trouble for the day. He arrested John the Baptist. He did so for her. Apparently, she still found fault in his actions and a mere glance at Salome shouldn't bring another tirade especially when John was in his dungeon. He walked to her chaise and promptly reminded her she was still attractive to him. Herodias didn't speak the rest of the evening, her smile one of victory.

Malchus saw a change in Selah. She hummed more. His dinner was always ready when he arrived. He could smell fresh herbs before he entered. She had a green thumb. His house was clean and she made it very comfortable with remnants from Kezi's shop. He had lots of pillows. Allowing her to help Kezi had done wonders for her he realized, and he regretted his selfishness and yes, stubbornness at times.

"Dinner smells wonderful," he reclined now watching her set the table.

"Oh, my bread!" She hurried to turn the fresh baked pieces one last time.

"It's done you well wife to have time away from the house in the mornings. You may continue if that's what you desire."

She turned to look at him. She couldn't begin to tell him what her time with Kezi and Simon meant to her.

"I do like it Malchus. I've been meeting people and I like learning about money and business. I still leave all the selling to Kezi. I don't feel comfortable yet to negotiate prices." She laughed at the ease Kezi had. No man or woman could take advantage of her. She was ruthless, but in a good way. She was fair and honest and provided good products. Kezi began to let her sew and most of the pillows now filling their home were practice items.

"This one has eight different materials," he laughed and gave it a little toss.

She picked it up and fluffed it with care placing it back behind his right arm. "But yet, that's the one you always choose."

"It's my pillow of many colors, like Joseph's coat!"

They laughed together. They were growing in their marriage. She began to understand more about his life. Everyone knew him and he knew everyone. She didn't ask if he heard anything about Kezi. He may not let her continue to work if he thought she might still be "working". She wanted to tell him it had been almost a year since she moved here, how her life had changed. Kezi told her that day when they first met, as she was relaying the story of when Pilate came with his soldiers, she was shaking inside when they came into her tent. She didn't know if the soldiers were coming to taunt her or God forbid, ask for her services. She stood confident that day. She knew in her heart that part of her life was over, dead. They had no interest in her and she was relieved!

They became like sisters. Mornings were the best! Simon came every day and they were becoming close friends. They would catch him several times during the week close to the shop, standing guard. He remained obsessed with the statement Jesus made to Nicodemas and this also was a morning ritual. Kezi promised Simon the next time

Jesus was in Jerusalem they would ask him the meaning of this term "born again".

Selah studied Kezi. She was a couple years older and most of her acquaintances also. She hoped to learn from each woman. Most were married, others widowed. They all had a story. Some afternoons she would have to pull herself away, and run home in time to make dinner, so engrossed in listening. One woman named Joanna who came often to purchase Kezi's beautiful scarves was the wife of Herod's steward. Once out of sight, the women would talk about her imagining all sorts of things she may be privileged to see in Herod's house.

Kezi grew somber then. She told them John the Baptist had been arrested and thrown in the dungeon at Herod's home. Cries of shock followed.

"How long will they keep him?" one asked.

"What was he arrested for?" asked another.

"Kezi, what can be done?"

They turned to Selah. "Your husband, Malchus, can he speak to anyone?"

Selah stuttered, "I don't know," she looked at Kezi for help.

"We don't have details. I'm not sure Selah's husband would either but perhaps she'll speak to him about this man and when we meet again, we can discuss if there's anything we could possibly do." In her heart, Kezi thought probably not.

Chapter Three

It was a little over a month Mary had been home. Her father met with a few local fishermen and she went with him, had begged him to take her in their boat across the sea. She had battled her emotions for some time, and nothing could bring her comfort. Her mother agreed seeing the despair in her face, she was just happy to have her back home.

"The sea air will do you good Mary," her mother packed a lunch for them and Mary simply nodded.

She only wanted to be free. Free from the oppression she felt. She thought she might scream some days but always managed to remain detached to her surroundings. She let the rhythm of the waves and the heat of the sun bring her to the closest edge of peace she felt in a long time. Her father never took his eyes off the clouds searching for any signs of an impending storm. He was going to meet Zebedee of Bethsaida. She sat with her arm draped over the boat attempting to reach the surface of the water, staring into the depths, mindless. An occasional splash from the oars would jolt her out of her daydreaming and she would lift her head to check all was calm.

But it wasn't. She heard the sounds of several boats and the creaking of wood, men yelling to each other, and she stood for a better look. Losing her balance, she landed hard, her father turned and called out.

"Mary, look! I've never seen anything like it! That boat appears to be sinking, look at that catch! His nets are breaking! It's the heat of the day, look at those fish!"

She never saw her father so alive! Over fish! It was the family business after all. Finally, able to secure her footing, she came close to witness the vessel leaning to one side with its net full. Another boat was fast approaching and as she and her father were still some distance away, they watched the entire rescue at sea, the fishermen laughing, rejoicing and shouting with the exception of one. She was on her feet caught up in the enthusiasm and pure joy of the men when she saw him. He was on his knees, head bowed. *Why wasn't he jumping and shouting or helping to bring in the catch?* As her father maneuvered their own boat closer, she saw Jesus. It was Peter at his feet, a myriad of emotion. Still on his knees, hands lifted high, now rejoicing, but somehow, she knew it wasn't because of fish. Even from this distance, she sensed a peace she longed for. Peter was at peace. *What did Jesus say to him?*

The boats were abandoned, all on shore listening to Jesus. She found shelter under the shade of a tree. Several people gathered and she blended in with the women who began separating the fish in their baskets. She didn't take her eyes off Jesus. And it seemed to her he didn't take his eyes off of her. Her heart was pounding. Her legs were weak. She thought she might faint. She couldn't move. He was walking towards her. Her knees gave out and as she sank to the ground, he called to her, "Mary". *How did he know my name?* She was shaking. She felt she had no control over her mind or body. He took her hand and strength was restored. His eyes were full of compassion. He spoke. She heard his words but to this day she couldn't recall them. She only knew she was free! He delivered her from all fear, doubt, anxiety, depression, loneliness and mental anguish she lived with the last year. She felt loved. Unconditionally. Her heart was full. She didn't understand what happened. She didn't know anything about this man, but what resounded in her soul was she knew beyond doubt she would spend the rest of her life finding out.

Shavuot was approaching. Caiaphas made it abundantly clear he wouldn't tolerate any interruptions at the Temple. The guards had strict orders. Any hint of disturbance on their watch would result in their dismissal. Malchus missed being home. Caiaphas had him engaged twenty-four hours a day, six days a week. He was looking forward to summer. Maybe he and Selah could go away for a few weeks. He would take her to the sea. He needed to be far removed from Caiaphas, the Temple, the guards, politics, and all the nonsense. He was tired of listening. He wanted, no he needed someone to listen to him. He heard about Kezi. At first, he was outraged. Selah hadn't mentioned her background. Giving her the benefit of doubt, he inquired with his sources and was assured it was past history and he need not worry. Kezi was actually quite respected in the community and no one thought any less of Selah or him at the friendship with her.

Everyone has a past. He knew his Selah. The past couple of months had been wonderful! Their lives seemed to be in harmony. He smiled at her innocence. He struggled with his own. He knew too much! His head was full. He couldn't empty the contents at home. Selah wouldn't understand or comprehend the munitions of Caiaphas' world. He didn't want her to know. He heard so many contradictions, he now questioned everything. *Who was right?* The Pharisees were passionate about the law. He was conflicted. There were choices in life. Barabbas and his followers would shout they had no choice! They didn't choose Rome. John the Baptist was the topic for a week when Herod arrested him. He didn't have a choice. Kezi, raped by a Roman soldier, didn't have a choice either. He felt his heart beat a little faster. There was a time not so long ago these things wouldn't affect him the way they did now. *Jesus.* That day still haunted his dreams. *Who is this man?* Caiaphas warned everyone not to speak his name. He was in good spirits as there had been no sight of him.

Kezi and Simon now had their shops next to each other. Simon offered his fellow merchant a small percentage of his profit to allow him to be close to his girls as he now referred to them. He reminded his friend, "I've only a little time left. I wish to relax in my old age, maybe take up fishing." They both laughed. Simon was born a salesman, not a fisherman. He would like to putter around a garden and sit in the square with the sun warming his bones.

"Balaam my old friend!" Simon gave the donkey an affectionate hug around his neck. He always made sure he had Balaam's bag at the ready with apples and pears. Kezi was displaying her latest tunics and had been busy sewing beads on pillows. He scratched his beard upon first sight of them.

"They have tassels."

"Yes, Simon, they're fancy pillows."

"Well, we'll see how many you sell today. Want to place a wager?"

Kezi was careful to arrange them so each color and fabric would compliment its neighbor. Selah, the student, took note of all. Malchus mentioned a small trip over the summer and as much as she longed for the sea, she would miss her new life with Simon and Kezi. They were her family. Simon secured Balaam and they sat down for their morning fellowship. The city had begun to swell again from those coming to celebrate. They cut their morning time down by half to take advantage of the opportunity to sell.

"Shalom." Kezi didn't turn around, she just called out she wasn't ready to open yet.

"Kezi," the voice was familiar. She stood up.

Simon and Selah continued to eat their breakfast and heard Kezi crying or laughing. They couldn't tell from inside the tent, and before they could stand, Kezi returned and announced, "We have a visitor!"

"Shalom everyone."

"Mary?" Selah couldn't believe it! This was not the girl only a couple months ago hardly looked at anyone, hair down in her eyes, always, she didn't want to say it, "lurking" in a corner or behind a door. This vibrant, young girl, a smile from ear to ear wasn't Mary. Simon thought he should leave to let the women talk but Mary wouldn't have it. Kezi couldn't let go of her, the shock and surprise overwhelming her this morning. No one knew what to say first.

"I already said hello to Balaam," Mary said. "He of course looked disappointed I didn't have a treat for him," she looked at Kezi, "I have much to tell you."

Kezi insisted she stay with her and invited Selah and Simon for dinner. "Wait, how did you get here? Who are you traveling with?"

"I'll speak with you tonight. I'll explain everything later." She looked at Selah, "You will come, won't you Selah?"

"Of course!" Malchus would be busy. She would get word to him today.

"Simon, will you come also?" Mary asked.

"I'll be there, and I'll bring the food!"

She was beaming. They didn't want to let her out of their sight. "I'll see all of you in a few hours," she hugged each one and quickly left. Kezi and Selah, mouths open, just stood there. Simon clapped his hands to bring them out of their stupor.

"Come now, we have work to do. You have many pillows to sell today," he picked up a blue one and discovered Kezi had sewn beads on each tassel and as he shook it, the beads clicked in unison.

"How is a man to sleep with these noisy beads at his head?"

"They're for decoration Simon, not sleep!" Kezi took it from his hands as he couldn't stop shaking it. He was entertaining himself with a thought that had his laughter filling the tent.

Nicodemas eyed Malchus a little suspiciously as he watched him run up the remaining steps to where he was standing. *What did Caiaphas want now?*

"Greetings Nicodemas. Do you have a few moments?"

"What's this about Malchus? If Caiaphas has another meeting, we shall all be asleep for the feast from pure exhaustion."

"No, this is personal." They walked to a private area. Malchus didn't know what question he wanted to ask first.

"Tell me Malchus, what is it you would like to know?"

"This man Jesus, who do you think he is? What do the Scriptures say? He said that day the Temple was his Father's house. I know this is God's house, but he called God his Father, and Nicodemas, I was there that day as you know, when he said it, I can't explain it, but he said it with such authority."

Both men looked around to see if anyone was eavesdropping on their conversation. Nicodemas' palms began to sweat. *Did Malchus know he went to meet Jesus that evening? Is this a trap Caiaphas has set?*

Malchus continued, "I've heard many stories about this man. They say he heals the sick, performs miracles and even casts out demons. You're a learned man Nicodemas. Where in the Holy Scriptures does it speak about such a man?"

Nicodemas saw he was sincere. It wasn't a trap. "We know God uses men to do His work, great prophets. Think of Elijah and Elisha. They performed many great signs. Perhaps this Jesus is another prophet God is using to speak to His people at this time."

"Some say he is Messiah." *What did he just see in Nicodemas? A glimmer of hope?*

"Malchus, this could become a lengthy conversation. We don't have enough hours in the day left for this topic. Caiaphas must have plenty for you to do and I must leave for another meeting." He placed his hand on his shoulder, "Only time will tell if this Jesus is Messiah," Nicodemas was careful with his words. "This requires much study, yes?"

"Yes, it does. That's why I wanted to speak with you. You have studied. Do you think he's the one to come?" They both saw Caiaphas at the same time. The conversation ended at that moment. Nicodemas waved at Caiaphas and hurried down the steps before he could call him.

"What did Nicodemas want?"

"He had no request Caiaphas. He only stopped to say how wonderful the Temple looked and is looking forward to Shavuot," Malchus was convincing.

"I shall need you to stay at my house the next few days in final preparation. Please inform your wife. You may take time to go into the market to let her know."

"Caiaphas, your home is not far from my own."

Caiaphas put his hand up to prevent him from saying anymore. "I know this is somewhat of an inconvenience, however, I need you to be close should any rumors about Jesus and his follower's surface and even Barabbas for that matter. They like an audience and during the feast we need to be on guard," he was walking away before Malchus could respond.

He took his time walking to Kezi's shop. He knew Selah would understand his absence again as Caiaphas became more paranoid during the feasts. *Time will tell*, that's what Nicodemas said. He thought it wasn't a very wise answer from one who had the chief seats in the synagogue. Who was he to turn to? How much could he learn once a week at Sabbath services? Even during Sabbath, he remained servant to Caiaphas. A servant. *This is all I am to be?*

He had to admit he relished the attention at the market, in and around the Temple. He felt pride. He wasn't pedaling vegetables from some old broken-down cart. *Simon.* This man had pride in doing exactly that. He saw it when Simon was able to offer the best melons and fresh greens each day, treating each piece of produce as it were a trophy, an award given for his achievements. It was a cucumber for land's sake! An old man and his garden and he appeared happy and at peace. He didn't need accolades of others. Kezi and Selah fussed over him and since the two women had come into his life, even the other merchants said it was like he was a new man! *Like he was born again.* He stopped. *Where did those words come from?* He swore to himself! Malchus, you're hearing things. He stood in the middle of the market trying to reconcile his own ramblings. He knew deep in his heart these words held a far greater meaning. He would ask Nicodemas when they spoke again. Perhaps he would get a better answer.

Mary was waiting at Kezi's house. Simon arrived first.

"Well young lady, it's good to see you! Kezi and Selah should be here soon." Simon was awkward around her. Mary helped him with Balaam and he noticed she didn't divert her eyes anymore. She gave him direct contact, engaging in small talk, patting Balaam's head, almost giddy.

"Mary, tell this old man what's happened? It's obvious to all of us you're a different person!"

She didn't hesitate. "Jesus!" she said. "I have met Jesus."

A tear rolled down Simon's face and overwhelmed with the warmth of her voice, he grabbed and hugged her and spun her around like his own granddaughter. They were both crying with joy when Kezi and Selah reached them.

"Are we celebrating something?" Kezi now joined in the circle as they danced around.

"We're celebrating Jesus!" Mary cried.

Selah observed them for a few seconds before becoming a part of the circle. It was strange to her. This girl who never spoke, had peculiar behavior, hair always wild and loose without a covering, was smiling, laughing, dancing, all with clarity and joy as if she discovered a treasure.

She soon found out this treasure was Jesus. *Jesus,* his name on her lips brought wonder.

They couldn't sit down for a long time, the joy genuine and heartfelt. Mary shared the day at sea she was freed from bondage. Her account had them sitting straight up, leaning in, every detail they wanted to taste and place deep in their heart. They begged her to repeat some parts of the day so they wouldn't forget the moment she saw Jesus. Dinner was untouched. Balaam was stuffed! Kezi then shared the night she surprised Simon and Selah when they followed Nicodemas. Mary was just as attentive as they were when she shared her life changing day.

"Wait! You have all met Jesus?" Mary looked at each face, not wanting to miss one reaction.

"Yes," they said together. Kezi asked Mary if she recalled the day two men had come to her house.

"Andrew and Phillip! They are here!"

"Where?" Kezi was on her feet.

"They're here for Shavuot. We're here for the feast and then we'll go back to Galilee."

Now Selah spoke, "Mary, when you say all are here, is Jesus here?"

"Yes, and many followers, myself included."

They could only stare at this transformed young woman who in a short time had gone from troubled soul to follower of Jesus, no doubt in her mind, no question in her heart, no fear of the unknown, completely at peace.

"Kezi, I'll stay with you and then I must leave. I owe you so much! Your kindness to me I shall never forget."

Simon and Selah were excited beyond anything they could imagine. Would they be able to speak to Jesus? Could they really ask him questions?

Malchus, Selah whispered to herself.

"Nicodemas," Simon was thinking out loud.

Pilate returned to the city. He was beginning to loathe these feasts; however, he was expected to keep order. Claudia heard about the arrest of John the Baptist and Pilate was nonchalant, callous even. She was disappointed at her husband's indifference.

"Claudia, don't start. We're only here a few days and hopefully it will be quiet and trouble-free."

"Is there no compassion left in you husband?"

He walked away. The city put him in a bad mood. She had to admit during the celebrations, it wasn't pleasant for her either. He would have meetings all day. There was nothing for her to do. She went to the balcony and looked over the market. A sea of people, animals, shops, colors and smells. She would go shopping. She would disguise herself and leave through the kitchen where staff entered. She would take advantage of Pilate's foul mood, the influx of people and walk the streets. *Walk the streets* she said out loud and began to laugh. She couldn't dress fast enough. Her maid had clothes laid out for her.

"Not these Avi, please find me something more comfortable." Claudia looked at what she was wearing. Again, she addressed the girl. "Bring me a tunic and outer garment like you're wearing."

"I don't know if you have something this plain." Avi rushed to her wardrobe and began sorting through blues, purples and greens. No dull brown or grays could be found. She held up a cream-colored tunic and quickly made a sash.

"Perfect." Claudia slipped on her shoes and told Avi she was dismissed for the afternoon. Avi didn't leave her chamber.

"I'll be in the garden today. I want to sit in the sun and relax. I don't require your service for the better part of the day," Claudia motioned for her to go. There were only two servants in the kitchen when she walked in. She observed the table with lunch preparations and pretended to look for fruit she knew would be out of season. She moved around baskets and lifted a few trays and finally spoke.

"Yes, I'll be in the garden, please bring me fresh melon and perhaps some mint." All she had to do now was wait. As the two servants left to go to the market, she did also about twenty paces behind.

The shimmer of silver caught her eye and Claudia found herself among several women almost in a frenzy pulling colorful scarves and sashes between them. There were small bottles of perfume and wonderful pillows and sachets. She picked up a silver sash and held it up to the sun.

"It's beautiful!"

Kezi replied, "Yes, and it's the only one left."

"I'll take it!" She then realized she had no money. "Oh no, I've forgotten my purse."

"I can hold it for you for a little while."

Claudia cut her off, "No, I can't ask you to do that."

"You didn't ask," Kezi smiled.

Claudia smiled back, "I'm not sure when I'll be here again."

Kezi folded the scarf and placed it in her hands. "It's yours, a gift. Enjoy it."

"I couldn't possibly. You don't understand. I have money, but I left so quickly I forgot my purse."

"I believe you. I own the shop and it's my way to say welcome to hopefully a new customer."

Nothing like this ever happened to her before. She was uncomfortable. She was humbled. Mary and Selah were busy keeping garments in place and a watchful eye on the jewelry. Unfortunately, annual celebrations brought out the worst in people. Claudia continued to admire Kezi's things. She saw a pair of earrings she would send Avi for later. She knew she should go back but she was enjoying herself. She never did anything like this or hadn't in this city. No one recognized her. No one would be looking for her in an open market. Kezi was staring down and she followed her gaze. *Oh, my sandals!* She had forgotten about her slippers. They were a dead giveaway.

Roman, Kezi thought. Not only Roman, but influential Roman slippers embroidered with jewels. She locked eyes with Kezi and both women seemed to acknowledge this revelation. No other words were spoken, she hurried home praying the kitchen door would be unlocked. Kezi watched the woman, head down, travel towards the Temple. She would look for those slippers again. Someone else was watching too. Simon. Without Kezi noticing, he followed the mystery woman.

Simon realized she was heading directly to Pilate's house. *It can't be.* Only a woman of stature would have the type of embellished slippers she was wearing. A servant wouldn't, but yet this woman was walking quickly to access the servant's quarters. He kept out of sight and was able to see her outside the entrance to the rear of the city house. He saw her take the silver scarf and tuck it in the sash hiding it. She was careful to smooth it out and draping her outer garment over her shoulders, she casually walked to the door. As she pulled it open, he thought he could detect the slightest curl of a smile on her lips. She looked over her shoulder ensuring no one saw her but he did. *Claudia.* He sucked in his breath.

Yesterday was the last day Mary was in the shop. There were no words for the transformation that had obviously taken place in her life. Kezi understood. Selah was trying to. Both Mary and Kezi tried to explain to her it was personal, a "personal" revelation of who Jesus is and although they didn't have all the answers, one thing they did know is Mary was no longer a depressed, emotional mess and Kezi no longer a prostitute. It was as simple as that. They were no longer what they once were. This is what she struggled with. What was it about her life that no longer should be? As she meditated on this, her frustration grew. She and Simon discussed this several times. He would shrug his shoulders, tell her not to think so much and they would talk about it later. But she was consumed. She saw it in Mary. The woman she knew in Kezi, she couldn't imagine her former life.

"Mary doesn't like goodbyes. She told me to tell you she'll see you soon," Kezi said.

Selah attempted a smile. They walked to the market, Balaam in tow, and were surprised Simon hadn't arrived. He showed up at lunchtime to escort Selah home. He told her he would wait until Malchus arrived if she needed him to.

"Where were you this morning? We missed you."

"I waited for my friend Joses. He brought me some berries that grow close to where he lives," he wasn't sure if he should mention Claudia.

He wanted to be certain it was her and if anyone else noticed the Prefect's wife roaming the streets of Jerusalem unattended.

"I missed Mary this morning. She left before I woke up," she stopped walking and looked at him. "Mary's so different. It continues to amaze me. I've never seen such a change in someone's behavior, why her whole appearance has changed."

He nodded in agreement. She was tapping her foot. He thought that helped her concentrate.

"She's a new person Simon. Doesn't it astound you at the change in her?" Before he could respond Selah clapped her hands and said, "I've got it! She's born again!"

Simon shouted, "Yes, that's it! She's new, like she's just been born. You're right Selah! It's not the outside that's new, it's the inside! Her heart and mind are all new! The Mary we knew doesn't exist anymore. She's new! Like she was born again!" They ran back to Kezi's shop.

Malchus wanted to go home. The Temple guards were suffocating him. Caiaphas was in charge of the treasury and as his attendant, he was never far, and when money was involved, Caiaphas was surrounded. Accountability. Little did most know Caiaphas held all his dealings in the privacy of his own home. Pilate would no doubt have a new list of those he would appoint as tax collectors and Caiaphas would be privy to the list before said appointments were made. *Accountability?* Malchus smirked. Who's holding Caiaphas accountable? Annas, his father-in-law? Doubtful. He most assuredly got the first cut of profit. He knew too much. He shouldn't have any protest when he requested his travel plans. He would be home the day after tomorrow and would tell Selah he wished to go away, to take her to the sea. They would be gone several weeks. He knew she would miss Kezi. Maybe he would invite her to travel with them. He didn't know if she could afford to close her shop for the summer. Many did. He wasn't fond of the journey, but once at sea he would relax. He closed his eyes. No matter how hard he tried, he couldn't erase the image of Jesus, with this righteous anger overturning the money changers tables, the Temple livelihood, and with a passion he hadn't seen in a very long time. He hoped for passion in his own life. He opened his eyes; both Caiaphas and Nicodemas stood before him. He thought he was dreaming. Caiaphas, arms folded, just stared at him.

"Sleeping Malchus?"

Caiaphas actually sounded pleasant. He had to admit he held many meetings this past week. He and Nicodemas both chuckled.

"Go home to your wife."

He never saw Caiaphas jubilant. *What's happened? Did both he and Nicodemas make a small fortune this Shavuot? Did Pilate go back to Caesarea? Was Barabbas dead?* For both of these men to stand side by side joking around with a servant, something was amiss. He would find out.

"I'll be off then."

They turned their backs and were engaged in conversation before he hit the second step. Selah should be home, but he would cut through the market anyway. He saw Balaam first; Simon and Selah were speaking with someone. Simon looked animated in his actions, they didn't notice him, so he walked around the merchants still packing up to see who they were speaking with. It was Kezi. As he drew near, he began to hear their conversation.

"And that's when I think I understood," it was Selah speaking. "Mary was new. The old Mary was gone. It was like someone or some-thing had made a new Mary, like she was born again!"

Simon just smiled, the grin wide and sincere. Kezi had her hand over her mouth, her other hand on Simon's arm.

"You must be born again," Simon spoke the words slowly, methodically.

They all stood and nodded their heads like they just discovered the secret of the ages. Malchus thought he might still be dreaming.

Kezi went home to an empty house. In the quiet of her surround-ings, her thoughts went to Mary. She was thankful several women were traveling with her. She knew firsthand the benefit. She couldn't imagine being with Jesus every moment. *She will have great things to tell us upon her return.* She began to sort out material and a small bag of assorted beads fell and scattered everywhere. As she picked them up from the floor, she saw her own shoes left by the door. *Those slippers! Who did they belong to?* She had admired the symmetry of the workmanship which drew her eye to them in the first place. They were not the kind of shoes you typically see in Jerusalem, especially given the attire of this woman. She was hiding something or hiding from someone. She sat there, rolling one bead between her thumb and finger, watching the sun go to sleep. Darkness. She could move around the city easily. She remembered a place close to the market where servants would stop before going to their respective homes. There they shared wine, food and gossip. She brought the bead with her, a story forming in her mind.

Malchus waited in the shadows. His head hurt from thinking so much these past few weeks. He wasn't ready to talk about words he was hearing from thin air. What had him gripped in complete bafflement was Selah repeating those same words. *How could she possibly know this same phrase? She couldn't!* This mystified him even more. It was simply impossible! Yes, they needed time away. He would discuss it with her tonight. He began his walk home.

Selah had dinner ready. She missed her little house. She missed Malchus. He seemed uneasy around her lately. She recognized that faraway look as soon as he came in the door. There was no hiding it.

"Welcome home!" she would be as cheerful as she could. It's good to be home, even though I enjoyed Mary's visit and my time with her."

"Yes, Mary. Where did you say she went?"

"What?" She was buying time; this was a question she didn't expect.

"This Mary, where did she go?"

"I'm not certain Malchus, she said she was going to Galilee."

"Who is she going with?"

She sat down. *Did Caiaphas ask Malchus to find out information about Jesus?*

"She's traveling with Jesus and his followers."

He waited for her to continue but she was finished. She wasn't going to volunteer any information.

"When did they leave?"

"Malchus, why are you asking? Did you meet Mary? Is she in trouble or in some kind of danger?"

"I was curious, that's all. I know nothing about her. Come, let's eat. I want to talk about us going away. I thought we would go and see your family," he studied her face. He didn't get the reaction he thought he would.

"Yes, that would be nice Malchus. How long would we be away?"

"I don't know, I think the better part of summer."

"Caiaphas will allow you to be gone that long?"

"Is there a reason you don't want to go? I thought you would be anxious to see your family and you've told me how much you enjoy the sea."

"I do, it's just I like working and I wouldn't want to leave Kezi alone that long. Mary may not be back for some time."

He was biting his tongue. He had questions he wanted to ask. He didn't have to, she continued talking.

"She received an inheritance. Her father, when she went back home, saw such a change in her and when she told him she was going to follow Jesus and support his ministry, he gave her the inheritance."

"What?" He was shocked.

"She didn't expect to receive it, but Malchus, an incredible thing happened to Mary when she went home and her father was with her! I wish she could share her story with you," she tried to read his blank look. "Of course, I know you didn't know Mary, but Malchus, even in the short time I knew her, I saw a miraculous change!"

"Miraculous? Really Selah?"

"Yes, I think so."

Now what did he see? She looked sad. "What have I said?"

"You don't seem to believe what I'm saying. She's a different person. Like she's...she didn't finish."

"Like she's what Selah?" He was holding his breath. *Would she say it?*

"Like she's born again."

"Born again?" *Did you think of the words born again? What do you mean by that?*

Selah didn't like his tone. "I meant it's as if she's a new person, that's all."

He knew better. The three of them heard the phrase somewhere, otherwise they wouldn't have discussed it among themselves. He pressed her.

"It's those two words together, born again. You didn't answer me. Did you hear these words and you're repeating them or is it something you thought of?"

She was shaking a little and prayed he didn't notice. *What does he know? Don't lie Selah!* He walked towards her.

"I guess I overheard them. It's an unusual phrase I agree. How can a person be born again? It sounds a little silly. It's just this young girl Mary, Malchus, I can't stop thinking about the change in her and that phrase fit perfectly, that's all," she felt his breath he stood so close. "What is it Malchus? Do these words trouble you? I won't speak them again if this upsets you. You look displeased."

"Forget it, I'm not upset," he helped her clear the table all the while asking about her childhood, did she have a favorite place she went to, anything to keep him from thinking.

He made her uncomfortable. Her heart sank at the thought that somehow, he found out about the night they went to find Kezi and met Jesus and to everyone's shock, saw Nicodemas. She wanted to tell him. She would ask Kezi what she thought she should do. She would also tell Kezi that he wanted to go away for the summer. She wasn't looking forward to either conversation.

Kezi was out most of the prior evening attempting to find any information she could on any Roman women who were in the city. She dared to even visit one location where some women she had known from her past were still in the business. She had an eye for quality leather, materials and craftsmanship. No one she knew would be able to spend money on slippers of this quality with families to support.

Simon and Selah just arrived. She stepped out to greet them. "You two will not believe what I did the other night!"

"A couple of days ago a woman came to the shop and she picked out a silver scarf to purchase."

"I remember the silver one! It was one of my favorites," Selah said.

"Yes, mine too Selah, so, I was folding it and the woman realized she had no money."

"Do you think she was trying to take it?"

"No, I don't. There was something different about her, I don't know why I did this, but I gave it to her and said it was a gift."

"Kezi, that's so nice," Selah said. Simon just listened.

"But then I noticed something a little unusual. She had on very costly slippers. No ordinary person would have this kind. They were beautiful with a pattern of blue, gold and silver embroidered thread with gemstones perfectly symmetrical."

Simon couldn't hold his tongue any longer. "I followed her."

"What? You don't know who I'm talking about!" she looked at Selah like Simon had too much wine.

"I saw you looking down at the ground. At first, I thought you may have seen a coin or perhaps this woman dropped her money. Then I saw the slippers."

"Simon! You followed her? Why did you wait so long to tell me?" she gave him a little push on his shoulder.

"She went to Pilate's house."

"Pilate's?" Kezi repeated.

"She entered through the kitchen, the servant's entrance."

"No servant would have those slippers unless," she didn't finish her sentence.

"Unless what Kezi?" Selah wanted to know.

"Unless they were a gift, or perhaps payment," Kezi looked at Simon. They weren't sure if Selah comprehended what they were saying.

"She turned as she was going in," Simon told them. "I think she wanted to make sure no one saw her but I briefly did. I believe it was Claudia, wife of Pilate."

"No, it couldn't be! She would never be without Roman escort," Kezi was certain of this.

"I didn't want to say anything until I was certain it was her," he looked at both women.

"Simon, do you really think it was Claudia?" Kezi was intrigued. *And she gave her a scarf!* She thought at first the woman couldn't afford it. She put her face in her hands.

Simon was shaking his head. "These are strange days, yes? Nicodemas sneaking out to see Jesus and now the wife of the Prefect out in an open market, no money, no escort."

Kezi and Selah both stood at the same time. They knew they would study every detail of every woman who came to the shop from now on. Kezi's mind was racing. What must this woman, if indeed it was Claudia think of her giving her the scarf, presuming she couldn't buy it, that saying she had forgotten her money was something she heard a thousand times. She didn't know if she was mad, sad or glad. Mad that perhaps she was tricked by a Roman governor's wife, sad that maybe she was truly lonely and escaped the confines of her home for an afternoon, glad she treated her with kindness. Now she was more curious than ever! When she looked up, she saw Simon staring at her and knew he was just as curious.

Nicodemas let the sunlight refresh him. He'd been reading for days, weeks with a new hunger. Jesus' words gnawed at him. He replayed that scene over and over from the moment he addressed him and the words that followed, 'Except a man be born again, he cannot see the Kingdom of God'. *Not only did Jesus say I couldn't see the Kingdom of God, he also said I wouldn't enter it either unless I was born again.* The rest of the dialogue was too wonderful! He could only concentrate on those first words. Jesus called him a master of Israel. He should know these things. He was teaching others! And yet he sat, surrounded by scrolls, searching to understand and discern words spoken to his very core. It made his bones weak. The sun was not helping. Caiaphas' house was literally a stone's throw from his and he wrestled with himself to walk over and somehow bring up the subject of the kingdom of God but he wouldn't. The words awakened his heart! His thoughts turned to Malchus. The words he heard must have stirred him as well. *Who is this Jesus?* All his studies didn't point to this man as Messiah. Or did they? He looked around his room. It was dimly lit, the sun now hidden behind soft gray clouds. So much to reason, so many questions. He thought he may never leave this room again.

Joanna and Avi were friends. They seldom were able to shop together but today they both happened to reach the Essene gate at the same time. The small enclave where Jerusalem's wealthiest lived found them in close proximity, but their duties kept them indoors most days. Today was an exception and a surprise.

"Avi, it's been weeks since I've seen you. How are you my friend?"

"I'm well, and you?"

Joanna adjusted her belt and apron. She had much to shop for this day. "Things have quieted down, however, Herod has almost gone mad by John the Baptist and his constant shouting, even in the dungeon he continues to shout for Herod to repent! I've also heard Herodias has threatened him she will leave and take her daughter if he thinks about releasing him," Joanna looked around for any listening ears. "That daughter of hers, she's trouble Avi. Everyone sees how Herod looks at her, even Herodias."

"She's young, isn't she?" Avi asked.

"She's her mother's daughter. I've seen her paint her eyes!"

"No! I've only seen my mistress paint her eyes for a party!" Avi couldn't believe a girl so young would do this.

Joanna turned to her, "How's the wife of Pilate?"

Now it was Avi's turn to make sure their conversation was private. "The other day she dismissed me for the afternoon saying she wanted to sit in the garden," she leaned in closer, "but Joanna, she asked me to find her something plain to wear and I never left the quarters. She wasn't in the garden. Later she came in through the back and hurried up the steps. She had something hidden in the girdle I tied around her garment. When I approached the room, she was hiding something and never spoke to me."

"What was it?"

"I don't know. I saw her holding up something, but I didn't want her to know I was at the door," Avi stood and extended her hand to her friend. "Come, let's get our shopping done."

Joanna let Avi pull her up. "Do you think she left the house?"

"Well if she didn't, she hid pretty well."

"But why would she want to wear plain clothes?" Joanna asked.

"She actually said she wanted a tunic that looked like mine!" Now the two women laughed.

"What are you shopping for today?" Joanna inquired.

"Pillows," Avi said with delight in her eyes.

"Pillows?"

"Pilate and my mistress are going home. She wants new pillows for her litter."

"I know just the place," Joanna led her to Kezi's shop.

"Look at this one!" Avi shook the pillow enjoying the colors of each tassel. Selah was smiling. She helped Kezi braid the tassels, several of which they had to do over before Kezi sewed them. She liked everything perfect. Joanna came around the corner and both Kezi and Selah said hello at the same time.

"Shalom, shalom," Joanna turned to Avi and introduced her. "We're shopping for pillows today!

"These are so pretty Kezi. Do you have another one like this?" Avi wasn't letting go of her find.

Kezi went to another section of her tent where she found the matching one. "I have it!" She turned the pillow to let the tassels dance as she brought it to the women.

"What do you think Joanna? Should I get two that match?" Avi loved them.

"Yes, I think she'll like them."

"Oh, they're not for you?" Kezi asked.

"No, I'm shopping for my mistress. She's leaving tomorrow and asked for new pillows, ones that hadn't absorbed all this dust is what she said." The women laughed again.

Kezi laughed too. "Anything for you Joanna?"

"Not today. I have other things to shop for and Avi and I don't see each other very often so when we ran into each other today and she told me the Prefect's wife wanted new pillows, I brought her right over."

"Did you say the Prefect's wife?" Kezi and Selah both stood still.

"Yes, Claudia, the wife of Pilate. I'm her servant," Avi looked at Joanna nervously. Kezi and Selah were looking at her a little strangely. Joanna noticed too.

"Kezi, is something wrong?" Do you not wish to sell to a Roman?" Joanna asked.

"No, you know I sell to the Romans. I've never met anyone who actually worked at the Pretorium, especially inside the private rooms of Pilate's wife. She must have beautiful things," Kezi decided this was her chance.

"Oh yes, she does," Avi said. "It takes me an afternoon to pack her chest. The sandals alone! She has a pair for every outfit!"

"I would love to rummage through her things," Selah now spoke. "Does she wear the sandals of Rome or does she import them from the East?"

Avi and Joanna were having fun. They seldom spoke about their employers.

"Most are slippers. Some have small bells so you can hear when she's coming, and some have perfume so when my lady walks, you smell cinnamon!" Avi said in delight.

"You're kidding!" Selah exclaimed.

"No, and she has several pairs of beautiful embroidered ones covered in gemstones, they glisten and shimmer. Why just this morning when I was cleaning her room, I picked up a white pair she must have worn recently. They're so soft, hand sewn leather with blue, gold and silver thread," she looked at Joanna. "You don't know how many times I've wanted to try them on."

They all laughed but Kezi and Selah were certain now of the mystery woman who had Kezi's silver scarf.

Chapter Four

Kezi would love to go to the sea. Home. Selah caught her off guard at the invitation to travel. She was thankful she had time to make a decision. She was a business woman. There would be opportunity on the trade routes, especially at Decapolis. She wanted to buy more silk and of course spices that were hard to find in the city. She heard both Simon and Selah arrive.

"It was Claudia!" Kezi broke the silence.

"How do you know?" Simon asked.

"My friend Joanna came to the shop with the woman who serves her. One thing led to another and we have no doubt it was Claudia. She came to buy pillows. Pilate is leaving for Caesarea soon."

"Perhaps we should all go to Galilee for the summer. It seems everyone is headed that way. Pilate, Claudia, Mary, Jesus," he looked now at both women, "Me."

"You will go Simon?" Selah grabbed his arm.

"If Kezi goes, I'll go. It will be another adventure."

"I will go." Kezi's words were out before she knew it. "Selah, I'll need a few days to prepare. Speak to Malchus tonight, ask him when he wishes to depart, and who's traveling with us?" The three embraced and Simon called after Selah to bring Balaam tomorrow, he missed the donkey. Selah smiled all the way home.

Malchus met Caiaphas in his home. He confirmed his travel and was a little taken back Caiaphas didn't flinch when he told him he would be gone at least six weeks.

Caiaphas handed him a small purse of coins. "There will be taxes to pay, especially around the port cities."

"I'm fine Caiaphas, there's no need for your assistance."

"I insist Malchus, besides think of this as a bonus, for a job well done. I've heard many will be traveling, even Pilate will be returning home. I hope you'll continue to be alert."

He understood now. Payment for continued listening. He held out his hand for the money.

"Should you see Jesus or any of his followers, I hope you'll take note of their actions."

"Don't you have others already in the region to report to you?" Malchus asked.

"What the Pharisees do and their account of this man is not reliable. I need someone I can trust to give me accurate information," Caiaphas smiled as warmly as he could muster. "I'm only saying should you hear of any so-called miracles this Jesus is doing, I would be interested in knowing. Pilate himself also expressed he's counting on me to keep order. We have our feasts to think about. It's a solemn time. I won't have this man stirring up the hearts of the people with falsehoods."

"What does Nicodemas say?" Malchus grew bold.

"Excuse me?"

"What does Nicodemas think of Jesus? He's a chief ruler, a Pharisee. Is he concerned?"

Caiaphas didn't answer. "Have a safe journey Malchus. I'll see you in six weeks," he turned and walked away.

"Yes, I'll let myself out," he muttered under his breath. He made his way to Kezi's shop. He looked at Selah to ask with his eyes if she spoke to Simon.

"Malchus, I have another cart we can take, Selah asked me first thing this morning."

"Good, thank you. We'll need to carry water pots. It's the dry season. I thought we would leave after Sabbath. That will give us four days to prepare. Is that enough time for you Kezi?"

"Yes, I think that would be fine. Simon will help me and I asked if I could borrow Balaam for a day."

"Balaam has a lot of new friends," Malchus laughed. Kezi and Simon never heard him laugh. Selah noticed their reaction to him. "We'll travel north along the river. It should only take three to five days to reach Tiberias."

"It sounds perfect!" Simon told Malchus he never traveled to the area and was looking forward to a boat ride, something else he never experienced. He would bring his cart tomorrow.

"Great, that will give me time to prepare," he forgot he was officially off duty. He told Selah he would be back later and decided to go for a walk. He headed to the valley. He was greeted by several men as he made his way outside the city's gate. He wouldn't go far, he would find shelter under the olive trees, maybe close his eyes and take a nap. He hadn't been able to enjoy this sanctuary for a long time. He came here right before he left to bring Selah to Jerusalem. He took off his outer garment and spread it on the ground. He leaned against the strong trunk of the tree. The olives wouldn't be harvested for several months. It was quiet now. He closed his eyes and fell asleep. He didn't know how long he'd been sleeping when he heard footsteps. He carefully opened his left eye, so slight he would still appear asleep. He felt around for a rock. His heart was beating faster as he waited for the next step to determine which direction the person was coming from, behind him or hidden by another tree in front. He didn't move. He could feel no rocks. He had removed most before spreading his garment.

"Malchus." He opened his eyes.

"Nicodemas! What are you doing here?" he stood looking for Caiaphas.

"I'm alone," Nicodemas uncovered his head. "Please sit. Truly this is a nice place to rest. I thought we could finish our conversation. I saw you leaving Caiaphas' house earlier so I followed you."

He was stunned. Nicodemas brought bread, cheese and wine.

"Shall we?" Nicodemas gave a blessing and he took the bread. "Please forgive my intrusion to your afternoon. I'll ask you to keep our meeting private." Nicodemas wasn't convinced he could trust him.

"Of course, yes," he still expected to see other Pharisees or Caiaphas himself.

"I can assure you Malchus, I haven't been followed. I myself have to take certain precautions." They ate in silence.

"So, where did we leave off?" Nicodemas hoped he would open up to him.

"That day at the Temple, it changed me somehow. I can't express it in words." Malchus continued, "It was the way Jesus handled himself. Everyone let him go through the Temple and didn't attempt to stop him, not the guards, not Caiaphas, not even you Nicodemas. It was as if we were intruders." The two men sat enjoying the quiet, each lost in their own thoughts.

"I've been reading Malchus. Isaiah speaks about a voice in the wilderness proclaiming to prepare the way of the LORD. I've heard many stories about John the Baptist. Was he not a "voice" in the wilderness? Did he not proclaim to make a way for the LORD? I heard he baptized Jesus at the Jordan and some say," Nicodemas cleared his throat, and Malchus still waiting for Caiaphas to appear leaned in closer, "some say they heard a voice from heaven."

"What did the voice say?" Malchus needed to hear it again and from the mouth of Nicodemas.

"This is My beloved Son in whom I am well pleased," Nicodemas let out his breath.

"I don't understand Nicodemas. How can God have a son? Where in the Scriptures does it say God has a son? God is one."

"It is indeed complex and much meditation and prayer is needed along with study. I have many questions myself. Who can know the mind of God? We must be patient. I believe God will confirm the words of His prophets. Yes, there's much to consider. I didn't follow you to engage in a deep discussion on such a fine day. I only wanted to let you know none of us have all the answers. We all have questions. We shall speak again."

He didn't know how to respond. He thanked Nicodemas for lunch. He sat under his tree and thought to himself, he didn't learn anything. He reasoned that even the most learned man of Israel had doubts and uncertainty. He sat under his tree until it was time to walk Selah home.

Selah and Malchus were ready. It wasn't an easy trip. The roads were a worn dirt path in most places and rocky, but everyone thought it worth it to reach their final destination. Malchus knew travel was a hardship. Selah had voiced her concerns to him at the end of the day. She brought up Simon and the rough roads. Malchus assured her others would look after him.

"What about water?" she asked.

"The wells are marked and if they're dry, that's why we're taking our water pots."

"What if we have trouble? Robbers!" He replied there were many able men going, not to worry.

"And animals!"

He assured her any animal would be more frightened of the group than they would of them. She felt better after she voiced her anxieties. He held her close that evening. They talked about the sea and how Simon was set on a boat ride, with the condition of the sea being calm. She and Kezi didn't want to tell him how fast storms could develop. He wanted to keep everyone in the group together as much as possible especially for their return. He knew Pilate already left for Caesarea so it was unlikely they would cross paths. She didn't mention Mary anymore. Malchus knew she was traveling with Jesus. He thought there might be a chance of seeing them in Galilee. He heard Jesus stayed in the area. He wasn't sure how he felt about the possibility. He was interested. Yes, that's what he told himself, he was merely interested in what Jesus had to say. It wasn't for Caiaphas, it was personal. He made a living listening to what others said. He developed a good sense of when people were truthful or making false statements. He listened to Selah's soft breathing. It reminded him of the breeze through the trees when Nicodemas followed him to the groves. He obviously trusted him to not mention their meeting to Caiaphas. *Why did he trust me?* It warmed his heart and that surprised him.

'*But thou Bethlehem, Ephratah, though thou be little*', Nicodemas read this portion of Scripture over and over again. Jesus was from Nazareth, not Bethlehem. He resolved in his mind Jesus couldn't be the Messiah. He breathed a little easier. Everyone knew Bethlehem was the city of David's birth. He put his hand over his mouth as he said the words out loud. *Born. Where was he born?* He realized he knew little about Jesus. He looked at his writings, he would make a list of all the Scriptures that were messianic. He could then check off all that didn't apply. It was a simple, reasonable solution.

Born in Bethlehem. This was his first entry. From the tribe of Judah. Seed of David. Will enter the Temple. Will perform miracles. Enters Jerusalem on a donkey. He had a dilemma. He very well couldn't approach Jesus and ask, "By the way, were you born in Bethlehem?" Bethlehem was only five miles away. Perhaps he would journey there and inquire. This was becoming a frustration to him. He looked at his list. Will perform miracles. Most heard about the water to wine miracle at Cana. He wasn't sure if he believed this story. The people were looking for someone to rule Israel and break the stronghold of Rome. They would believe anything now. But he heard other stories. Even at the council meetings, Jesus' name came up often. Caiaphas would dismiss all as heresy. He was miserable. It was that night. Jesus challenged him, looked at him as if he knew beforehand he would be coming and addressing these very questions, and with a sympathetic look, knowing I should know the answers if I am who I say I am, Nicodemas, chief ruler of Israel, a learned man, influential teacher of the Law, and he spoke to me about the wind! He looked up in surrender, *I know nothing!* He began to read again.

Malchus thought this group assembled resembled a small exodus. Children were running and laughing keeping the few animals their families were bringing in order. Carts overflowed with grain and supplies for their travel. He saw apprehension but he also saw excitement in the faces of those who never left Jerusalem. The law required them to travel to Jerusalem, not from it. But here they were gathered, twenty-two men, seventeen women and forty-eight children. What was he thinking to embark on this journey with all these people? He should have just left with Selah, however he admitted to himself that wouldn't be the wisest decision. All these children! He suddenly felt responsible for them. And Simon. He was like a child himself! He and Kezi were at his home before the sun was warm on his face. Balaam let him know they were there. Even he seemed anxious to go.

The men prayed and began their slow march east of the Jordan River. They would take their time searching for the easiest way following the river north. He figured it would take them a week with all these children. The men positioned themselves accordingly, Malchus volunteering to stay in the back, watchful behind them. It was a pleasant day and they hoped to walk at least ten to twelve miles. He saw how easy Selah interacted with those she never met. Everyone had a light heart.

They chose the highest point of land along the banks of the river looking for the slightest slope to the water. The sky painted soft shades of lavender and pink proving a calming effect on the children as most sounds now heard were from the adults. Each man brought a small ram's horn, the best way to alert the group of any signs of trouble. He felt peace. No one followed them. He and Selah could hear Simon asking Kezi about the sea.

"What color is it? Does it change? Can you smell it? Will I see fish? How deep do you think it is? How many boats have you ever seen at one time?"

Kezi was patient and answered as best as she could. She was tired and his questions didn't cease. Selah buried her head into Malchus' chest so they wouldn't hear her laughing. Just as he was ready to doze off, he heard Simon call for Kezi with one last inquiry.

"Do you think Jesus will be there?" He found himself replying for Kezi, *I hope so.*

Kezi saw them first, the dust from the horses unmistakable. They stood looking west, the horses at a steady run, this small group of Romans had purpose and she knew this usually meant trouble. They had been traveling five days and were only another two from Tiberias. She watched the centurion and his guards until they disappeared near the first ridge. She was familiar with this activity, most likely a trusted messenger of Pilate on a run to deliver a personal invitation or inquiry on Rome's behalf. She knew Pilate and Claudia had returned and wondered if Claudia had worn her silver scarf. Selah confided to her how she surprised Malchus with her first purchase and she now thought of Claudia doing the same for Pilate. She chided herself for a wicked imagination, Selah shouldn't have shared this intimate moment she had with Malchus, but she was young and it amused her to see his reaction. She was a newlywed, she had no one else in Jerusalem to talk to. Kezi enjoyed their closeness. Women talk. She was banking on it. She would find out about Claudia and she would find out about the centurion who just raced into the sun this summer evening. They would camp here tonight. Simon continued his ritual of nightly questions.

"Had Kezi ever swam? Would the water be cool? Did she think Balaam would like to sit in the water?" He was tenacious!

One night after the round of questions she finally said, "We'll get on a boat, you can peek over the edge and see if there's any fish. I'll push you over and you can tell me how cool and deep the water is and if Balaam comes to rescue you, we'll know too that donkeys can swim."

Malchus and Selah laughed so long and hard that both Kezi and Simon joined in until their stomachs hurt. They were becoming a family. They embraced the idea without having to consider it. It had been a natural process. Simon hadn't spoken with Malchus. He fussed over the women while Malchus kept several paces back. They had gone at a leisurely pace which Simon was grateful. They would reach Tiberias the next day and spoke about going to Capernaum.

Despite the work of setting up camp and the physical exertion, Malchus enjoyed the time with Selah. Kezi and Simon loved her. Not many truly cared for his well-being. He knew Simon wanted to get to know him better and he found a way to avoid time with the older man so far. He saw a tenderness in him, he had peace in his heart. He found himself jealous. He wanted to strike up a conversation. He was miserable sometimes at his own procrastination. His sleep remained compromised at his questions and uncertainties. *Does anyone really, truly know the truth of all things? And why did he care so much now?* Life wasn't bad for him. He had a beautiful wife, they had a home, they had money, children would come and he didn't worry about his position with Caiaphas. Should anything happen, he thought himself resourceful.

Selah was laughing, a rich, joyous laugh. Her head was back and she and Kezi looked like sisters enjoying a familiar story shared as young girls. It warmed his heart. He turned and saw Simon noticed the women also and now waited on his acknowledgement. He smiled and gave a half wave to Simon which prompted him to stroll over.

"Tomorrow I shall see the sea," Simon looked in the direction in which they would find their first short stay. They decided to stay in Tiberias a few days, go to Magdala and then Capernaum. He stood wiping his brow.

Malchus surprised him by not leaving. "I would like to try my hand at fishing."

"I want to go on a boat! Simon replied. Both men laughed and began talking about the weather and how they were enjoying the journey.

"Are you missing your fellow merchants and business of the market?" Malchus asked.

"Yes and no. A man gets used to things, routines, but I've never gone on a journey such as this and I would give up one month's profit anytime to see the country!"

"I appreciate all you've done Simon, the help with your cart, all your provisions, watching after Balaam."

He decided there was no time like the present. "I hear that man Jesus stays frequently in this area."

Malchus shifted his weight. He looked north as Simon did earlier. "Yes, Selah mentioned the young girl Mary was traveling with him and headed this way."

"Have you ever seen him?"

"Yes, at the Temple," Malchus had no emotion in his voice. He continued, "The day there was so much trouble, the day you rescued Balaam and I guess Selah too."

"Yes, yes, I remember like it was yesterday. What a day it was indeed! Men I know lost a lot of money that day," Simon noticed he still showed no emotion. He was difficult to read.

Malchus suggested they sit. "Caiaphas was beside himself!" He actually began laughing.

Simon joined him, "You should have seen his face!"

"I have seen it!" Simon struck his knee and both men broke out laughing again.

"Do you know Simon, that day at the Temple when Jesus came through, not one person tried to stop him."

"Where were the guards?"

"They came running when they heard the people yelling, but when they saw Jesus with that whip in his hand, they stopped in their tracks and watched him."

"Where was Caiaphas?" Simon asked.

"He was right behind the guards and he only stood and said nothing."

Simon asked, "What about the Pharisees?"

Malchus looked down and shook his head. "They seemed confused. Jesus was shouting and the merchants were calling for help, no one did anything. Even I just stood there."

Simon didn't know if he should dare ask another question. He couldn't help himself. "Where was Nicodemas and the other rulers?" There, he included others, the focus off Nicodemas.

Malchus was careful. Simon couldn't possibly know of any communication between him and Nicodemas, but he was hesitant. Simon tried to appear indifferent with this last inquiry. He was biting his lip.

"Nicodemas was there also. They were all there Simon as I said, it was a strange day."

"How do you mean?"

"This man Jesus, no one challenged him. I told," he caught himself, "I thought to myself it was uncommon that no one spoke a word to him. We all came running to see what was taking place and Jesus, he was, I can't explain it," he stared up at the sky to think about his next words, "It was like all these people came into his house while he was away and he came home to find strangers doing things that he would never allow, and he was mad and began to tell them to get out, this was not their house, it was his." He now turned towards Simon for the first time during this unexpected time together. "Simon, he said it was his Father's house."

"His Father's? What did he mean?" Simon placed his hand on Malchus' forearm unknowingly.

"I don't know Simon. What do you think he meant?"

"The Temple is where we go to worship God. David commissioned his son Solomon to build God a house, so it's God's house."

Simon was still talking when Malchus interrupted. "Jesus said it was his Father's house, so he's calling God his Father?"

"He's the God of Abraham, Isaac and Jacob. Did Abraham call God his father? Do you know Malchus?"

Both men were silent. The sun was setting and the smoke from the fires swirled up to meet the orange sky. They would retire early tonight, everyone looking forward to their arrival in Tiberias. Kezi and Selah saw them talking, Selah hadn't seen Malchus have a one on one conversation with any man on this trip, he was usually with a group, and she was happy it was Simon. She hoped he would get to know him as she had and would come to love him as she did. She waved the two men over. She wouldn't ask him about this visit. She would wait for him to tell her. She hoped he didn't make her wait too long.

The entire camp fell asleep it seemed at the same time, the promise of the sea the next day making everyone want to rush the morning. They crossed the river at its narrow point and followed to where it entered the lake. Simon was practically skipping which made all the children giggle and he called to each one to hurry and run alongside him. Up until now there had only been a few falls, a couple of scraped knees, all were in good spirits.

Both Kezi and Selah smelled it. They were close. The sea. Kezi ran ahead of the children to take in the tranquil view she had missed for several years. As she stood, the sun kissing her face, the water greeting her with thousands of lights, she felt a single tear roll down her cheek. She fought to keep the past buried. It's where it belonged. She could hear the children's excited voices behind her. They would reach her in a few moments. Magdala wasn't far and she thought about going ahead of the group to have a private moment, conquer any last remaining anger that might attempt to rob her of her new life. The water was calm and she breathed in its strength. She heard Simon before she saw him.

"Woo-hoo!" he was shouting and she thought he might run and dive in! Malchus and Selah were right behind him and the entire group stood with lifted faces to inhale the fresh water, taking in the panoramic view, smaller boats seen in the distance. They could have remained for hours but begrudgingly moved on as they were anxious to reunite with family members.

Selah arrived at her childhood home to find no one there, many of the neighbors also absent. It was as if the entire village disappeared. An older woman finally appeared from the roof of one of the small homes.

"They've all gone to see Jesus!" she yelled as she waved her hand towards the north. Simon began walking towards her. The older woman began to descend. She didn't wait for him to say anything but simply repeated what she already said.

"They've all gone to see Jesus. They say he healed a leper! Touched him and everything! They say he's healing everyone! The village has traveled to Capernaum to hear him teach. They're carrying the sick," she looked at Simon. "Are you sick? Are you following him too? Well speak up old man!"

"How long ago did they leave?" he asked her.

"Three days, maybe four."

"Why didn't you go with them?" He wondered if she was truly all alone in the village.

"Do I look sick to you? Did you not just see me climb down from the roof?"

He asked if she needed anything, told her they had traveled from Jerusalem. He walked back to where Malchus and Selah stood. Selah looked alarmed.

"Everyone has gone to Capernaum to hear Jesus. She said they left three or four days ago. Where's Kezi? I thought she was right behind us."

"Malchus, what should we do?" Selah clutched his arm. They waited for Kezi and the others before making any decisions.

"There's no one here," Kezi turned in a circle to emphasize her claim.

"They've all gone to Capernaum! To see Jesus!" Selah seemed more excited now than upset Malchus thought.

Kezi looked at them. "Everyone?"

"I think most, Simon said. They've taken all who need healing. He healed a leper!"

"What? A leper!" Kezi directed her gaze at Malchus. "Malchus, what do you think we should do?"

He wasn't used to giving direction, only following Caiaphas'. He wasn't sure. Why would that woman remain behind if everyone else left?

"Kezi, do you wish to stop in Magdala and rest or go right to Capernaum?" Selah asked.

"I don't know Selah. Your family has gone to see him. Can you believe this? He's healing people from leprosy! What must Malchus be thinking? This is incredible! Selah, do you believe Jesus is the Messiah?"

There was an awkward silence. She wasn't sure. She looked at both Kezi and Malchus nervously, "I don't know, he's performing miracles, healing a leper. Doesn't our Scriptures say the Messiah will do these things? Malchus?"

He never felt more vulnerable in his life. They were waiting for his answer, for direction, guidance, wisdom, something, anything. His mind was racing. Then at a moment of clarity, he quoted the words of Nicodemas, *'Time will tell'*. The simple answer seemed to temporarily satisfy them. He neither confirmed nor denied. They ate quickly, most of the group deciding to stay in the heart of Tiberias instead of the smaller villages. Simon asked Kezi if she would like to walk down to the sea and they left Malchus and Selah to have some privacy.

"Would you like to go on to Capernaum Selah?" his voice was soft, caring. She was reclining on his shoulder.

"I will do what you think is best Malchus. We've come a long way. We could stay here for a few days, however, it's strange how many people have gone. Perhaps if we went to Magdala, Kezi may see some of her family and," she hesitated.

"Mary might be there," he looked down at her.

"Yes, but I think if Jesus is in Capernaum, that's where we'll find Mary."

He wrestled with his thoughts. Jesus touched a leper. The Pharisees would be ready to stone him, cast him out and call him unclean too! He kissed the top of her head and she snuggled into his side closer.

"I'll tell Simon and Kezi we'll stay here tonight. Simon can enjoy the sea tomorrow, we'll go to Magdala and on to Capernaum. Simon and I will inform the group and make arrangements to meet back here to travel home." He made a decision. He was taking charge. He wanted to see Jesus.

Simon and Kezi were thrilled with his decision. They walked back to the sea and watched the sunset. Malchus thought it might have been one of the most peaceful, beautiful days he ever had. Simon insisted Balaam stand in the water and with a little prodding was able to coax him in. The water wasn't cold and Balaam seemed to enjoy it. Simon began to splash him which he didn't seem to enjoy, and in a rush to escape Simon's onslaught, knocked him down. They laughed at Simon sitting in the shallow water, the soft waves rolling over his tunic.

"Light a fire Malchus, I'm soaked through!"

They didn't see any boats, Selah wondered if everyone was in Capernaum. The old woman was nearby when they returned. She brought hay for Balaam and also wine, fresh goat cheese and figs. They invited her to join them but she had things to do, wanted to gaze at her stars she told them. The four of them watched her climb up to her roof and she gave them a short wave before disappearing into the night. Simon looked up at the stars. How many nights did he not appreciate their majesty? He would bet his good cart the old woman thanked God every night for them. He thought he should begin this practice as well.

Caiaphas was troubled. He heard Jesus healed a paralytic, but the news of him actually touching a leper, he was disgusted! He was anxious for Malchus to return. He wanted details. This man was gaining popularity. They said multitudes were following him now. And if the multitudes were following, and he came to the Temple, he foresaw a disaster. *This was his time of year. He was High Priest!* He found himself pacing a bit faster and the confines of his inner chamber felt like a prison cell. He needed to expose Jesus as a worker of iniquity. He shuddered at the thought of touching a leper! It must be a rumor.

Nicodemas heard rumors too. He and Caiaphas had dinner together, a rarity. It was a quiet summer and they took advantage of the long, lazy days. Nicodemas didn't bring up Jesus. He knew Caiaphas' feelings towards him. He was still assessing his own. His list was growing. The book of Isaiah had become torture for him. *Who is Isaiah speaking about, wounded for our transgressions, pierced for our iniquities, by his stripes we are healed?* Some said they heard Jesus called the Son of David. This had him searching the Scriptures until the early hours of the morning. He too was anxious for Malchus' return. He hoped for a firsthand report. He needed facts, not idle gossip. Until then, he tried to not let his thoughts consume him.

Malchus watched Kezi leave early this morning alone. They arrived in Magdala yesterday afternoon. Like Selah's village, the people had gone to Capernaum to see Jesus. Every time he heard or spoke his name, he felt his heart beat faster. There was no doubt they too would see him. She began running and he became alarmed. As he was about to go after her, Selah came from behind him.

"She's fine Malchus, she needs time alone this morning."

"Is she alright?"

"Yes, she gently squeezed his arm, just old memories, that's all."

Selah didn't know he heard about Kezi. He didn't know the details. He didn't need to know, and now getting to know her, his distaste for the Romans grew.

"We could be in Capernaum by early evening. We'll leave when she returns." He was direct. Selah liked him taking the lead.

"I imagine the rest of those traveling with us are already there. Where's Simon?"

"He's watching Kezi."

They shared a moment of complete understanding which was new for them. He had come to like the old man. He smiled as he openly called and addressed Simon that way now. It was one of admiration and fatherly. He knew Simon genuinely cared for them. He was probably awake before Kezi and followed her without notice to ensure her safety, and would stay back to give her privacy. *Old man.*

Selah purposely stayed away any time she saw Simon in close proximity. Malchus softened towards him and friendship was growing. It brought joy to Selah's heart. It was answered prayer. She enjoyed when the two men would banter back and forth on how to load supplies on Balaam, or which way the wind was blowing to start a fire.

She was ready to go to Capernaum in hopes of seeing her family and of course Mary. The days were growing hotter. She walked the shoreline cooling her feet and ankles. She lifted her tunic to her knees when no one was looking and waded in a little further. She would love to sit down and let the waves drench her garment. It would dry quickly. Both Malchus and Simon had gone waist deep but then a fish nipped at Simon's feet and he was back on the shore in seconds. She and Kezi took every opportunity since then to tease him.

"I need a boat! No fish will try and nip at me then!"

But when Simon saw how far the boats launched from shore, he wasn't sure he wanted to get in one. They slept in an abandoned barn. Kezi didn't want to enter the small village in the middle of the night. They had taken their time walking, stopping often to simply stare at the sea. They skipped rocks, something she taught them to do and they would sit in silence listening to the waves lapping the shore.

Kezi was gone only a short time. Selah didn't think she would be long. It was too painful. Simon returned slightly out of breath.

"Kezi will be here any moment, I ran ahead of her," his breathing was labored.

"It should be a beautiful day," Kezi said.

Selah saw a calm in her face and knew she had completely forgiven the soldier who victimized her. She wouldn't be here perhaps at this moment and life was like that, unexpected, challenging, not in our control. She made peace on the grassy hilltop where her innocence was compromised. She wouldn't look back. She was ready to move forward.

The travel up the coast was indeed pleasant. They began to see smaller boats as they journeyed north. They looked for a flat area to stop and eat. Malchus went up a smaller hill to see if he could find shade. That's when he saw them, hundreds, no, thousands. The hills were moving before him with people! He shaded his eyes. He searched the horizon. He could see movement on every hilltop, every slope was filled. He couldn't believe what he was seeing! His gaze went down to the sea and he gasped. He couldn't number the boats! He stood there, mouth open straining to take in the image. It was the water. He saw multitudes like this in Jerusalem but somehow the sea made it glorious, the sun reflecting off the water made it the color of, Selah, the color of her eyes!

They were waiting for him. He motioned he was coming back down. His legs felt weak. *Jesus.* Jesus was in the midst of that great crowd. He kept his eye on Selah. He was warm with emotion, this sudden discovery pushing him forward, Selah watching thought he was going to come down the hill head first.

"Hurry! Come and see! Drop everything! Hurry Selah! Come Simon! Kezi, hurry!"

The three of them ran to meet him and he grabbed Selah's hand and began running back up the hill.

"Malchus, what's going on?" She was doing her best to keep up with him.

"Malchus, wait, you're going too fast!" He kept pulling her up, his eye on Simon and Kezi also as they stepped over rocks, Balaam left behind to stare after them. Just when he knew they would see this incredible sight, he shouted for them to stop.

"Close your eyes!" he commanded them. "Selah, keep them closed!" He guided Kezi and Simon to where she stood and positioned them all in a row. They were laughing at his excitable state and Selah now echoed his shouts to hurry.

"Malchus, what is it? Is it a large boat?"

He stood beside her and grabbed her hand, "Now, open your eyes!"

No one spoke. They couldn't. Simon fell to his knees. He never witnessed such a sight! Kezi began dancing. Selah looked at Malchus and they embraced for a long time. No one could explain what the other was feeling. Joy. Amazement. Wonder. One thing they all had in common, they all knew this was about Jesus.

"Let's go!" Simon was rolling down the hill.

"Malchus, help him. He's going to hurt himself!" Selah and Kezi both began to chase after him.

"How far do you think we are? When do you think we shall reach the crowds? One hour, two?" Simon moved around Balaam so fast Selah thought he must be getting dizzy.

"I can't tell old man," Malchus laughed at the sight of Simon trying to decide which way to go.

He thought this must be how people felt when they made their first pilgrimage to Jerusalem and their first glance at the city on the hill. You wanted to get there as soon as you could to see what wonders were contained. The people were moving in the same direction. They were following. Following Jesus. The things they heard must be true!

He could reason about how many people he saw. There were thousands. He thought of Caiaphas. Another report he won't want to hear. He didn't want to think about him. He supposed all who lived close by were on these hills. He didn't know what to expect once they arrived. Would they begin calling out for the family of Selah and Kezi? Their travel companions? Would the women only want to find Mary? And be closer to Jesus? His heart began to beat fast again! He heard that inner voice asking questions. *What about you Malchus? Who will you search for? How close to Jesus do you want to be? Do you only want to gaze at the crowds? What are you coming to see? To hear?* He stopped walking and leaned on his staff. He didn't know how long he stood, but it must have been several minutes because Simon was calling for him.

"Malchus, are you alright? Do you see something else?"

"Can we stop?" He needed a quiet moment. When they reached the crowds, it would be anything but quiet.

Simon came to him first. "Son, are you feeling well?"

He began weeping. Selah and Kezi rushed to him.

"What is it Malchus? They looked at each other in confusion. He was crying. Selah never saw him shed a tear! Simon held him as he wept on the old man's shoulder. He looked at the two women as if he understood this sudden outburst. The women left them alone.

"Now, what is it Malchus? You can tell this old man," he patted him on the back trying to console and comfort him.

"You called me son," he looked at Simon, his face wet with tears, his eyes searching his for loyalty.

Simon pulled him into his chest tighter.

"I do think of you as my son Malchus," he wouldn't let him go. "I never had a son. You know I love Selah, think of her as my own daughter, Kezi too. I've grown to love all of you. You've made this old man's heart glad. I was lonely Malchus. I consider you family," he released him enough so he could look at him. "I'll do anything I can for you and Selah, anytime, anywhere. You have my word."

Malchus could only shake his head. They stood until he was ready to speak.

"Simon, who do you think Jesus is? We've traveled many days and we're about to join thousands of people to go listen to a man. Who is this man? Why am I so emotional?"

"Indeed, why are they following him? I think none of us really know for certain, but he's giving our people hope. You saw him that day. This is a man of passion! Let's not think too much on what we're doing now, walking all these miles to sit at the sea and relax, but it seems our God has other plans for us. Whatever is driving these people seems to also be guiding us. We may walk away and say, this Jesus, he's a nice man, but I think we need to find out who he is for ourselves. Now, let us continue, Balaam has eaten all my dates and I hope to find some merchants in that crowd!"

He laughed and hugged Simon once more. He called for Selah and Kezi and they joined the men. Simon looked at each face. He saw hope, anticipation and also uncertainty. He prayed they would all have their questions answered, that peace would be in their hearts and the question many had would be answered. Who is Jesus?

Claudia sat at the base of Mt. Hermon looking at the snowcapped mountain. Pilate had been agitated for several days. They were back a little over a week when she heard him swearing. He heard a report of a centurion seeking Jesus to come and heal his servant. What angered him was this Roman officer sent some of the Jewish elders to beseech Jesus to come to his house, that he himself didn't feel worthy. *What kind of officer serving Rome doesn't feel worthy?* To ask others to go and beg for this man of the desert to come to a Roman house, Pilate was incensed!

To make matters worse, the servant, who supposedly was close to death, now is well. She heard him shouting at the messenger. Did this Roman officer throw Jesus a party? A parade? Has a shrine been erected? She couldn't understand why this bothered him. There were rumors and stories of all sorts the past year, and he was never angered as he was now. She hoped they would have a relaxing summer, perhaps another party, maybe even a trip to Rome.

Jesus was gaining the support of the people. She heard the servants speaking about him all the time. He wasn't far from their home. There had been hushed whispers and gasps every other day it seemed of Jesus healing someone, casting out evil spirits, even touching a leper and healing him! Pilate had received an earful from the Pharisees, 'He's confusing the people again. He's breaking the Law of Moses!' Pilate repeatedly told them he didn't care about the Law of Moses; the only law was Roman law and they needed to be mindful of who governed Judea.

She was certain the pressure of dealing with the customs of these people had caused his irritability. She was becoming irritable now waiting for her servant to assist her, this one not as efficient as Avi. The girl had proven to be a treasure. She didn't know how she managed to always be at the right place at the right time. She came to rely on her.

It was quiet here. One night, the moon seemed brighter than usual, there wasn't a leaf moving, the air still. She heard a roar. It echoed around the mountain. She walked to the edge of the terrace and strained her ear. It was cheers of people! She backed in the house with her hand over her heart. *Jesus.* The people were cheering Jesus. She didn't need to ask anyone if he was nearby. She knew.

They reached the sea. This time it was a sea of people. Simon agreed to stay with the women while Malchus found out as much as he could. He knew how to move quickly through small groups listening to more than one conversation. He developed an ear to catch certain words. He looked for any familiar faces. He heard many from Jerusalem were following Jesus too. He couldn't believe what he was seeing. How would they be able to find anyone? They were sitting on the lake bank waiting.

"What did you find out Malchus?" Selah asked.

"How many people do you think are here?" Simon wanted to know.

He looked at Kezi waiting for her question. "Did you see anyone we know?"

It was overwhelming. They were used to crowds but this was different. The men agreed it was the landscape, the sea, something about the water and how sound traveled across the stillness. He could hear with no effort. He and Simon hooked the cart back up to Balaam and made a horizontal path up the side of the smallest incline they could find. It wasn't long that other men stood on each side ensuring Balaam had success. Kezi and Selah stood for several minutes taking in the expanse of the people. How would they ever find their family members?

Malchus had an emotional journey. He busied himself to avoid having too much time to think, even though that's what he hoped to do on this trip. Sit and think. He saw Simon, this gentle old soul watching over him. Simon loved him like a son. His heart believed this.

"What do you think Simon?"

Simon scratched his beard and scanned the horizon.

"We have maybe four hours of sunlight. Perhaps we should walk towards the west where most people seem to be gathered."

Kezi and Selah nodded they could walk awhile and they slowly made their way over the terrain. The women searched the faces hoping for a familiar smile. Simon also looked in all directions. Their eyes met and he shrugged his shoulders, "I see no one I know."

Selah also searched for those they traveled with, someone from her village, everyone was a stranger. She stopped and looked at their surroundings. It was beautiful. The sky had begun to welcome the soft colors of sunset. Malchus knew they should stop for the night.

Kezi broke their silence. "I can't believe we haven't seen one person we know. None of us!"

Simon thought he would walk a bit further while they settled to see if he could find out any news, and assured them he wouldn't be more than an hour. He walked quickly, it was growing dark and he looked for landmarks along the way. He halfway counted on Balaam's braying to guide him back.

"Jesus went to his house!" Simon stopped to listen.

"A tax collector!"

"Yes, a tax collector. He made a great feast and I heard there were many publicans there."

Simon walked up interrupting them. "Shalom, peace to you. My name is Simon, a merchant from Jerusalem. I overheard you speaking about this man Jesus. My friends and I are seeking him and have traveled a great distance. Can you tell me, do you know if he's expected here?"

The small group welcomed him. He sat and heard a marvelous story. It was dark now and the unfamiliar land was aglow with cook fires. Malchus stood waiting. Simon heard the sound of Balaam's bell. He added it to Selah's scarf before they left. The clear tone of the solitary bell he would recognize anywhere.

"Simon, sit and eat while it's hot," Kezi fussed over him and Malchus lowered the covering of their tent.

He devoured two pieces of bread and started talking before he swallowed the last piece.

"A tax collector named Matthew gave up his post and followed Jesus! He gave a great feast in his home and many publicans were there!"

"What? Malchus didn't believe it. Simon, you're certain this is what you heard?"

"Yes, I sat down with a small group of men who stopped to pay the tax, and Jesus was passing by, you know the main highway into Capernaum, when they say he looked at this tax collector and said, 'Follow me' and he did!"

"What else Simon?" Selah handed him a cup of wine.

He looked at all of them, hesitant to speak. "They say many sinners were there and they were eating and drinking in this house of Matthew."

"I thought Jesus was supposed to be a righteous man," Malchus seemed angry. How could he sit with a tax collector? Are they not the same as the money changers, the same men whose tables he overturned? And sinners? What do you mean Simon? What did these men tell you?"

Simon shook his head no, he didn't want to say in front of Selah and Kezi, but they knew.

Kezi laid her hand on his arm. "Simon, are they certain it was Jesus?"

"Yes Kezi, his followers ate at the table too. The Pharisees were there also."

"Pharisees?" Now Selah had questions. She glanced at Malchus. "Were they part of this feast?"

"Selah!" Malchus now stood up. "Of course not, were they Simon?"

"No, they only saw him. They've been following him. I want to say what the men told me. I have been repeating their words all the way back. They began to question his followers. They asked, 'Why does your teacher eat with these'?"

"Right, why would he?" Malchus was pacing now. His hope was diminished. I can't believe one who comes and says all these words, all these things we've heard, miracles, healing, and then he sits and has dinner with tax collectors! I'm very troubled by this!"

Kezi and Selah looked at Simon, soft pleading in their eyes, praying he wouldn't say anything else to further upset him.

Kezi spoke. She didn't want to put Selah in an awkward position with her husband. "Is there more Simon? Did they answer?"

"No."

Malchus pointed his finger at all of them and said, "See, even his own followers disagreed. What man would sit with sinners and those who don't follow the law? The Messiah. No messiah would sit with sinners and tax collectors!" He made a spitting sound. "I don't understand," he made a sweeping motion with his arm, "Why would all these people follow this man? They must not know who he really is! I bet they don't know, but as soon as they find out, they'll all return home," he looked at Selah, "and that's what we shall do tomorrow."

"Tomorrow? But Malchus, we've just arrived. I thought we agreed to wait."

"Wait for what Selah? To chase down this imposter messiah? To see those who are following? Mary? Your family? I'm certain all will be returning to their homes."

Simon needed perfect timing to finish all he'd been told. He waited for Malchus to sit down and Selah poured them each another cup of wine.

"It wasn't his followers that answered the Pharisees," he paused to see if Malchus was truly listening. "It was Jesus who answered. He said, 'He didn't come for those who are whole, who are well but for those, no, wait, let me think, he said, 'It's not those who are healthy who need a physician, but those that are sick.'"

"What does that mean Malchus?" Selah looked directly in his eyes.

He heard the wisdom of the words and bit down on his lip. Simon hoped he would ponder these words before he spoke. The words were fire in his heart.

"I guess he means," he looked at all their faces, why was it up to him to interpret what Jesus meant? "I'll think about it. I'll sleep on it," he rose to prepare to retire for the evening.

Selah rose too and began to speak but Simon had his finger to his lips for her to keep quiet. No one slept. Malchus tossed and turned.

He was talking in his sleep. At one point, Kezi asked Selah what he was saying.

"I don't know," Selah whispered, "he's mumbling."

"Do you think he wants to go home in the morning?"

"I don't know Kezi. Perhaps Simon can speak to him. What do you think?"

"I think you two better get some sleep!" Simon sounded like a father telling his daughters to go to bed!

Selah whispered again. "Simon, the words of Jesus, do they make sense to you?"

Simon actually did see the meaning. If a person was living according to the law and not committing any sin, they didn't need someone to tell them they were fine. He thought a lot about Jesus using the word physician. After much thought, he understood. He hoped Malchus would too. He spoke softly to the women explaining what he thought Jesus meant. "Now please let us get some sleep. There will be decisions to make in the morning."

"Goodnight Simon, thank you," Selah was sleepy.

"Thank you? Why are you thanking me?"

"Because you're so kind to all of us, Malchus, me, Kezi, we love you Simon, goodnight."

They were surprised in the morning how many people left. Malchus stretched. He looked back at Selah and Kezi packing items preparing to travel.

"What do you think old man?"

"Let us walk a little Malchus," Simon began in the direction of the small group he spoke with last night.

"I heard what you said Simon."

"Heard what I said when?"

"I heard you tell Selah and Kezi what you thought Jesus meant," Malchus was abrupt.

"And you disagree?" Simon was cautious.

"No, I agree Simon." They stopped walking and the two men faced each other.

"It does make sense, Malchus started. I'm confused by this man. He does one thing and just when I think I've convinced myself of who he isn't, he speaks words I can't deny the wisdom. It's a hard place I find myself in Simon. What happens when we go home and I go back to Caiaphas? You and I both know he'll want to hear all about Jesus and what people are saying. I'd like to tell him I didn't hear anything, but how do we live as we have knowing this man is healing people and these crowds that are following him? He'll return to the Temple, I'm sure of that. And then what? How do I not do what Caiaphas tells me? He doesn't like Jesus and is planning to discredit all he's done. I've heard the council say he's using sorcery. I'm here in Galilee, wanting to do the right thing for my wife, to search for her family and part of me wants to see Jesus and hear his words for myself and the other," he didn't finish.

"And the other part?" Simon wanted to push him into realizing his own belief.

"If I don't hear, then I can stand before Caiaphas and not tell a lie, that I didn't see or hear Jesus."

Simon began slowly walking back. He put his hand upon Malchus' shoulder.

"So, what shall we do?"

"I don't know Simon."

"I will say follow your heart."

Malchus stopped again and looked around as families were beginning to move west.

"Let us follow."

Chapter Five

The men Simon met waited to see if he would pass by. When Simon reached them, he introduced Malchus, Selah and Kezi. The youngest of the group said they would like to join them, help them try and locate their family and talk about the words of Jesus. They had more to share with Simon and the others if they would like to hear.

"We would," Simon didn't look at Malchus.

They told them Jesus passed by their village and healed many. Someone from their village was on the road to Capernaum when Jesus met Matthew the tax collector. The whole group walked steadily as the youngest man recounted his friend's words. Malchus wanted to know everything, every word that was spoken and asked the young man to tell them all he remembered.

"We're from Decapolis. Merchants in our land began talking about this man Jesus. We heard he was performing miracles. My little cousin was sick. No one knew what troubled her. So, we brought her here and it happened that Jesus passed by and she was healed! My family took her home, a few of us decided to stay. After a few days we rested here and that's when our friends told us about the Pharisees who began to question Jesus openly at this house of the tax collector."

Simon asked, "The one they call Matthew?"

"Yes," the young man answered, "This is when they asked Jesus why he ate with sinners, and his answer '*That those who were sick needed a physician*'."

Malchus nodded. "Go on please."

"Jesus said he came to call sinners to repentance," Kezi spoke for the first time. "The man at the river, John the Baptist, also told people to repent. He called Herod a sinner."

"Yes, people say he's the voice in the wilderness," the young man looked at the elder of his group for approval to continue, "from the writings of Isaiah, *'The voice of him that crieth in the wilderness, prepare the way of the LORD'.*"

"Wait, Malchus said, are you saying this John the Baptist is who Isaiah is speaking about?"

Kezi and Selah searched the young man's face. *How would he react to Malchus?*

"This is what the people believe, yes."

"Tell me, Malchus said, do you know where Jesus is from?"

"Nazareth. Jesus of Nazareth," the young man continued. "The Pharisees seem to be against all this man is doing, even asking why his disciples didn't fast?"

"His disciples do not fast?" Simon looked at Malchus.

"Jesus said, 'While the bridegroom is with them, the attendants of the bridegroom cannot fast, can they? So long as they have the bridegroom with them, they cannot fast'."

"Malchus, what does this mean?" Selah hoped he could answer, it was a strange saying to her. The young man spoke before he could answer.

"The bridegroom is a wedding of course, a celebration. So, no one fasts at a wedding when you're eating and drinking, but when the wedding is over and there's no bridegroom and reason to celebrate, then you have time and reason to fast and pray as you normally would."

Simon nodded yes, "That makes sense to me."

"Yes, I understand too!" Selah was delighted at this young man's easy way of speaking. She encouraged him to keep talking. "He tells stories in a way people can understand, but there must be," she looked at Kezi for help.

"A deeper meaning?" Kezi said.

"Yes," Simon agreed. "What's he really saying?"

The young man was nodding too, "He speaks in parables. Look, we're heading home. You can turn south to Tiberias."

"Simon, what do you think? Should we journey west or head back to Tiberias?" Malchus asked.

"This land is beautiful and I've enjoyed it. I feel bad the women haven't seen their families or Mary, but our group will be expecting us. Jesus could be anywhere. It seems we've been right behind him. The women are tired. I still haven't been in my boat!"

Malchus laughed, "And I haven't caught a fish!"

They decided to return to Tiberias. They departed early. The women were thankful it wasn't far. Sabbath was the next day so they walked at a fast pace. Tiberias was alive with people! Simon explored the markets and port and came back with fresh fruit and vegetables, wine, grain and of course managed to find Balaam his apples. He also found a fishing boat he and Malchus could go out on in the morning, plenty of time before Sabbath, he told them. He would get his boat ride and Malchus the chance to fish.

Malchus and Selah enjoyed a quiet morning. They heard the calls of the fishermen. He wanted to prepare all he could before Sabbath. The next day they would go east and wait for their group. He was anxious for the trip back. With the growing number of people following Jesus, he knew that meant there would also be growing numbers of robbers along the road. He and Simon discussed it. They needed to have the group together, strength in numbers Simon said.

Selah didn't think Malchus had ever been on a boat either. She hoped he wouldn't get sick. Some did. The sea looked calm and the sky clear. She was ready to shop with Kezi. Malchus brought quite a bit of money with them, all they had in fact. The women would wear it fastened to the inside of their garments today. She didn't want it lost at sea. The way Simon and Malchus joked with each other, it wouldn't surprise her if they both ended up in the water today. Kezi made note of several places she and Selah would shop. Simon was pacing, losing patience while Malchus finished preparing for their day.

The women watched as they boarded the vessel, the two men like young boys exploring a new cave. Selah wanted to know how far out they were going and the owner assured her he was an experienced man of the sea, fished his entire life and his family also. It was all he knew. He watched as she scanned the horizon.

"We'll have fair weather, nothing to concern yourself with. Let's be off now," and they began rowing out, Simon and Malchus with fixed smiles as they waved at the women.

"Come Selah, don't watch them out of sight. We'll do some exploring ourselves."

As they led Balaam through the streets, Selah saw children point and laugh at his scarf and they laughed along. She caught Malchus straightening it giving Balaam an affectionate pat. They enjoyed their late morning together. Kezi wasn't upset they didn't stop at Magdala. She was ready to go home. The four of them had grown closer and she couldn't imagine her life without any of them, even Malchus. This trip had changed things. There was freedom in their conversations now. Selah matured in a way that surprised her. She was more inquisitive, wanting to learn, especially when it came to the Scriptures. They were both learning and this new-found love for the word of God brought them closer.

It was a heart issue. It forced them to examine the true intent of their motives, and the person they were becoming. It wasn't an easy process. They both found things they didn't like about themselves. They both wanted to change those traits that were not appealing and Selah called almost shameful. They would hold each other accountable. When Kezi grew impatient with people, Selah had permission to gently place her hand on her arm and tell her to relax, count her beads or walk around the shop to straighten pillows, anything to keep her from speaking unkind words to a customer.

Selah judged people too quickly and hated that she did. Kezi would remind her of her own past and how she would have probably judged her. Selah had actually begun to cry as she realized the truth of her statement and how much she loved her friend. It had grieved her, so if Kezi noticed her looking at someone with disdain, she would simply point to herself. Selah cried several times. They were both experiencing hard lessons. Selah was tired of sniffling and Kezi was tired. She had practically walked the entire city of Jerusalem it seemed when Selah found her pacing in front of indecisive customers.

The two women with Balaam in tow weaved through the merchants with carts laden with every fruit and vegetable. There were painted clay pots and large, beautiful rugs and they touched everything. Kezi heard the sound before she saw the source of it. Shells. They were shiny and polished, different colors, shapes and sizes. One woman emptied out a rather large basket into another and the sound enticed her. She could make earrings and bracelets, necklaces and decorate her pillows. She ran over and scooped up a pile with both her hands.

"How much for the lot?"

The woman turned. "I have many, would you buy the entire sea?"

"Yes! Kezi said, I believe I would!"

She ended up with two large bags and it was the only item Balaam ended up carrying the entire day. They sat and people watched and made note of what the women were wearing, the most common color and what head coverings were most popular. They settled in a spot out of the way.

"I can't believe we didn't see Jesus or Mary," Kezi made sure her bags were tightly secured. She also untied a small lunch they brought. There were many people here, the streets crowded and the Roman influence evident everywhere. They searched the faces for anyone from the group they came with.

"I thought we would walk back to the harbor and watch the boats come in," Selah was excited to see Malchus and Simon's reaction.

"Let's go Selah, the men should be coming back soon."

Simon and Malchus were unsure climbing into the boat, but the depth was about four feet so when they sat down, they felt better. The rocking took a while to get used to and when others climbed in after them, they both grabbed the side and held on. There were ten men going out and Malchus saw the boat could probably hold a few more. There were nets and hooks and even two spears. This was a ride of leisure, not fishing. They both let their hands drag the sea as the men rowed out. At one point, Malchus watched Simon as he was halfway leaning out and poked him giving him a start, and the shriek from the old man made everyone laugh out loud. He sat back closing his eyes letting the sun warm his face. This was a nice start to the day. The steady rowing and the sound of the oars could put him back to sleep.

"I see one!" Simon's excited voice made Malchus sit up.

"Where?" Malchus scooted over closer to Simon.

"It was silver, I saw it!" Simon didn't take his eyes off the spot hoping to see it again.

The owner of the boat said he might have seen a sunfish; they would have to go out a little further and maybe they would let the net down but didn't expect to catch anything this time of day. Malchus thought the owner and the two men rowing were fishermen. The rest of the men on board, like he and Simon, were just enjoying a boat ride while women shopped.

Simon studied the faces of the men, making up stories in his mind for each one, amusing himself. But there was one man he found he couldn't look away from. He hoped he wouldn't catch him staring. He had been standing the entire time with the owner. He looked overjoyed, yes, Simon thought, this too must be his first boat ride! He had a smile on his face that was permanent, as if nothing could erase it. He spoke to the owner in low tones and the owner simply nodded pointing north. And the man would smile bigger.

"What is it Simon?" Malchus caught him staring. "Do you know that man?"

"No, but look at his face. He's been smiling and standing the entire time. Even when the boat wasn't too steady, he was laughing, rocking with it almost as a challenge. Did you notice?"

"Yes, but," Simon didn't let Malchus finish.

"Look now, do you see Malchus? It's as if he knows something that none of us on this boat does."

He looked up. He wasn't a young man, he couldn't deny the man had a joyful expression. They were careful and whispered to each other hoping the sound traveled behind them. They sat in the opposite end of the vessel. He thought they might be in the middle of the lake. It was calm and the rowers stopped. The owner searched the water, would look at the sun and sniff the air. Malchus and Simon found themselves repeating every action. When they discovered this and all the others, the men burst out laughing. Simon wasn't shy.

"This is my first time on a boat! I'm an old man, I've traveled from Jerusalem with my friend here. He's never caught a fish!"

Malchus felt at ease with these strangers and replied, "And I don't think I shall catch one today."

The two men who rowed had the oars out of the water and were passing around cups. The men drank wine with bread and dried fish. Another man shared figs and walnuts he purchased at the market.

"My friend from Jerusalem, this too is my first time on a boat."

Simon hit Malchus' knee, "I knew it! See I was right!"

"I'm not as old as you but I'm not a young man either."

"Where are you from?" another asked.

"Capernaum," he answered. The owner of the boat remained silent.

"Capernaum? Friend, there are many boats there. Why travel here to Tiberias?"

The man looked at the owner. "May I?"

The owner spread his hands looking right and left, "You have a captive audience."

"Nine days ago, several of my friends came to my house and told me about a man who was healing people." Malchus and Simon stopped eating.

One man asked, "Was it the one they call Jesus?"

"Yes!" the man standing said.

"Did you have a family member sick?" the man asked.

"No, it was I. My friends, they carried me to the place where Jesus was."

"Carried?" one replied.

"Yes, carried," the man said.

"So, you were sick?" The men shifted in their seats a little, wondering what kind of sickness had befallen the man.

"You could say that. My friends, they were convinced if they could get me to Jesus, I would be well. It was so hot outside, I wanted to stay inside on the floor as I was accustomed," he looked up and all the men on the boat, including the owner did as well thinking the man saw something. Simon knew he was collecting himself.

"The crowds, oh the crowds, they walked through carrying me on my mat, so many people, all crying out for Jesus. We couldn't see the house where he stayed. I told my friends, please, let us just go home. It's useless. We can't get near. They wouldn't hear of it! One of my friends saw his younger brother and called to him. He also came and they forced their way through. They were pressed in all about and then something quite amazing for my friends to do, they lifted me to the roof!"

"The roof!" one of the men said.

"Yes, they knew Jesus was in the house and there was no way we could approach, so they tore off part of the roof and lowered me down. I didn't know whose house it was. I looked at my friends in disbelief they would risk falling themselves and of course tearing the roof off of a stranger's home, but then I saw him. Jesus. Others in the house were shouting and some helped lower me to the ground while my friends stared down the hole they created." Simon was gripping the side of the boat with his left hand, his right gripping Malchus' arm.

"I was paralyzed," the man said.

"From fear?" the youngest man asked.

"No son, I was a paralytic. I couldn't walk, that was my sickness."

All the men began talking over each other and the man held up his hand. He looked at the owner of the boat.

"This man knows my family. He can tell you I speak truth. Jesus looked up at my friends and he smiled. I thought he would be angry, we interrupted his teaching, his dinner, my friends made quite a mess, but Jesus smiled. He looked down at me and said, 'Son, your sins are forgiven!' I didn't move. I just laid there and those gathered around the house began shouting and questioning the words he spoke and he said to them, 'I know what you're thinking, but to show you the Son of Man has the power to heal, I say, rise, take up your mat and walk!' Everyone must have been looking at me but I kept my eyes on him and I'll never be able to explain what I felt, but I rose and took up my mat and walked out of that house praising God!"

Simon jumped up rocking the boat and shouted, "Praise God!" Malchus said nothing.

The men were all astonished! They had several questions, all of them asking at the same time. They gathered around the man and Simon sat back down. The owner walked towards them.

"His words are true. I've known his family a long time. I've fished off the shores of Capernaum many years. The talk of Jesus is everywhere now. We've all heard many stories, truly miracles, wouldn't you agree?"

Malchus and Simon both said yes.

"This man, he walked here from Capernaum. He hasn't walked for many years. He wouldn't even sit as you could see in this boat. He doesn't even want to lie down to sleep! He has good friends. They had faith, enough faith for him when he didn't have any. He's telling everyone he meets his story. He told me he was following those who were following Jesus."

"Jesus was here?" Simon asked.

"No, he's west, on his way to Jerusalem through Judea."

"How long ago was he in the area, do you know?" Simon was ready to jump off the boat.

"I think two days."

"Malchus!" Simon shook his arm a little. "We should leave in the morning, don't you think?"

"Yes, that was the plan. We'll go to the village to meet our group."

"What if they're not there?" Simon seemed worried.

"Why would they not be there?" Malchus hadn't taken his eyes off the man who was healed. If he was a paralytic, he too would be walking everywhere showing himself to those who knew he couldn't walk. It was the words, 'Son of Man' that stirred him. Jesus called himself Son of Man and those at his baptism said God called him Son. *Son of God or Son of Man? Which one was it?*

The oars were put back in the water. Malchus forgot all about fishing. It was a now or never moment. He stood and carefully walked to the other side of the boat. Simon watched him. The man stood smiling as Malchus approached.

"That's quite a story!" Malchus figured the man to be about fifty years of age.

"I'm not sure I would call it a story," the man responded.

"Right, I see your point." The man couldn't help notice Malchus looking at his legs, his feet and making an assessment.

"I wasn't always a paralytic," the man spoke directly to him. "When I was about thirty, I went to rise one morning and couldn't. My legs, they simply stopped working. No doctor could make me well. Some said I had a demon. I grew weaker of course and have been confined to my couch. When our village heard all Jesus was doing, it gave me hope. Have you ever longed for something that seemed impossible? I wanted so much to hope for the impossible, to take a walk with my wife and take care of my family. It's been a hard life. My friends, I bless them every day. They had hope when I didn't. When they lowered me down through the roof of that house, it was as if, I don't know, like thousands of needles pressing into my skin but it didn't hurt. It tingled. I could feel it in my feet. I think my faith began to grow that instant. I would never believe something like this could happen."

"Did Jesus lay his hands on you?" Malchus was almost whispering.

"No, he only spoke."

"Can you tell me again exactly what he said?" his palms were sweaty.

"He called me son. He said, 'Son, your sins are forgiven.'"

"Why would he call you son? And only God can forgive sins," he diverted his eyes from the man.

"Yes, Jesus caused quite a stir with these words, it was like he could read what was in their hearts. Pharisees were getting angry, but they were quiet when he spoke. Like I said before, he told me to rise and go to my own house!"

"And you were able to rise on your own?" Malchus asked.

"Yes! Immediately! That feeling I can't explain, it was powerful! No one helped me, I was made completely whole. My family, we've been blessed, touched by God to have this man Jesus make me whole with just his words."

Malchus looked down, shaking his head. "It doesn't make sense to me. How can a man heal someone with words?"

"I don't know, but what I do know is I can walk and move and jump on a boat and I will tell anyone who will listen about Jesus of Nazareth. There's no doubt he is from God. He healed a leper! Did you hear about that?"

"Yes," Malchus' words were barely audible.

The man now placed both his hands on his shoulders. "Do you believe?"

"Believe what?" Malchus asked.

"Believe in this man Jesus and what he's doing."

"I don't know, I guess I do. You're standing here. You're a stranger, but yet I have no reason for you to tell me an untruth," he turned to look at the owner. "The owner says he knows your family, but..."

"But what?" the man didn't want him to get off the boat without his faith renewed or awakened.

"How can a man do these things?" Malchus' voice was a little stronger.

"I believe it's God who is working through him. Could Moses part the Red Sea on his own?"

Malchus had a hint of a smile. "No, I suppose not."

"If God could use Moses, why couldn't he use Jesus?"

Before he could respond, the man embraced him.

"I think God put me on this boat today for you, to tell you my story. Somehow, I feel you need to hear the good things Jesus is doing. What he did for me, I believe he will do for all, whatever it is you need young man, do not lose hope. Listen to your heart. Don't listen to what man says, follow your heart."

Malchus simply nodded. He made his way back to where Simon sat, they could see the shoreline wasn't far. He stared out at the sea. Jesus was out there somewhere walking towards Jerusalem. His Jerusalem. His city, his home, and now in a few weeks he would most likely return for the fall feasts. *Would he look at him differently?* A leper, a tax collector, a paralytic. It made his head hurt. *'Follow your heart.' Why did the man say that? And then embrace him that way?*

The women were waiting. Simon saw only two bags on Balaam. He asked Malchus if he wanted to share this wonderful story or could he tell Selah and Kezi?

He mumbled, "I shall tell them."

Simon jumped up as the boat drew near and waved at the women like he had been on a long voyage. Kezi and Selah looked at each other and smiled at his enthusiasm.

"At least it doesn't look like he fell in," Selah laughed at Kezi's remark.

"No, and Malchus," Selah squinted her eyes to see him, he remained seated. His head was down. She hoped he didn't get sick. The harbor was busy, otherwise she would make her way down to the boat. He was talking to a man and Simon was halfway across the area that separated the dock from where the women stood.

"Just wait until you hear what happened!"

"Simon, tell us!" Selah kept her eyes fixed on Malchus. "Is Malchus alright? Why is he still on the boat? Who's that man he's talking to?"

Kezi looked at Simon for assurance everything was fine. His big grin said it all.

"Did you have fun Simon?" Kezi wanted to know every detail.

"It was wonderful!"

"Your clothes are a little wet. Did you fall in?"

"No, I didn't. The oars splashed water on me. It was great! The water was cool and I was hot."

"How far out did you go?" Kezi asked.

Malchus now joined the group and answered for Simon. "The owner said we were about in the middle."

"That far? Did you see any fish?" she asked them.

"I saw one!" Simon had his hands out to show Kezi how big it was.

One look from Malchus and the women knew he was exaggerating. Simon patted Balaam as he always did and then the bags. "What's this?"

"Shells. I will have the finest earrings in Jerusalem," Kezi said.

Selah grabbed Malchus by the hand and gave him a gentle pull back. "Is everything alright? Who was that man you were speaking with so long?"

He looked back and he was gone. "I never asked him his name."

Kezi and Simon walked back to join them.

Kezi asked, "Is something wrong? Are you feeling poorly Malchus?"

It was hard for Simon to remain still but when Malchus didn't embark from the boat and he saw he spoke again to the man, he decided to let him tell the women. He wanted to see how he would retell the story.

Malchus looked for a place they could sit and led the way. His head was down as he watched his feet take every step. He had taken walking for granted. He noticed how little puffs of dust would shoot up on his toes and settle for a short ride as the sand and rocks moved under his sandals.

Selah looked at his feet too. *Did he hurt them jumping from the boat?*

"That man I was speaking with, he was on the boat with us."

"Yes, we saw him," both women nodded.

He was almost wringing his hands, he believed the man...but how did this happen, 'Follow your heart', the man told him again before they departed. "He was a paralytic!"

"What do you mean Malchus? That man?" Selah saw Simon's grin and if Malchus wasn't so serene right now she might have thought they were playing a trick on her.

"The man couldn't walk Selah, for years. He was confined to his couch, his family and friends carried him everywhere."

She looked behind her to see if she could see the man again. "How does he walk now?" she looked at his face. She saw his jaw had clenched. He was struggling with what he was about to say. "Malchus, what happened to this man?"

"Jesus." One word. One name. That's all he needed to say.

Kezi had her hand at her mouth, eyes wide. "Malchus, tell us!"

Simon could see he was indeed having difficulty. He didn't ask what the man said to him. He looked at Malchus and he nodded for him to go ahead.

"This man lives in Capernaum," Simon told them.

"Capernaum," Kezi said. "What's he doing here?"

"Hold on, hold on. He hasn't been able to walk for many years. His friends heard about Jesus healing people so they went to this man's house and carried him to the place Jesus was. Oh, I wish you could have heard him tell his story!"

"When did this happen?" Selah asked.

Simon looked at Malchus. "What did he say, about ten days ago?" Malchus nodded.

"He said there were many people surrounding the house. They couldn't believe how many were there. We told him we saw the crowds too. He told his friends to take him back home, there was no way for them to get close but they were determined he said. What friends! We all need friends like that, yes?"

"And then what? What did they do?" Kezi and Selah both were leaning in close to Simon.

"His friends went up to the roof of the house! This man said they began digging through and they made a hole for him to be lowered into the house!"

"No! Oh, my goodness!" Selah looked at Malchus again. His face was blank.

"His friends tore up a stranger's roof and lowered this poor man down! He was in disbelief of what they were doing and as his mat met the floor, there was Jesus. What the people must have thought!" Simon looked up imagining what had taken place.

"Go on Simon, finish the story!" Kezi was even closer now not wanting to miss a word!

"He said the room grew quiet. Jesus finally spoke and looked down at him and said, 'Son, your sins are forgiven.'"

"Son. He called him son," Malchus finally spoke. "This man was probably fifty years old, but yet he called him son."

The women looked at Simon to say something. "Yes, we all found that to be curious."

Malchus continued, "It wasn't that so much as he said his sins were forgiven. No one but God can forgive sins," he looked at all of them waiting for them to agree.

Kezi and Selah were afraid to speak. Simon was scratching his beard, a sign of him contemplating his next words.

"It's a strange remark and this man said that's when the Pharisees and others began to question him. They said the same thing, basically, who do you think you are? This man lying on the floor didn't speak. He told us he kept his eyes on Jesus. And he said, what was it Malchus, he said he felt like a thousand needles were pricking his feet but it didn't hurt."

Selah and Kezi exchanged looks. They knew one needle caused a little pain and discomfort.

"Then the man said it was as if Jesus could read their minds."

"He said their hearts," Malchus interrupted.

"What Malchus?"

"The man said it was like Jesus could read what was in their hearts."

"Yes, yes, you're right. And then this man said Jesus looked straight at him and told him to get up and take his mat and go home!" Before Kezi and Selah could respond, Malchus did.

"And he did," his comment was void of any emotion.

Kezi jumped to her feet! "I want to go find this man! What a miracle he's had! C'mon Simon, let's go! Praise God!"

Simon stood now too. "He's probably halfway home to Capernaum! This man didn't sit the entire time we were on the boat. He's walking the shoreline telling everyone what happened to him."

"Oh Selah, do you think Mary was there?"

"I'm sure she was. If not in the house, close by. Oh, what a sight that must have been."

Malchus remained seated for a few minutes. "Jesus is heading towards Jerusalem." Again, the somber tone.

Both women gave a little scream that startled the men.

"Selah!"

"Malchus, I'm sorry, but I'm excited. Mary may be only a day or two ahead of us. We could possibly travel all the way home with Jesus!" And that's exactly what was troubling him.

"Malchus, can we leave now?"

"We need to stay the night; the hour is late. We'll go to your family's village in the morning and wait for our group."

"How can we sleep? Malchus, it's not far. Why can't we go now? If those who traveled with us are there, then we'll leave at first light," she saw no reason to stay.

Malchus looked up to the sun. He knew there was a few hours of daylight left. He looked at all of them and with the same somber tone said, "We cannot, it's Sabbath." He was right of course. The four of them slowly walked back.

Balaam's plodding had slowed. They would be at the place they camped in a few minutes. Malchus and Selah walked arm in arm, something they didn't do often. She wanted to ask him so many questions but she would wait. She was the one now who needed patience. They sat around the fire with their own thoughts reflective of the journey so far, the travel before them. The cart lay unattended. Their days hadn't been planned according to Sabbath. She could leave now. She didn't care about Sabbath. She knew she was supposed to but right now she didn't. If Jesus could read her heart she thought, then he would know. She and Kezi went outside the camp to relieve themselves.

"Is Malchus alright Selah?"

"Yes, I think so. He hasn't said much, has he?"

"Did you ask him what the man said?" Kezi asked.

"No, he'll tell me when he's ready."

"Oh Selah, can you imagine what that must have been like to watch that man lowered through the roof!"

"I know, Malchus would have had a fit as much work he has put in on ours," the woman giggled.

"If we don't see Mary on the road, I know she'll see us once she reaches Jerusalem."

"Yes," Kezi said, "but wouldn't it be wonderful to walk back with her? She must have several stories to tell us."

"Can you imagine Malchus telling Caiaphas about this man; a paralytic! Or that we heard Jesus touched a leper! Caiaphas would rend his garment!" They giggled again.

It wasn't funny but the mood had been too quiet and serious for them. Malchus and Simon could hear the women. Malchus was staring into the fire, Simon gazing at the sky.

"Malchus, you know we'll be here for one more day. Why did you not tell Selah that we couldn't travel?"

"Let me ask you Simon, would it be so bad if we did? Selah, her eyes, she wants so bad to reach her friend Mary."

"Yes, Kezi too," Simon agreed.

"Would you be opposed to travel tomorrow?"

Simon looked away from the stars. "Let me think about it for a while."

Malchus leaned closer, "I will need to tell, remind Selah that we'll be here one more night."

"Are you going to tell this old man what that man said to you? What has you troubled son?"

He almost wished Simon didn't address him as "son". Everyone was "son". Even a fifty-year-old paralytic! "He told me to follow my heart."

"Wise words. Is that all?"

"It's enough," he gave Simon that look, don't ask me anything more right now. "Well old man, do we travel on Sabbath?"

Without hesitation and rising at the same time, Simon replied, "Follow your heart."

"Are you going to sleep already Simon?" Kezi asked.

"No, I'm just stretching my legs. Look at that moon!"

"I know, it's beautiful to see it by the sea. I've missed that."

"Are you tired Malchus?" Selah searched his eyes.

"No, I was just thinking, we're all anxious to get home."

"Yes," she said.

"We are," Kezi agreed, "Simon and I both actually miss the market."

He now looked at Selah only. "You know Sabbath isn't over until sunset tomorrow."

Simon was behind Malchus. He saw anguish in both Kezi and Selah's face.

"Yes husband, I know."

"However."

"Yes, however what Malchus?" Selah was hopeful.

He laughed for the first time this evening. "I was thinking it wouldn't hurt us to travel the short distance to your family's place. If the group is there and they wish to wait until the next day, we'll wait."

"And if they're not there?"

"If they don't arrive first thing in the morning, I thought we would seek out the nearest synagogue and ask," he swallowed, "we'll ask if Jesus has been there and if you feel comfortable to travel without the group, we'll continue. What do you think?"

"If you think we'll be fine traveling without them, then I trust your decision," Selah replied.

"Kezi, are you comfortable going without the group should they be delayed?"

"Yes Malchus, I have faith we'll be fine. I know these roads. I don't think we'll be alone. Many will begin the journey to Jerusalem for the feasts."

"It's settled then," he said.

The women went inside their shelter and Simon walked back over.

"A well thought out plan Malchus," Simon smiled.

"Just following my heart old man."

Simon stayed outside a while longer. He inhaled deeply. The moon shimmered on the water, the stars were bright and a soft breeze cooled the evening. He was thankful. "God of Abraham, Isaac and Jacob, thank you for our safety as we journey home. Thank you for my friends.

Thank you for my boat ride," he chuckled a little. Here I am, a grown man thanking God for my boat ride. Yes, he thought, God likes it when we thank Him even for the little things. He thought about Sabbath and his heart grew heavy. He closed his eyes listening to the waves. *They don't stop. The wind. It didn't stop blowing. They both were working during Sabbath.* He said thank you again and promptly fell asleep.

"Do you believe we're created Malchus?"

"What kind of question is that first thing in the morning?"

Simon was doing his best to remain serious. "It's a simple question. Did God create us?"

"Yes, satisfied?"

"Did He create this beautiful sea, and the sun and the moon?"

"Listen old man, we don't have time this morning for your silliness," Malchus was hiding his smile.

"Last night as I watched the waves roll in, the stars shining and that magnificent moon, I thought to myself, God has created all, just like us, and yet the sun comes up every day."

"Yes, yes, what's your point Simon?"

"They do not get Sabbath rest."

Kezi and Selah clapped their hands and Malchus couldn't help laughing out loud.

Simon gathered them together. "I don't think our God will be angry with us if we lift our bags and carry water today. He knows our hearts. He's merciful. I'm not going to worry about such things. Let us go now."

They found the area as quiet as when they first arrived.

"How long shall we wait Malchus?"

He looked at Selah. "If they're observing Sabbath, they won't be here until morning. We'll just sit here until then I guess. What say you Simon? What do you think we should do?"

"Why stay here? Let us continue south. The group may be ahead of us! If they're observing Sabbath, we may catch up to them. If not, we simply keep going. Look around. There's no one here."

"You're right," Malchus looked behind him. No one was coming west. The day was uneventful which the men were thankful. The walk along the shore to the river was easy. They didn't see any of their travel companions. They may have decided to extend their time with family. He couldn't worry about them. He needed to focus on his family, Selah, Kezi and Simon. The land became more familiar and they found the river narrower and shallow. They crossed easily and found caves in the rocks for shelter.

"If you're able Selah, we could be home in four or five days," Malchus scanned the area, staff in hand, listening for any movement from animals.

"Do you think that will be too fast of a pace for Simon?"

"He's truly amazed me. We can take our time. Caiaphas will just have to wait for my return."

"This is the first time you've mentioned his name."

He turned now. "Truly I'm not ready to go home. I like being out on the hills, climbing and relaxing by the sea."

"You know Malchus, John the Baptist was in this area baptizing," Simon spoke.

"Yes, I've heard."

"The people say he baptized Jesus not too far from here."

Malchus nodded.

"Did you hear some say they heard a voice?" Simon asked.

"What?" He needed time to respond. He had heard.

"It's been said that when Jesus was baptized, a voice from heaven," Simon looked up and Malchus followed his gaze, "the voice said, 'This is my Son in whom I'm well pleased'. Can you imagine?"

"I heard people say it was thunder."

"Perhaps the voice was thunderous in the way it sounded!" Simon made his voice as deep as he could and bellowed out the statement that both Kezi and Selah left what they were doing to see what Simon was doing.

"This old man is now imitating the voice from heaven!" Malchus slapped his knee.

"What are you talking about?" Kezi stood, hands on her hips.

"I told Malchus I heard when Jesus was baptized, people said they heard a voice from heaven and he said he heard it was thunder. I was simply trying to make my voice sound like thunder!"

Kezi was shaking her head laughing at the two men but Selah wasn't laughing.

"Malchus, didn't you say you heard about this voice?" she asked.

"I think all of Jerusalem did."

"Do you think it was only thunder?"

"I don't know Selah, I wasn't there. Some say they didn't hear anything."

"Don't you find it odd how some heard a voice and others heard nothing?"

"Perhaps the people who didn't hear anything were all standing further away. We have seen how sound carries over water; I don't know Selah."

"What did the voice say Simon?"

Simon became uneasy. Selah had such a tender heart.

It was Malchus who repeated the words. "This is my Son in whom I'm well pleased."

"And this voice was the voice of God?"

"Well, the people said it came from above," Simon didn't want to say too much.

"And that is why some said it was thunder?" she asked.

"Yes," Malchus answered.

"But how does thunder sound like words? If it was only thunder, how could people say they heard those same words?"

"I believe they heard those words," Kezi said. I think if your heart is right and pure, you somehow hear. The people who heard nothing, I don't think they wanted to hear. They were there perhaps for the wrong reason. John the Baptist caused a lot of trouble, why the way he dressed and the stories that went around the market that he only ate grasshoppers and honey, people were making fun of him, and then all his shouting at Herod! Who does that? This man is wild in his nature. I think people went to see him to laugh at him. Their hearts were not pure nor did they have any desire to really hear what he was saying. He was telling people to repent! No one wants to hear that. As far as the thunder, I think people heard what they wanted to hear."

Malchus looked at Kezi with his mouth open. She was right! "Kezi, those words are from your heart. How could you know such things?"

"I don't know Malchus. We've been hearing many things. The Pharisees are following Jesus, but they're following for other reasons. They were at the river when Jesus was baptized. I bet they were the ones that said they heard nothing. I...I want to finish my sorting. Selah, do you need help cooking?"

"No Kezi, I'll call you when we're ready to eat."

Simon and Malchus stood there amazed at Kezi's words. Selah felt joy in her heart. She stood silently blessing her friend.

"I guess I'll ask my last question for another time," Selah turned to finish their dinner.

"What question is that wife?"

"Can God have a son?"

Five days later they were back in Jerusalem. The neighbors didn't seem to take notice of their absence. Everyone has their own life Selah thought. It was a strange time mostly because of Jesus, but no one wanted to discuss him like she did. The topic of conversation was always Roman oppression and taxes. She admitted she didn't know much about the one to come, Son of David, the Messiah, but she didn't think he was coming just so they wouldn't have to pay taxes. Malchus was moody all the way home. She knew he was frustrated. Simon became the closest person to him and he had come to respect his honesty. He left to buy fresh hay for Balaam and told her he may let Caiaphas know he was back. Sabbath was the next day. At least he would have one more day to rest and decide what he would tell him of his journey. She suddenly thought about John the Baptist. Had he been released? She couldn't wait to be back at the market. The women would have all the latest news.

Malchus was careful. He didn't want anyone to see him. It was hot, he missed the sea breeze. He was lost in his thoughts walking and went past Kezi's house. He found himself east of the Temple, and pulling his outer garment over his head, went through the gate to his favorite place. He could see the slopes of the Temple mount behind him and he walked until he was hidden within the groves. At least here he would find shade. His tree. He loved the shape of the branches. As a young boy he would climb and sit for hours and let his imagination wonder about far lands. Now he thought he might break a bone if he attempted this feat. He sat as he always did, his outer garment removed and spread on the ground. He wasn't tired but closed his eyes, the sun filtering through the boughs of the trees. He thought of Selah. She'd been quite remarkable, never complained once on their journey. It was long and hot; she didn't see her family and they didn't see Mary or Jesus.

He heard the flutter of wings and watched a flock of sparrows as they flew towards the Temple. He thought of Simon's conversation when they left Tiberias on the Sabbath, *all created things, they do not rest*. Even the birds were busy, something so simple and yet he was conscientious that Sabbath was a few hours away and he needed to collect Balaam and the hay. He couldn't be seen on the streets of the city carrying anything. Yes, Simon was right, the sun came up every day but did it not rest when it set? Simon had said, 'No, I think it's just shining on another land'. He shook his head. It was too much to think about. Like Selah, he longed for the sea. It had calmed him too. He and Simon spent hours on the shore resting, the waves growing as the wind picked up from the east. He was thankful for the calm day they went out. He could almost feel the movement of the water below him, the sounds of the oars as they sliced through the coolness beneath.

He and Simon both had let their hands down feeling the pressure and strength of the sea. He laughed out loud at Simon's fish story. The only fish he saw was for sale at the market. Simon's purchase of salt enabled them to bring some home which he assumed would be part of dinner tonight. *Dinner!* He rose and gathered his garment. He would go to Kezi's first and get Balaam and then the hay. He had plenty of time. He found Simon at Kezi's. He was working on a small cart for her to use back and forth to the market. He invited both over for dinner.

"Relax Malchus, we'll come another time. Enjoy your privacy and your home, maybe pick up some flowers for Selah."

"Flowers?" he repeated with a raised eyebrow.

"Yes flowers. The man that has the hay will also have flowers. Do you have enough oil?"

"I didn't check anything! I'll pick up oil. Anything else old man I should bring home?"

"Just don't forget the flowers."

"Poppy's! Malchus, they're lovely. So many different colors! I shall use them as our centerpiece. What else did you bring?"

"I ran into Simon and he reminded me to buy oil."

"Simon was at Kezi's?"

"Yes, he's building her a small cart."

"Did you stop and see Caiaphas?"

"No, I'll see him soon enough."

She arranged the colors so each one could be easily seen.

"Let me tend to Balaam and wash up and then we'll eat."

She pulled the purple flowers up a little higher in the arrangement, he watched her from the door. She was humming. A good sign he thought. He looked around their cozy room and caught a glimpse of silver in her sea colored scarf. He began to whistle as he walked around the back.

Caiaphas saw Malchus. He was hard to miss pulling that donkey of his. He had been walking home from the Temple, as always there were many preparations for the feasts, but this one, the most solemn, the most important. He needed to keep himself pure. It could mean his death if he didn't. He wouldn't call out to him like a common man. He had others to do his bidding. He needed to remain calm no matter what controversial stories were swirling around and he heard plenty. He could only assume Jesus would return to the Temple for the Day of Atonement. He knew his popularity was growing. Hundreds had become thousands. He had been proactive already commissioning Pilate to return to Jerusalem ahead of schedule demanding the security of the Temple, explaining the feast the most reverent of the Jewish people, that he wouldn't tolerate anything less than the total cooperation of Rome. He smiled to himself knowing he probably tossed his request in the fire but he would have the victory. Pilate had to govern. Keeping peace was under his purview. He would take every precaution to keep Jesus from causing any disruption. He wouldn't allow one man to unravel all he had trained for, all he had at risk. One Galilean would not undo him.

"So Malchus, you had a good rest?" Caiaphas didn't look at him.

"Yes, well the journey was long but we took our time."

"What day did you return?"

He was smart enough to know Caiaphas already knew. He wouldn't lie. "Two days ago, before Sabbath."

Caiaphas didn't waste time. "Did you see the Nazarene?"

"No, I did not."

"There are reports of thousands now following him and yet you didn't see him?"

"I didn't Caiaphas. We did see the crowds for a few days while we were in Capernaum."

"There are many new stories circulating, I'm certain you've heard."

"Yes, I've heard some."

"Would you care to elaborate?"

Malchus twisted in his chair. Caiaphas was standing by the window, he hoped he didn't notice.

"They're just stories Caiaphas, I can't tell you if they're true."

"I know they're just stories, however some have been quite disturbing," he turned away from looking outside and sat opposite Malchus. "It's been reported this Nazarene healed a leper, actually touched a leper! Can you believe that Malchus? This man who wants to lecture us on the law himself touches a leper!"

"Yes, I heard. It's unbelievable," he thought it better to be in agreement. He didn't know if this was true but, in his heart, he knew it probably was. Caiaphas had a point. Why would Jesus touch a leper? It was against the law.

"What else?"

"What else?" Malchus echoed.

"Yes, what else did you hear?"

"Mostly that he's teaching in the synagogues and many are following him."

"That's all?" Caiaphas asked.

"That's all I've heard," he saw that look numerous times. Caiaphas didn't believe him.

"I have it on good authority that a man named Matthew has left his position and now follows this man."

"I know no one named Matthew," Malchus replied.

Caiaphas' face was turning red. "The tax collector Malchus! Matthew, the tax collector! Pilate himself stationed him in Capernaum! You're going to sit there and tell me you didn't hear of this feast this man held for Jesus, that publicans and sinners joined his table!" he was pounding his fist on the table and Malchus saw the vessel in his temple throbbing.

"Caiaphas, I'd forgotten that story. A tax collector? I heard it, but I for one don't believe it. I didn't see this feast. I don't know of this man Matthew. Why should I trouble you with these falsehoods? I see how upset you're getting. Have you spoken with Pilate? Do you know this to be truth?" he was trying to calm him down.

"No, I haven't spoken with Pilate."

"Caiaphas, you said yourself this man Jesus doesn't follow the Law of Moses. Those who are following him will soon see the truth about him. I'll find out what's true, and what is false. You have much to prepare for. Why take time to discuss such nonsense?"

Caiaphas' breathing was becoming normal. He sat back in his chair and studied Malchus again for a few moments. "Yes, find out what you can and report back when you have proof."

He was out of his chair and down the hall before he had another outburst. He wished he was at the sea. No worries there, no pretenses, freedom from Caiaphas. As he left the Temple area, he thought about the paralytic. If Caiaphas found out he kept this from him; that would be the end. He couldn't bring it up now. It's not something that slipped your mind. He would have to deny the day at sea. He would ask Simon, Selah and Kezi not to repeat the story to anyone. He would tell them how important it was for them to never admit that he and Simon were on the boat with the man who was healed. Selah wouldn't like the deception. This was his life. She would have to understand. He would have to start sharing truths about Caiaphas. He tried to keep his private life private and his work hidden from Selah. He was beginning to find this would now almost be impossible. He wished they would have stayed in Capernaum the additional weeks he planned. He now comprehended the allure of the sea. A man could think. The closest place of refuge, his tree in the groves. He couldn't keep running and hiding. He wasn't the most honest man; he simply kept his mouth shut. Especially at home. With Selah. His wife. He looked to the groves, but today he wouldn't go. He would speak with Simon. He remembered he was building a new cart for Kezi. Perhaps he would let him help.

The two men assembled the cart. It took them the entire afternoon. Simon had everything ready. Malchus assisted mostly by holding the wood in place. The women were inside making jewelry. Selah helped Kezi and watched every move, asked a lot of questions and learned something new. Kezi was not only a perfectionist, she was creative. Throughout the day she would stop, look at her materials and as if dancing, would move picking and choosing a bead here, a shell there and have Selah hold things up to her ears, her waist and change tunics to see what color jewelry would look best. Selah was having fun. She draped Kezi's most costly silks and other fabrics across her while holding shells to her ears letting Kezi hold up necklaces and slip on bracelets.

Malchus and Simon could hear the women and their comments about each color.

Selah would say, "Oh Kezi, this is a beautiful color with those pretty white shells you bought and wouldn't this look nice with that scarf that looks like the color of a sunset."

Malchus smiled. He knew what his favorite color was.

"Owww!"

"Simon! What did you do?"

"I hit my thumb! You weren't paying attention!"

"I'm sorry, let me see, are you alright old man?" Malchus was chuckling.

"Yes, hold that still for me. We're almost done. Where's your head at son?"

"At the sea," he responded. "Well the color of the sea anyway."

Simon shook his head. "Caiaphas didn't have anything for you to do today, is that it?"

"Aren't you glad so I could come and help you?"

"Some help! That thumb is going to throb all night!"

The women came out to see why Simon was yelling. He held up his thumb and the two of them fussed over him for several minutes. Malchus sat back and smiled at the attention he received. It wouldn't surprise him if he hit the other thumb on purpose. Kezi insisted everyone stay for dinner and they recounted the fresh memories from their trip, mostly funny stories with Simon. The women still giggled like young girls when they asked about the fish he saw. Kezi said next time he told the story they would have to move outside as the size of the fish couldn't fit in her house.

"Yes, ha ha Kezi, it was longer than the boat!"

Selah was happy to see Malchus enjoying himself, but then his face turned serious.

"I'm glad we're all here, there's something I need to ask all of you."

"What is it Malchus?" Selah laid her cup down.

"It's Caiaphas. Some days he's just impossible!"

Both Kezi and Simon also sat up a little straighter. He never spoke freely about Caiaphas.

"Malchus, is everything alright?" Selah could hear a stutter in her own voice as she said, "Are you still in his service?"

"Yes Selah, nothing like that. Today he asked me..."

"Asked you what?" she was impatient.

"Asked me about Jesus."

"Jesus?" Simon looked at both women.

"He wanted to know what I heard about him while we were on our trip. He actually asked if I saw him. Of course, I said no. Caiaphas, he looked at each of them again, "he has people who report to him."

"Like what you do?" Selah kept her eyes down.

"Yes, like I do. He asked if I knew about Jesus healing a leper and I said yes, we heard and we did happen on the crowds at Capernaum. He then asked if I heard anything else and I said no. He brought up the man, the tax collector and he got so angry," he was up now pacing. "I said I forgot about him, why trouble him with these tales when I don't know if they are true. He didn't believe me."

Simon could see he was troubled. "But you don't know Malchus. He shouldn't be angry at you."

"This is what he pays me to know Simon."

Selah and Kezi sat, not moving. Did Malchus just admit that he's paid to bring information to Caiaphas?

He read their thoughts. "Yes, this is what, well part of what I do. It's politics. It's Rome. It's not something I enjoy." They all nodded not knowing how to respond.

"He kept pressing me, 'Is there nothing else'?" He turned to Simon. "I sat there wondering, what does he know? If he asks me about the man on the boat, what shall I say? Simon, I was sitting there trying to remember every man's face on that boat. Did someone recognize me? Has someone already reported to Caiaphas I met a man, a man who was paralyzed and this Jesus, this Jesus that he calls the enemy, healed this man and I took a leisurely boat ride with him? I thought, he's set a trap for me! I'll have to deny all! Which brings me to ask you, all of you, to please not repeat this story to anyone. We were not in Tiberias. I was not on a boat. This is important. I'm not asking you to lie, I'm asking you to not speak of that day. It's important!"

Simon was the first to speak. "Say no more Malchus, we shall not speak of that day."

Malchus looked at Selah, "I'm sorry to ask you this, I'm in a difficult position."

"I understand Malchus. I'm glad you told us what happened today. It's been my hope you would share with us about Caiaphas. Perhaps we can help you in other ways."

"Kezi, is this too much of a burden for you? I know the market is where everyone speaks of all they hear."

"Malchus, don't worry. As Simon said, we will not speak of that day."

They saw his shoulders drop in relief. He sat down exhausted.

"Perhaps we should go home Malchus, it's been a long day. Kezi, let me help you clean up," Selah was up clearing the table before Kezi responded.

Simon was looking at his thumb. The swelling had gone down considerably.

"Thank you for your help today," he stuck his thumb in the air and both men began to laugh. They went outside to admire their handiwork. "This Caiaphas, he really thinks of Jesus as his enemy?"

"He does Simon. I think that day at the Temple during Passover when Jesus overturned the tables," he looked at Simon now, "it cost him a lot of money."

"I see," Simon thought he said enough for one evening. He wouldn't ask any more questions. He knew both women were as thrilled as he was that he opened up and seemed to trust a little more. He did want to encourage him before he left.

"Caiaphas sounds like a difficult man to accommodate, no matter what his position, makes no difference to me," he put his hand on his shoulder as he now was accustomed to doing and said, "Malchus, you can always tell this old man what's on your mind if you need to talk, you know where to find me. I think you've found I'm a good listener too."

He embraced Simon. Selah and Kezi saw them from the doorway. Kezi squeezed Selah's hand. Both women knew what the other was thinking. Malchus and Selah walked home holding hands.

Chapter Six

Selah had never been left alone at Kezi's and she was nervous. A few women already stopped by and when they didn't see Kezi, left. She went around the tables, everything was folded, centered and color coordinated. Simon had smoothed out small twigs and fashioned little wooden pegs to hang jewelry on. Kezi said he was very clever and asked him to make larger ones for her necklaces and hanging shells.

"Finally!" Selah sighed in relief.

"Finally?" Kezi teased her. "We haven't been too delayed."

"How's Malchus today?" Simon looked toward the Temple thinking of his new friend.

"He's fine Simon, he's still worried that Caiaphas knows he hasn't told him everything."

"Yes, with all the Temple preparations and Pilate arriving back, maybe Caiaphas will forget about this."

"Pilate is back?" Kezi asked.

"Just arrived yesterday I was told," Simon knew what she was thinking. "Yes, Claudia is here."

"Good. She can be the first to buy my new wind chimes."

"Wind chimes," Simon repeated.

"That's what I'm calling them because they chime when the wind blows." Kezi loved the business of the market. She never grew tired of the commotion. There were always new people and days went by quickly. She couldn't imagine Selah only here in the mornings, she needed her all day. When she sold her first pair of shell earrings, she felt she was selling her own child. Silly she knew, but she wrapped them as she would a newborn, only for the woman to say she wanted to wear them now!

Simon finished for the day. He came and sat next to Kezi.

"By the way, who told you Pilate was back?"

"A woman, she said she knew you. She came to buy flowers."

"Avi?" Kezi asked.

"Yes, that's her name!"

"Is that all she said?"

"Yes, she remembered my place in the market was next to yours and that I often had fresh flowers. She was in a hurry. I didn't want to keep her. I'm going home. I'm tired today."

She looked him over. "Do you need anything Simon?"

"Yes, rest. I want to be rested up for all the celebrations!"

They listened to the blasts of the shofar from the Temple with reverence. It was a holy time for everyone, a new year to reflect and repent. Caiaphas would enter the Holy of Holies to atone for the sins of the people. Selah knew she would hardly see Malchus during this time. There was a calm in the city unlike any time both women could remember. It was eerie. Yes, the people celebrated but were pensive. Most had hopes of a new year without the Romans. Many were questioning doctrine. Simon knew many were looking for Jesus. There had been no sight of him. People were discouraged, especially Kezi and Selah. There had been no word from Mary. The last they heard Jesus remained in Galilee. Jerusalem was crowded. They heard many in the market with the accent of those from Galilee, but no Jesus. Kezi only saw Avi at a distance. There had been no opportunity to speak with her. She didn't see Joanna either. *Where was everyone?*

Selah suggested Simon and Kezi come to their home for dinner and talk about their shelter for the feast. It was a week-long festival, they needed to make plans. It was an exciting time for all who came to the city. Summer ended; the harvest was ready. Malchus' trees were stripped of their fruit. The people were joyous! She loved this time of year. The menorahs would be lit around the Temple at night and the whole city illuminated. People danced and sang and played instruments, it was a celebration she looked forward to each year.

"Do you know Selah, I was counting the poles as we laid them out and I told Simon, "I think you cut too many."

"No, he said, I have the perfect amount."

That crazy old man is building Balaam his own booth!" Malchus slapped his knee.

"He loves that donkey!"

They were enjoying the end of the day ready for the celebration to begin. Kezi brought olives for Selah to press and Malchus sat back and watched her use the small stone.

"This will take me all night!"

"That's why we buy our oil. If I waited for you, we would never have bread!" he helped her with the last of the basket.

"Kezi's going to decorate our booth. I better tell her she will be decorating two!" She looked at him in the soft light of the only lamp burning. She could see the young boy she met in his expression.

He caught her staring. "What?"

"I was just remembering the first time I saw you. Some days it doesn't seem that long ago, others..."

"Like years?" he laughed.

"Time doesn't stand still, does it? I can't believe I've been, well we've been in this home a year and a half. I love it here Malchus. I didn't think I would. Everyone comes to Jerusalem! It must have been exciting to grow up here, see all the people from so many different places. I can't imagine! I knew the same families all my life. No one moved to my village."

He was glad Selah was happy. He worried she wouldn't adjust to the lifestyle of the city but she had and quickly! It was Kezi. She would be homesick had she not met her he thought.

"I'm happy you've come to love this place as much as I. Yes, I couldn't count the people I have seen move through the walls of the city, especially of course during the feasts."

The lamp was low. He felt safe in the shadows of the room.

"Selah, remember I told you about my favorite place I like to go?" He didn't wait for her to respond. "There's one particular tree I climbed as a young boy, and Selah, I think some days I sat up there until sunset. Every now and then I still go."

"You climb the tree?" she put her hand up so he wouldn't see her smile.

"No, I don't climb the tree," he knew she was smiling. "I sit and think. It's my...my sanctuary."

She gave him a look of encouragement to continue speaking.

"When I was young, during Sukkot, I would climb my tree and watch the priests come from the Eastern Gate. They would cut willows and line up in rows to start the procession back to the Temple. They would wave the branches, and the sound, it was like the wind, and the High Priest and the flute player, everyone would make their way back to the Temple, and all the people were shouting, it was such a joyous time," he looked at her now, "I was happy in my tree." They both heard Simon arriving.

"I don't care if he's just a donkey, I'm building him his own booth!" Simon knew they teased him out of their love for him.

"Which one Simon, purple or blue?" Kezi danced in front of him twirling ribbons. "Is Balaam partial to blue? Does it match his eyes?"

"No, his eyes are brown."

Everyone laughed with Simon. It was a time of joy. They constructed four booths with one roof. Kezi hung her wind chimes and thread different colors of ribbons through the palm branches. Simon placed hay all around Balaam's booth. The donkey too would celebrate this feast. Selah made juice from pomegranates, baked bread and small cakes of dates and raisins. Balaam already consumed one. She knocked it on the floor so she would have an excuse to give it to him. The four of them walked in front of the courtyard and surveyed their handiwork.

"I think we're ready!" Selah clapped her hands in delight and when Balaam casually walked into his own booth, they all began laughing slapping each other on the back.

Malchus saw Nicodemas a few times, always at a distance and didn't initiate a chance encounter. He hadn't told a soul about their meetings, not Selah or Simon, the only two people he would confide in. He wanted to tell Selah but was reluctant to express his deepest questions and doubts, fears and anxieties. *Didn't everyone who ever lived wonder about eternity, God, truth?* He did. He wanted to speak to Nicodemas again. Several more times actually. The more understanding he could glean, the easier he thought it would be to share with her. He wanted her to learn from him, be proud of him and most of all respect him. He was uncertain if he met any of these conditions.

Nicodemas had grown fond of Malchus' tree. In his absence over the summer, he found himself walking to the grove often. The early morning was quiet and he moved throughout the city unnoticed. He carried nothing. He simply sat. As the days grew shorter and summer was ending, he knew he could no longer indulge in this solitude. Harvest season would begin and the curtain of olives would be laid bare, his shelter and covering stripped. The summer was uneventful. No Jesus. No uproars. No trouble. Even Caiaphas seemed under a false sense of utopia. But with the fall feasts arrival and all the pomp and circumstance which Pilate liked to refer to it, the reality of Caiaphas' position awakened his temporary stupor. That's when the impromptu dinners started. Nicodemas was surprised at the first invitation and even more surprised when he suggested dinner the following week. Now in the confines of his own house, the streets swelling with pilgrims, he sat. His desk was littered with scrolls. He thought of the scribes who toiled to copy them, thankful for their dedication He walked over and moved the weight he placed on an open scroll. King David had written, 'They will pierce my hands and feet'. The scroll laid open for weeks now to this passage. Beside it lay open the Book of Isaiah. He ran his fingers over the sacred words. He prayed God would reveal to him the connection. *Who were both David and Isaiah speaking of?* Servants brought in more tables to allow several scrolls open at the same time. He would walk from surface to surface repeating the passage as he read the next. He was determined to reason these words until they came alive in him. Days turned into nights and summer passed with no new revelation but he wouldn't be moved. He asked for another table.

Simon and Malchus rested under the shade of Malchus' extended roof.

"So, tell me son, will Caiaphas expect you to be by his side at all times?"

"He hasn't made clear yet what my participation will be this year. I'm sure he'll want me close by in case."

"In case of Jesus?" Simon asked.

"Yes."

The two men waited for the other to speak. It was Selah who broke the silence.

"Sukkot will begin soon. No more work for you two. Come inside. The house is cooler this evening. We'll have our dinner together. Tomorrow we'll celebrate!"

They watched her as she joined Kezi. She had been light hearted and excited for the feast for days. She wanted to get close to the Temple to watch the procession and Malchus obliged. He knew the priests would enter both the East Gate and Water Gate and he admitted after all these years, he was filled with joyful anticipation. The lighting of the menorahs was his favorite. The city basked in a golden glow and from his tree he thought Jerusalem must be paradise. The people were exuberant! Everyone was thankful. It had been a good harvest. It was a new year. He felt like a new man. This past year he gained a father, a friend, and had grown closer to Selah. He hadn't thought about politics or taxes, he was enjoying his life. He told Selah later while they were gazing at the stars how happy he was. He also reminded her from where they were, they would be able to hear the procession in the morning from the pool of Siloam. Tonight, the sky was clear, the sound of music filled the air, his wife was at his side and he was happy.

Simon was singing. Kezi attempted to sing wrong words loudly over him just to hear him bellyache. She scolded him earlier for drinking too much wine. It only made him sing louder. It had been a wonderful day. Selah turned to find Malchus fast asleep. Kezi's chimes were playing a simple melody, one which put Simon to sleep as the women both heard his steady snoring.

"Selah, are you still awake?" Kezi whispered.

"Yes, are you comfortable?"

"I'm fine, yes. Do you find it strange Jesus is not here?"

"Yes, I thought Mary would be here. I expected her to show up at the shop."

"Maybe they're delayed in their travels. I've been asking around the market, no one has seen him."

"We have six more days, maybe he's on his way."

"I hope so. Goodnight Selah."

"I need to report in," Malchus said.

"You're going back to the Temple?"

"No Selah, I'm going to Caiaphas' house. We have only two days left. I need to see if he requires anything," he looked at each of them. "I should only be gone one hour. Caiaphas has been in a pleasant mood. No Jesus I guess."

She nodded. He knew the women had searched the crowds for any sign of Mary, they only wanted to make sure the young girl was well.

"We shall wait until you return for our dinner. They will be lighting the menorah soon."

"I'll be quick!"

She watched him moving towards the sun, she shielded her eyes until she could no longer see his familiar walk.

"He won't be long," Simon assured her. He started a fire. They would feast tonight with beef stew. Selah had the largest cooking pot out for the occasion. They filled it over half way. Spices were thick in the air. The whole city rejoiced until the splendor of the night sky kissed them goodnight. They sat listening to laughter and the sounds of children playing.

"Don't you wish every night could be like this?" Selah had her knees drawn up under her tunic, making a rocking motion close to the cooking stew.

"Every night? Simon repeated. I guess that would be pretty close to a perfect life!"

"Like paradise," Kezi added.

"What do you think paradise is like Kezi?" Selah turned to her friend while stirring the stew.

"Whatever it is, I think it will be wonderful!"

"So, you believe it exists?" Simon sounded doubtful.

"Yes, what would we have hope for if we didn't?" Kezi leaned in to inhale the aroma. She hadn't had any meat for some time. When there were sacrifices at the Temple, she thought all of Jerusalem smelled like beef stew and it made her mouth water.

"What about the Sadducees?" Simon asked.

"What about them Simon?" Selah didn't know anything about Sadducees.

"They don't believe in eternal life, nor angels or anything!"

"Why?" Selah couldn't believe it.

"Actually, I'm not sure Selah. Perhaps Malchus knows. Caiaphas is a Sadducee."

"Caiaphas! I thought he was a Pharisee."

"No, Nicodemas is a Pharisee."

"This is confusing," Selah looked at Kezi for clarification.

"Does your heart tell you there's a paradise that awaits us Selah?" Kezi spoke in low tones.

She didn't hesitate, "Yes."

"That's it then! Let us not speak about others and what they believe or don't. I suppose one day we'll all know truth."

Tomorrow would be the last day. Selah didn't want it to end. They would hear the shofar in the morning and would gather at the Court of Women. *The water and the wine offering.* She would ask Malchus to explain to her again the significance. She hoped he wouldn't fall asleep right away. She wanted to understand what they were doing and why. She looked around. People camped wherever they could. Everyone was happy. She breathed in the night air. This to her was paradise.

"Malchus, can you tell me again about the water and wine and what it means?"

He looked at her in the moonlight of their temporary shelter and saw the woman behind eyes who did wonder and question, and he admired her for wanting to learn.

"The drawing of the water is like the pouring out of God's Spirit, just like when God breathed into Adam's nostrils and gave him life. It's God's Spirit, poured out, the true source of life. The wine is joy. When the priests pour out the water and wine, it symbolizes the life and joy of the Holy Spirit."

"Why do we remain silent after singing?"

"We listen for the wind, the breath of God. We hope to feel and hear the Spirit of God."

Simon now spoke. "I understand the wind. What I'm having difficulty with is the water. How does the wind and water connect?"

Malchus knew it was from the book of Isaiah. "Simon, it's about drawing water out, the refreshing we get from water."

"I don't get it."

Malchus continued, "Well, we know how important water is."

"Yes," they all said.

"We draw water to refresh ourselves. It's living water. We sing the song, 'We will draw out of the well of salvation.'"

"But the wind Malchus?" Simon replied.

"The priests waving the willow branches sound like wind. They're bringing wind and water to the Temple. I think they both represent the Spirit of God and the prophecies about the outpouring of His Spirit. I'm ashamed I don't know more."

"Malchus, don't say such a thing!" He could tell Simon sat up. "I now make the connection! I've heard this talk of living water. I think many of our prophets spoke about it. Both water and wind can be symbols of the Holy Spirit," Simon laid back down and looked at his stars. For some reason he thought of the old woman who told him she needed to see her stars. He heard a still small voice, words he heard only one time, *'Except a man be born of water and the Spirit, he cannot enter into the kingdom of God'. Water and Spirit. Water and breath. Water and wind.* "Praise God!" he said loudly, I get it!"

"What Simon?" Malchus asked.

"I'll tell you another time. Let us get some rest." He started his false snoring just to hear Kezi and Selah giggle. "I love you my family."

"We love you too Simon, they said together."

He stared up at the stars a long while. He heard Kezi's chimes, only a small melody tonight as the air was still, but now whenever he felt the slightest breeze, he would inhale the very breath of God.

Caiaphas was ecstatic! The feast was successful. Nothing could damper his spirits on this last great day of Sukkot. He saw Malchus at the Pool of Siloam and again at the Temple. He had a keen eye. Even with the crowds and celebrations, Malchus watched for any signs of trouble. By all accounts, the city and its people rejoiced! There were no shouts of "Barabbas", no threats against Rome, no angry mobs shouting about taxes and no Jesus. He received a personal note from Pilate congratulating him on a successful fall season.

He would ensure the guards were recognized and duly compensated. He carefully put the note in his private chamber running his fingers over Pilate's seal. He would see Malchus at the Court of Women and tomorrow they would all rest. His father-in-law neglected to send acknowledgement, but he wasn't moved by his selfishness. The sky was blue, the people cheered as he performed his duties, the city was alive with music, and it was a perfect day. The priests had completed their rotations and he was ready to join in the celebrations in the role of spectator, not participant.

The final push of the people towards the Temple filled his heart with pride. The representation of the Law of Moses, the Temple practice, the daily sacrifices and rituals, all had been received by the inhabitants of the city with complete acceptance. He gave them what they expected. He thought Nicodemas haughty, only a mere nod of approval as he paraded by the group of Pharisees that he seemed to patrol. *Jealousy, pure and simple. He was High Priest, not Nicodemas.* He sat through three miserable dinners and learned nothing! The man had no news to offer and seemed awfully curious about Malchus and his return. He wouldn't share with him all Malchus reported to him in private. This was coveted material indeed. He felt a smile begin to surface on his face and quickly regained his pious composure for the throngs that awaited a glimpse of his pageantry.

Kezi and Selah gave Balaam a new scarf. The previous one had become worn and frayed. They chattered away all morning while waiting to walk to the Temple. They agreed it had been a fun, exciting week and had gone much too fast for Selah's liking.

"Sabbath is tomorrow Selah. I'll help take everything down before it begins and then of course back to work the next day!" Kezi knew the people that traveled would remain awhile. She had much to sell!

You could feel excitement in the air. The city was exploding with celebration! Selah was positive everyone felt like her, not wanting the party to end.

They made their way through the lower city towards the Beautiful Gate. The atmosphere was magical! Selah couldn't remember a Sukkot celebration like this ever. There wasn't an empty space in all of Jerusalem! She didn't realize how awe inspiring her home truly was. Her ears were hurting from the shouts of all the people but she loved it! Not one person wasn't caught up in the climax of this feast. Malchus was making her dizzy looking in every direction, waving at people he knew, checking the positions of the guards, standing tip-toe to get a better look at the priests as they entered their respective gates. It wouldn't be long until they circled around the altar seven times signifying the end of the feast, but more importantly, proclamation asking the Holy Spirit of God to come upon the city.

The last water ritual was performed, the anticipation was extraordinary as this multitude of people would all in one accord be silent, the customary hush as they listened for the wind, all of them taught about the significance of the water, and this, the last poured over the altar. The stillness escaped no one who was in attendance.

Suddenly a loud voice cried out! "If anyone is thirsty, let him come to Me and drink! He who believes in Me, as the Scripture said, 'from his innermost being will flow rivers of living water.'"

"Jesus!" Selah didn't realize she screamed his name.

There he was right in front of them! The sound of the entire Temple changed in an instant! People began shoving and crowding towards them and Malchus grabbed her as Simon took ahold of Kezi's hand and they stood their ground. They heard cries from every area of the Temple.

"Jesus!"

"Prophet!"

"He is the Christ!"

Malchus was paralyzed. He stood, eyes fixed on Jesus. He knew the guards would be there momentarily, Caiaphas also, the Pharisees, yes of course, but he didn't care. Not today. He was consumed with awe and wonder of this man.

Selah turned to Kezi, "Do you see Mary? Shall we call out for her?"

Selah was afraid. The reaction of the crowd began to shift. Different groups were shouting at each other. She had folds of Malchus' garment firmly in her hand. Her knuckles were white.

"Shall the Christ come out of Galilee?" someone shouted.

Many voices now echoed throughout the court. "No!"

Malchus heard the guards, still he didn't take his eyes off this man called Jesus. People were raising their hands in praise, others their fists in defiance crying out also in their loudest voices, "The Christ comes from the Son of David and the town of Bethlehem, not Galilee, not Nazareth!"

Simon watched everyone. What a day this has become! He searched the crowds for one man, Nicodemas. The guards stood before Jesus, listening, doing nothing. They looked like they were waiting for more authority.

Caiaphas. Where was he hiding? 'If anyone is thirsty,' Malchus mouthed the words, 'Let him come to me and drink'. He didn't understand. He bit his lip in frustration.

"Malchus!" He looked to his left and one of the Temple guards was calling him. He saw the Pharisees and Caiaphas making their way and he simply directed the guard to look behind him.

There were crowds behind Jesus shouting and the officers speaking to him just looked at each other. Malchus couldn't believe they weren't removing him; he was causing an uproar! Surely Pilate could tell the difference from people celebrating to this confusion. When Nicodemas arrived and those with him began berating the guards, he watched. He didn't know Simon was in front of him watching and listening too.

Nicodemas raised his hands to ask for silence, "Does out law judge any man before it hears what the man has done?"

Some then shouted even louder and to Malchus' surprise called back to Nicodemas, "Are you also of Galilee, search the Scriptures, no prophet comes out of Galilee." After that the noise level became unbearable, people were pushing and shoving and Jesus disappeared from Malchus' sight. He was concerned for Selah and Kezi's safety and began shouting for Simon when he didn't see him.

"I'm here! Malchus, what should we do?" Simon was concerned too. He expected the Romans any moment.

He tried to take in what was happening from every direction. He wasn't sure who saw him and who didn't. Selah had ahold of him tighter than before. They couldn't speak. They wouldn't be heard. He pointed back towards home and they began a very slow decline to escape the frenzied crowd. Kezi and Selah kept their heads down, moving behind him as he led them down familiar paths. Selah was crying. Kezi put her arm around her.

"We'll be fine Selah, don't cry. You'll be home soon."

She shook her head. Malchus suddenly turned sharply almost running. He led them to a small concealed space to ensure Selah was alright.

"Selah, what are you upset about?"

"Everything! It's been a beautiful day and now Jesus is here and all the people ruined the last day of celebration. I couldn't see if Mary was here, and now we're going home and I don't understand what just happened!"

He didn't know what to say. He squeezed her hand and said, "I know, let me think a minute." He thought it best to go home.

It was Kezi who began to speak first. "I don't feel safe going out right now."

"Kezi's right," Simon agreed. "Let everyone calm down. Malchus, did Caiaphas see you?"

"I don't think so, but one of the guards did."

"Malchus, did you understand Jesus' words?" Selah asked.

"No, I didn't."

"Did you Simon?" he looked to him for help.

"It was strange words! I'm not sure what he meant. What did he say exactly? There's been too much excitement! I can't remember what he said."

"If anyone is thirsty, let him come to me and drink," Kezi repeated.

"Is it a riddle? What's he saying? How do you drink from a man?" Simon questioned.

"Water is the source for life. That's what we're celebrating, water for our crops and when the priest pours the water on the altar as an offering," Selah stopped talking, Malchus was looking at her in a very strange way.

"Go on Selah."

"We're asking God to continue to bless us, that we depend on water, it's our source of life and Jesus said, 'Come to him if we're looking for water, he will give us water', he's our source, our life source!"

"Selah! I think you have great understanding!" Kezi was on her feet now pacing. "It's almost as if he was saying to rely on him for our water, for our substance. Malchus, Simon, what do you think?"

The two men sat and stared at these two young women, unlearned in Scripture, yet what they understood Jesus to be saying had Malchus' head spinning.

"What did he say after that?"

"After that?" Kezi asked.

"Yes, he said something else," Malchus said.

"I don't know Malchus. It got so loud and when I realized it was Jesus, I started looking for Mary and I couldn't hear."

"He said if we believed in him as the Scripture has said, out of our belly shall flow rivers of living water." They all looked at Selah again as she repeated the words effortlessly.

"As Scripture has said, Simon repeated. I wish I knew more of what the Scripture said. We need to speak to someone like," Simon didn't finish.

"Like who?" Malchus asked.

"Never mind Malchus."

"No, Simon, who were you thinking of? Another rabbi?"

"Yes, someone who is learned and has studied the Scriptures. I know we're waiting for Messiah to come. I would like to know what the Scriptures say about him. I want to know if Jesus could be him."

"Malchus," said Selah, "Do you know what the Scriptures say about the Messiah?"

Her voice was soft and sincere and his heart ached. He didn't. He only knew he had hope that one day he would come. All that he overheard through the years while serving Caiaphas, he had to admit he didn't pay attention. His goal was to advance his position and he'd been selfish reveling in his personal recognition. Everyone knew him. Everyone sought to get his ear, whisper their own ambitions to him in hopes to advance with Caiaphas just as he did. The Scriptures didn't help his cause. Now, in the quiet of his home, all searching his face for some word of wisdom, hope for understanding, an explanation of what had taken place today with this man Jesus once again challenging all who had gathered to celebrate, he hung his head, ashamed, angry and confused. He didn't want to care about what any rabbi, teacher, Pharisee or zealot said. What did it have to do with him? He only cared about what Caiaphas could do for him.

The house he was sitting in was only possible because of Caiaphas. His dreams of a better life for him and Selah were determined by the generosity of Caiaphas. His social standing, Caiaphas. He was a slave to Caiaphas. Jesus was the enemy of Caiaphas. Her eyes made him grip the sides of the table they sat around. Her steady gaze and the love it reflected made him feel less than a man at the moment.

Simon moved slightly to break the silence. Malchus finally spoke.

"What I know is the Messiah will bring freedom and peace and will restore our people and our land. I know he is to come from the line of David." He realized that was all he knew.

Selah looked at Simon now, "Simon, do you think Jesus could be the Messiah?"

"I think time will tell."

"What did you just say?" Malchus asked.

"Time will tell if Jesus is the Messiah, and like I said earlier, we need to be taught by someone. I don't know about you but I only remember hearing mostly about the Law of Moses. Some spoke about the Prophets; I can't recall what they said. I'm old, my memory isn't so good," Simon laughed a little, it was too solemn for his liking. The past week had been full of laughter and wine and eating and celebrating and this wasn't comfortable.

"Malchus, you hardly ate anything," Selah waited to take his bowl.

"I'm not hungry," he kept looking at the door.

"Are you expecting someone? What is it Malchus?"

"Caiaphas will be looking for me."

"But it's Sabbath. Surely he doesn't expect you to be at his home on Sabbath."

"Usually not, but," he didn't finish.

"Jesus," Selah said.

"Yes, Jesus."

"But what does Caiaphas expect you to do now?"

"It was because Elias saw me."

"Who?"

"One of the guards. Believe me Selah, he's told Caiaphas I was there and did nothing."

"Are you sure he saw you?"

"Yes, I'm sure."

"And you think Caiaphas will be angry?"

He laughed now. "Well, let's say he won't be happy. I should have done something; at least stand with the guards to show I was behind them."

"Don't worry about Caiaphas this night. We'll go to Temple tomorrow and you'll speak to him then."

"And if Jesus shows up?"

"Would Caiaphas ask you to do something to stop him from speaking?"

"I don't know. Why does talking about Jesus make my head hurt?" He knocked the bowl of his uneaten dinner to the floor.

"Malchus!"

"Selah, please, I don't want to talk about it. Give Balaam my food! And by the way, the name Balaam has a bad notion about it."

"What?" She was upset now. She was halfway listening.

"Balaam, he used what God gave him in a negative way."

"Malchus, I don't know what you're talking about. What are you saying?"

"You want to know about Scripture? I remember Balaam was hired to curse Israel. It's not a good name."

"So, you're telling me to change Balaam's name?"

"I don't know what I'm saying, I'm sorry Selah. I'm just going to step out. I'll take this to Balaam and I may just walk for a bit. I won't be long. I need to think."

He didn't come back until the sun was up. She felt frightened for him. *Did his whole life hang on Caiaphas?* That's how he made it sound to her. She was anxious to get back to the market. She didn't care about wealth, position, power in society. She was happy. And she wouldn't change Balaam's name. She didn't care what it meant. When she named him, she just thought of the story she heard as a young girl about a talking donkey. There wasn't any good or bad associated with it. It hurt her heart when he said that last night. She went out to check on him. She saw a half-eaten pomegranate on the ground and by the way Balaam was tied and the impression in the hay, she knew Malchus slept out here. Now her emotions ran all over the place. *Did he choose to sleep outside instead of the warmth of their room? With her?* She picked up the fruit. Balaam didn't want it either. She was ready to go to the Temple today. She and Kezi would search for Mary.

Malchus hardly spoke. People greeted him as they walked through the crowds and he only nodded. Selah smiled at those who acknowledged him and remained silent. She was looking down at her feet when she heard her name.

"Selah, hurry! Jesus is here!" It was Kezi. She was on the steps, Simon nowhere to be seen. Kezi waved her to hurry and then she saw Malchus. Had he stopped moving? People were swarming all around him and Selah looked panicked.

"Malchus, where's Caiaphas today? Jesus is teaching again!"

"Find Caiaphas Malchus, this man is deceiving the people!"

Selah became separated and Kezi watching felt helpless. More men were now addressing him. She took one last look and when he didn't call for her, she quickly began pushing her way towards her friend.

"Are you alright?"

"Yes, Kezi let's go. Where is he?"

"He's teaching. We'll get as close as we can."

Selah never looked back. Malchus was on his own. Last night and today with his behavior, she started to think he preferred it that way. "Where's Simon?"

"He's there, listening." A great commotion was heard and they ran with the people.

"Kezi! Look! A woman!" The men were all shouting.

"This woman was taken in adultery, in the very act!"

Selah gripped Kezi's arm. "Oh Kezi, will they stone her?"

Kezi wasn't breathing, her eyes fixed on the woman. "Selah, I know that woman."

"Can you see Jesus?" she was on her tip toes.

"Selah, I think they've thrown him to the ground! No, wait, now I see him! They're leaving."

Selah began to nudge the woman in front of her and she and Kezi inched closer.

"Kezi, look! Nicodemas!"

Kezi again searched for Simon. They would never hear what Jesus was saying. People were arguing and the women couldn't concentrate.

"Oh no!" Kezi had her hand over her mouth.

"What did I miss?"

"They're picking up rocks! Oh Selah, there's nothing we can do!" They couldn't see Jesus and they soon discovered no one else did either. He had disappeared in the crowd.

"Come Kezi, I want to find Malchus and Simon. The women stayed by the gate hoping Simon would return. They waited over an hour.

"There! Selah, there's Malchus."

"Where?" Selah looked in the direction Kezi was pointing. *Caiaphas!* He was with Caiaphas and they were surrounded by Temple guards and Pharisees. She watched him carefully. He stood, never moving a finger. He didn't utter a word, he just stood behind Caiaphas.

"What shall we do? Malchus could be here all day!" Kezi exclaimed.

She continued to watch him. He wasn't looking around for her. Maybe he was mad that she left him with all those people but she couldn't breathe! Both women still looked for Simon.

"Where do you think he is? Come with me Selah. I have a feeling Simon will know we have gone to either your house or mine."

Malchus was exhausted. He hadn't slept the night before and he stood in the center of a growing group of men all talking at once making his head hurt worse than the previous evening. *Selah.* She won't understand. She would be unhappy with his decisions today, but it couldn't be helped. He didn't think he moved a muscle the entire morning. He knew the vein in Caiaphas' temple would be throbbing. It took on new life when the guards came back to report Jesus simply disappeared. Nicodemas was absent. The scribes were debating with the Pharisees, the guards were pointing fingers at each other; he heard about the woman caught in adultery, and throughout the entire chaos and confusion that now always surrounded Jesus, not a stone was thrown. He wondered what Selah and Kezi heard. He was getting an earful now. Everyone had their turn repeating to Caiaphas the words Jesus spoke and what they said to him. He kept his mouth shut. He didn't react to any dialogue. He stood thinking he would like to be witnessing this all from above, sitting in his tree. He was numb to their repetition. Yes, Jesus speaks contrary to the law. Yes, he confuses the people. Yes, he causes trouble. Yes, the people love him. Yes, more and more are following him.

"Malchus, why are you so quiet today? Are you persuaded by this imposter?" Elias the guard was only a few feet from him.

"I think Elias you should think about what you just asked me."

"I saw you yesterday when Jesus disrupted the celebration. You were there, as close to him as you now are to me and you did nothing!"

Caiaphas turned to Malchus waiting for him to respond.

"I was waiting for you Elias. I was counting how long it took you and the others to arrive. I didn't know if Caiaphas was safe, I wasn't going to leave Jesus out of my sight until you arrived. I had no weapon. I was with my wife. And I'm a servant of Caiaphas, not you."

Caiaphas' smile was all he needed. He accepted his answer.

He knew he just lost a friend. He told himself he didn't care. Caiaphas was pleased. Right now, that's all that mattered. The Pharisees that came to complain were relentless. They wouldn't leave until Caiaphas addressed all their concerns. He kept his eye on Elias. He did have weapons. He assumed Pilate himself could hear the roar of the crowds. It was when Jesus spoke, the people cried out. They wanted to believe he was the Christ. He stood in the folds of the most learned men of Israel. They all said he wasn't the "one". They called him an imposter, mocked that he was from Galilee, said he had a devil. He saw the face of the paralytic man who had been healed. *How does someone who has a devil heal a man and why would he?* Everyone was still bemoaning their complaints to Caiaphas, a constant hum in his ears.

"He said what?" Caiaphas' face turned pale.

"He said, 'Before Abraham was, I AM'.

He thought Caiaphas was going to faint. His hands were trembling from righteous anger. He was gritting his teeth and Malchus heard the sound of bone on bone.

"This is blasphemy! This man should have been arrested! Where is he now?" he looked at the guards. "Go! Find this blasphemer and bring him to me!" Caiaphas turned and Malchus thought every vein in his body was now throbbing.

"Malchus, follow me!"

"Shalom," Nicodemas greeted Simon.

"Greetings Nicodemas."

"You know my name but I don't have the pleasure of yours."

"Simon."

"You know Malchus?"

"Doesn't everyone?" Simon lifted his hands and smiled.

"Ah, yes. You've been watching Caiaphas and the others. Is there something you wish to ask?"

"No, I was," and now Simon was reasoning again, *Do I let him know I know Malchus and consider him a friend?* His hesitation indicated to Nicodemas two things. He knew Malchus and for some reason didn't want to divulge this to him or he may be one of Jesus' followers sent to report if there were plans to arrest him. Simon decided there was no time like the present.

"I know Malchus. I know his wife. She works at the market. I'm also a merchant."

"I see, and you were waiting for him?"

"Yes, I thought I would walk with him and perhaps discuss what's happened here the last two days."

"What's happened?" Nicodemas asked. Before Simon could answer, he simply said "Jesus."

"Yes, Jesus. His words are difficult for this old man to understand," Simon waited to see if he would take the bait.

"You're not alone my friend. There has been, and will be after today many discussions about Jesus."

"Did you hear him today?" Simon asked.

"Yes," Nicodemas said. He wasn't going to offer anymore Simon thought. He should just excuse himself now.

"What did you think of his words?"

Simon was shocked. He didn't know how to begin. He looked around a little nervously. He squared his shoulders and took a deep breath.

"Nicodemas, I'd like to know what Jesus meant when he said 'You must be born again', Simon thought he might have to reach out and steady him.

"Where did you hear this term?"

"One night during Passover, some friends were camped east and told me they saw a group of men who could have been followers of Jesus so I went in the direction my friends told me and overheard a conversation, and I've thought about these words often since then."

"They are indeed strange words," he had no idea if Simon recognized him from that night. If any of his peers found out that he purposed to go to Jesus, he wasn't sure of the consequences. *Who was this man Simon? He knows Malchus. Has Malchus told him I've also met with him? What does this old man know?*

"Please, let us sit."

Simon couldn't believe this opportunity. He continued to struggle to let him know all he knew. He needed time to think about this. Perhaps he was making a mistake. He might put Malchus' position in jeopardy. He couldn't be selfish, but oh, he had been dreaming about the chance to speak to him. He found himself shuffling his feet, stalling for time, giving a side glance to Nicodemas, yes, he was still there.

"Simon, I'm sorry, we'll have to speak another time. Look, the council is gathering. Caiaphas has obviously called a session. I shall inform Malchus of our meeting."

He was gone before Simon could respond. *What just happened?* He should have addressed the words Jesus spoke today and not brought up the night he followed the ruler. *He had to know that I saw him? Should I now tell Malchus everything? Selah.* He rushed to her house.

Kezi and Selah took their time walking home.

"Are you worried about Malchus Selah?"

"No, I'm a little mad at him honestly."

"Why?"

"You saw him. He left me on my own! And before that, there were several who greeted him as we walked, and he didn't acknowledge them! I greeted them; I don't know these people. I thought it very rude of him to ignore everyone."

"That doesn't sound like Malchus," Kezi didn't know what to say.

"I think he slept outside last night next to Balaam. He's upset about something."

She stopped walking and turned to her friend, "I think deep down he believes everything Jesus has done. But when he's around Caiaphas and others, they speak against him and give reasons why he can't be the Christ, the Messiah. I think he feels he's betraying both Caiaphas and Jesus at the same time. Kezi, I'm afraid for Jesus. I think they plan to arrest him. Some of the words we heard today would probably be enough for Caiaphas to give that order."

"I think Jesus is a very wise man. He saved that woman from being stoned to death! I just know it! I wish we could have heard everything he said." *Simon! Where was he? And where is he now?* "Do you think he's still at the Temple?"

"I don't know, I'm sure Malchus will be there all day."

They tried to piece together the words they heard. The past two days didn't seem real. Nothing was certain, people wore masks of doubt hiding behind tradition and lack of knowledge, the sky was cloudy and everyone was hoping for the sun to dispel the darkness and make clear what was happening in Jerusalem. They couldn't attain it.

"I think I better go home Kezi," Selah rose to walk home.

"You're not going home by yourself. Where do you suppose Simon is?"

"Did I hear my name?"

"Simon? Where have you been all day?" Kezi almost scolded him.

"Talking to Nicodemas."

"Simon, do you know where Malchus is?" Selah asked.

"I think he's still at the Temple, I don't know for certain. But you look tired, we're working tomorrow so I'm taking you home."

"Thank you, Simon."

"Simon...Nicodemas? And now you're leaving?" Kezi was tapping her foot.

"We'll have our morning session tomorrow," he nodded towards Selah as a reminder of how frail she seemed tonight.

Malchus was tired and hungry. He hadn't eaten all day. He sat, stood, paced and shifted his body in every position so he wouldn't ache from being in one place for such a prolonged time. He thought he might pull his beard out if he had to listen to the detailed dialogue of the scribes and Pharisees one more time. He lost count. Caiaphas had them repeating and retelling every word Jesus spoke. There was great commotion over the woman that was brought before him and Caiaphas stiffened when he realized Jesus wasn't so easily tricked when cornered by the Pharisees. He didn't want to bother with Nicodemas. He seemed to be enjoying the verbal sparring between Jesus and his fellow man that Caiaphas began to question his motives. He began to distrust everyone. He had too much at stake to let one man cause so much disorder. He read every face. He saw some of the guards were beginning to listen to the words of this Nazarene. He would speak to Pilate but first he needed something substantial to take to him so he would act on his behalf. Everyone was tired. Malchus thought he heard one of the guards snoring but surely, he wouldn't dare fall asleep. Nicodemas seemed to be the voice of reason.

"Caiaphas, Jesus is gone. Yes, I understand the disturbance he caused these past two days, yes, he has challenged the people but all great teachers should do so. No one here can deny he has great insight to the Holy Scriptures. We can't fault a man for wisdom and knowledge. It's been a long day. What is there to be done tonight? Jesus has probably had his dinner and is resting comfortably somewhere outside of the city. I myself am going home. Let us think about all that has been said and discussed and we'll return tomorrow to make good, sound decisions on how we might handle another disruption should it happen. Agreed?"

There were many who nodded and began to disperse before Caiaphas could respond. Malchus didn't move. Nicodemas was sensible. *Selah.* He suddenly felt like he was punched in the stomach. He knew Simon would have kept both her and Kezi in his sights all day. He wasn't worried about her and he should be. This disturbed him even more.

"Malchus, are you coming?" Caiaphas began to make sure everything was secure before leaving. Malchus followed.

Simon made sure Selah wasn't in need of anything before he left. He went to check on Balaam.

"Hello old friend! How are you this fine evening? What a day it's been Balaam! You should have been there!"

Balaam nodded his head, his bell ringing in agreement. Simon checked to see how much hay Malchus had left. Balaam began nudging his back.

"What is it Balaam? Are you lonely? Tell me Balaam, what should I do? Buy another donkey so you'd have company? Maybe you're lonely because we've been gone all day. Would you like to go for a walk?"

He didn't know if Balaam was shaking his head yes or he was moving it to convince himself to go look for Malchus. He untied him and went through the courtyard unnoticed and headed to the upper city. If he happened upon Malchus, he wouldn't lie to him, not after seeing how distraught Selah looked. He still didn't know if he should tell him about Nicodemas. He had no reason to walk in the upper city, not since he followed Claudia. He didn't like the abundance of Roman soldiers in this area and avoided it most of the time. He wondered where Nicodemas lived. He slowed his pace and adjusted Balaam's blanket.

"I feel pretty crafty tonight Balaam, and you're my accomplice."

It was early evening. Only servants were seen weaving in and out of covered colonnades balancing trays of food and drink, others following with lamps and basins. Simon could hear musicians playing in the distance, perhaps Pilate was entertaining. The streets narrowed and he decided this was a bad idea and turned to head back. He was out of his element. Shadows began to play tricks on him and even Balaam began to bray a little.

"Quiet donkey! We're going home."

A small boy ran up to them. By the looks of him Simon knew he was an orphan.

"Son, you startled us, are you running from someone?"

He had no shoes and looked hungry. Simon figured he was hoping for a handout as this neighborhood most likely had more to offer. He was small and could run and hide easily between gates and walls.

"What's your name?" Simon looked down on the dirty face. The little boy just stared, his hands behind his back.

"Where are you going?"

He didn't answer.

"Where's your family?"

"I have no family," the little voice finally answered.

"I see, can you tell me your name?" He patted Balaam and said, "This is Balaam, would you like to sit on him?"

The boy nodded enthusiastically and Simon lifted him up. Once settled the boy smiled and looked around like he was special. He was light as a feather.

"See there, Balaam likes you. Now my name is Simon. Can you tell me and Balaam your name?"

"Benjamin."

"Benjamin. That's a fine name for a young boy. How old are you?"

"I think I'm eight."

"When was the last time you ate? I imagine you're hungry."

He shook his head.

"Well then, we'll have to get you some food," he looked around. No one was coming to tell him who this boy might be. He knew he definitely didn't live here. He decided to take him to Kezi's. Perhaps as they walked back through the lower city the boy would begin to talk about anything familiar.

"Yes Benjamin, old Simon is hungry too. We'll both get something to eat and I know just the place."

He had the boy scoot up and took part of Balaam's blanket and draped it over the boy's shoulders. His dirty little hands pulled it close and Simon thought he might cry. He had no idea what he was doing. His first thought was to take him to Selah, it might be just what she needed to take her mind off Malchus, but Kezi would love this little Benjamin back to life! *Balaam! What if Malchus came home and found him gone? Selah didn't know he took him. Ah, what a mess!* Now he didn't want Selah to see the boy. All women liked to fuss over children. He decided the boy needed food. He hoped Malchus would be too tired to check on the donkey.

"Where are we going Simon?"

"We're going to my friend's house. Her name is Kezi, we work beside each other at the market. Have you been to the market?"

"Is that the place where everyone has food?"

"That's the place!"

"I like that place! Do you sell food?"

"I do," Simon said.

"Oh boy!"

Benjamin had an infectious smile, perfect white teeth. Simon missed his. The boy hadn't said anything, most kids noticed as soon as he spoke or smiled.

"We're almost there Benjamin."

Simon saw light at Kezi's house. She was probably doing last minute things getting ready for tomorrow. He lifted Benjamin down and tied Balaam up in his usual place and knocked softly on Kezi's door.

"Simon, what are you doing back?" And then she saw the large brown eyes peeking up around his garment, halfway hidden among its folds. She looked at Simon a little alarmed.

"Kezi, this is Benjamin. We've come from the upper city with Balaam. We're both hungry and I told Benjamin I knew just the place to go," he gave Kezi the look of I'll tell you everything later.

"Come in. Hello Benjamin."

He stood at Kezi's door taking in all he saw. She had material draped over her table and hanging from pegs and the breeze from the door and window breathed life into colors Benjamin never saw. He was still wrapped in Balaam's blanket. She put her arm around the narrow shoulders and guided him to a chair. She brought warm water and washed his face and then his arms and feet. She had soup and bread that she prepared for her own dinner and was glad she made a large pot this night.

Benjamin sat very still as he let Kezi bathe him. No one in a very long time had taken time to pay any attention to him. He hoped she wouldn't rush through the process. She examined his little frame as she carefully lifted his legs to wash the bottom of his feet. No marks. No cuts or open wounds. She dried his feet.

"I smell good," he smiled down at Kezi.

"That's because I used scented oils in the water."

She was in love. His innocent big brown eyes of wonder melted her heart. She was getting a lump in her throat.

"I have a new garment for you too."

"Just for me?" he asked.

"Just for you Benjamin."

"Did you know I was coming?"

"Yes, I think I did."

Simon had to step outside. He was bawling like a baby. Kezi set her table. She had fresh flowers and had already made a place for Benjamin to sleep without either the boy or Simon noticing. She had fresh greens and cucumbers with oil and vinegar, bread and lentil soup. Benjamin ate three bowls. She couldn't eat. She sat at the table and watched him savor the simple meal all the while studying every part of her home. Simon ate three bowls also.

"You boys were hungry!"

They nodded in unison as they sopped up the last of their soup with their bread.

"Simon, are you taking Balaam back tonight or maybe you can just bring him to the market in the morning."

"That's a good idea. That's what I'll do." They both turned to the boy.

"Benjamin, do you have some place to go?" Kezi asked in the softest voice.

Benjamin looked at Simon, then back at Kezi. She thought she saw his lip begin to quiver and his eyes grew glassy.

"No, but Simon can take me back to where he found me."

Kezi went over to him and got on her knees, eye level with this precious little one.

"Would you like to stay here with me Benjamin?"

He looked back at Simon who just smiled assuring the boy it would be alright.

"You would let me stay here, inside?" Kezi didn't know how much more she could take.

"Yes Benjamin, inside with me."

He threw his arms around her neck and buried his head in her shoulder. She felt his hot tears through her garment and hers rested on top of his head. Simon let himself out and sniffled over to Balaam and untied the donkey for their short walk home.

"Balaam, it surely has been some day we've had."

Kezi didn't ask him any questions. There would be time for that later. She stroked his hair and covered him with the softest blanket she had. He fell asleep quickly with his right hand on her arm. He had thick, wavy hair and long lashes. He had a strong face for a young boy. *Who are you young Benjamin? And can I keep you?* She pulled herself away and secured the door. She didn't finish her preparations for the shop and looking around at material all disarrayed, for the first time in her life she didn't care. She slept soundly.

Chapter Seven

Malchus arrived to a dark house. Selah laid awake and heard him enter. He was mumbling to himself. This was becoming a habit.

"Selah, are you awake? Selah, wake up!"

She pretended to stir from being awakened. Her movement encouraged him.

"Selah, I'm home, wake up!"

"Malchus, it's late. Where have you been?"

"Shhh, it doesn't matter, I'm here now."

"Why are you telling me to be quiet?"

"Greetings my wife, aren't you going to kiss me? Come here Selah, give your husband a kiss."

"Malchus! What are you doing?"

He tried reaching for her.

"Malchus, have you been drinking?"

"It's alright. I'm home now to see my wife. C'mon Selah, kiss me."

"Malchus, you're drunk!"

"No, no, I just had a couple cups of wine with some friends, not drunk. I mean I'm not drinking. No, I mean I'm not drunk now. Oh, you know what I mean. Come here Selah!"

"No Malchus, I'm tired and you need to go to sleep. It's been a long day."

"I will sleep when I want to. You don't tell me when I'm sleeping, when I'm laying down."

"Malchus, you're not making any sense and you're slurring your words."

"So, what are you going to do about it? If you would just kiss me then you wouldn't hear my slurred words because I wouldn't be talking," he laughed now.

She never saw Malchus this way. She didn't like it. "Malchus, lay down and go to sleep."

"I am laying down, aren't I?" he laughed again. "Selah, what's the matter? Are you mad at me?"

"Yes, Malchus I am! But we'll talk about it tomorrow."

"No, wake up Selah. Let's talk now."

"Malchus, I'm awake."

"Right, so we're both awake. Why are you mad Selah?"

Her eyes began to adjust to the dark room, he was sitting up against the wall looking away from where they slept, his head bobbing up and down. He started snoring. She turned away from him and fell asleep. He was gone when she woke up. She laid there staring at the roof. She could tell he never laid beside her and wondered how he could sleep sitting up. Maybe he shared Balaam's hay. She went around back and stopped short when she didn't see either of them. He never took Balaam with him. Of course, he never came home drunk. Balaam was at the shop before she was. He looked at Selah a little puzzled.

"Oh, you think I don't care that you were missing," she patted his head. Malchus must be here waiting to greet her and apologize to all of them for his behavior. He knew Simon liked to have Balaam there and also Kezi could use him to carry her things back and forth. She tried to concentrate on this kind gesture before she entered Kezi's tent.

Sometime in the middle of the night, Benjamin managed to get underneath Kezi's own covering. His hair tickled her nose. His long lashes rested on high cheek bones and she noticed a few freckles across his nose. She thought him perfect. *Why today did this boy enter their lives?* As much as her heart ached for a child, it was many years ago and now, well this boy belonged to someone and she couldn't afford to get attached. His eyes opened and she smiled down at him.

"Good morning," he snuggled closer and closed his eyes.

"Benjamin, we need to rise, open your eyes."

"Do I have to leave now?"

"No, but we do need to go to work."

"Work?"

"Yes, I have a place at the market where I sell things."

"What kind of things?"

She pointed to her material strewn all over the room. "I sell fabric so people can sew garments and pillows," she smiled again as he had brought one tiny pillow with him that his head laid upon.

"What else?" he was smiling up at her, those perfect milk white teeth seemed to sparkle in the morning light.

"Get up and I'll tell you," she watched him go over to his mat, small pillow in hand and he drew it up to his face and seemed to inhale its memory.

"Kezi, I have to go outside."

She unlatched the door and showed him where water was kept for washing his hands.

"We're going to have our breakfast with Simon and another friend at the market."

"Is Simon going to take me back?"

"Back where?"

"Where I saw him."

"Do you know where you were Benjamin?"

"No, but there were big houses."

"How did you get there?"

He looked down at his feet. Kezi needed to get him sandals today.

"I don't know, I was just walking."

She gave him a handful of raisins. She would carry only a few things this morning and ask Simon to help her with her cart. She had him sit down and she took worn pieces of cloth and covered his feet with makeshift sandals. She tied and crisscrossed the leather strands on his ankles several times.

"Does that hurt? Step down. Now walk to the door. What do you think?"

"It feels funny."

"You don't have to wear them. Would you rather go barefoot?"

He lifted his foot high and then back down in slow motion that made Kezi laugh.

"I'll keep them on."

"We'll look for something more suitable today."

"Suitable? I don't know what that means."

"It means, we'll buy you a pair of sandals made for a boy like you."

He looked down at his feet and back at Kezi, "I've never had suitable sandals."

She couldn't breathe. She looked up so Benjamin wouldn't see the tears forming in her eyes. He followed her gaze and couldn't see anything.

"What are you looking for?"

"Answers."

"I don't think you'll find them in your roof."

She scooped him up and twirled around, surprising both of them. "You Benjamin I think are my answer."

At that very moment she realized the LORD had given her the answer to silent prayers she didn't know were buried so deep in her heart. *How would she ever explain it to him?* And with his hair tickling her nose again and his sweet laughter filling the room, she realized she just did.

Malchus sat under his tree. His whole body ached. He didn't remember coming home last night but this morning when he woke up, everything hurt, especially his neck! He slept sitting up. Selah was sound asleep. She didn't stir all the while he rummaged through the room looking for something to eat. He knew she was angry at him. He was angry at himself. The only good thing that came out of his dice playing, drinking evening was he made amends with Elias. The guard thought his position in jeopardy, that his influence with Caiaphas would end his service. He was ambitious but he told himself not at the expense of someone he considered a friend. He couldn't sit here too long. He would have to report to Caiaphas soon.

He saw Balaam tied up at Kezi's. When he found the donkey missing this morning, it was the first place he thought he would be. Simon would have made sure Selah got home safely, more than what he did. *What in the world happened yesterday? Why was he in such a foul mood? It was Jesus. No, it was Caiaphas. It was both of them.* Complete opposites he thought and he found himself in the middle of both their personas, their ideology, their beliefs and passions. He heard both voices in his head, trying to discern truth, attempting to understand things he was never taught, it was a battle between heart and mind.

This is what drove him to drink so much last night. He was forced to sit for hours and listen to every person in the room's opinion. 'Jesus said this, our law says that' 'He's a liar'! 'He's a blasphemer'! 'He's a prophet and teacher from God'! 'He performs miracles'! 'He has a devil'! 'He's the one we're waiting for'. 'He's a Nazarene'. Malchus thought if he had a skin of wine, he would drain it now to silence all the voices. It's what he did last night and now he had to go and listen again. It was pointless.

Pilate's name came up several times and he knew Caiaphas would want a meeting with the Prefect, possibly today. The Feast of Dedication was soon and he wouldn't tolerate another scene at the Temple. Malchus didn't think he was causing that much of a scene and when he said so, it was the last thing he said. After that he listened and drank. Today he would simply nod his head in agreement with all Caiaphas said. It would make his life easier. He would go home before going to the Temple. He would tell Selah he was sorry and would walk her home this afternoon. He looked up at the gnarled branches, empty of its olives and thought perhaps they were lonely. *I know the feeling* he said out loud as he rose to walk.

The sun warming his back, he began his walk home. He looked at the Fort adjoining the Temple and wondered if there was one Roman soldier who was watching him this very moment. He knew they stood guard at their post, even the high slope of the eastern side. He doubted they would ever have to be concerned with someone breaching this side. He had the advantage with the sun behind him. From that position the guards could see a great distance. They probably could see Jesus and his followers moving through the valley. Any movement would be detected. A lone traveler. A Pharisee. A servant of the High Priest. He waved at whoever might be watching. For some reason it made him feel better.

Kezi slowed her pace this morning with Benjamin just in front of her. She wanted to see if he lingered in any one place or if anyone would call out to him. He asked if he could bring his little pillow.

"Of course, you can," she told him.

He held it close to his face. Now in the cloth covered feet holding the pillow in front of him with both hands, she didn't know what to think. *How could this little one capture her heart so quickly?* Several times he looked up and flashed her that smile, dimples and all, and she thought if he batted his eyelashes, she would never let the boy out of her sight. She wanted to ask him questions but would speak to Simon first. She knew where most of Jerusalem's elite lived and needed him to tell her exactly where Benjamin had run up to him.

"Balaam! I see Balaam!" Kezi watched as Benjamin ran to the donkey. Simon turned and tousled the boy's hair.

"Look what I got, my very own pillow! And look at my feet!"

Simon did look but his eye was on Kezi. She looked radiant! He patted his heart and nodded and she smiled.

"Benjamin, did you greet Simon?"

"I showed him my pillow."

"Yes, but when you see someone you know, you greet them. You would say, "Good morning Simon.""

Benjamin repeated her words and turned back to her. "Good morning Kezi. I didn't say good morning to you."

"And good day to you Benjamin. Now, why don't you go inside this tent and find a place to put your pillow and look around at everything."

Kezi and Simon both watched as he pulled back the flap. He didn't go inside, but just stood there with one hand clutching his pillow and the other holding the edge of the worn tent. He looked back at Kezi and inside again.

"This is where you come every day to work?"

"Yes."

"Wow!" and then he disappeared.

She put her hand to her mouth and laughed. Her tent probably resembled a magical place for a small boy. With Simon's help they hung bolts of material, only the most colorful from the top of the tent. Her shell chimes hung between them. Selah helped coordinate all the pillows and scarves around the perimeter of the tent carefully selecting complimentary patterns and colors. When they opened both sides of the tent, if there was the slightest breeze, the sound of the shells and her fabric flying like flags were captivating. She was proud of what she had accomplished in a short span of time.

"Business first Simon, have we paid the man you retained to stay here every night?"

"Yes, I paid him before Sukkot."

"Please tell him how much I appreciate him."

"Now, can we talk about the boy?"

"Oh Simon, this dear, precious boy. Where do you think he comes from?"

"I don't know Kezi. His speech has no regional dialect, of course I never heard that word he just used."

"Where were you last night when he ran up to you?"

He came in closer. "I was on my way to the house of Caiaphas. I thought I might see Malchus. Selah wasn't in a good place last night. Have you asked the boy any questions?"

"No, he was tired and hungry and Simon, we're strangers!"

"Yes, but it seems he's used to strangers."

"What shall we do Simon?"

He studied her and the toothless grin surfaced. "Ah, but you've already decided. Why bother this old man?"

She couldn't help herself and hugged him tightly. "What would I ever do without you?"

He helped her pull her "money changing" table out. She chided him every time he referred to it that way. She began to tie up purchases with the closest matching ribbon she had and would secure a small sprig of dried flowers on hand. It was a treat when she was able to use lavender, sage and pine. She knew the customer would smell the fragrance back to their homes and hoped it would remind them to tell their neighbors about her shop.

Selah was late. She worried about her friend. *Malchus!* He needed to make amends with her and now she finds out he wasn't home, that Simon went to look for him. But as she watched Benjamin asking

Simon questions about all his food, she was happy Malchus was late getting home.

"Simon, don't give him too much fruit!" Benjamin looked at the pear in his hand.

"This is for Balaam."

Fast thinker, she thought. She knew the market would be busy today. She wanted to see if anyone would call out his name. She hoped not.

Malchus was making his way, his pace much slower this morning. Selah was still annoyed with him. He apologized for deserting her, that's the word she used. She knew he didn't remember his amorous advances last night so she didn't bring them up. She did know he was hurting. He had complained about his back and his neck and she had no sympathy. He put the blame on Caiaphas and his obsession with Jesus. He told her Caiaphas had everyone in Jerusalem tell him exactly what Jesus said, over and over, hours of the same conversation.

"That's what caused you to have too much wine?"

"Yes Selah, that's why I drank too much. I didn't want to hear any more words! I told you I was sorry, let's not discuss it further."

She saw the clenched jaw and thought that was probably not helping his sore neck. *Men! They bring their own misery.* They didn't pay much attention to the boy petting Balaam. Most children in the market gravitated towards him.

"Good morning Selah, Malchus."

"I'm sorry I'm late Kezi."

"You're not late, don't worry. I do expect a busy day however. Malchus, do you have time for breakfast?"

"Not today. I wanted to tell you I'm sorry I wasn't around yesterday. I know I could have helped get you and Selah through the crowds faster."

"We were fine. Maybe we can all have dinner soon."

"Yes, and the old man over there. Who's the boy? Someone you know?"

"Yes, his name is Benjamin," that's all she was going to tell him and in reality, that's all she knew.

Selah had been standing by Simon and her missing donkey and was now speaking to Benjamin. She was bent low so she could see his face.

She stood suddenly and looked at Kezi. *The boy must have told her he stayed with me.* Malchus said goodbye and waved at Simon as he went.

"Kezi, you want to tell me what's going on?"

"Sure, do you want to tell me what's going on with you and Malchus?"

"Malchus came home drunk, slept sitting up and disappeared again this morning when I woke up. He said he was sorry and that's it. Your turn."

"Oh Selah, isn't Benjamin the most handsome boy you've ever seen? Simon found him last night. Well the boy actually ran up to him. Selah, he was dirty, no shoes, all alone and Simon figured he was an orphan so he brought him to my house."

"Where has he come from?"

"We don't know."

"Has he mentioned his mother?"

"No."

"Kezi! How long will you let him stay with you?"

"As long as he wants."

"You're busy. The boy will need," Selah didn't finish.

"What Selah? Love? A home? A mother?" All these words seemed foreign to Kezi but yet she spoke with ease.

"I don't know about many things, but this boy has brought me joy in one night. Simon is going to retrace his steps and tell me where he was when he saw him. Today, this week, I'll bring him here every day and see if anyone recognizes him or calls his name. What else can I do? Please don't ask him any questions. Let me do it when the time is right."

"Those dimples will be dangerous for the girls of Jerusalem in a few years."

Kezi hugged her friend. She knew Selah would support her decision.

"Today he can stay close to Simon. We'll watch the women buying from him and see if Benjamin talks to anyone in particular."

Kezi stayed outside to keep watch as much as she could. Simon was teaching him about all his fruit and vegetables. He stood behind Simon when customers came but by early afternoon Simon had him picking up anything that jostled off the cart. Anytime Kezi looked over, he smiled and waved. After a while he came and laid his hand on her arm.

"I'm tired Kezi."

She made a place for him behind her inside the front of the tent and he was hidden within the hanging fabric.

"I have my own tent!"

He retrieved his pillow and she let him pick out more so he was surrounded by comfort. Selah watched her with him. She hoped her friend wouldn't get too attached. She couldn't imagine where he came from. He had to be an orphan, nothing else made sense. If he was lost or ran away, his parents would be looking for him. It was just a matter of time and then Kezi's heart would break. The streets had quieted. Both women sat at the table watching Simon.

"Why was Simon out last night? Kezi, don't pretend you didn't hear me."

"Alright. He was looking for Malchus. Selah, he was concerned. It was a difficult day, was it not? You know Simon cares for both of you. He just wanted to make sure he was alright."

"Oh, he was alright, you can say that!"

Kezi leaned in, "Were you awake when he got home?"

"You know I was! He kept calling my name, "Selah, wake up, kiss me," both women were laughing now and Simon wanted to know what was so funny.

"We were remembering how your loud snoring kept us awake during Sukkot!"

"That was Balaam you heard!"

The women laughed even more. Benjamin, his little pillow tucked under his arm laid there listening to their laughter. His tent was blue and purple and he heard the faint sound of shells. Dust coated the inside of his nose but didn't prevent him from smelling all the spices and food that permeated the air in this open market. He could see Kezi's feet through a small gap at the bottom of the tent. He hugged his pillow a little tighter and drew it again closer to his face. Of all the smells in this place, he liked his little pillow the best. It smelled like Kezi. He closed his eyes and slept.

Simon liked having Benjamin around, attracted the ladies he told the women. Selah waited for Malchus and they took Balaam home much to the disappointment of Benjamin. Simon let the boy help him pull the cart to his house. His small frame strained with the weight. Kezi thought in just a few months she would fatten him up and it wouldn't be long before he could manage the cart on his own. She insisted Simon join them for dinner. She purchased some fish. The boy needed protein.

"Simon, did you notice if anyone thought they knew him today?"

"No, no one. We need to think about what we want to ask him."

"I know, I don't know where to start. Did he say anything?"

"Not really. You saw him. He hid behind me most of the day, of course later he didn't seem so shy. It's a mystery."

"Benjamin, let's go!" Simon called for the boy to come out of the house.

He looked at Kezi, "Are we going home now?"

"Yes, and we're going to have fish for dinner. Have you had fish before?"

"Maybe once I had it."

"Did you like it?"

"I can't remember."

Kezi didn't ask him anything else but Simon couldn't help himself. "You were a big help to me Benjamin, I may have to pay you wages."

"What's wages?"

"Money so you can buy things."

"I could buy my own food?"

"Yes, you could buy your own food. Have you never been to a market before to buy food?"

He stared at his feet. Kezi shook her head no to Simon indicating to stop asking questions, but Benjamin was only trying to remember.

"I used to go sometimes with all the women."

"I see," Simon obeyed Kezi and didn't ask who the women were.

"One woman was mean to me."

"Benjamin," Kezi bent down to hold him, "I'm sorry someone was mean to you. That will never happen in my house. Do you understand?"

"Yes, you're not mean," he looked at Simon, "and you're like the men who came to see the women."

Kezi's heart sank. She knew exactly who this boy was. Benjamin wasn't finished.

"But the mean woman went away."

"Away?" Kezi asked.

"They threw rocks at her and the other women told me she wasn't coming back, that she went away."

Kezi did her best to hold back her tears. "Look, we're home, now go with Simon and wash your hands and feet." She laid her bags down and lit two small lamps. She looked for the thickest piece of fabric she could find and buried her face where she wept.

"Why are your eyes red Kezi?" Benjamin asked.

"Well, I was cutting up these onions and they sometimes make your eyes water."

"Onions. We sold some of those, didn't we Simon?"

"We did. Wait until you taste them!"

"Simon, will you bless the food?"

Benjamin listened to every word. When Simon and Kezi said amen, he repeated it. He took the tiniest piece of fish and put it in his mouth.

"This is good! I like it! I never had this before."

They ate while Benjamin asked about every ingredient. Simon said goodnight and Kezi began to clear the table. Benjamin stood by his mat, his little shoulders shaking. He was crying.

"Benjamin, what's the matter?"

"I forgot my pillow!"

"Oh honey, that's alright. I have plenty of pillows."

"But I want that one."

She glanced around, most of her pillows were at the shop. "We'll find you a similar one."

"But it won't," he was still crying.

"It won't what?"

"It won't smell like you," he was sobbing and she held him until he settled down.

"My pillow smells like me. Do you want to share it tonight?"

He nodded, sniffling, looking over her shoulder to the place she slept.

"That's better. Now, how about a small raisin cake with honey and then we'll go to sleep."

He could only nod. She pulled his mat next to hers and laid her pillow right in the middle. Benjamin laid down and smelled the pillow.

His smile was all she needed. She kissed his forehead and said good-night. He was asleep before she covered him.

Malchus and Selah walked slowly home that evening. She fixed him dinner but she didn't eat. She was no longer upset with him, there had been too much happiness today with Kezi and Benjamin to think about her own disagreement. Malchus apologized again which she knew wasn't easy for him. She removed water from the fire. She asked Kezi for scented oil and put a few drops in. The room quickly filled with spikenard. She took linen strips of cloth and braided three together and submerged them. She waited several minutes for the water to cool down and then wrung the cloth leaving her with a damp, warm compress. She walked behind him and gently laid it upon his neck and pressed the heat into his soreness. She was humming. He let her massage his shoulders while the heat of the compress relaxed his muscles. Between the low light, the fragrance of the room, and the unconditional love of Selah, he closed his eyes and thanked God for His mercy and grace. He felt unworthy to have this blessing he called Selah, his wife. He reached for her hands behind him and pulled her down to his lap. No words were spoken until the small lamp released its last flame. He would remember this night. He would do his best to place himself in this quiet, dark room, completely at peace, the fragrance of spikenard buried in Selah's hair, the warmth of her breath on his cheek, the promise that all was well.

Claudia was bored. It was winter and there would be one more feast in a few weeks and then nothing until spring. She longed for Rome.

"Leave the doors closed Avi, I feel a coolness in the air today," she watched her. The young woman was fluid in her movements. "Tell me Avi, this next festival of your people, how long does this one last?"

"Eight days mistress."

"After this you have no celebrations until spring?"

"No, nothing until Passover," Avi wasn't used to Claudia conversing with her and she became leery of her questions.

"Have you ever traveled outside of this country?" Claudia asked.

"Do you mean outside of Jerusalem?" Avi replied.

"Have you ever been to any other Roman province or perhaps down to Egypt?"

"No mistress," Avi answered.

"Would you like to?" Claudia asked.

"Go to Egypt?"

"Egypt, Rome, Gaul, anywhere really."

"Why?" Avi became concerned.

"Why not? Wouldn't you like to see other countries, experience other cultures?"

"I never thought about it," Avi said.

"Have you never left Jerusalem?"

"No, it's my home. My family is here," Avi replied.

"That will be all for now, thank you. I will stay in my quarters today."

"I'll be just outside." Avi walked backwards out of the room as she always did. She surveyed Claudia's quarters. She couldn't imagine the kind of life she lived. The small glimpse of her time here she thought was lonely. She hoped she would need something from the market. She hadn't seen Joanna for weeks and she was restless. Claudia probably wouldn't leave her bed all day. She would bring both lunch and dinner. Pilate on the other hand busied himself the entire day finding time for baths and much grooming. She didn't understand the Roman men's need for such detail. He had those who even plucked the hair from his legs! It took much discipline for her not to stare at his exposed legs, the Roman attire much different than the robes of the Jewish men. She tried to imagine friends she grew up with in these short tunics with bare, hairless legs and began to laugh. The sound echoed throughout the hall and she quickly raised her hand to cover her mouth. She wondered how men in all the countries Claudia mentioned dressed. She closed her eyes, leaned back in her chair and began to daydream.

Kezi let Benjamin sleep a little longer. The boy probably hadn't slept at ease in a long time, fearful of the men who came around not knowing from one day to the next where he would be. She would bet his mother, the woman who gave birth to him traveled with the Romans or another caravan throughout Judea, maybe even Samaria. He could be Syrian for all she knew. It didn't matter. He was safe here and he would remain with her.

"Good morning," Benjamin rubbed his eyes. "Are we going back to the market?"

"Yes, we go every day but Sabbath."

"I need to go outside."

She loved to hear the patter of his feet. He liked to go barefoot. She thought he'd already grown accustomed to his nightly foot washing and oil she would massage into his feet. She had a small bowl of dates and leftover bread on the table.

"We need to go soon," she told him.

"Can I help Simon again?"

"I'm sure that will be fine."

"Is there any more fish?"

"No, you and Simon ate all we had. We can buy more today."

"I liked that fish a lot! I think I did have it before when I was by the water."

She stopped what she was doing. "You did? Do you know how long ago that was Benjamin?"

He held out his hand to his side, "I was this big."

"Do you like the water?"

"I don't know."

"Did you see any boats?" she asked.

"Boats?"

"Do you know what a boat is? Men catch fish from boats on the water."

"I don't remember."

"That's alright. Maybe one day we can go see some boats."

"Have you seen one?"

"Yes, I grew up by the sea. It's very pretty up there."

"Up where?"

She took the cup on the table and said, "Pretend this is where we are right now in Jerusalem." She took the small bowl of dates and moved it above the cup, "This is where the sea is."

He studied the table for a long time. He looked up at Kezi, "I'm in Jerusalem?"

"Who is that boy?" Malchus asked.

Selah acted like she didn't hear him.

"Selah, did you hear me? Who's that boy?"

"Oh, his name is Benjamin. I think he's the grandson of one of Simon's friends, I'm not sure. Shall I look for you today at the market?"

"You know I'm usually there every day."

"I know Malchus, I meant will you stop by to have lunch and walk us home."

"Us?"

"Me and Balaam."

"Yes, come now, we need to go," he stopped at the door. "By the way, who taught you about putting that hot towel on my neck?"

"No one. I just know sometimes when I feel the sun, it makes me feel better. Does your neck feel better?"

"It does, thank you," he kissed her then standing in the doorway.

"Malchus, the neighbors."

"I don't care about the neighbors," he kissed her again.

"Malchus!"

And then he spoke loudly, "Look neighbors, I'm kissing my wife!"

She ducked behind him.

"Selah, no one is paying any attention to us," he went around to get Balaam. She closed the door and stepped out into the courtyard. Several women smiled behind their hands. They were paying attention. She blushed a little, and as she waited for him, she began humming.

"Malchus asked about Benjamin today," Selah said greeting Simon.

"What did you say?"

"I told him I thought he was the grandson of one of your friends, that I wasn't sure. I've never seen Kezi so happy. I don't think it was a coincidence you running into him. The boy needed someone, and Simon, I think Kezi did too."

"Well he's a fine boy. We're watching to see if anyone recognizes him or calls to him while he's in the market. So far no one has."

"It's curious isn't it, where do you suppose he came from?"

"I don't know. Let Kezi tell you all she has learned."

"Has she found out something?"

"Ask Kezi."

"Simon!"

"Look, we're here already."

Kezi and Benjamin only too just arrived. "Balaam!" The boy ran to the donkey.

"What about me?" Simon asked.

"Good morning Simon, good morning Selah. Simon, Kezi said I could help you again today. Is that alright?"

"Yes, of course, a man has to make a living," he showed him how to secure Balaam away from the cart so he wouldn't eat all his profit.

Selah and Kezi began their routine of setting up.

"How's Benjamin today? He seems fine."

"He slept well," Kezi replied.

"Simon told me you found out something."

Kezi checked to see where Benjamin was. "Come inside."

"Kezi, what is it?"

"Oh Selah, this poor boy. First, I don't know how old he is. He told Simon he thought he was eight. I'm not sure. He's so small, he might be younger."

"How would we ever know? Go on Kezi."

"On our way home, he told us a woman was mean to him and the men that came to see the women were also mean."

"Oh Kezi, no."

"And then he said they threw rocks at the mean woman. Selah, I think he was born traveling with, like I used to. This mean woman obviously was his mother, a prostitute who got tangled up with the wrong man and was stoned."

"Oh Kezi, you don't think he saw it happen, do you?"

"I don't know, he's so young he must not remember. Last night we had fish for dinner and he said he might have had it before by the water.

I told him I grew up by the water, asked if he knew what a boat was and this morning, I tried to show him where the sea is. He didn't know he was in Jerusalem. I have no idea where he's from. Selah, I don't think anyone will come looking for him. He most likely wandered off one day, perhaps came across others traveling and people just assumed he was with their group."

"Bless his heart. Kezi, he needs you."

She nodded.

Selah put her arm around her friend, "And you need him."

Kezi let her tears flow freely.

Benjamin stood at the tent entrance. "Why are you crying Kezi?"

She wiped her eyes quickly. "Come here Benjamin," she pulled him to her. "I'm crying because I'm so happy you're here, in Jerusalem."

"And I can stay with you?"

"Yes."

"And this will make you happy?"

"Yes, it will."

"Does that mean you'll be crying every day?"

She held him tighter, "Probably."

Selah was crying just as much. She was truly happy for her. To see such life and light in both Kezi and Benjamin's eyes would make anyone want this connection. She hadn't thought too much about her own family. She trusted things happened when they were supposed to, just like meeting Simon, Kezi and now Benjamin coming into Kezi's life. She wondered if Malchus thought she might be barren and didn't know how to approach her. Did he want children, she didn't know? They hadn't talked about their future and now Kezi's was changing. She needed to speak to her about what to say to Malchus about the boy. She didn't want to hide anything from him. Benjamin was with Simon and no customers had yet come.

"Kezi, what shall I say to Malchus about Benjamin?"

"Tell him the truth. In fact, I'll tell him, I think that might be better."

"Benjamin is a very fortunate boy," Selah hugged her friend.

They paid close attention all week to every person who passed by. Not one person seemed to recognize him. Kezi let out a sigh of relief. In just a few days she had grown attached to him. She asked Malchus if he had ever seen him around the Temple or by Caiaphas' house. No one had ever laid eyes on him.

The Feast of Dedication was only a week away. Kezi wondered if Mary would be back to stay with her. It dawned on her Benjamin heard of Jerusalem. *I wonder if he's heard about Jesus.* She may bring it up at dinner tonight. He kept a close eye on Simon's cart. Any thief attempting to steal food would be met by innocence with dimples and she suspected already there were several who dropped their spoils hoping the boy wouldn't tell Simon. His nimble fingers sorted out beads and Simon began teaching him to count. She loved to request ten blue beads or five small white ones to see his brow concentrate on the task and then the delight of his achievement. She made him a leather strand bracelet with two red beads. She didn't have to tell him what it represented. When she tied it on his wrist, he hugged her and kissed her cheek. It was her first kiss from him. He didn't linger but hurried off to show Simon.

"What do you have there Benjamin?"

"A promise."

"A promise?" Simon repeated.

"Yes, see these two red beads? That's me and this one's Kezi and it's a promise we will always be together."

Kezi and Selah had to go inside the tent again even though Benjamin would just think they were happy. They both laughed and cried more as they wiped their eyes. They saw Simon also had to turn from the young boy.

"Big baby!" Selah yelled.

Nicodemas walked the market this day. He rather enjoyed it. Most everyone in Jerusalem knew who he was. He couldn't deny the attention he received made him feel the work he did was worthwhile. Simon saw him from where he stood. There was a hush and then a celebratory sound that moved through the marketplace when someone with stature made their way through. He recognized Simon and stopped.

"Friend, we meet again," Nicodemas said.

"Good morning Nicodemas. Can I interest you in some fine oranges?"

"No shopping for me today, just a stroll through on my way to the Temple. It's a beautiful day."

"Kezi, Selah, come." Simon introduced them to Nicodemas. "Kezi is my business partner, and Selah is the wife of Malchus."

"Greetings," Nicodemas had nothing else to say.

Benjamin stayed hidden behind Kezi. Many approached the ruler and he nodded and went on his way.

"That was strange," Kezi spoke first.

"Strange in what way?" Selah asked.

"He usually isn't alone; they travel in packs."

"Kezi!"

"Simon, you know it's true. I think it strange he said nothing, not even when," she looked at Selah.

"Not even when you introduced me as Malchus' wife?"

"Yes, I'm certain he sees Malchus often. Simon, do you agree?"

"Too many listening ears in the market is what I think."

"I know that man," Benjamin's little voice from behind Kezi had them all turn at once.

"You do?" Kezi asked.

"I've seen him before."

She adopted a habit of stooping down when she spoke to him to be eye level. "Where have you seen him?"

He looked at Simon and his little brow furrowed as he thought. He had an orange in his hand that he tossed back and forth. They were waiting for his answer. He looked again at Simon.

"It was by where you found me, I saw him at a house with that other man."

"What other man Benjamin?" Kezi asked.

"The nice man."

She looked at Simon and Selah to see if she should continue asking the boy questions. They both shrugged their shoulders.

"I'm glad the man was nice Benjamin. What made him nice?"

He didn't know if he was in trouble. She hadn't asked him so many questions. He started peeling his orange with much concentration.

"He gave me money and said to give it to my mother. When I saw you Simon, I was trying to find the nice man's house. I ran up to you to see if you were him."

"And you got an old man with a stubborn donkey!"
"I like you better, you're nice to me too."

Nicodemas was gracious to all who greeted him. He didn't know what drove him to walk through the market. He wanted to be among real, hardworking people, no one looking to gain his favor, no debates, no arguments, just people making a living honestly. He found it curious Simon worked right next to Malchus' wife. Selah, a pretty young woman. There was softness in her eyes, unlike the other woman at the shop. He doubted anyone fooled her. He saw Caiaphas earlier and knew he wanted to follow him. He'd been avoiding him whenever possible. His obsession with what everyone else was thinking was driving him mad. He was looking forward to a few months of quiet where he could reflect on his own thoughts. He respected the merchants as did everyone. They provided goods and services to the city. Walking through the market witnessing the joy on people's faces who worked hard for their living and how Caiaphas and his father-in-law ensured they paid their taxes made Nicodemas ill. It was business. The treasury of the Temple, the whole of Jerusalem counted on it. The annual dues were collected, the workers paid, the priests accommodated and Caiaphas lived a very luxurious, comfortable life as did he.

He wondered how well Selah knew Malchus. *Did he tell her all the minutia of the Temple? Did he himself understand the financial dynamic, the wealth and control of Caiaphas, his father-in-law and the deals that were sealed behind closed doors? Did Malchus know the degree of venality that Pilate exhibited?* Yes, in the stillness of his inner room, he felt ill. He also was part and parcel, his own life tightly interwoven through the fabric of deceit, greed and hypocrisy. Jesus had opened his mind and heart to truth. He struggled with this self-realization, and at this junction brought his own self-loathing. He knew he was an honest man, but when he meditated upon the words of Jesus and weighed them against the actions of his life, he became confused and even depressed. This he knew would need to be remedied immediately. He could hear the shuffling of footsteps in the hall outside his closed door, his servants ready to carry out the smallest request, and at the moment he could think of nothing he could ask that would ease his conscience, so he sat in the stillness of his room listening to the rain.

Chapter Eight

It was winter. Jerusalem settled for a nap. Avi had time on her hands. Pilate and Claudia left and she was unemployed. She hoped to see Joanna to ask if she knew of any positions available, not for Herod but perhaps a family in the upper city. She didn't want to sit at a loom and weave like so many young women making curtains for the Temple. She thought of Claudia. She asked if she would like to travel. She should have inquired. Yes, her mother needed her, but if she could ensure her needs were met, did it matter where she was? Jerusalem. She wouldn't leave. She picked up her pace. She was uncomfortable on certain streets, especially where the craftsmen seemed to gather.

The man was staring at her. She wanted to walk away but couldn't turn from his steady gaze. She looked behind her, maybe he was looking at someone else. When she turned again, he was smiling, pointing at her to confirm his attraction. She found herself smiling back. How could her face feel warm on this cold, wet day?

"Avi!" "Avi!" It was Joanna. "I've been calling you. What has you distracted? She saw the young man. "Ah my friend, I see Marcus has caught your eye."

"Marcus?" "You know that man?"

"Yes, I've seen him at Herod's court."

"Herod!"

"Have you forgotten who my husband is?" Joanna smiled.

The women found shelter out of the rain and Avi told her she too was hoping to find work and purposely came out in hopes of finding her friend.

"But now, I'm not so sure."

"Because of Marcus? Did he say something untoward?"

"No, I just...he makes me a little uncomfortable."

Joanna laughed, "He makes you uncomfortable, is that it?"

Avi now laughed. "It's his eyes! They seem to look right through me! It's unnerving."

"Let me ask Chuza what he knows of this man."

"Joanna, do you think you could find work for me?"

"What happened with the house of Pilate? Claudia dismissed you?"

"They left. Pilate wanted to leave before the roads were too muddy. Do you know before she left, she asked if I had a desire to travel? I think she might have been asking me to go with her as her personal maid. I can't leave my mother, my family." She now wondered what Joanna was doing in the lower city.

"What are you doing here?"

"What?" Joanna asked.

"You're never down in this part of the city. What brings you here?"

"I was looking for someone."

"Looking for someone among the craftsmen in the rain?"

"Yes." Joanna was abrupt.

"That's all you're going to tell me?"

"Yes. Now listen, I must go. Give me a few days, let's meet after Sabbath at the market where I took you to Kezi's shop. Do you remember the one?"

"Yes, I remember!" Before Avi could say anything else, Joanna covered her head and walked quickly back to Herod's palace.

Malchus was soaked. He had been walking around the markets both in the lower and upper city. He enjoyed watching the craftsmen since he was a young boy. He knew most everyone and they knew him. He wasn't naïve, he knew not all trusted him. Some would simply nod their head in acknowledgement, no verbal greeting, he didn't fault them. It was in the dark corners, the rear of these shops that he knew the real trade was commencing. The Romans knew it also. He wondered if they moved through the shops looking for a cache of weapons as they collected the taxes. Barabbas had been known to favor this area where he could easily hide among men of the same caliber. He heard the warning song of the craftsmen when the Roman guard began their descent to the southern part of the city, the pounding of metal on an anvil, the thumping of a fuller's mallet, the banging of the wooden shuttle, all orchestrated to sound the alarm.

He needed to get home and out of his wet clothes. The sky grew darker and he hoped Selah would be home before it rained harder. He wasn't looking forward to smelling a wet donkey but knew she would insist Balaam stay indoors. The warmth of the animal he couldn't deny was welcomed during the winter months. He missed Simon. He needed to talk. He would go to his house early one day soon.

Selah was ready to go home. It was quiet in the market. Benjamin stayed in Kezi's tent all day leaving Simon to fend for himself. She noticed the boy had put on a little weight and seemed to have grown an inch or two, standing taller having a sense of belonging. He began interacting with some of the boys his age and to hear his laughter brought both women to tears. He had been delivered from a nightmarish life which resulted in him living on the streets. She caught him several times during the day staring at Kezi, looking at his clothes and then he would take the two red beads in his bracelet and turn them all the way around his wrist. Once they returned to their original place, he would smile, jump up, run to Kezi and hug her legs, even if she was with a customer. Kezi never minded and would always tousle his hair and smile down at him.

There had been a few inquiries of who he was and Kezi didn't know how to respond. At first, she said the boy was a child of friends but when she saw the look of confusion on his face, she knew she needed to speak to him about this. It wasn't long the next customer asked who the boy was and Kezi without hesitation said, "This is my son Benjamin." It was settled in that moment. He never left her side the rest of the day.

She walked as fast as she could. Her feet were cold. She was pleasantly surprised when she discovered Malchus home, a fire lit and the small house warm.

"When did you get home?"

"About an hour ago. My clothes were soaked! And you need to put on dry ones now."

"The fire is nice, thank you for bringing Balaam inside."

"He's warming up the place faster than my small fire!"

"The market was quiet today."

"Its winter, people aren't traveling." He actually prepared dinner. He said he cheated.

"What do you mean?"

"Our neighbors brought over soup. They had plenty. I think she felt sorry for me soaking wet with a donkey dripping all over the floor."

"The bread too?" she asked.

"Yes, I thanked her, told her my wife was a working woman and didn't have time to cook for me."

"Malchus, you didn't!"

She told him how Kezi now introduced Benjamin as her son, how happy she was, how everyone loved the boy.

"What about us Selah?" he laid down his cup.

"What do you mean Malchus?"

"Children."

Her heart began to beat faster, "I, well, I mean are you concerned Malchus I haven't conceived?"

"I know we've talked about children. I always thought we would have children and start a family."

She grabbed his hand, "Me too Malchus. I'm surprised I haven't conceived. I thought maybe you were disappointed."

"I'm not Selah. Perhaps the timing isn't right."

"Oh Malchus, that's what I thought too. The LORD knows when the best time will be. Do you agree?"

"Yes."

She couldn't tell in the dimly lit room if he was a little disappointed and he didn't want her to feel anxious. He gave her hand a squeeze.

"The LORD knows. We'll wait for His time. Now I think we should go to sleep; I have an early morning."

He rose early. Selah was in deep sleep. He was happy they brought up children. It was a start. They seemed to be in agreement, this would be the LORD's doing and they both were at peace without having to discuss it further. He didn't want her to feel pressure. He tied up Balaam and decided to pay Simon a visit.

Simon was awake and outside and saw Malchus walking towards him.

"Good morning! What a surprise! Is everything alright?"

"Yes, I just wanted to see you and catch up."

"I know we haven't known each other long, but I know you wouldn't leave the comfort of your wife and warm home to come see this old man and catch up," Simon watched for his agreement.

"Come, let us go inside." The two men shuffled around, uncomfortable at the intimacy.

"What's on your mind Malchus? Is something troubling you?"

"I'm not troubled Simon, I just would like to understand."

"Understand?"

"God."

"Oh, well how much time do you have? This could take the rest of our lives and we would still be no closer to knowing His ways."

"I'm ashamed Simon I haven't been as zealous as I should be."

After talking for an hour or so, the two men went their separate ways. Malchus hoped to bring Caiaphas good reports today. There were many stories that found their way to the Court of the Priests from Galilee. Jesus wasn't anywhere around Jerusalem but yet his presence filled the chamber and this was driving Caiaphas literally up the wall. The sky was clear today but he didn't think it would stay that way. More rain likely. He looked around. Every man was busy about their own business. He silently uttered a prayer asking God to help him. He stood gazing at the sky. He hoped no one noticed him just standing there looking up, but someone did. Nicodemas.

Selah wasn't used to waking up alone. She knew Malchus had to be at the Temple early many mornings but this morning when he left, it was dark with no hint of the sun. Balaam was outside. She could hear his bell. She stretched. Kezi would be counting on her to be on time. Benjamin had taken priority in her daily routine and some mornings Selah arrived before her. The absolute joy she saw in both their faces made her jealous, but she knew no other two people who deserved such happiness. Kezi had a rough start to life and Benjamin apparently too. There was a kindred spirit, a bond between them that would be difficult for anyone to attempt to break. She stared up at the roof. Did she feel that bond with Malchus? Yes, he was her husband, they willfully entered into their marriage covenant but that unconditional bond of love and trust, she gasped that she didn't think they had reached it yet. But she knew they would. The past few months were promising.

Simon was at her door calling her name, the sound of Balaam's braying also mixed in the startled sounds that woke her. *Oh, my goodness!* She jumped up and called to Simon from behind the locked door.

"Simon, hold on!"

"Are you alright?"

"I fell back asleep!"

"We were worried. It's the third hour."

She saw Kezi's relief and genuine concern for her.

"I overslept!"

"That's not like you. Did you and Malchus have a leisurely morning?" Kezi grinned at her.

"No, he was gone when I woke up. I can't believe how long I slept."

They missed their early morning time together and now took advantage of a quiet market.

"I've never seen this place so empty this time of year," Simon was inspecting his cart, he had a large quantity of parched corn to sell.

Kezi agreed, "Why do you think it's been so quiet?"

Simon was scratching his beard, Kezi and Selah gave each other the familiar glance they shared every time he did this.

"I think the weather has a little to do with it but people need to eat! Our customers will not go to the other market. It's curious. Listen, I've been thinking," Simon wasn't scratching his beard, Kezi knew he had already made up his mind about something. "I think we should tell Malchus about our night of silence."

"Is that what you're calling it now?" Kezi laughed.

"I think Malchus should know especially since both Selah and I have met Nicodemas face to face."

"Oh Simon, I don't know," Selah was shaking her head no. "I don't think we should."

He looked at Kezi, "What's your feeling?"

"Do you feel it's important?"

"Yes, I don't like keeping things hidden," he looked at Selah. "Malchus has become like a son to me. Yes, it's still rough around the edges, our friendship, but if he found out, his trust would be hard to gain again."

"But how would he find out?" She didn't like this conversation and where it was heading.

"We don't know everyone who was there that night. You know people talk. If he gets angry, I would rather have all of us there to reason with him why we didn't tell him. Agreed?" He waited for their answer.

"Agreed, they said."

"Now the only question is, when do we tell him?"

"Tell me what?" Malchus stood at the tent entrance in disbelief. His wife, friend and this man who he confided to just this morning were all in agreement to disclose something to him they had kept hidden. Selah sat there in shock. Kezi looked to Simon to speak.

"Malchus," Simon stood and greeted him as he would any day hoping he would understand he hadn't told the women of their early morning visit. He saw Benjamin was fine and the streets still quiet. Kezi squeezed Selah's hand to reassure her all would be well. Malchus nodded to Kezi and sat down next to Selah.

"Tell me what Selah?"

"Malchus, I forgot to mention that I met Nicodemas."

"That is all?"

Simon spoke, "I introduced him to Selah."

His eyes were fixed on Kezi. "But that's not all, is it Kezi? I don't believe meeting Nicodemas is what you were discussing, am I right?"

"Yes Malchus, you're right," Kezi didn't play games. Life was too short.

Selah pleaded with her eyes to be careful. Simon only gave her his encouragement. Malchus may be softened with a women's tale of the events that night.

"Last Passover."

"Passover!" He looked a little agitated now. They had kept something from him all this time.

Kezi kept her voice calm. "Yes Malchus, it was during Passover, it's when I first met Selah."

Malchus glanced at Selah, her head was slightly down.

"She stopped by my shop and I sold her a scarf," Kezi saw him relax. "As you know Malchus, it was chaotic, mostly because of Jesus."

"Jesus?"

"Yes, when he was at the Temple."

He nodded his head. "What does this have to do with me?"

Selah spoke, "It was the night I met Simon, when he helped me with Balaam."

He was angry that night, more worried, and all these emotions now flooded his mind and they could see it on his face. Selah turned and placed her hand on his.

"Remember I just wanted to see Kezi. She was so nice to me and I needed a friend and then the people, the crowds and Balaam getting away from me."

"Yes, yes I remember. Simon, what is it you're not telling me?"

"That night," he looked around, maybe someone else now stood at the tent's entrance, "I saw Nicodemas."

"Nicodemas?" Malchus now leaned in closer to Simon.

"Yes, Nicodemas. We followed him."

"Followed?" "Wait," he looked at Selah and Kezi, "you all followed Nicodemas?"

"No, it was just me and Simon Malchus," Selah kept her voice low.

"Where? Where were you Selah?" his voice was becoming stern. "Simon?"

"We followed Nicodemas east of the Temple," Simon answered.

"Go on," Malchus said.

"Nicodemas went to meet Jesus."

"What? I don't believe it. How do you know?"

"Malchus, we followed him. We heard his entire conversation with Jesus." Selah and Kezi were shaking their heads in agreement.

"Did Nicodemas see you?"

"No, we were hidden among the trees."

They sat there waiting. Malchus was quiet. He looked at each of them, a direct stare left to each one's interpretation.

"Why did you keep this from me?"

"We didn't want to Malchus, especially Selah. This has burdened her. But I just met her, I didn't know you. I knew of you, but we both know there's a difference. We were in shock seeing Nicodemas. Poor Selah, she didn't know anything about him. It was me Malchus, I was obsessed! Here's Nicodemas, and I catch him sneaking in the middle of the night to find Jesus! And especially after the day at the Temple when Jesus caused so much trouble. Can you understand why I had to follow him and see where he was going?" Simon asked.

Malchus said nothing. Simon continued.

"Selah didn't have a choice. I literally dragged her through the olive groves. We, the three of us agreed to wait to tell you because of your position." He put his hand on his shoulder and he didn't flinch. A good sign they all thought.

"That day at the Temple, it was like no other. I've been in this city a long time. I listen to what people are saying. The Romans and their taxes, their brutality, the politics. Malchus, we don't know all the connections, we didn't want to cause you any trouble with Caiaphas. We didn't know what to do so we didn't do or say anything. We love you, all of us, and after a short conversation this morning, we agreed we needed to tell you. Let me be the first to apologize for keeping this from you. It was never any of our intention to do so; we were concerned of your position." Simon exhaled.

No one could read his face, not even Selah. *Was it the calm before the storm?*

"Can you forgive us Malchus?" Kezi looked right at him.

"Of course, I understand your hesitation," he looked at Selah.

"Selah, I'm not angry," he saw her body relax. "I'm just as shocked as you all must have been that night. Let us not speak about this."

"But Malchus, aren't you curious?" she asked.

Malchus put his finger to his lips to silence her. He rose suddenly and went to leave.

"Selah, I'll come to walk you home."

"Kezi, what a strange morning! First sleeping so late, Simon coming to check on me and now Malchus. I almost fainted when he appeared. I can't believe we didn't notice him standing there. I hate he found out this way but I'm glad you and Simon spoke. That night wasn't planned. I think he realizes the circumstances and we told him the truth. I'll know when he comes back if he's alright."

Malchus arrived earlier than Selah thought. She heard him before she saw him. He and Simon were talking and she saw him give Benjamin an affectionate hug.

Kezi joined the group, "What's everyone doing for dinner?"

"Eating," Simon made Benjamin laugh.

"I'm inviting everyone to my house for dinner."

Benjamin ran over to Malchus. "Will you come and bring Balaam?"

He looked at Kezi, "Are you cooking?"

"Yes, we're going to have beef stew if you're interested."

"Beef?" Simon replied. "I'll be there!"

Benjamin looked again at Malchus, "Do you like stew Malchus?"

"I do. Thank you Kezi, we'll be there. Now if Kezi doesn't mind, you can ride Balaam home and we'll see you in a couple of hours."

Selah looked nervous going home. Everyone was unsure of his reaction and now she had to go it alone. Her body was tense. Malchus put his outer garment around her. Kezi saw her shoulders release her anxiety and husband and wife walked quickly home. He wanted to get inside the warmth of their home. He was glad to not have Balaam to contend with and he found himself thinking about beef stew! He couldn't explain it, but he felt as if a weight had been lifted off his shoulders today. It didn't make sense since it was Selah, Simon and Kezi who should have felt relief. He understood completely their reasons for not telling him. He saw Selah stealing glances at him and he hugged her tighter. They were almost home. He thought about Nicodemas the entire day. He actually couldn't wait to hear all the details of that evening. He wouldn't press her. He would wait for everyone to be together, perhaps tonight at dinner. As soon as he secured their door, he brought her close and kissed her as a husband kisses his wife. He led her to the place they slept and they remained there until it was time to leave for dinner.

Kezi had stew, bread and wine. She also had cakes with assorted dried fruit. Benjamin watched her prepare everything. He sat on a small stool as she stirred the stew and leaned in to smell the aroma.

"I think we'll add just a little more pepper."

"I'll get it!"

"Be careful Benjamin, that's hard to come by."

He walked back slowly holding the container she kept it in with both hands.

"Do you want to crush it between your fingers?"

"Yes!"

She let him take one small peppercorn and release it into the boiling pot. He replaced the lid and put the container back.

"Can I check on Balaam?"

"Let's wait for Simon to get here, it's dark out there Benjamin."

"I'll be alright, I got used to being in the dark."

She quit stirring to look at him. "Come close to me Benjamin. Whatever you used to do, whatever happened in your life before you and I met, I want you to know you don't have to be in the dark anymore. I'll always be here. You have Simon and Malchus and Selah, we all love you and you never have to be alone. Do you understand what I'm saying to you?"

"Yes, my life is with you now and I never have to be by myself."

There was a knock at the door and Simon whistled.

"Simon!" Benjamin ran to him, "Can we go check on Balaam?"

"Benjamin! Let Simon get in the door."

"No, that's alright. You can help me with his hay. Dinner smells delicious!"

"Malchus and Selah should be arriving soon. It should be an interesting evening. Simon, do you think Malchus was really surprised about Nicodemas?"

"Yes, I do."

"I felt sorry for Selah but when I saw how tender he was towards her, I felt better. I thought he would be upset. We've all seen his temper."

"C'mon Simon!" Malchus and Selah were at the door when Benjamin opened it again.

"Mother, Malchus and Selah are here," Benjamin ran out pulling on Simon's sleeve.

Kezi stood, her hand on her mouth. "Did he just call me mother?" she let her tears flow freely.

Selah ran to embrace her, "Yes, he did!"

Malchus thought he should go join Simon and the boy.

"Malchus, I'm fine. Don't go back out, come in and sit," she wiped her eyes and made them relax while she poured them a cup of wine.

"So, did you have a restful afternoon?" she saw the flush that came on Selah's cheeks.

"We did, it was a nice afternoon to take a nap."

"A nap, hmmm. Selah, you overslept this morning and still needed a nap!"

Malchus threw a pillow at Kezi. They all laughed and Simon and Benjamin came back into a house full of joy.

"Kezi, this was so good!" Selah made sure she got every drop of the stew in her bowl. Benjamin was eyeing the cakes.

"Yes, you may, but eat slowly." Kezi knew he was getting sleepy. She closed the curtain to his sleeping area and told him to say goodnight to everyone. She followed him with a small lamp.

"Are you tired?"

He nodded barely able to keep his eyes open.

"Did you say your prayers?" He smiled and nodded again.

"Did you pray for your own donkey?"

His eyes grew wide. "How do you know so much?"

She kissed his forehead and he grabbed her neck, "Goodnight mother."

"Goodnight my son."

Selah cleared the table and Kezi rejoined them. There was love and peace in her home and she basked in its embrace.

"There's more wine, help yourselves," she sat back down and looked to Simon to speak. But it was Malchus who began.

"Kezi, what a wonderful dinner, thank you for having us tonight." He took a sip of wine. He looked at each one. He leaned back on one elbow and said, "Tell me everything."

Simon began recalling helping Selah try to find Kezi, that before they knew it, they were moving through campsites, his friend Joses noticed a large group of men and decided it had to be Jesus and they began to make their way towards the group. That's when to their shock they saw Nicodemas.

"We hid in bushes," Selah said.

"We did and your wife kept "shoosing" me! When Nicodemas revealed himself to Jesus and all those with him, I tell you Malchus, I could hear my own heartbeat! He called Jesus Rabbi, said everyone knew he was a teacher from God."

"Nicodemas said that?" Malchus asked. "Go on Simon."

"He said no one could do these signs unless he was from God, and then the strangest words." Malchus noticed both Kezi and Selah were nodding waiting to hear them again. "Jesus said to Nicodemas, 'Unless one is born again, he cannot see the kingdom of God.'"

"Born again," Malchus whispered the two words as if they were a long-lost memory.

"Yes, born again. What can this mean? 'How can you be born again', Nicodemas questioned Jesus and oh, what a conversation they had!"

"Do you remember all that was said?" Malchus sat up now.

"I think between me and Selah, yes."

He turned to Kezi, "Where were you?"

"In the bushes with Simon and Selah."

They all laughed and Malchus listened to them recapturing every detail. He could hear his own heart beating. *Do I tell them about my meeting with Nicodemas? Should I wait for another time? Is it too much for one evening? I'm now the one hiding things from them.*

"Malchus, are you alright?" Selah looked to Kezi and Simon for support.

"Yes, I was just thinking. This is a lot to take in. I don't know how to, I mean Nicodemas!"

"It's clear he didn't want anyone to see him. I think with everyone here for Passover, he knew it would be a good opportunity to hide among the crowds at night."

He looked at his wife, "You're right Selah. No one would be paying attention to one man."

He took a deep breath. He could see no one expected what he might say next. He had sucked in his breath so hard when they repeated the words born again, he thought surely Selah would notice but she didn't. He knew she was more concerned about his reaction to their covering up the events that took place that evening.

Kezi and Selah began to chat about Benjamin in soft whispers, Simon was staring directly at him. He was almost in agony. He felt he would betray Nicodemas if he made their meeting known but this was his family. He was squirming in his seat. He thought of a different way to approach things. It would take the focus off of himself temporarily to the overheard dialogue of Jesus and Nicodemas.

"What is it Malchus?" Selah turned completely around to give him her full attention.

"One afternoon I was walking home from the house of Caiaphas and," he paused, *would anyone believe him?*

"What Malchus, what happened?"

"I heard the words born again."

Kezi spoke now, "Malchus, I don't understand."

"I heard those two words in my ear. No one was around, it scared me. Then I was on my way to walk you home and I overheard your conversation, all of you," he spread his hands to leave no doubt he was including all three.

"Overheard what Malchus?" Kezi asked.

He turned to Selah, "I heard you telling Simon and Kezi what you thought Jesus meant when he said 'You must be born again'. You were talking about Mary."

"Oh, my goodness Malchus! Why didn't you say something?"

"I was still in disbelief myself I heard these words. Truly they're strange words. I know I didn't overhear them from someone else. This troubled me greatly, and when I heard all of you talking, I thought, how could this be? Where did they hear these words? It was one of the strangest things that ever happened to me."

Kezi reached for another lamp. The room had grown dark, the oil burning quickly or the time later than she thought. Malchus wanted to say more. *Now that Nicodemas had met both Simon and Selah, should he be bolder about them wanting to learn? Would Nicodemas carve out time for them and would he trust each one not to tell anyone?* He didn't know. He needed time to think about the consequences. In the meantime, the four of them crossed a new threshold and he hoped Selah would have patience as he collected his thoughts. Jesus had messed up everything. He wondered if Nicodemas felt the same.

Nicodemas saw Malchus briefly not having opportunity to speak privately with him. He sat now in the hall alone wondering about him. There was a sensitivity to the things of the LORD he had buried. He thought he probably kept them there his entire life. He saw a willingness to learn, a hunger for truth and his frustration at not knowing where to turn and he knew he was the one to help him as much as he understood which had put him in a quandary lately. *What did he know?* He had grown frustrated as well. He didn't realize how personal a man's faith and understanding were. *What is the kingdom of God?* Jesus' words were like a knife in his heart, 'Except a man be born of water and of the Spirit, he cannot enter into the kingdom of God'. *Did Jesus mean after death man would enter the eternal kingdom? Or could he access the kingdom now, in the present by being born into it, born again, alive to the things of the Spirit of God, not of the flesh, the laws or the humanness of the world? What else did he say? If I didn't believe what he told me of earthly things, how would I accept anything he said about heavenly things?*

"Ah, who is this man?" He didn't realize he spoke out loud.

"Who were you speaking to Nicodemas?"

Caiaphas. He had a bad habit of showing up at the worse times.

"Caiaphas, was I thinking out loud? I didn't wish to disturb you."

"You didn't, I was passing by and heard someone speaking. So, tell me, what man are you speaking of?"

"Jesus," he saw Caiaphas clench his jaw. "You know we've never had a conversation about him between just the two of us."

"Nor will we, he's an imposter and a troublemaker! I'm glad the people don't speak of him as much as they were," he held both his hands up knowing he didn't agree. "Yes, I hear the occasional story. I know he continues to teach. I'm surprised Nicodemas my friend that you would ponder this man's words."

"He speaks like no other we've heard."

"Words of a madman! Go home, relax. Enjoy this day. It's not raining now and I for one will go home for refreshment before the evening sacrifice and would advise you to do the same."

He left before he could respond. Another bad habit he had. Nicodemas sat unmoved. That night in the garden changed him. He had no idea what Jesus meant. *Who is this son of man in heaven he spoke of? How can he be in heaven when he is sitting in this olive grove speaking to me?* 'God so loved the world' he said 'that He gave His only begotten Son'. *Son!* This had caused many sleepless nights. God had a Son. His name is Jesus. He sat unable to move for hours.

Marcus waited to see Avi. He knew the way and the time she usually walked past this area of the market. He hadn't asked a soul about her. It wasn't something he would do. Besides, he was only traveling through. He wasn't enjoying the weather. He had come to Jerusalem out of curiosity. He studied art, music, theatre and had been obsessed with chariot races his mother told me from a very young age. He heard Herod liked them too and since he arrived, he was able to procure a seat to engage with other travelers and inhabitants of the city. He had especially grown fond of the common man and their dedication to their craft. It was here in these open shops when he first saw her. She was slender, dark almond shaped eyes and her hands those of someone who served in a house, not grinding grain all day. She walked quickly, her head down usually, but the day at the carpenter's shop he caught her looking at him. There was something in her eyes he hadn't seen in other women he'd known. It haunted him for several days, weeks now until he found the word he was searching for. Peace. She had peace in her eyes. Complete contentment. She never looked anxious. He wasn't certain of anything. He had a life of luxury compared to these small one room stone houses. He would look for the quickest route out of these poor, muddy streets. There was no sun today, no shadows to hide in and he didn't want her to think he was deliberately stalking her. But he was.

It started to rain. It wasn't heavy, but it was cold and he felt ridiculous standing out in the open. The men of the shops motioned for him to duck under their coverings but he didn't want any encumbrance. The low roof lines of these open shops would block his view. He would stand in the rain. His hope was this woman would think him an idiot for not taking the offered shelter. There was no sign of her. He heard several men laughing behind him. He was soaking wet. His hair now hanging in his eyes, he found he was laughing at himself. The sky was relentless. It had been well over an hour. He began to shake a little, the chill in the air becoming quite uncomfortable.

Avi had been watching him. She had hidden herself out of his view. She was cold too. She knew he was waiting for her. She felt nervous when he looked at her. They both couldn't stay out in this rain much longer. She was flattered. He was growing weary. He was allowing a perfect stranger to cause him discomfort. He turned! She began walking towards him.

"Greetings. Can you stop for a minute, well please, can you just come under here?"

She looked at him.

"Do you not know my speech?" Several shop owners began greeting her and calling her name.

"Avi, that's your name?" She nodded.

"I'm Marcus. May I escort you to where you're going?"

She began walking. She couldn't look at him. Even with his matted down wet hair and the faint sound of his chattering teeth, he was handsome. She felt bad she waited so long to reveal herself.

"I was hoping to see you today. Where are you going?"

She hadn't realized she was leading him to her home. She stopped suddenly.

"Why did you want to see me?"

He stood, the water dripping from his hair down his face, his clothes stuck to his body, his hands starting to feel sweaty.

"I, well I thought...I think you're very pretty and I wanted to meet you."

"Jerusalem is filled with pretty women, why me?"

He smiled. Avi returned it. He pointed at her, "That's why, your smile intrigues me."

"Next, you'll tell me my eyes are like deep pools," she couldn't finish, the rain falling harder and a clap of thunder startled her so she jumped!

"Let's go!" He grabbed her hand and shouted over the rain, "Lead the way!"

She was only a few blocks from her home, she led him there. Her mother and siblings were huddled around a small fire. They expected her home any minute so she wasn't surprised when the younger of her brothers and sisters didn't turn away from the fire to greet her. It was her mother who spoke.

"Oh my, you're both soaked through! Come Avi, close to the fire. Children, grab dry clothes. Hurry!"

"We're fine mother, just wet. This is Marcus."

The room was dark. There were small lamps burning and the light from the fire barely illuminated those standing near, but it warmed him. The floor beneath his feet was solid. He knew it was the earth, hard packed, the musky smell filled his nostrils. Avi's mother handed him a dry tunic and pointed behind him. He found a smaller adjoining room and stripped quickly of his wet clothes. Avi's brothers and sisters were young. He wondered how old she was. She was responsible for them; of this he was certain. He picked up his wet clothes and came back around the corner. Avi was sitting on a small stool, her sister drying her hair. It was as black as his, shiny and thick. Her mother motioned for him to sit next to the fire opposite Avi. A cup of warm broth was placed in his hands and he let the steam warm his face as he brought it up to take a sip. Avi watched him inhale the simple onion soup.

"Thank you, I don't think I could have waited for you another hour."

The room was brighter now. A new lamp had been lit and the fire stirred.

"When the rain stops, you'll have to go," her tone not harsh, just factual.

"Isn't this your rainy season? I could be here for several weeks!" He heard laughter behind him and when he turned, she tried to hide her smile behind her cup.

"Who are you?"

"I told you, Marcus."

"Where are you from?"

"Greece."

"Why are you in Jerusalem?"

"I've never been."

She tilted her head. He wasn't going to offer any more information unless she asked for it.

"So, are you traveling the world, going to all the places you've never been?"

"Wouldn't that be fun?"

She thought of Claudia. "Would you like some more soup?"

"Yes please," he emptied the second cup. "Well I feel better."

"I'm glad. Is this your habit Marcus from Greece when you travel to places you haven't been to meet women?"

"You mean to stand in cold rain for half a day and risk illness?"

"Yes, that's what I mean."

He loved the corner of her mouth and how her eyebrow would lift in conjunction when she was toying with him.

"Is it your habit Avi of Jerusalem to hide in shopkeeper's tents and watch strangers stand in the rain only to bring them to your home for soup?"

She dropped her cup. She looked at him and couldn't speak. He was grinning. She burst out laughing and her entire family joined in.

"Please, come and sit with us by the fire," Marcus implored them.

Avi's mother wouldn't let him leave, not until he had dinner and his clothes were dry. He had an easy way about him. He asked Avi's siblings their names and would repeat them over and over mixing up the first and last parts on purpose she thought just to hear them giggle and correct him.

"Where are you staying?"

"I'm a guest of Herod."

"Herod! Really? You've been in his palace?"

"Yes, he has many apartments, I came with a group who are studying the arts. Herod's been gracious and loves to be entertained."

"How long will you be here?" She didn't want him to see her eyes so she looked down.

"It depends," he said.

"Depends on what?" Now she looked directly at him.

"The rain. I've heard they expect a long, rainy season this year."

"I hope so," she replied.

Marcus smiled.

Avi didn't sleep. How could she? This dark-haired stranger had seized her heart. She had to send him back out in the rain. When he stepped outside, he spread his hands wide while looking up at the dark clouds above him, smiled and then bowed, a gesture that made her laugh out loud.

Her mother watched them closely. Avi was beautiful her mother thought, and in the company of this Marcus, she glowed. She was falling for him. She wasn't sure how she felt about this. A Greek. He had knowledge of things they never heard of. He had studied his entire life thus far. He told them he was interested in medicine. She was relieved when Avi told her she had seen him for several weeks around the market and her friend Joanna knew of him. Her mother finally went to sleep and as Avi slowly drifted into her own slumber, the sound of the rain brought a smile on her lips.

Marcus hoped gaining access to his rooms wouldn't be difficult, there was certain protocol. He was soaked again. He tried his best to stay close to the buildings as he made his way back through the upper city. He would speak with Chuza in the morning and hoped Joanna would be around as well. Surely, they would have some influence to secure Avi work. She told him she served in Pilate's house. He was surprised. How could this precious flower be subject to the cruel atmosphere of Pilate? He shuddered from both the thought and the cold. He had decisions to make. He couldn't wear out his welcome here, however he thought Herod oblivious to his houseguests. He was tempted to stay until someone said something, at least through the rainy season. He looked around at his accommodations, a far cry from the two-room stone house. Yet here, he felt cold, lonely and empty, unlike the warm, joyful house of Avi's.

Chapter Nine

The following days turned into weeks and spring would soon make its appearance. Malchus would be on high alert, watchful for any signs of trouble. Jesus and his followers would be returning to Jerusalem. He could feel it in his bones. Claudia saw the permanent pout on her husband's face. This time she wasn't as distraught to return to their city residence. John the Baptist remained in Herod's dungeon and Pilate heard the wild man continued to torture Herod with his words of repentance. Joanna was pleased she was able to assist in securing employment for Avi. She was also pleased in the relationship between the girl and Marcus. She wondered if Claudia would insist Avi return to her service. Currently she was overseeing the kitchen staff and doing a good job. Marcus missed his home, Avi the only reason he stayed. He wanted to continue his studies. He knew he would leave soon. He heard stories of Passover and now he could experience it firsthand should he extend his time here. He would speak with her this evening.

Everyone was anxious for spring. Avi brought Marcus to Kezi's and both Kezi and Selah never saw her happier. Malchus and Simon spent a lot of time with Benjamin teaching him to read and write. They were still unsure of how old he was, they all agreed he was between eight and nine. He was growing. Simon kept track by making a small notch on the inside of Kezi's doorframe, he had grown one and a quarter inch.

"That's not much!" Benjamin had cried.

Simon told him to wait until summer, then he would shoot up three inches! He had friends now and Kezi allowed him to play around the market, but had to check in often. She couldn't imagine her life without him. She knew she said this often and Simon and Selah always agreed. He'd been a blessing to her, to all of them. He had grown close to Simon. He was good with the boy, extremely patient. He told Kezi he would leave all that he had to him.

"It's not much, but he'll have it as an inheritance."

Kezi chided him for speaking of this. She couldn't imagine her life without him as well.

"I think I would like to have a party."

Selah stopped what she was doing. "A party?"

"Yes, winter is over and before we're all so busy, I want to have a party. I'll ask Simon and Malchus if they have time to set up a tent next to my house."

"Who would you invite?" she asked. Kezi had a smile on her face that Selah hadn't seen before. *What was she up to?*

"I would ask Joanna and Chuza, Avi and Marcus, Simon's friend Joses and his wife, some of the families that Benjamin now plays with their children, and I wanted to ask Malchus if there were some families we traveled with last summer he would like to invite, and I would also ask a few of the merchants we have come to know."

"What's the occasion?" Selah asked.

"Spring. Life. Celebration."

"I'm not buying it Kezi."

"And it would be an opportunity to see what the other merchants are doing and thinking about for Passover, Joses provides a lot of Simon's goods and the friends of Malchus…"

"Kezi! The friends of Malchus who are at the Temple can direct the travelers to your shop!"

"Oh, I didn't think about that!"

"You're something else! How soon would you have this party?" Selah was laughing.

"Two weeks."

Passover was in six. She would need to plan accordingly. She needed to keep things simple. Yes, she admitted she had ulterior motives. She would love to hear what other merchants were thinking especially after their fill of good food and wine. She hoped Joanna and Avi would share their description of the inside of Herod and Pilate's house, what the women wore, did they paint their eyes, what was their favorite fragrance. She hoped to learn of any news of caravans and trade routes; were there new spices or dyes being used, but truly she wanted to share her blessings, have fellowship with those she loved. She would ask Simon what he thought. Selah would ask Malchus. She would make her final decision before the end of the week. She thought it a very enterprising idea.

Joanna saw Marcus as he walked the gardens just north of the property. Avi wasn't working today. She went down to join him.

"There's not much to look at this time of year," Joanna startled him.

"I've found it a great place to think."

She looked around. No one else was here at the moment. "You're leaving?"

"How did you know?" he replied.

"I can see your turmoil from my balcony, and a woman knows," she smiled.

"Do you think Avi knows?"

"Probably, but she's most likely thinking of your return."

"I'm perplexed by this place," he told her.

"Herod's or Jerusalem?"

"Both. I'm surprised I don't feel alone. Our philosophy has made its way here."

"Yes, first the Romans, now the Greeks."

She made Marcus laugh. "You're uncomfortable with both?" he asked.

"Not uncomfortable, no, but we all have our traditions," she said.

"Yes, tradition is prevalent here. Your god is the most confusing," he watched her carefully.

"Yes, I imagine to your culture this would sound absurd. We know the Romans too have many gods."

"But you hold true to one?"

"Yes," Joanna said.

"Avi too?" he asked.

"Yes, Avi too."

They walked a little further.

"Passover is soon Marcus. Will you think about staying until then? It's a great feast, one that all males are required to travel for. Perhaps you'll discover our passion and understanding of a monotheistic deity instead of your polytheistic view."

He raised his eyebrow, "You baffle me Joanna."

"How so?" she retorted.

"I've found most women here don't comprehend cultures of other nations as you do," he said.

"We comprehend, we simply dismiss them."

He laughed out loud and she reminded him to consider waiting until after Passover. Like Caiaphas, she knew Jesus would be here. *Let's see how he comprehends him, she thought to herself.*

Chuza watched his wife ascend the stairs, a smile fixed on her lips.

"What has you amused today? The Greek?"

"Avi has fallen in love with him. He'll be leaving soon. I was only trying to convince him to stay awhile longer," she answered.

"By that smirk on your face I think you've convinced yourself a victory."

She glanced back at Marcus, his head down, walking at a slow pace. "We shall see."

"Benjamin, how would you like to have a party and invite some of your friends to our house?"

"I would like it! Is it my birthday?"

"No honey, we're just going to celebrate how good our life is. You and your friends can run and play and we'll have food and perhaps music!"

Simon looked at Kezi. "Music would be nice, my friend Joses can help with that."

"Oh Simon, does he play an instrument?"

"Yes, his whole family does!"

"Wonderful!" Kezi was getting excited. "Simon, which merchants shall we ask?'

They discussed the pros and cons of those who sold closest to the Temple. They needed to be careful in their selection. They didn't want to offend anyone and strategy was involved. Simon scratched his beard, Benjamin turned to Kezi.

"He's thinking mother."

"Yes, I know."

The boy had picked up on subtleties from everyone. He would hum when Selah did and they would try and out hum each other until Kezi had to ask them to stop. "You sound like locusts!"

He knew when Malchus had a lot on his mind. He had short sentences and wouldn't look at anyone directly. He knew his mother was impatient and he would bring his dimples over to a customer who was indecisive and just look up at them and say "That's pretty" or "I like the blue one". They couldn't resist, and he was sincere. Some days she kept him right up front. The only guests Kezi wasn't sure how to inform were Avi and Joanna. She didn't want to take the chance of them stopping by. Malchus and Selah brought Balaam which made Benjamin's day.

"Can Balaam come to the party? My friend Nathaniel has a donkey, we could race!"

Malchus was smiling, he missed being a boy. "I think that sounds like fun!"

They decided on the day. Malchus would invite his friends from the Temple, Simon would see Joses, he and Kezi would confirm the short list of merchants and the women would figure out how to reach Avi and Joanna.

"I see Chuza, Joanna's husband."

"You do? Where Malchus?" Kezi asked.

"At the Temple. He brings tribute from Herod."

"We wish to invite Marcus as well, Avi's friend," Kezi yelled as he hurried off.

Marcus played dice and drank wine with the other guests and lost track of time. It was too late to go to Avi's. He'd been selfish this evening. He missed action! This country was quiet. Jerusalem the last couple of months was wet, cold and a mixture of gray and brown. Should he begrudge himself a few drinks and a dice game? A few laughs with the men? She would have been waiting for him. He didn't intentionally want to disappoint her, but he needed a night to not think about his future, her or this dusty city! The men were losing their money as fast as they were draining their cups and their betting and drunken outbursts were beginning to give him a headache. He got up to retire to his quarters.

"Marcus!" "You can't leave!"

"Where are you going?"

"It's early! Give me a chance to win my money back!"

He ignored them and waved them off as he climbed the stairs. His head was pounding. He actually cursed as his steps only brought more discomfort. Perhaps medicine was the right avenue. He would find a cure for this dreadful pain. The shutters were open and the cooler night air made him feel better. He stood at the open terrace doors and breathed in as deeply as he could. Passover. He read about it. He didn't think a few more weeks would present any problems with his travel. There was a challenge in Joanna's words. He had no idea what she meant for him to learn or perhaps discover at this celebration. The entire animal sacrifice was somewhat gruesome even for him. He had to admit he had no deep understanding of its true meaning. *Malchus. I'll speak with Malchus.* He left the doors open. He could hear the faint sounds of the men still gambling. He had taken a considerable amount of their money. They would all have headaches tomorrow when their wives realized their pockets were empty.

He arose early and decided to go to the Temple in hopes of seeing Malchus. He was told he couldn't enter certain areas as he was a Gentile, upon death the signs read. He would believe it when he saw it.

Chuza greeted him as he was ready to leave, "Young Marcus, I heard you did well last evening. The men are complaining you retired early and didn't give them a chance to win their earnings back."

"Is that so?"

"Yes, already I have advanced wages this morning. Where are you off to?"

"The Temple."

"This is where I'm going. Do me the honor of walking together."

"Herod, I've hardly seen him. Does he live outside the palace?"

Chuza answered, "Yes, he sometimes stays in Jordan."

"He's Jewish, correct?"

"Yes."

"But he does not abide by your law?" Marcus asked.

Chuza smiled, "The men not only lost their money, but sounds like they also lost the control of their tongues."

Marcus now laughed, "No, I've heard many stories in the courts of Herod and elsewhere."

"Elsewhere?"

Marcus spun around, "This city, people are free to speak. I find they're most willing to share their opinions in the lower city."

"Ah, Avi."

Marcus shook his head, "No, not Avi, the craftsman. I've enjoyed watching the men work. I find them honest and sincere."

"And these honest, sincere men have told you these stories?"

He was careful, "I've heard a story of a man Herod has locked up somewhere for reminding him it's against your law to marry his brother's wife."

"This is true," Chuza responded.

"This man, he's here?"

"No," Chuza said. "He's in Jordan; he's been there now a considerable time."

"What's his name?"

"John. They call him John the Baptist."

"What's his crime?" Marcus asked.

"That's complicated. Tell me, why are you coming to the Temple today? You will not be able to go past the outer courts."

"So, I've been told. I wish to speak to a man I've met. I want to discuss this Passover feast you will soon celebrate."

Chuza stopped, "Who is this man?"

"They call him Malchus."

He stopped again, "This is the man I'm going to see. I'll inform him you're waiting to speak with him."

"What about you Chuza, do you celebrate Passover?"

"Yes."

Marcus looked for an area to sit before they reached the Temple, the streets were filling quickly.

"Enlighten me would you as to the significance of this feast?"

"It's the time we remember and commemorate when God delivered us from Egypt."

"The parting of the Red Sea," Marcus said.

"And tell me, should we look to Poseidon for this miracle?"

Now Marcus laughed, "I'm sorry Chuza, we all have our myths, our gods."

"We have only one God, that's the difference. Moses led our people out of the bondage of Pharaoh. We were slaves. We believe our one God delivered us and in obedience, our ancestors placed the blood of a lamb on their doorpost so the death angel would "pass over" the house as the firstborn of every family and even the animals were killed that night. It was the final plague that befell Egypt and Pharaoh. Each year we celebrate this deliverance, that's the short version."

Marcus had no comment. He didn't want to offend this man or their traditions.

"On second thought, I think I'll walk down to the lower city. I want to be back to spend time with Avi. We have lunch in the garden."

"Yes, I know."

"You know?" Marcus asked amused.

"It's my business to know the affairs of Herod's house."

"Thank you Chuza for my lesson, no need to tell Malchus. I'll see you later."

"You're invited to a party," Malchus oversaw the exchange of money in the treasury between the steward and Chuza.

"What party?"

"Kezi, a merchant of the market. My wife works with her and they know Joanna."

"How nice, I'll inform Joanna."

Malchus gave Chuza the details, "She asked me to extend the invitation to Avi and her friend Marcus."

"I was just now walking here with Marcus. He was on his way to see you."

"Me?"

"Yes, he wanted to know about Passover."

"He's Greek, he wanted to know about our customs?"

"I think the customs name is Avi." The two men shared a chuckle.

"I think he's extending his stay to experience the celebration."

"You think?" Malchus smiled.

"Yes, my wife, she likes Avi. She has proposed for Marcus to stay. Young love, sounds complicated."

"She has no family?" Malchus asked.

"She takes care of her mother and brothers and sisters."

"She sees a future with this man?"

"This I don't know. My wife hasn't told me yet."

They both laughed again and said their farewell.

Avi sat opposite Joanna. She was biting her lip so she wouldn't cry. Joanna could read her better than anyone and it only took one look of concern from her friend to evoke all she had kept inside. Her emotions were all over the place. *Was she in love with Marcus?* Her mind said yes, her heart was uncertain. Or perhaps her heart said yes, but her mind was indecisive. She was confused. *How could it be both? Who was she kidding?* She knew the cause of her turmoil. He was Greek. How could they overcome so many hurdles? She wouldn't leave her home. Marcus missed his. She held to her heritage, traditions, it was who she was. His mind seemed to be open to endless possibilities.

"How can you follow one god that you've never seen?" he asked her one evening. "What makes you so sure he exists? What proof do you have he's the only one? Why would you close your mind with this narrow-minded way of thinking? Can't you see how ridiculous it seems?"

"No." One word is all she had afforded him and she walked home alone. She wouldn't speak against all he believed and what consumed his thoughts. She wanted to, but she was in the habit of biting her tongue. Many times, she tasted her own blood. She thought he truly wanted to know about her culture, but after several weeks, something changed. Herod didn't live according to the law, his household was filled with many Romans under his employ, even Chuza and Joanna were said to be Roman. Marcus undoubtedly saw the hypocrisy. He drank with those who came to Herod's to amuse themselves with all manner of entertainment.

Joanna studied Avi's eyes, the younger woman was troubled. She loved a man who was going away soon. She wasn't feeling well today. She hoped to rest this afternoon.

"Are you in love with him Avi?"

"Yes, I think so."

"You're not certain?"

"Yes, I am. Oh Joanna, what shall I do? He's leaving."

"Would you wait for him?"

"He hasn't spoken of a future, has given me no promise."

"I see." Joanna could see the anguish of her heart. She thought this might be the first man she ever deeply cared for.

"What does your mother say?"

"She doesn't say much. It's my life, my decision."

"But what decision has to be made if he's promised nothing?"

The tears now flowed.

Joanna put her arm around her, "Avi, we've been friends awhile now. I pray we'll always be close. You're like my little sister. I hope you know I'll always listen. I can see you're greatly troubled by your feelings for him. We've all come to know him the few months he's been here. I think he would have returned home much sooner if it were not for you. He obviously cares deeply for you."

"He's Greek. He doesn't understand our ways, I'm not sure if love can conquer all these differences between a man and a woman."

"Perhaps only time will tell. There will have to be compromise. This is what I would call the stumbling block. Will you compromise?"

Avi looked pale, she nodded her head no.

"Ah, well yes, I expected as much. You'll need to speak with Marcus. You need to be honest and tell him how you're feeling."

"But Joanna, how can I? He hasn't told me himself of his feelings towards me. I would feel foolish."

"He has said nothing?"

Now she blushed.

Joanna lifted her hands, "You need not tell me."

"I must go Joanna, they'll be looking for me," she wiped her eyes and was out of Joanna's sight before she could think of anything else to say to her.

The sound of her husband's voice was at the door, "We've been invited to a party!"

"Really? Who's having a party?"

"Kezi, a merchant by the Temple."

"Kezi! Yes, I know her! How wonderful!"

"I also was asked to extend an invitation to Avi and Marcus. Kezi didn't know if she would see Avi beforehand."

"Perfect," Joanna smiled.

"Perfect?"

"Well, interesting."

"I'm not following you Joanna."

She smiled as she rose, "A party is just what we all need."

Kezi and Selah worked hard preparing for the party and were excited to gather with the small group invited. Malchus expected three of the families who traveled with them the past summer and Simon had been instrumental in providing the food and musicians. Benjamin was anxious for the day to begin. There would be many boys his age coming. He asked Selah every day up to the party if Balaam would be there.

"Are you only thinking about your donkey race?"

"Yes! We're going to win every race!" he exclaimed.

The weather cooperated and the temperature was perfect. Simon had gone to a butcher to select what they needed and the men carefully guarded the main course. The smell was incredible. Avi and Marcus arrived with Chuza and Joanna. Simon's friends were right behind them and music filled the air as soon as they greeted everyone. It was Marcus that stood out. He greeted his host.

"Thank you so much for your invitation, this all looks so wonderful! I can't believe we're outside. It's been a cold, wet winter. I love the fresh air."

"Well please enjoy yourself," Kezi spread her hands indicating a welcome to all. "Avi, you look beautiful."

"Thank you Kezi, it was a great surprise to receive your generous invitation. I seldom have the opportunity to attend a party."

As the families came, the music grew louder. Simon blessed the food and everyone began to fill their bowls. Most of the children ate on the run, Benjamin's donkey races were the hit of the day. As usual, the separation of the men and women found the men at one end and the women closer to Kezi's house as they reclined to eat and talk. Kezi and Selah easily engaged the women in conversation admiring each other's jewelry and Kezi was surprised a few of the women didn't know she had a shop at the market. Both women had purposely worn shell earrings and newer bracelets they had made, Kezi thankful for the slight breeze that allowed her chimes to join the musicians. Avi noticed Marcus sitting between Simon and Malchus. He was smiling and seemed to be having a good time.

Selah turned to her, "My husband likes your Marcus."

Avi blushed, "I can't say he's mine, it's been difficult knowing what kind of relationship this is. He'll return to Athens soon, after Passover. We're taking things one day at a time. We care for each other but," she glanced back over at the group of men, "I'm not certain this will work."

The children were getting tired and a few families began gathering their belongings to travel home. Malchus lit torches and brought more wine to the table. The sun would be setting soon. Joanna was relaxed. She filled her cup.

"Kezi, this has been so nice, I think we all needed a break."

"Splendid party Kezi!" Malchus raised his cup.

"I couldn't do it without you, Simon and Selah."

The others called out their approvals. She placed small lamps on the table. It was an intimate group.

"Marcus, I understand you may stay in Jerusalem for Passover," she hadn't had much time to speak with him during the day.

"Yes, as of now I have extended my stay," he felt everyone waited for him to say more. "I hope to learn more about your Passover celebration and Avi tells me the city will be filled! I didn't know this was a requirement for the men to travel here every year."

Everyone began talking at once. Simon made sure they wouldn't run out of wine and filled their cups. Marcus was having a pleasant evening. He watched his consumption.

"So, what can you tell me about this man Jesus?" No one spoke. "I'm sorry, did I say something improper?"

Chuza spoke, "No Marcus, I'm sure you've heard his name while staying at Herods. There are many marvelous stories about him that have circulated throughout all Judea."

"Jesus is very controversial Marcus," Simon wasn't sure he wanted to begin this conversation. "There are many in Jerusalem who would rather not have him here."

"Why? What has this man done?" Marcus looked at each of them.

"He confuses the people," Chuza offered.

"I'm not confused." Chuza looked at Joanna a bit taken back. She matched his look, "No, I haven't had too much wine."

"I've heard he's performed miracles! Is this true?" Marcus didn't know where to direct his question.

"Yes, it's true," Malchus now spoke. "There's many witnesses to these miracles."

Kezi and Selah both looked at Marcus nodding their heads in agreement, a little shocked Malchus felt comfortable speaking in front of Chuza.

"We were in Galilee last summer and the crowds following him were unbelievable. I've seen him at the Temple twice," Malchus said.

"Dare I ask what everyone thinks of him?" Marcus looked to the women first, "Avi?"

"Like you Marcus, I've heard many stories. I don't know much more than that," she didn't want to jeopardize her position. Chuza didn't look happy to have this as the topic of their conversation.

"It sounds like everyone who has met this Jesus has a story. I would like to meet him," Marcus was filling his cup.

"As I told you earlier Marcus, you cannot enter the Temple," Chuza looked at Malchus and Simon for help.

The women were now talking amongst themselves and Malchus thought it best to change the subject, but Marcus wanted clarification.

"I thought I could enter so far."

"Yes, that's true, the outer courts, the Court of the Gentiles," Malchus answered.

"That is where I will go then on your Passover."

Avi studied Marcus. *Did he truly desire to understand what this meant to her and her people?* He watched her as he raised his cup to drink. She could only see his eyes now, pools of brown and gold, she couldn't see any life in their depths. She shuddered.

"Are you cold Avi?" Kezi moved the lamp closer.

"No, it's been a wonderful day, I've never eaten so much!"

No one wanted to leave. Kezi thought the party successful.

"Leave everything for tomorrow, go home all of you and rest."

Simon, Malchus and Selah along with Balaam walked home under soft moonlight. It was Malchus and Selah now ensuring Simon got home safely. There was no need for a long farewell, they would see each other the next day. Marcus and Avi followed Chuza and Joanna back to Herods. Joanna insisted Avi stay there so she wouldn't disturb her family at such a late hour.

"Are you angry with me Avi?" Marcus tried to walk arm-in-arm with her.

"I'm not angry Marcus."

"What is it then?"

"We're too different Marcus. You'll be leaving soon. What's there to discuss?"

"Us," he said.

"There is no us, it's me and you. I live here, you live in Athens. How can there be us?"

"We may end up in Rome or Greece. Are you telling me you'll never leave Jerusalem?"

She felt her heart miss a beat. "Marcus, this is my home, my family is here. How could I leave?"

"What about me? I know you care for me as much as I do you." He stopped walking and took her in his arms. "I understand this is your home and your concern about your family. Your family can be wherever we are. Is not our happiness more than this? Do you love me Avi?"

"I think I do. I've never had feelings for any man. I'm saying I'm not sure," she saw his disappointment. "Joanna thinks I've fallen in love with you," she smiled hoping he would soften his expression.

"Have you fallen in love with me? Look at me Avi."

Joanna turned and whispered to Chuza to hurry around the corner to allow them privacy, she would wait until the young couple began walking again. Marcus saw a slight tremble in her lower lip. She has probably never been kissed. He felt shame for his past behavior. He didn't want to bring offense to her however he was a man, a man in love who wanted to show her his affection. He lifted her chin and kissed her.

"No one has seen us, Marcus we must go," she grabbed his hand.

He drew her back and kissed her again.

"Marcus, we mustn't, people might see."

"See what, two people in love?"

"Marcus please," she was smiling though and he took advantage all the way back to Herod's several paces behind Chuza and Joanna.

"He kissed you, didn't he?" Joanna's smile warmed her heart.

"Several times. I've never been kissed. I don't think I should have let him kiss me so much, especially out in the street!"

Joanna laughed, "I'm sure much worse has happened in the streets than one young woman receiving her first kiss."

"Joanna, it was wonderful!"

"Yes, I'm sure it was, however," she laughed again which made her coughing start, she patted her chest. "It's nothing, just a little cough."

Avi looked around her room, "Shall I close the shutters?"

"Yes, perhaps you should, thank you Avi," Joanna continued to cough.

"We shouldn't have stayed so late and Marcus and I taking our time walking home."

"Walking home, is that what they're calling it?"

Both women we're laughing but this seemed to aggravate Joanna's coughing.

"Rest now Joanna, we'll speak tomorrow."

She only nodded and Avi left to go to the room arranged for her. She knew Marcus wasn't far away and the thought of him so close comforted her. As she closed her eyes, she didn't think about the kiss they shared, she had the image of him at the table, cup raised to his lips with only his dark eyes looking at her. It troubled her then and it did so now as she tried to force the image from her mind.

Joanna's coughing echoed through the halls. Marcus was concerned. He would speak with her in the morning and inquire how long she'd been coughing. He heard her before from his afternoon walks in the garden, but it had grown worse. He also heard Avi laughing with her but it didn't bring a smile. She was refraining from truly giving her heart to him. He believed she wanted to, but something held her back and it wasn't this city or her family. It was much deeper. He wasn't a patient man. He would depart this city after this Passover feast with or without her, and at this moment he didn't know if he would ever return.

It had been weeks since Kezi's party. This city was expanding as normal and markets were non-stop with activity. Simon relied on Benjamin this year to be his eyes and his legs. The boy could move through the crowded square with ease letting Simon know what other merchants were selling. Selah had been exhausted each night and slept soundly, Malchus too was very busy. Joanna's cough worsened. Avi went by the shop to let the women know of her condition. She remained at Herods; she wouldn't leave her friend in her time of need. Marcus made his arrangements; he would sail back to Athens one week after Passover. With Joanna's illness, he and Avi hardly spent time together and when they were able, it was strained. He was bitter. He was used to achieving his goals. He had pursued this young woman and had failed. His heart hardened against this city, its people and traditions, their law and regiment. People had begun to speak of Jesus. He overheard the soldiers at dice games talking about possible trouble, and again, he didn't understand how one man could cause all this disruption. Malchus shared the story of the previous Passover when Jesus went through the Temple and caused all manner of chaos. When Malchus shared how he knocked over tables, money flying and everyone scrambling, Marcus thought he saw admiration for this man. Kezi and Selah told him about Mary, the young girl who now was a follower of his and he thought it a remarkable story, but it was just a story.

He was surprised at the people pouring into the city. It was loud! Between Chuza, Malchus and Simon, he expected the onslaught, but to be on the streets in the midst of the anticipation, he began to sense the rhythm. He found himself loitering quite a bit at Simon and Kezi's place at the market. He wished he was an artist to capture the swift movements of the people, loose chickens playing hide and seek with their frantic owners, children singing and playing souvenir flutes. Spices clung to the inside of his nose and the creaking of the merchant's wooden carts made him smile. *Avi.* He could see how she would miss this mayhem, but every city had a market and chickens and spices and their own temples, so what was it that kept these people in its clutches? God. Everyone said the same thing. It was a one-word utterance that he couldn't wrap his head around. This is why he extended his stay. He would observe them celebrating God.

He met some friends here. He admired Kezi. She told him a little of her background and how Benjamin had become part of her life. Who didn't like Simon? He was one of the most generous men he ever met. Malchus and Selah were somewhat of a mystery to him. They didn't fit, yet somehow it worked. It gave him hope for a future with Avi. Selah had been very kind to him, always making time to listen and truly had a sympathetic ear when it came to Avi. She told him how she left her family to come to Jerusalem for Malchus. To his dismay, she had grown to love the city and couldn't imagine leaving.

"Perhaps when I'm older I'll return to the sea," her eyes would twinkle when she spoke about the sea. Marcus loved the water. He couldn't wait to sail. Malchus and Simon shared their sea adventure. He held his side when Malchus relayed Simon's fish story and how the old man screamed like a little girl when he poked and startled him.

"In front of those men!" Malchus had laughed. He didn't mention the real story to Marcus, he was in Herod's courts and he knew he spent a lot of time with not only the other Greeks, but the Roman soldiers too. He would take no chance of Pilate hearing a tale to irritate Caiaphas. Passover was in four days. They told Marcus even more pilgrims would be coming.

"Where do they stay?"

"Any place they can," Selah had him turn to the north and the east. "They will be camped everywhere."

He was anxious to witness this city at the height of this annual feast. Avi wasn't sure if she should invite him to celebrate Passover at her family home. She knew he was accustomed to the finer things and his ease at the courts of Herod proved her assumptions. She purposed to keep her distance. He was leaving. Her friend was ill. Her family needed her. She couldn't afford to dream right now. Her desires were put on hold.

"What are we to do Marcus?"

"I don't have the answers Avi. I have to complete my studies. I must return to Greece."

"I'll wait for you," she hoped he would see promise in her eyes.

"It could be years Avi, you're willing to wait for uncertainty?"

"Are you not willing to keep me in your heart?"

He looked away from her, "It's a long time Avi to hold to possibilities."

"What is time when there is love?"

He had drawn her closer, "I know there's love; I'm concerned with the time."

"Is there someone in Greece who waits for you Marcus?"

"No." "Avi, this separation, I can't see how it will work."

"I don't understand, I've told you I'll wait."

"You don't understand, I'm saying I'm not sure I can."

"I see."

"No, I don't think you do. I want you to come to Athens, begin a life with me there. We will marry and we can bring your family."

"My mother wouldn't leave Jerusalem. I'm not ready to leave either," she wasn't sure what else she expected him to say. She wouldn't be the reason to keep him from his passion, he wouldn't become a wedge between her mother, home and family.

"So, this is goodbye."

"As I said Marcus, I will wait."

He had no more to say this night. Joanna's coughing distracted Avi and she turned to leave. He didn't stop her. She cried on the way to Joanna's room and stood outside her door until she composed herself. Her friend took one look at her and summoned her to her side.

"He'll be back," her labored breath barely audible.

Avi laid her head down and sobbed.

Malchus began to make his way to the bridge. This is where security needed to be priority. Herod would use this to access the Temple. From this point he looked every direction. Soon the city would be overflowing with yet another celebration. The Greeks had their games, the Romans their parties and they had their feasts. *Was this life? One big party after another?* He knew the significance of each feast and yes, he understood the importance of God's command to remember all he had done for his people but now what? They had been waiting, God had been silent until this wild man John the Baptist began proclaiming the kingdom was near, and then of course Jesus and the rumors surrounding his baptism. He didn't want his head to hurt again from thinking on those words that supposedly some heard coming down from heaven, and where is John the Baptist now? In Herod's dungeon the last he heard. What did he think now about the kingdom coming near? What does that mean? And what did he think about Jesus while he lived in isolation in a dark cell under Herod's house? He made his way across the bridge to Caiaphas' house. He was anxious to get home and hoped Caiaphas wouldn't require him to stay at his. Unfortunately, he thought the latter.

"Malchus, I will ask you to accompany me to the Temple. I have word Jesus is already here in Jerusalem, I need you to be diligent in your observations of the people tomorrow." Caiaphas didn't sound as upset as he normally did when speaking about Jesus and Malchus relaxed a little.

"Of course," he replied.

"I want to be informed of his every movement and where he is at every moment."

Malchus knew this would be easy. He would look for the crowds.

"I hope you've already inspected the crucial areas."

"Yes Caiaphas, I have."

"Take men with you in the morning to the Sheep Gate, I will not have the offerings jeopardized."

"It will be done Caiaphas."

He hadn't given much concern to the gate, the Fortress overlooked it; the Roman guard would alert the rulers if they suspected unusual behavior, they've been here long enough to know the difference. He didn't dare try and leave. He walked to his room that had been prepared since his service to Caiaphas began. It was comfortable, a small lamp and food were left on the table. He wasn't hungry. The sun was setting and he slept in the darkened room thinking of John the Baptist and his dark cell.

Simon took Benjamin to the men's court to find Malchus. As they got closer, the sound was deafening. Benjamin handed Simon the lamb and put his hands over his ears. Malchus was waiting for them. He had been waiting for almost an hour. Selah saw him first.

"Something's wrong."

Kezi drew Benjamin to her side, "Selah, why do you say that?"

"Malchus, I can tell by the look on his face."

They couldn't move any faster, the crowds were too large. Selah didn't take her eyes off of him. He was pointing east, the way they normally would enter. It was Marcus who reached them before they could ascend the steps.

"Marcus, what's happening?" Kezi searched the young man's face.

"A man who hasn't been able to move for over thirty years has been seen walking! It's incredible!" He was shouting at them. There was nowhere to go. They surrendered to the crowd. He turned to get his bearings. "Up there, some kind of pool this man was waiting to enter and your Jesus told him to get up and walk and he did!"

Selah looked for Malchus but he was gone.

Marcus continued, "This is unbelievable! Look at these people! And the animals! I've experienced anything like this and it hasn't even started!"

"Have you seen Jesus?" Simon shouted just as loud.

"No, this man, he doesn't know who it was but the people said it was Jesus."

"Marcus, is Avi here?" Kezi asked.

"I don't know. We made arrangements to meet at your house afterwards for dinner."

She turned to Simon and Selah, "'Malchus must expect trouble. I think he was warning us." She took charge, "Simon, you and Benjamin take Marcus to the Court of Gentiles. Selah and I will see if we can find Avi. We'll all meet back at my house when we can," and she was off making her way through. "Selah, hurry! I want to see Jesus!"

The sun was growing warmer, the sights and smells almost making Marcus sick. He had been forewarned, but here in the midst of this celebration, it awakened something in him. These were a peculiar people. As much as he could understand, today a man who hadn't been able to move close to forty years was now walking freely around the Temple, and instead of celebrating this miraculous healing, if these facts were true, he was rebuked for carrying his bed. It should be interesting conversation at dinner tonight.

Dinner! He was late! Sabbath had begun. They had practically pounced on the healed man the moment it started to tell him he was breaking the law. Marcus wanted to stay close to the Temple to ask questions, perhaps even speak with this man, but Avi and her family would be waiting. He was the last to arrive at Kezi's. He apologized. Selah took him by the hand to lead him next to Avi at the table.

"You're not the last, Malchus is not here."

"Shall we wait?" he asked.

"No, he might be delayed for some time."

He greeted Avi's mother and looked at each face gathered for this Passover dinner. Simon looked worried. He noticed how often he looked towards the Temple probably wondering if Malchus was caught up in some special council meeting. Selah had a calm about her. Chuza and Joanna were on the end, reserved. Joanna's cough had lessened but her pain and frailness didn't go unnoticed. Avi's siblings were well-mannered as their mother kept watch. Dinner was long and educational. Still no Malchus. Avi's mother and her siblings were escorted home by Chuza and Joanna. Avi protested but Joanna assured her she would be fine.

"You need time with Marcus."

Benjamin went inside and Kezi returned to the table when Malchus arrived. He sank to his seat. Selah began preparing his meal. Everyone waited for him to speak.

"I'm sorry everyone for being so late," he looked at Selah, "it couldn't be helped."

"Are you all right?" she searched his face.

"Yes, it's been a long day," he began to eat. Simon and Marcus sat across from him. He knew they all had questions. He finished swallowing. "A lame man was healed today. He hasn't been able to walk for thirty-eight years."

"Thirty-eight!" Marcus repeated.

"It was Jesus. He was at the pool of Bethesda this morning. The man, he didn't know it was Jesus until later when he saw him at the Temple."

"I heard others asking the man who healed him," Marcus' voice was low, he purposed to say others.

Malchus nodded, "This poor man was harassed all day," he looked at all the faces hanging on to his words, "I would have just gone home or left the Temple area."

"Perhaps he had nowhere to go," Selah said.

"Perhaps," he continued. "Do you know what's most shocking to me? Caiaphas. He wasn't as upset as the Pharisees were. Our law prohibits to carry anything on Sabbath."

"This man Malchus, do you know him?" Marcus asked.

"I've seen him for many years."

"And this Jesus healed him today?"

"Apparently. What am I saying, yes, Jesus healed this man," Malchus held up his cup for Selah to fill.

"But how?" Marcus asked.

"I don't know. I don't think anyone knows. He doesn't touch them, he uses no medicine, he only speaks."

"Are you saying he has the ability, the power to heal people by his words?"

"Yes, it seems so," Malchus answered.

"We were traveling last year and heard many stories of people who were healed," Simon looked at Kezi and Selah as he spoke.

Marcus noticed alarm in Selah's eyes, but it went unnoticed by the old man.

"We heard he touched a leper."

"What Simon?" Marcus asked.

"Well he speaks to most and the one person you would think he would speak to, he touched! Our law definitely forbids that!"

"That's very interesting Simon now that you think about it." They all turned to Malchus again.

"All the miracles we've heard he's done was simply by telling people to rise, go home or get up and walk, no one has said that he put his hands on them except the leper." The last words were just a whisper that even Selah leaned in towards her husband.

"He does opposite of what you think, is that what you're saying?" Marcus couldn't grasp the law that held them in these chains of doubt and restricted their thinking. It was Avi now who spoke.

"I think he shows great love to people. The leper has to call out, warning everyone to not come near, but yet Jesus did and touched him. He brought the one thing the leper had most longed-for, human touch."

Kezi and Selah had tears in their eyes and Simon could be heard sniffling.

"I heard he also spoke to a woman in Samaria," she turned to Marcus, "Jews don't associate with Samaritans, but Jesus showed her love also. What man do we know would speak to a woman alone at a well, especially in Samaria? Everyone heard about the tax collector that now follows him. A tax collector! Are they not hated by our people? But Jesus called out to him. Why? Love. Jesus is a Jewish man. He grew up as we with the law, and yet he chooses to love the leper, the Samaritan and the tax collector, all those we avoid, so yes Marcus, he does the opposite."

No one spoke. Avi had captured the acts of this man Jesus in one word, love. Marcus felt a lump in his throat. Kezi and Selah had open tears falling down both sides of their faces and he knew they agreed with her assessment. Jesus was love. The realization of this love to the least of those in their eyes had been a rude awakening for all who shared this table. He diverted his eyes from the women and looked at Malchus. He was pale and trembling. Marcus thought for a moment he was becoming ill, but like the rest of the small group of friends, he too was overwhelmed with who this man Jesus was.

All their lives living under the constraints of their law and today on a Sabbath, Jesus healed a man who has been lame for longer than he and Malchus had been on this earth and instead of rejoicing and celebrating the miracle that this poor man could now walk and have a better future for himself, their chief rulers admonished this man for carrying his mat, the mat that represented thirty eight years of bondage and inability to do anything but beg strangers for mercy until Jesus. Jesus showed him mercy while they rebuked him. He began to tremble a little himself thinking these people with their law and traditions had just removed themselves from the one thing they claimed, loving their God with their whole heart and soul. How can you say you love and not speak or associate with certain people? You can't. And Jesus is traversing this country demonstrating their error and rubbing their faces in this truth. He's the example to follow. He's going against the grain by doing the opposite. He's living love, action, not just words. He looked at the bowed heads around him, each one in deep thought reconciling in their hearts and minds who they were and who Jesus is. He thought as Avi, Jesus is love. He didn't remember leaving, he only knew Avi was at his side as he walked her home. There was much to say but neither spoke. They would depart this night not knowing truly if they would ever see each other again. He stopped before they reached her home.

"Avi."

"Don't say anything Marcus, my heart can't bear it."

"I can't leave without you having some hope."

"Hope for you to return?"

"Yes, and for a future together."

"Marcus, I don't think this is possible."

"Because I'm not Jewish?"

She didn't like his tone. He didn't give her a chance to answer.

"That's it, isn't it? I'm a Gentile, not allowed to enter your Temple, not one who follows your laws, your rules so how could we possibly have a future?"

She began to speak and he actually took his hand and covered her mouth. She became fearful of him at that moment.

"Now it is I that will request you don't speak. My heart too cannot bear it. I fell in love with a woman who shows the same intolerance to those who are different. I suggest you seek this Jesus and take a few lessons from him. Goodbye Avi."

She stood unable to move. She could taste the salt on her lips. She fell to her knees and wept.

Avi's mother found her daughter just inside their door. She could still see moisture on her eyelashes, she had shed many tears. The children would be waking up soon, they would ask about Marcus.

"Avi, wake up," her mother sat on the floor near her daughter. She began to move the loose strands of hair away from her face. She opened her eyes to see her mother's concern and began to weep again.

"It will be alright daughter."

She could only shake her head no and cry, her mother's sleeve wet with her sorrow.

"He'll come back."

She shook her head no again. Her mother wiped her eyes and tried to comfort her firstborn.

"Marcus loves you, he'll be back," her half-smile offered no reassurance.

"No mother, I don't think so."

"Have faith my child."

"It's our faith that has pushed him away."

The two women sat on the earthen floor in silence. Avi had no more tears left. She sat in her mother's embrace feeling like a hypocrite. She then remembered Jesus called the Pharisees hypocrites and she began to vomit.

Herod made arrangements for all his houseguests to be escorted to their destinations with care and precision. Marcus didn't sleep. He would sleep later. He wasn't happy with himself, but he couldn't refrain from speaking his mind. He said goodbye to Chuza and Joanna, hugging the woman like his own mother wishing her well and promising to get word to her once he was home and had some semblance of his future. He had no idea what he wanted to do. He still had interest in medicine, however recent events challenged further study. Jesus didn't use medicine. *Was it mind over matter? Could one make themselves whole with positive thinking? With faith?* Faith. Avi now clouded his mind. He looked at the dust coming up from the wheels of the cart he traveled in. He couldn't wait to reach the sea and sail home. He closed his eyes never once looking back.

Chapter Ten

It had been one year since Marcus left Avi standing in the empty street, the darkness of the corners of her heart exposed by his words. She didn't like it and swore an oath to herself she would never be so vulnerable again. That morning lying in her mother's arms knowing he was on his way home stirred up a passion within her she was unfamiliar with. She wanted, no desired to know truth. She questioned her mother about their heritage and traditions. Simon and Malchus became like older members of her family, they didn't seem to grow weary of her constant inquiries. Even Benjamin had begun to ask questions, the simplicity of his curiosity refreshing.

Joanna had been healed by Jesus. This prompted Avi to diligently seek those who knew the Scriptures. Joanna was supporting Jesus and his followers with her finances, her healing made it easy for Avi to leave the employ of Herod and join Kezi and Selah at the market. Joanna knew Avi set boundaries concerning Marcus. She only told her he'd arrived safely and hoped to see him again, and after her encounter with Jesus, she relayed in detail to the young Greek that as with others, he simply spoke to her and she was healed, but encouraged him to continue with his studies as he did decide on medicine. Kezi and Selah become her mentors, sisters. Avi found herself at the table of Malchus and Selah often. There were many stories out of Capernaum and the surrounding area of Jesus and his ministry.

He had chosen twelve men. Joanna confirmed this. Out of the multitudes who followed him, he picked twelve men to be at his side, his disciples. Malchus seemed to be troubled by the way he was organizing and structuring his ministry.

"What is the purpose to choose these men," he asked Simon. "Do you think they plan a revolt?"

"Against who?" Simon asked. "Rome? With twelve men? I don't think so."

"So then why choose? He has hundreds following him."

Avi would be on the edge of her seat during these conversations. The women would offer their reasons and Benjamin would make them think.

"Aren't there twelve tribes we all came from? Maybe he wants one disciple from each tribe."

"Like he's speaking to all of Israel," Selah said.

"Yes, that's what I mean."

Kezi was proud of her son. He had grown this past year and after several pleas had his own little donkey. He and Balaam were fast friends. He called him Gray. He told her when he thought of a proper name for him, he would let her know, but right now he was just a little gray donkey bearing the name of the color of his coat.

Simon hadn't changed. His energy and enthusiasm were contagious. At one time Avi thought perhaps he and her mother would enjoy their latter years together but both were too set in their ways for compromise. She laughed and called him papa once just to get his reaction. He was a kind, giving man and she considered him family whether he married her mother or not.

One night they were gathered for dinner at Selah's, Malchus was unusually late. They knew Jesus wasn't in Jerusalem, it had been quiet. When he did arrive Avi saw that look, it was the same as the last night she saw Marcus. Something had gripped his heart.

"He has raised the dead."

Selah dropped the bowl she had in her hand.

"Malchus what are you saying?" Simon didn't believe these words. Malchus repeated them.

"There were many witnesses. A widow, her only son died. They were carrying him for burial. Jesus called for the young man to rise and he did."

"Where, where did this happen?" Simon was grabbing his heart.

"Nain. It was in Nain."

"He is the Christ," Selah sat next to Malchus. "Who else could raise the dead?"

All the prior stories of the lame and the blind being healed, rumors that he even spoke to the sea and the storm ceased, but raising the dead? Impossible! They were afraid to speak about it. Malchus said there were many witnesses. Selah hoped he would begin to trust his own convictions.

Kezi allowed Selah more control in the shop. She still didn't enjoy haggling over prices but discovered the women liked it especially when they thought they were getting a bargain. Avi had been helpful to both she and Kezi as she knew many of the women having grown up in the city. She would get first-hand information when Pilate and Claudia were in town and even Herod. They were devastated to hear of John the Baptist's death. It was gruesome and Selah excused herself feeling sick to her stomach when learning of the drunken party and result of one despicable woman. *What woman would use her own daughter in such a brazen way to have her revenge?* Kezi refused to discuss it stating she wouldn't give one breath to this woman by speaking her name. Selah thought Malchus indifferent when they talked about it later. He told her Herod was completely perplexed by the Baptist. He made the horrible mistake of voicing his thoughts about why Jesus couldn't raise him from the dead. Selah had gone ashen white and he cursed himself saying something so unfitting in his home to his wife.

"I'm sorry Selah, I don't know why I said that. All these things we're hearing secondhand and I'm confused by this man. It's been two years he's been causing strife among the people."

"Strife? The people? I think the strife he causes is within you Malchus," she bit her tongue. "People love him. They're calling him the Christ, one sent from God more and more. It's the rulers and the Pharisees and your High Priest that he troubles, not the people."

"Selah," he could see she was getting upset.

"All I know is wherever he goes he does good things. I can't understand why these Pharisees can't see his goodness, his works of healing and all the miracles he's done and only point out that his disciple's plucked grain on a Sabbath! That's ridiculous Malchus! Is that what you think? Do you agree with them?"

He raised his cup of wine and drank slowly. She watched him carefully place the cup back on the table.

"I'm going for a walk."

"At this hour?" she asked.

"Yes, don't wait up for me."

"I won't."

"Good."

She waited until she heard him close the gate and then picked up his cup and hurled it at the door, the broken clay pieces resembling her broken heart. He always left! She wanted to scream at him sometimes, *"Be a man Malchus, get angry, yell back; tell me what you're really feeling. Are you happy? Sorry you married me? Mad at Caiaphas and your life? Struggling with your faith? Just say something!"*

She was tired of hearing what Caiaphas said, what Nicodemas thought. *What is your opinion Malchus? Do you have one?* She gave the table a little push, enough to make another cup fall off. She rested her head on her arms, "God of Abraham, I believe in Jesus. I believe you sent him to us. I don't understand everything but I know he's changing people. Let our hearts be right. Help us. Help Malchus."

He had been gone about an hour. She knew she hurt his feelings. There were contradicting voices filling their heads, she was tired of always defending her own. She thought him double-minded. When he was with Simon, Kezi and now Avi, he was patient and kind with a peace about him. She looked forward to their time spent asking each other questions, discussing what Jesus was doing, what the people at the market were saying, rejoicing at Joanna's healing, their hearts stirred when a new story reached them of the great crowds and miracles. But when it was just her, and he came home from Caiaphas and those he served alongside all day; he was a different person, cynical, short tempered and she had enough of it tonight.

How could one man cause so much division? But Jesus did. You either believed him or you didn't. It was simple. She chose to believe. She wanted him to make his choice. She could live with whatever he chose, *just make a decision!* His own words condemned him. There were several witnesses. Selah thought it was more like hundreds. *Why would a miracle anger him? What was buried in his own heart that needed to be resurrected?* She was willing to find out. She asked for complete honesty. They all had doubts. They were all skeptics at one time or another. *Caiaphas!* Malchus couldn't get away from him. He loathed Jesus. She couldn't imagine what was said behind closed doors. What did he think of this last report, a boy raised from the dead? No one could deny the miraculous. She heard movement outside.

Malchus stood at the gate. He knew Selah would be waiting. He had walked to Nicodemas' house. He stood in the shadows debating to knock on his door. Nicodemas had avoided him. Everyone was becoming paranoid. The more news they received about Jesus, the more distance Nicodemas kept. He felt foolish hiding and thought of the night Nicodemas himself hid in the dark seeking Jesus. One day he would tell the ruler he knew about his secret visit. Even the most learned instructor had sought instruction that night while he himself lived in the shadows of doubt and that's where he found confusion. He wrestled with his thoughts the entire day. *How could a man speak and command the dead to rise?* But it happened. He was standing behind Caiaphas when they were told of this latest phenomenon. He saw Caiaphas sway and thought he might fall back. Some days he wouldn't mind if he did hit the floor. Nicodemas smiled at the news. He found it odd. What was he thinking at that very second that brought a smile to his face when everyone else displayed shock and anger?

He tried to imagine himself at the city gate in the burial procession when in the distance Jesus and his followers began to come into focus. *Did the widow know who he was?* Sure, he healed people but my son, my only son is dead. *Did she think he stopped just to pay his respect?* They were told he touched the bier, told the young boy to rise and the boy sat up! He got chills.

The walls of Nicodemas' house felt smooth and he edged closer to the front. He couldn't bring himself to knock on the door. *What if Caiaphas was there, then what?* He could feel his heartbeat in his ear. It was a strange sensation. This past year had been strange. He couldn't count how many times he went to his tree waiting, hoping Nicodemas would come so they could speak. He actually thought they might become friends. He was mistaken. If anything, he seemed reluctant to acknowledge his presence. He started acting differently the day Simon spoke with him at the Temple. Perhaps he was protecting not only himself but all of us from the wrath of Caiaphas. He didn't fault him for his aloofness, he was too busy to let it bother him, but today, that smile, he couldn't keep it hidden.

He thought he was the only one who noticed. Nicodemas figured out the riddle. The smile was pure satisfaction, one that belonged to him only. It was to be kept stored, locked away until he deemed it useful. He enjoyed a good riddle, he hoped maybe if he happened upon him walking to or from his house, he would seize the opportunity to coax the ruler to spill it. The throbbing of his heart continued to echo in his ear. He wouldn't wait much longer. Nicodemas had probably retired for the evening. *Selah*. He needed to go home. He would apologize. This too was becoming a bad habit. Just because he was tired and frustrated when he arrived home didn't give him the right to take it out on his wife. She was tired too, on her feet most of the day saving what she earned so they could have a comfortable future and he walked out. She made his home a refuge, and he chose to stand in the dark in the middle of the night hoping to ask a Pharisee why he smiled. He cursed himself. Why he reacted the way he did baffled him. He pushed off the wall to walk home.

Simon was on his roof looking at his stars. He knew sleep wouldn't come easily. *A boy raised from the dead. How could anyone sleep?* He thought of the young boy, he wished he could speak with him. He had a few questions. That could have been Benjamin. He thought of Kezi and the absolute grief and sorrow turning into complete joy as life came back into the young body. The thought made him tear up. He had come to love his little helper and the day she let him take the boy to pick out his own little donkey was one of the best days of his life. The two had been inseparable. It had taken Kezi several weeks to convince Benjamin Gray could walk on his own. The small donkey gathered in his arms would actually rest his head on the boy's shoulder. He had never seen anything like it. He thought about picking up Balaam and he laughed out loud, *"Oh God I needed that laugh. It has been much too serious lately.*

We, I, can't understand what is happening in our land. What is my part?"
He fell asleep on his roof that night, content with his stars thinking
about each member of this new family of his.

They all had dreams, fears, worry and doubt but together they were
strong and he prayed he would have several more years with them. Kezi
and Selah had become true daughters, and he would do anything for
them and Malchus, the son he never had. The young man was troubled
in his mind but all men had their battles. He would sort it out one day
and he hoped soon especially for Selah's sake. She had changed the
most this past year. Kezi taught her the skills and savvy of a true merchant. She had gained confidence in her marriage and didn't shy away
from asking Malchus point blank questions about his daily activities.
She had taken Avi under her wing, the youngest of the women heart-
sick for Marcus. She had taken no interest in any other man. When
Selah voiced her concern, she would simply nod in Kezi's direction. She
was happy, had her own business, a son she would lay down her life for
and no man was involved. Selah couldn't argue.

Caiaphas lie awake, his wife's tossing and turning not the culprit
of his sleepless night. He was grinding his teeth until his jaw hurt.
*Madness! This is not a great prophet as Elijah, but it happened. Just as
Elijah raised the widow's son, now this Jesus did the same. What will he
do next? What could he do more miraculous than raising the dead? This
man needed to be stopped!* Preferring the region of Galilee was the only
good news Caiaphas had received as of late. The scribes and Pharisees
were making his life miserable. He agreed with most of their dissent.
The letter of the Law, it was their life and their breath. God. Not a man.
*This man Jesus was becoming dangerous, practically claiming he was equal
to God. Elijah didn't make these claims. How could these people be fooled?
What must he do to prevent any more deceit?* The moonlight streamed
through the terrace doors. He squinted observing his personal effects.
He loved this room, his home and the life he was living. There was
only one solution to ensure his comfort and sanity, get rid of Jesus. He
would seek every opportunity to discredit all he said and the works he
did and have Malchus begin to identify those closest to the Nazarene

while in Jerusalem. There had to be something, someone that would allow him to make his case against him. Until that day he feared all his nights would be restless.

Nicodemas lay awake also so his servants would gain no rest this night. He was cautious lately keeping to himself. He started preparing new lists. The writings of Daniel had gripped his mind as of late. Between Isaiah and Daniel, he lost sleep, weight and a few close friends. He had no social life. He sat now with his parchments covering his entire desk. He pulled out his most recent list.

Simon Peter and Andrew, brothers, fishermen from Bethsaida. James and John, brothers, sons of Zebedee, also fishermen. Philip from Bethsaida. Thaddeus and James, brothers. Bartholomew. Thomas. Matthew the tax collector. Simon and Judas Iscariot.

Three sets of brothers, uneducated, common men. He heard Jesus picked these twelve from all those following him. He chose men who were not learned. They left their livelihood to follow this man. *What was the intention?* He didn't think it had anything to do with Rome. No, this was from God. Healings were now commonplace. Jesus had raised the dead! He was casting out demons right and left and some said he even spoke to the sea and it obeyed. Surely God was with him but his words were becoming more controversial. It kept a man awake at night.

He felt lonely, sleep evading him every night this week. He wasn't prone to taking naps but fell asleep twice in meetings this week which didn't go unnoticed by several members including Caiaphas and Malchus. He caught Malchus staring at him. He attempted to smile and nod but it was insincere. Malchus hadn't done anything. It was unfair to treat him as insignificant. He didn't like living his life not trusting, always wondering what the true motives were of his contemporaries. He wasn't paranoid, he had nothing to hide with the exception of his secret meeting with Jesus. He suspected Malchus knew. He could only assume the friend Simon somehow overheard rumors in the market. He had no idea who was gathered that night around the fire. Should this Jesus become more radical in his speech, who knows what Caiaphas might do and all those who followed and were connected to him could face consequences. *Would he be included in a sweep of the city?*

"Who is Jesus?"

Kezi turned to see the big brown eyes of her son Benjamin.

"Mother, did you hear me?"

"Yes, what do you know about him?"

"I've heard you speak of him often and Selah and many others at the market."

"What do they say or what have you heard?"

"I've heard some call him a troublemaker," he said.

She gave a short laugh, "Go on."

"My friend says his father talks about him all the time, he's told me stories."

"What kind of stories?"

"He helps people."

"Yes, he does."

"Nathaniel's father said he raised someone from the dead. What does that mean?"

She sat down across from him. "We're born Benjamin and one day we will take our last breath and no longer live."

"We die? That's what Nathaniel told me."

"Yes."

"And a boy who was very sick died and Jesus brought him back to life. How did he do that?"

"I don't know Benjamin," she watched as he thought on her words. His brow would come together to meet his hairline.

"If he can bring people back to life, then why doesn't he do that for everyone? Nathaniel's grandmother died and she's still where they put her. Why doesn't Jesus bring her back to life? Nathaniel misses her."

"That's a very good question son and one I can't answer."

His large brown eyes stared past her. He was tapping his fingers on the table. "I also heard he can speak to the wind, to make it stop."

"Yes, I've heard this too."

"Do you believe that Kezi?"

Kezi. Why did he address me as Kezi, not mother?

"Yes Benjamin, I believe this to be true. All the stories, the things that have been said about Jesus, there are many witnesses, people who were there when these things happened."

The finger-tapping became harder. "He's only a man, how can a man do these things?"

"What do you think?"

"I don't know mother, that's why I'm asking."

Kezi's heart leapt, *he called her mother again.*

"What does your heart tell you Benjamin?"

"Nathaniel's father says he's from God. I think he must be. What do you think God is trying to tell us?"

"What do you mean?" she leaned in across the table.

"If Jesus is from God, and he's here doing these things that no one else can, why is he, I mean what is he, wait, I forgot what I wanted to say." He stopped tapping and rested his face in both hands, looking down at his feet.

"There's a reason he's here, that's what I wanted to say. Why is he here mother doing all these things? Did God send him here? Where did he come from? Do you think if he comes back to Jerusalem, I could ask him these things? Do you mother?"

"These are big questions you ask. I wish I had answers for you. What I do know is that God loves you very much, and I'm so thankful he sent you to me, and when he comes back to Jerusalem, I think he would love to answer your questions."

"You think God sent me to you?" She could only nod.

"I hope he does come back. I have many more questions."

The chains around Barabbas' wrist made him curse out loud, his fellow prisoners in the same agony. They laughed as he tried to escape the iron clutches. He wondered who sold him out. He knew his friends would vehemently deny any betrayal. The Romans and their smugness made him spit. His plan had been thwarted. He never expected to be arrested. He was knocked unconscious when brought before Pilate after his guards supposed he lurched toward the Prefect in an attempt to do bodily harm. How he wanted to wipe that smirk off his face permanently. He was hopeful the uprising and movement he started would be carried out even though he was unable to lead locked in these chains. He was hungry. The city had begun to welcome all those making their way to celebrate Passover. He could smell cook fires through the only small opening above his head. He expected only some stale bread and a cup of sour wine. The stench of his cell was overwhelming and caused him to vomit over the last occupants. He slid down the wall feeling hopeless.

Malchus and Selah sat under his tree, the sun warming their faces. This would be the last opportunity until after Passover, the streets already swelling with their countrymen.

"I could stay here all day."

He looked at his wife. Her eyes were closed, her face lifted up to receive the sun's rays. She looked beautiful today. Her face was peaceful. She had no lines, no freckles; her youth still prevalent. They were not alone otherwise he would have kissed her just then. His grove was a favorite to camp. They both would be busy this next week. He didn't want to think about work on such a lovely day. Caiaphas expected trouble. For once it wasn't all about Jesus, but Barabbas who stirred the people. They shouted their discontent when they felt safe to do so with no risk of being arrested or brought before the council. He heard they wanted to make Jesus king and now this loudmouth, brazen Barabbas had turned the people's hearts towards violence. There was great confusion in the city. Some hoped for a complete overthrow of all Roman presence. He knew this wouldn't happen. The followers of Jesus hoped and prayed he would be the "one" to right all wrongs. He didn't think this would happen either. Caiaphas would see to it and quite possibly have Jesus arrested and thrown in with Barabbas, and let the best man win.

"What are you thinking about?" she began to unpack their lunch.

"I was thinking how beautiful you look."

"You were not thinking of me just now, I can tell."

He lowered his voice, "I have a bad feeling."

"What Malchus?"

"This Passover, I think there will be trouble."

"Why?"

"Do you really want to discuss these things on such a wonderful day?"

"You're right, I don't. Can I ask one question?"

"Of course," he replied.

"Is it because of Jesus?" she watched his eyes for any hint of doubt, anger or annoyance.

"They want to make him king. This has not set well with Herod, Caiaphas or anyone."

"What do you think?" she asked.

"About possible trouble?"

"No, about Jesus."

She saw the clenched jaw, the annoyance she hoped was in the past. "Malchus, he's raising the dead. This man Lazarus, his friend, many know him and," she stopped.

"Selah, I do not wish to speak about this."

"He is coming."

"What did you say?"

"He'll be here soon. Many are talking at the market. I'm frightened for him Malchus."

"What have you heard?"

"I thought you didn't want to talk about him," she saw the flash of anger in his eyes. "This man has done incredible things. There are stories he has walked on the water! He has to be from God! I don't care if you want to call him King, the One, the Son of God, the Christ, Messiah, it doesn't matter to me. I believe he is all."

He swallowed.

She continued, "No one can deny his words and his wisdom, let alone the miracles, and I want to know, no, I need to know Malchus, what my husband thinks of this man," she came closer spilling the cup of wine he poured. "This is important to me Malchus. Who do you think Jesus is?"

The look that was now in his eyes made her sit back. She had crossed a line. It was too personal for him, especially here, exposed and in his safe place, his tree, a place he felt vulnerable, a place he had coveted, one he freely was now sharing with her and she just ruined it. This wasn't a conversation he wanted to have in his sanctuary. She invaded his space, his mind, his heart and he didn't like it. He rose up quickly and she knew their afternoon was over.

"Malchus wait!"

"No Selah, I want to leave now. I'm not hungry and I just wanted one day away from everything!"

"I understand Malchus but I'm your wife. Can we not have a conversation?"

"We can, but not about Jesus."

"Why do you have such difficulty speaking about him with me? A husband and wife should be able to openly talk about anything. We made a covenant agreement when we married."

"You don't have to remind me of this. Why is it so important to you to know how I feel about everything all the time?"

"Malchus, I don't ask you about everything all the time, but..."

"But what Selah?"

"Never mind, let's go home," she gathered their things and begin walking as quickly as she could. She could hear him scrambling to keep up and this would have made her smile but not today. He kept her at arm's length, she wanted more intimacy. If they couldn't share their desires, their private thoughts and their hopes and dreams, she might as well be single. They didn't speak all the way home. She kept her head down. She didn't want to speak to anyone. Except Kezi. She could always talk with her friend.

She felt like telling him to go home without her so she could go to her house and vent! *What had turned her husband's heart cold? Caiaphas? The Pharisees? Had they poisoned his mind with their self-righteous works? Where was their love for the common man, their concern for their neighbor?* She didn't understand his hesitation to talk about Jesus. It was just them, alone under his tree, enjoying a sunny day. She heard a few people greet him as they approached their neighborhood. He grunted his reply.

He slammed the door when he came inside. She turned.

"You don't walk away from me!" his face was red. She knew it was from anger, not the sun.

"I didn't walk away Malchus, we were walking home. You were the first one to stand up to leave," she stood her ground.

"Why is it so important to you to know what I'm thinking about all the time?" he asked.

"It's not."

"Then why did you get upset and storm off?"

"I didn't."

"Selah you're making me angry!"

"Well Malchus you make me angry sometimes also."

"Why are you so obsessed with Jesus?"

She just stared at him. *Is he out of his mind?* She didn't know where to begin.

"Malchus, you're the one who tells me how Caiaphas is the one obsessed with him and the Pharisees and that's all you hear all day so I don't think I'm the one obsessed."

"You don't know what you're talking about."

"Are you serious Malchus? Every night when you come home you mumble about your long meetings with Caiaphas complaining how everyone talks about Jesus, what he's done, what did he say, where is he now. Is this not true?"

He stood, his hands at his side. She softened her voice.

"Why are you so upset? I just want to know how my husband personally feels about Jesus. That's all. We've spoken about him these past years with our friends and all the wonderful things he's done, why does this question bother you? I don't understand."

He didn't either. He wasn't mad at her. He was mad at himself. He didn't understand his outburst either.

"I'm going out," he slammed the door again with the same intensity.

She sat and looked at the door. She didn't want to take her problems to Kezi. She busied herself preparing her home for Passover. She wondered if he would go back to his tree. She was tempted to go there herself. It was a peaceful spot until today. Maybe that's why he got angry, she brought discord to the place he called his sanctuary. Still, his reaction was unwarranted. She rested her head on her arms and tried to block out the noise from outside. The sun remained strong and streamed in, basking her in its warmth. She needed this hug from a friend. Her afternoon turned cold. She raised her head and looked at their home. The latch on the door looked broken from his hasty and loud exit, the rug lying at the base seemed incapable of catching any fallen pieces of splintered wood. Her curtains were faded. She remembered the day she hung them.

It was home, and it had been filled with laughter and love. At least she believed it had. *Had she been a fool? Was he pretending all this time in their marriage?* Her mind was swirling, connecting every moment, every part of this life in Jerusalem and she began to question every motive, every decision. The women often stared at her almost in disgust as she went to work outside of the home and God forbid, she didn't have children and would buy bread and oil. She loathed the olive press. It took forever! Why waste time when she could purchase it every day if needed at the market. Did he care that she wasn't home barefoot and pregnant huddled around a courtyard fire gossiping with the neighbor women? Kezi understood exactly how she felt about these things. She thought maybe one day she would return to the sea and open her own shop. She sat up abruptly. *Malchus wasn't in her future!* Her vision didn't include him. She panicked almost as if wherever he was at this very moment, he could sense she hadn't included him in her seaside future. She sat with her mouth open staring at nothing. She sat this way the rest of the afternoon.

Marcus stood looking directly at the sun. He missed Avi. There were several ships in the distance. *Would one carry her to this rocky shore?* Her Passover ceremonies would begin soon. He needed to make a decision. *Would she be happy to see him? Has she found another?* His letter from Joanna he carried with him, the parchment cracking when he read the words she penned. She is well. Her heart longs for love. The letter was written several months ago. Marcus hoped her longing remained. He couldn't bear it if she married and started a family. He truly believed they were meant to be together. Through time, they could work out their philosophies and differences. Her passion for her faith in this unknown god is what attracted him to her and after spending time with the small circle of friends at their Passover dinner, he realized they all shared the same passion. This unity was their strength! Avi wouldn't be moved. She was as solid as the rocks he stood upon. He glanced around. The women here were moved by the latest show performed at the local theater. He shielded his eyes, the sun's reflection off one of the ships coming into port temporarily made him divert his gaze out over the endless sea. He breathed in the air and listened to shouts behind him as men became alert at the approaching cargo. His palms were sweaty, not from the heat of the day but from his decision. He would go to Jerusalem.

Kezi was so happy, she thought it might be a sin. Business was good, Avi and Selah were dear friends, Simon like an old crotchety father to her and Benjamin, her heart, her joy, her everything. He had literally shot up like a weed the past summer and now taller than her. No one came to her shop to see her anymore. They all came to see him. He was a handsome boy. He preferred selling vegetables to beads and that was fine with her. There were many days she and Simon sat watching and observing his natural abilities in the market. He knew the people. He knew what they liked and everyone loved him. She smiled to herself. She taught him to be respectful, polite and he had a charm about him no one could deny. One flash of a smile and direct look with those eyes and even the "experienced" women of the city would blush. Simon and Malchus spent considerable time with him teaching him all they knew. He could build anything. She had come home to small cages and other creations on more than one occasion.

"Really Benjamin, what do you plan on doing with all this?"

"I don't know, I like to work with my hands and build things."

His donkey Gray had benefited the most. He had his own house. She made him share it with her cart and liked the extra storage, and of course, Balaam had his own room when he was an overnight guest. No one would believe she had an inn for donkeys. He kept it clean; he and Simon would spend hours hammering away. For her birthday he made her a beautiful olive wood bowl and fashioned a metal handle for carrying it, but the feature that made her gasp when she opened it, were the beads he had threaded the metal with so the handle was smooth and decorative. She sold dozens during the fall feasts. She gave him all the proceeds and began to teach him the art of buying and selling. He was anxious to travel to discover exotic items he only heard about.

"When will the men from the East be here?" he asked her over dinner.

"From the East?" she asked.

"Yes, the caravans that bring goods on the trade routes."

"Would you like to travel to meet them on the main roads they enter?"

"Yes! Can we? When? Show me mother on the table where this road is!"

He handed her his cup and cleared the area between them as she used the items on the table.

"Decapolis," she stated.

"I would like to take two cages with me."

"Do you plan on trapping an animal?"

"Mother." "Simon said there were birds, colorful birds and some who could talk! I would like to see a talking bird. Can you imagine mother?"

"No, I cannot. All this time Simon has never mentioned a talking bird."

His eyes would light up when he dreamed about seeing places for the first time. Marcus told him how he crossed the sea to his home and of course Rome. Simon explained the aqueducts and other architecture and achievements of the Romans and he couldn't imagine what the city must look like. Yes, the Temple was magnificent, but it was only one building. He desired to see a whole city of splendor. He was very curious. He would ask questions and if someone didn't have the answer, she saw frustration and disappointment. This is life she would tell him. We all have questions that remain unanswered. His inquiries of God, Moses and the Law became more frequent. She was thankful for both Simon and Malchus to address them, but she continued to see the same frustration.

"What about Jesus?"

Both Simon and Malchus looked at each other waiting for the other to answer.

"Unfortunately, Benjamin, there are many questions about him also left unanswered."

He could rattle off a dozen questions not giving them time to answer one. They would look at Kezi to intervene but she never did.

"Where is Jesus now? Where does he go when he leaves Jerusalem? Have you ever spoken with him? How old is he? Where's he from? Why does he make so many people angry? Did he really raise the dead? What do you think he wants? Who are those men that travel with him? Does he work? Is he rich? Do you think he's the Messiah?"

He wore everyone out. Simon and Malchus were patient. They would try to remember all his questions in the order he asked and attempt to answer the young boy. Simon loved him like a grandson. He would rattle off his answers as quickly as he could knowing Benjamin got a kick out of him.

"I don't know where Jesus is right now. I've heard he travels all over teaching and preaching. I met him, but have never spoken with him. I don't know how old he is but I would say he's younger than me. He's from the region of Galilee, grew up in Nazareth I've been told. He doesn't make everyone angry. I think yes, he did raise the dead. Maybe he wants a talking bird."

"Simon!" Kezi began to laugh with Benjamin but he got back on track.

"The men are his disciples, like all rabbis have. Like you Benjamin, I heard he was a carpenter, likes making things. I don't think he's rich. I know many people give him money and support what he's doing."

"What about my last question Simon?"

"Yes, a difficult one. I don't know for certain Benjamin but I do think we'll know soon."

Malchus turned to his friend. "Why do you say that?"

"How long can this go on? You yourself have said they've tried to arrest him several times. Sooner or later something has to take place that we'll know exactly who he is."

"I think Simon is right," Kezi said. We know how Caiaphas feels about him and his influence. It's just a matter of time."

Her eyes told them she didn't want them to say anymore in front of him. He was smart but this political climate with Rome and the economic ramifications didn't need to be discussed with a ten-year-old boy. She placed her hands on his shoulders as he sat at the table.

"It's complicated son. We must wait sometimes for answers to our questions. Why did Simon go out that night walking with Balaam?

Where would you be now if he didn't? Can I ever love anything or anyone more than you? That's the only question I have an answer to."

"Mother," he promptly kissed her cheek and the frayed leather bracelet with the two red beads she held against her other cheek. Without turning around, he called out to Simon, "Big baby".

Simon's sniffles and Malchus' laughter were the last two things she heard echo through her home as the men departed.

Caiaphas waited until everyone was seated. He'd given tremendous thought over the last year to the consequences of his life as he knew it would be if compromised. It was abundantly clear to him Jesus was compromise. He couldn't afford to dip into the treasury much more to go unnoticed. Malchus had no idea why he called this meeting. It was late. He heard grumbling from every man as their dinner plans were interrupted. They slowly sauntered in, their faces clearly displaying their disdain for the personal intrusion this night. Caiaphas stood waiting for complete silence. He wouldn't repeat his words. He convinced himself his motives were for the good of Israel, that's all that mattered. Nicodemas and the others sat waiting. Malchus exchanged greetings with all of them, Caiaphas didn't.

"Gentleman, Passover is only a few days away. I intend to arrest Jesus for blasphemy and have made arrangements with one of his disciples for the opportunity," he held his hands up to quiet the murmuring. "Every time this Nazarene comes to Jerusalem, its complete madness and I will put an end to it! Many of you have spoken with me privately and I know you're in agreement."

Many were now turning in their seats, Malchus kept his eyes on Nicodemas.

"I've spoken with Pilate; he has guaranteed his full cooperation to control the crowds. I will not have this, this liar, blaspheme our God one more time. That is all. Goodnight."

Malchus was torn. Did he run after Caiaphas or stay and listen to the others and report later? Nicodemas hadn't moved. Caiaphas' words hung in the air and those who already digested them at a prior meeting were on their feet, nodding their agreement. He understood his point.

It was sickening to him, but he understood. They would arrest Jesus; he would settle down after time in prison and then hopefully return to Galilee and conform. He thought this the best solution. Nicodemas slipped out and he waited until all left the inner chamber. He prayed Jesus wouldn't come, or that he would simply celebrate Passover like everyone else. The city had been quiet, Barabbas was still being held; his followers not seen for several months.

The Pharisees said most of the stories that reached the city were false claims, however many still hoped and believed. He now sat alone letting Caiaphas' words sink in. *What did he expect of him? What was his involvement? Selah. This will devastate her and Kezi, Simon, Joanna, and Mary. I can't be involved. What do I do?* It was dark now. He relished the quiet. He listened. He could hear the night rounds of the priests beginning to prepare the Temple for its slumber. He loved the stillness of the room. In a few days no, hours, the noise of the city would chase all stillness away. He needed to speak to Caiaphas. *Was he lying? One of Jesus's disciples had made arrangements to provide the opportunity to betray Jesus? When did this occur?* The Pharisees no doubt knew of his movements, where he spent his time when coming to Jerusalem and Bethany. Perhaps this disciple went unnoticed, traveled to Jerusalem to seek Caiaphas out. Caiaphas must have been fooled! He would ask the name of this disciple. *Would Caiaphas lie to the Sanhedrin? To Nicodemas? Probably.*

Last week when Jesus rode into the city upon that donkey, the crowds went crazy. The people were shouting, waving palm branches, some calling him King of the Jews. When news got back to Caiaphas, he immediately went to Pilate, no doubt that's when the plan to arrest Jesus was finally made plausible for both political and economic reasons. Perhaps one of his disciples had second thoughts about who he was. There was much confusion surrounding Jesus. He believed God was using him, but the Messiah? People in the markets were saying he was fulfilling prophecy. He had more followers but could they overthrow Rome? He didn't think so. Maybe he should tell Simon and Kezi about the risk of him coming back for Passover and they could travel to Bethany and warn him. He wouldn't have to be involved any further with whatever took place. The stillness enabled him to think. He sat for another hour.

Simon felt lonely today. Even in the crowds at the market he felt lost in a sea of uncertainty. This was unusual for him and unwelcomed. His life had been full the past few years so he didn't understand this sudden emotion of loneliness, almost abandonment. He tried to shake it off but couldn't. He asked Benjamin to watch the cart and found a place to sit literally in the cracks of a wall, hidden from the pushing crowds. He hoped for an escape for just a few moments to clear this oppression. He looked at the sky. It was clear. He expected dark, gray ominous clouds covering all of Jerusalem. He began searching the faces of those in the market today. Most were focused purchasing their needs for the Passover celebration, watching over their children, the stresses of the day apparent only on a few. Simon thought some looked as despondent as he was feeling. *What is it God?* He closed his eyes to concentrate. The noise of the market a slow hum in his ears. There was fear in the street. Only a few days ago it was joy! Young boys had run into the market shouting, "He's coming!" "Jesus is coming!" "Hurry!" "Come and see!"

They were not prepared to see the people lined up waving palm branches as Jesus rode upon a donkey, everyone rejoicing, some began to lay down their coats. They were shouting, "Hosanna! Blessed is he who comes in the name of the LORD!"

Some called him King of Israel! There was majesty in the air. He couldn't think of another word to describe what he witnessed. It had been unlike any other celebration he attended and now this heaviness. *Most unfortunate* he mumbled to himself. He noticed several older women pointing at him. Benjamin was probably wondering about him. He would think on this later if the feeling didn't pass.

Kezi watched Simon. She had the advantage. He had wedged himself between two stone walls and found a temporary hiding place until the owner could repair the crumbling limestone. She worried about him. He was quiet this morning, leaving the women to chatter on about the events of the last few days. She caught Benjamin staring at him too. Now he seemed to be talking to himself which wasn't unusual, but when he dropped his head into his hands, it took all her strength not to rush to his side. If he wasn't feeling well, he would tell her. He liked to be fussed over. She smiled at this thought while never taking her eyes off her precious friend. Selah and Avi were busy unaware of her post. Both Balaam and Gray were brought to the market today. There were too many travelers in the city to leave them unattended. Benjamin had them positioned around Simon's cart.

He turned now and looked to where Simon disappeared and then back to Kezi. He too had been watching. She only nodded. Ever since this boy came into her life they could communicate with a simple nod. Her life began the night Simon brought him to her door and all the years before him were a faint memory. *Simon.* She thanked God for him every day too. He was more visible now but still he sat. He was looking at the people. She turned. It was a normal day at the market. He was talking to himself again. She knew him well enough this wasn't his enduring mumbling about Balaam eating his profits or Malchus calling him an old man, this was different.

She could see from this distance the confusion he wore. Again, Benjamin looked at his mother. There were no customers and she shook her head no. That look asked, *Should I go see what's wrong?* The boy loved him and she watched him pretend to adjust the donkey's tethering so he could move closer to his retreat. She almost burst out laughing at both her son's antics and his slight rebellion. Balaam's braying had Simon on his feet and he slowly walked back. She would invite him for dinner this evening. Perhaps he was lonely. They all had been busy and tired and went home each evening without any fellowship. Benjamin's smile warmed her heart. He said something to Simon that evoked the wide toothless grin. Selah was calling for her but she stood. *What did Simon see?* He was looking at the sky again and she did also. The sun hurt her eyes, the sky clear, not a cloud in sight, but Simon, he looked as if he expected a storm any minute.

Malchus went home to rest. He hurried inside and latched the door. Selah wouldn't be home for hours. He undressed to lay down. He closed his eyes but his mind was racing and he knew sleep wouldn't come. *Caiaphas!* He wasn't a smart man but he saw right through his intentions and motives. What troubled him the most is he not only would benefit from this selfishness but somehow would use him in this last attempt to arrest Jesus and hopefully somehow banish him from Jerusalem. He thought anything was possible, Herod held John the Baptist for almost two years and his end was tragic. *Is this what Caiaphas had in mind?* Arrest him, not allow visitors, weaken his spirit, his resolve, to silence him and eventually all those who professed him to be the Christ?

His eyes were heavy but now as he laid here in the quiet, he wanted to devise a strategy. How could he say no to Caiaphas? *Breathe Malchus,* he told himself. Caiaphas may have other plans and duties for you. His life was not his own. Caiaphas would expect him to remain at his side or go wherever he told him to personally witness his orders were carried out. He and Pilate were much alike in that regard. He saw a hint of respect in the soldiers who were commanded to enforce the Prefect's whims. He hoped it would be a simple arrest and with all the celebrating no one would notice. Perhaps Caiaphas and Pilate had joined efforts and Jesus would be escorted to a prison far from Jerusalem. It would only be a matter of time when he would be forgotten and everyone could resume their lives.

He finally closed his eyes. Images danced before him. Selah, her eyes wide with wonder as Mary recounted the past couple years traveling with Jesus. The man on the boat challenging him to follow his heart. The blind man walking through the Temple declaring he could now see. Jesus overturning the tables. Nicodemas meeting him at his tree. Simon calling him son. The disciples surrounding their Rabbi as the crowds became unruly. Kezi and Simon celebrating Sukkot at this very house and the nights filled with love and laughter. He laughed, but the stillness of the room swallowed his outburst. *Jesus.* Quiet. *Jesus,* he repeated. He kept his eyes closed. The last image he remembered was Jesus riding on that donkey, the people calling out his name as they showed honor waving palm branches. He turned to Caiaphas to see his stone-cold expressionless face, his eyes as black as pitch.

Selah knocked on the door several minutes until Malchus finally unlatched the door.

"What's going on Malchus?"

"I was sleeping."

"Why were you sleeping?"

"I was tired," he responded.

"In the middle of the day?"

"Yes."

"What aren't you telling me?"

"Nothing."

"Have you been drinking?" she asked boldly.

"What?"

"Drinking, with your so-called friends."

"Selah, I haven't had any wine today, don't start."

"Is that a warning? You know Malchus you're unbelievable!"

"Selah, I told you I was just tired. I came home to take a nap and if I want to have a cup of wine with my so-called friends I will. Its Passover week, a time to celebrate."

She wanted to wipe the grin off his face. He had been drinking entirely too much for her liking. He embarrassed her in front of Kezi and Mary the evening Mary came to visit. It had been a memorable day, Jesus and his followers parading into the city with shouts of praise and he came home drunk! Kezi saw Mary's reaction to his slight swaying and garbled speech and quickly gathered her things to leave. She was so angry asking why he drank so much she could hardly make out what he was saying.

"I saw a monster!" He was leaning on the table trying to remove his sandals. "He was scary looking!" he began to laugh but she wasn't amused.

"Malchus, poor Mary, you just frightened her!"

"Well the scary monster frightened me!" he fell to the floor.

"Malchus!" She helped him to the mat. "Just go to sleep Malchus."

"Don't leave me Selah."

"I'm not going anywhere."

"Lock the door!" he shouted.

"Malchus, are you in trouble?"

"No monster here."

"What monster Malchus?"

"Black eyes."

"The monster has black eyes?"

"Yes."

She removed his other sandal and brought him some water. She held his head as he emptied the cup. He looked over her shoulder at the door.

"Don't let him in Selah."

"Who Malchus?"

"Caiaphas."

Now as she stood toe-to-toe with him, he didn't smell like he'd been drinking. Perhaps he was telling the truth.

"Malchus, I'm only concerned, the other night."

"Yes, the other night I had been drinking, but today I haven't."

"Are you hungry?" she finally laid down her bag she came home with.

"No, I still feel tired."

"How long have you been home?" she examined the room, he caught her.

"What are you doing Selah?"

"I'm not doing anything Malchus."

"Why are you looking around like you're trying to see if I'm telling you the truth? How could you possibly tell how long I've been here by the mat on the floor?"

"Malchus, don't do this."

"I've been here for a while. How long, I don't know, but now I'm leaving."

"Leaving?"

"Yes, I'm going out to find some of my so-called friends."

"Malchus! Why are you doing this? You seem like you want to pick a fight with me. What did I do wrong?"

"You don't trust me."

"I want to Malchus."

"But you don't."

She stood once again to a slammed door and an empty house. She thought about following him, with the overcrowded streets he may not notice. She went around back. Balaam looked surprised, he just settled in from a long day at the market.

"Grab your blanket Balaam, we're going to Kezi's."

Courtyards were alive with children playing and women preparing dinner. She was approached as she had been previously by those looking for a place to stay. She kept her head down, the path to Kezi's one of memory now that afforded her time to think. Kezi would know what to do, what to say or not say. Benjamin came out of the house at the sound of Gray's warning they were approaching. And then she saw Simon. He took one look at her.

"Malchus?"

Her lips began to quiver. She nodded. He took Balaam from her and called to Benjamin. He didn't want the boy to see her upset and she hurried into Kezi's.

"Selah what a surprise, I..."

The tears were now flowing down her face.

"Selah, what's happened now?" she knew it was Malchus. She didn't look for him. "Did he come home drunk again?"

"No, but later may be a different story. I can't say anything to him without him becoming angry."

"Why don't you have dinner with us and then Simon can walk you home?"

She nodded and wiped her eyes before Simon and Benjamin walked in.

The two women embraced; their friendship strong. Hours passed and she became worried Malchus would come home to find her gone.

"Simon, I need to go now. I have Balaam, I'll be all right to go alone."

"That's not going to happen. We'll leave now. I need to walk off this dinner."

"What does that mean?" Benjamin asked.

"He ate too many honey cakes!" Kezi replied.

"Balaam can stay here with Gray and I'll bring them in the morning."

"Good idea my boy. I'll come by and help."

"I can manage Simon."

"Oh, you can manage, well I keep forgetting you're a young man."

"Thank you, Benjamin. We could probably walk faster without him."
Selah looped her arm through Simon's, "It's just me and you Simon."

"Just like old times. I'm worried about our Malchus."

"Simon, will you speak with him? He seems so angry lately, and I, I seem to make him angry."

"Passover is the day after tomorrow. He'll be busy," he looked down at her. He wanted to reassure her things would work out, but after today and the overwhelming feeling he had, he wasn't sure. He had retreated into a crack in the wall. Things were stirring in his heart he couldn't describe to anyone. He reasoned to himself all afternoon it was his imagination, yet this foreboding he couldn't dismiss.

"Where do you think he is right this very minute?" Simon stopped so she could have his full attention.

"I honestly don't know. It's like he's looking for an excuse to leave."

"To leave you?" Simon hated asking.

"Apparently so," she wanted to cry but tears wouldn't come. She was just as angry as Malchus had been. "It's this city!"

He stopped again. "Selah, what are you saying?"

"I don't know Simon. You remember how he was when we went to Galilee, Malchus was relaxed and different."

"We all were on a break from our lives. We've had fun here too! I don't think it's the city Selah."

"It's Caiaphas," she said.

"That could be true."

"It's these Romans and what does Malchus call it, politics! It's the Temple and the guards, Pilate, Herod, everyone, even Jesus," she almost whispered his name.

"Jesus?" He stopped again.

"I think Jesus upsets Malchus. He never wants to discuss him. I know how Caiaphas feels, but Simon, I truly believe Malchus believes in him. That man on the boat! All the marvelous things we've heard! So why does it upset him? He won't talk to me. He leaves mad and then comes home full of wine."

"It sounds like he's troubled about something. He's turning to wine so he doesn't have to confront it. And you think it's about Jesus? That's all?"

"Yes, what else could it be?"

"I don't know. There's much confusion lately. I have felt it. It's as if…"

"What Simon?" Selah needed answers that made sense.

"As if a big storm is coming."

"Simon! I just got gooseflesh!"

"Hurry now, let's get you home. We can't worry about what we don't know. Let's see if Malchus is home."

Malchus never came home. Selah didn't think she could live this way. She actually knew she wouldn't. She loved him, worried about him, but this anger, this temper of his she couldn't tolerate. She began to cry. She was at a loss of what to do. She couldn't breathe. She felt sick. Before she reached the door, she vomited. She began to cry again. Slowly she stood and filled a bowl with water, her tears like raindrops as they fell. She rinsed out her undergarment and dressed. She sat at her table in the early morning hours waiting for the sun. She would wait for him. She would tell him he could dismiss her because she would be leaving. She vomited again.

Chapter Eleven

Caiaphas rose early. Today was the day his trouble would end. He had thought this through, every angle he calculated. It would be a good day. How fitting it was Passover. His people were delivered from their enemy's centuries before, and he would be delivered from his enemy the same day. A smile formed at his lips. Thirty pieces of silver. The disciple of Jesus would inform him where this blasphemer was so he could be arrested. Money well spent he thought. The treasury could well afford this pittance of a sum. He found Malchus asleep on his porch. Faithful servant or drunken fool, it didn't matter today. Nothing mattered except his plan to be fully executed.

"Malchus!" "Wake up!"

He began tapping his foot in annoyance. It was dark when Malchus opened his eyes, an empty wineskin by his side. He soon realized the noise hurting his head was from Caiaphas' foot. He tried to hide the wineskin.

"Don't bother Malchus. Go home to your wife before the sun comes up and get some sleep. I need you back here later."

His eyes were blurry. He could hardly focus on his steps. He knew Selah wouldn't be happy. He hoped he would find her asleep. The neighbor women lowered their eyes when he stumbled through the gate. This behavior had become commonplace. He half waved at them and attempted to walk as straight as he could. He found the door unlatched. Perhaps she left early. The market would be packed today with travelers. He needed to sleep.

"So, you finally decided to come home," her voice startled him.

"Yes, and I'm tired so I do not wish to speak Selah. I need sleep."

He knocked over the bowl of water she placed on the table and cursed under his breath. His words were unintelligible. She was sitting up by the time he made it to the floor. He didn't look her way. He was asleep within a few minutes. She watched his body move under his heavy breathing and was amazed she still felt love for him. She was unhappy. She would tell Simon today that she would give him an ultimatum. Stop the drink, come home at a decent hour or choose her. Quietly she dressed and left.

She walked with confidence. She didn't want to leave but her pride wouldn't allow her to stay if he didn't change his ways. She wondered if he would wake up soon or sleep the day away. Surely Caiaphas needed him at the Temple. Maybe she should ask Simon to check on him in a couple of hours. No. He was a grown man! This is what upset her. He was acting like a child. He couldn't engage in conversation without getting mad and storming out. He was on his own today. He had displayed irrational behavior. She felt sick again. Her nerves were on edge. She never knew who or what to expect when he came home. She hadn't realized she was a few steps from Kezi's when she heard Avi calling out to her.

"Good morning!"

"Good morning Avi, are we the first ones here?"

"Yes, I think we're going to be busy today."

"I hope so, Kezi is already making plans for new merchandise!"

The women knew what to do. They started bringing items to the front table when Kezi arrived. Shortly after Simon and Benjamin came with donkeys in tow. The day flew by. Selah didn't have a chance to speak to Simon or Kezi and none of them discussed Passover dinner. It was late afternoon when Simon came inside Kezi's tent leaving Benjamin at his cart.

"What's everyone doing for dinner?" he looked at the women who stopped what they were doing at his inquiry.

"I hadn't thought about it!" Kezi looked at Selah.

"I'm not sure when Malchus will be home. I guess I didn't think about it either."

"I'll be home with my family," Avi said. "Everyone is welcome."

"Thank you Avi, I'll need to check with Malchus."

"I may need to leave a little early Kezi to let my mother know," Avi seemed nervous to have invited additional people.

"Well none of us prepared. I can't believe it! It's been so busy this year and I thought perhaps," Kezi didn't finish as a man entered the tent.

"Joses!" Simon went to embrace his friend. "What are you doing here?"

"Inviting everyone to my home for Passover!"

"We were just discussing how none of us planned this year."

"Then it's settled! We have plenty! Everyone please, come."

"Can you believe Selah, none of us prepared for Passover? Where's Malchus? Will he be home soon?"

"I should probably leave to find out. I don't know if he'll want to go to Joses' house. Will you go Kezi?"

"Yes, and you should too."

"Malchus may have duties."

"Caiaphas would keep him through dinner?"

"Probably, who knows?" She didn't want to have this conversation. She could feel the emotion start to rise again.

"Why don't you go, see if he's there and we'll come to get you. We'll have time," Kezi watched her gather her things.

It was obvious she wasn't happy or not feeling well. She took a quick look at the shop before leaving. Avi had been doing a great job. Everything was in order except the young girl's life. She didn't seem happy either. Something was going on with Malchus, and Simon! She still hadn't spoken to him about his behavior. Dinner somewhere else would hopefully take everyone's minds off of whatever was troubling them. She called for Benjamin and Simon. The three of them hurried through the crowded streets.

Rumors were flying all day about men who followed Barabbas starting an uproar to challenge his release. Mary told her she was concerned for the safety of Jesus, and his disciples asked him to not come to Jerusalem. It had been a strange week. Benjamin ran and knocked on the door. Selah looked like she had been crying, her eyes red and puffy. Malchus stood behind her.

"Hello Malchus!" Benjamin went in to greet him.

Selah looked at Kezi, "Malchus has to go back to Caiaphas' house, he won't be joining us for dinner."

"Oh, I'm sorry," she tried to not stare at Malchus. Simon was speaking with him. "You're still coming, aren't you?"

"Yes, I don't want to stay home alone," Selah half smiled attempting to show her she was fine.

Kezi turned to Malchus, "So, Caiaphas doesn't allow his servants to celebrate Passover with their families?"

"Kezi, it's not that. I can't speak of the reason he wants me close by."

"We'll miss you," Benjamin finally said. "Shall we bring you some food?"

"Thank you, Benjamin, but I'm sure I'll have something to eat."

"Malchus, is there anything we can do?" Simon seemed concerned.

"We should go," Kezi began walking towards the door to leave, Selah and Benjamin right behind her but Simon stayed at his side. He placed his hand on his shoulder, something he hadn't done for a long time only because he hadn't the chance.

"Are you alright son?" He noticed he just stared after Selah waiting until he thought she or Kezi couldn't hear them speak.

"What is it Malchus? Are you in trouble?" He kept an eye on the door for the women.

"No, I just, I don't know Simon; I'm in the middle of things."

"What things?"

"I can't say."

"Can't or won't?" Simon was a little offended at his lack of trust.

"Listen, go enjoy your friends. If I can get away, I'll join you."

Simon didn't move. "It's Passover Malchus. Is there anything I can do?"

"No."

"This week has been difficult," Simon wouldn't release his hand off his shoulder.

"What do you mean Simon?"

"I don't know. I feel as if something big is going to happen."

Malchus wanted to sit, he felt his knees give way.

Simon continued, "Like a storm is coming."

"A storm?"

"Yes, you know when the wind ceases to blow and its still, and you sense the slightest drop of temperature and sometimes you can smell the rain, but that calm before the storm, that's what I have felt all week. It's unnatural."

Malchus only listened. He knew the old man had more to say.

"All these people in our city coming to celebrate, the streets are crowded, there's, what's the word, anticipation, yet there's this heaviness."

"Heaviness?" Malchus asked.

"I can feel it Malchus. I can't explain it. It's almost as if I'm watching a play," he looked out to see Kezi and Selah talking. He turned back to Malchus.

"The other day, I sat and watched the people in the market, like I wasn't there, but I was. I kept looking up at the sky waiting to see dark clouds race to shower them with thunder and lightning, but the day was clear and beautiful."

"Simon, I don't know what you're talking about. Perhaps I should be asking you if you're all right."

Malchus led the way hoping his old friend wouldn't tarry so he could lock the door and walk to Caiaphas' house. He had a feeling it was going to be a long night. He took one last look at his tidy little house and latched the door. He saw Simon disappear around the corner, his wife, friend and Benjamin following. He should be with them celebrating. Instead he thought he would be waiting, for what, he didn't know, but he had no choice. How he wished for freedom at this moment. Freedom for all of Israel. Caesar and his Roman army could go back and stay in Rome and let Jerusalem breathe. Simon's words were fresh in his mind. Perhaps Barabbas was smart enough or popular enough that his followers had devised an attack. *Is this the storm Simon sensed coming?* He looked up to see if his dark clouds were on the horizon. Sunset was only a few minutes away. He hurried to the house of Caiaphas. He found himself checking the sky several times as he made his way. It wouldn't surprise him if the dark, gray clouds of Simon's storm rested above the High Priest's house. He almost expected it.

Avi and her family had a quiet dinner. She heard the story of Passover her entire life, but tonight as her mother shared the events that took place so long ago, she watched in amazement how her younger siblings sat straight up paying close attention. As she ate the bitter herbs, she held back tears at the bitterness she felt in her heart. *At least I can rest tomorrow.* She would sleep in and let her brothers and sisters bring her lunch and fuss over her. There was quiet in their neighborhood as everyone settled for their dinner. She knew children everywhere would listen to the retelling of their generations leaving Egypt, free from slavery. She wondered if they would be as astute as her siblings seemed to be this evening. The tiny rooms held them captive. She saw numerous soldiers today, suddenly she felt a chill on the back of her neck. *We're still slaves!* Her mother noticed her shuddering.

"What is it Avi?"

"I'm just tired mother. I think I'll try and sleep now."

With Kezi's help, she now had privacy. There was a small alcove they had fashioned her own room. Several pillows and thick curtains divided the rest of the house and helped with the sound. Simon and Benjamin made her a small table and she lit the small lamp she placed there. She arranged the pillows all along the walls and propped herself up so she could look out the small upper window, the only fresh air that reached her private space. The stars were still sleeping as the sun had only gone down a while ago. She could hear her mother telling the children to be quiet so she could rest. She brought her hand to her mouth to stifle any cries. She had chosen her mother and family over Marcus, over traveling with Claudia seeing the known world. The first star made a bold appearance, the silver sparkle brighter than the oil lamp beside her. She began to weep. Her soft sobs actually a comfort. It was a release. She was happy but not content. She had peace but not love. She had hope but no promise. She stared at the lone star for some time, the solitary light fighting amongst the thousands that began to invade the sky and seemingly overtake the single representation of all her wishes. Her sobs became louder until silenced by her pillow she held firmly to her face.

"Do you want to tell me what's going on with Malchus?" Kezi and Selah walked arm-in-arm as Simon and Benjamin chatted away in front of them. They were walking Selah home. She didn't expect Malchus to join them so she wasn't disappointed when he didn't show up.

"I can't live with a husband who won't talk to me, comes home with too much drink, what kind of life is that?"

"What can I do my friend?"

"Nothing. This is all on Malchus. I'm going to tell him perhaps tomorrow, maybe even tonight that I'll be leaving unless he changes."

"Listen, this will pass. I don't want you going anywhere and where would you go anyway?"

"Home," Selah said.

"Home? Jerusalem is your home."

"No, I would go home to the sea," her faraway look made Kezi stop. Selah had thought about this.

She came home to an empty house. Again, she expected as much so she hoped the disappointment wasn't evident on her face. She thanked Simon and Kezi for walking her home and closed the door to loneliness. She removed her outer garment and vomited her dinner. She pressed a wet rag against her forehead even though she didn't feel feverish. She strained to hear the steps of her husband coming home. She laid there telling herself this could be the last night she slept on this floor, she couldn't be sick, she had plans. She needed to be strong. She knew she could stay with Kezi until she figured out how to get home if Malchus chose to ignore her concerns.

God, why is he doing this now? Has he fallen out of love with me? Is there another? This last question drew her to tears. She let her imagination get the better of her. It was wine, not women. She turned on her side away from the door. She attempted to calm her mind down. It was exhausting.

Malchus had fallen asleep and no one noticed. When he awoke, only a few servants and some of the Temple guard were in the room. Sleep had come to most after dinner and wine. He could hear men speaking but it wasn't Caiaphas so he didn't move. He continued to listen to the distant voices. *Nicodemas!* He got up and went closer to the door.

"Why have you called for me Caiaphas? The Temple? Now?"

His voice echoed down the hallway. The guards were now on alert and commotion filled the house.

"Malchus, come. We're going to the Temple."

Caiaphas didn't stop. He talked as he walked. Something's happened. He felt dread. He knew it was Jesus. His palms began to sweat as he ran after the High Priest, Nicodemas behind him looking straight. The guards seemed to know a secret. He couldn't read their thoughts but there was a menacing look in some of them. Other guards were gathered waiting. He noticed a few of the Sanhedrin were also there. *Caiaphas had called a meeting on Passover?* He was encircled by the council. They spoke in low tones. When they broke the circle, Malchus saw him. Judas. He was one of Jesus's disciples. *What was he doing here? Have they arrested him?* No, he was standing, free of restraints. He was pointing and nodding and he inched closer. He noticed other priests and Pharisees leaving. One was Caiaphas' attendant of the treasury. He heard footsteps behind him. Roman guards! No one could mistake their rhythmic marching, some carried torches; his head was spinning. He couldn't ask any questions. He had to wait to be told. Nicodemas seemed to be arguing with Caiaphas, and then his name was called.

"Malchus!" Caiaphas called.

"I am here."

"You are to go with the soldiers and my guard. Follow this man to where he leads you."

Caiaphas turned and walked away before he could respond. He was pushed along by the motion and movement of the men as they hurried down the steps, each man's sandals a distinct sound in his ear, the sand against the stone familiar. This Judas was moving quickly. He kept strides and when he reached the guard Elias, he finally found his voice.

"Elias, where are we going?"

"We're ordered to follow that man," he simply pointed to Judas.

"But why? Do you know why we're following him?"

"He's leading us to Jesus."

"Why?" Malchus was shoulder-to-shoulder with the guard.

"He's to be arrested for blasphemy."

His throat went dry. He couldn't swallow. *Why would they arrest this man in the middle of the night?* They were in the valley heading towards the olive groves. He felt sick. This was his refuge. *Jesus was here?*

He heard the disciple call out, "This way" and the men picked up their pace.

The line of torches could be seen as the men navigated the small hills. Where would they take Jesus? Caiaphas wouldn't want him at the Temple, or would he? The clanging of the weapons of the soldiers made him nervous. He carried no weapon. *How many followers of Jesus would be here? He wasn't prepared for this!* His heart was beating faster. *Jesus!* They, he, was coming to arrest him! He was sweating. There were more men than he thought following. He saw the Pharisees and officers of the Roman army. This was a well-executed plan. He wanted to run ahead of all of them and begin shouting for Jesus to escape, but no words would form on his lips, his throat unable to swallow, his mouth dry, his stomach turning. He was caught up in this madness, he had no choice. He only stared at Judas, unable to speak. They reached the garden, his beloved groves, his place of escape but this night there was no escape from the plans of Caiaphas. He heard the twigs snap beneath the men's feet, the smell of oil from their lanterns coated the inside of his nostrils. His breathing became labored.

"Rabbi."

He looked to see Judas greet Jesus with a kiss, a sure sign to identify him to those who came to arrest him. Jesus spoke and men were falling to the ground; he stood confused looking for protection, and when the men regained their footing, and he thought they had control of this late-night raid, one of Jesus's disciples burst forth, a large knife in his hand. He stood paralyzed until he felt the cold blade and the warm blood of his severed ear against his neck. The pain was incredible. He fell to his knees, his hand confirming the disciple's action. He was in shock. Things now were moving in slow motion. Blood was pouring through his fingers as he tried to put pressure on his open wound, the guards reaching for Jesus to take him away, some men dropping their torches for their swords and he on his knees in agony, looked up to see Jesus, who spoke with authority to all, commanding his disciple to put away his weapon, challenging those who came to arrest him, and knowing his time had come, and with nowhere to flee from this band of several hundred men, this Jesus walked towards him, bent down, and with humility and love as a fellow servant, touched the place of anger and brought healing and restoration.

The warmth of his hand on his while he lovingly moved it to the side left him speechless. The soldiers yanked Jesus away before he could do or say anything. The bleeding stopped. He reached up to caress the ear, not believing what just happened. His ear was whole. He was shaking. The men were heading back across the valley, the disciples of Jesus disappeared within the shadows of the trees. Except one. Peter. The one Jesus admonished for cutting off his ear. They looked at each other for several moments, he still on his knees, Peter's blood-stained knife tucked in his belt. Another disciple called for him and he turned and ran leaving him on his knees in front of his tree.

Grabbing fistfuls of dirt in both hands, he looked to the sky where he screamed and screamed until no more sound could be heard. He emptied himself of all he was.

Simon hadn't been on his roof for a long time. Tonight, it was clear and warm enough for him to enjoy his stars. He could see Balaam from this vantage point. He had brought him here as Kezi and Benjamin had their hands full with Gray and their merchandise. Besides he missed the donkey. If he had stairs to his roof, Balaam would be watching the stars alongside him. His worn wooden ladder was becoming more of a challenge to have these days. Maybe between Malchus and Benjamin they would build stairs. *Malchus*. Simon hoped he wasn't in any trouble. He prayed he was home by now and he and Selah were talking things out. Something lately had been missing. He knew she was frustrated with him, mostly his late nights with friends and too much wine, but it was something else. He decided to settle down and unrolled his mat.

Humming! That's it! Selah hadn't been humming. She wasn't happy. Malchus would seek him out when he was ready. He wouldn't push him. Selah was quiet through dinner. He caught her several times watching for him. She looked beaten, as if she had lost all hope in their future. *God of Abraham, bless my friends this night and guide them.* He didn't see many stars, only a few dotted the heavens this night. His eyes grew heavy. Joses had let the wine flow freely and Simon had his fill.

Caiaphas was wide awake, pacing the floor waiting for his prize. Only a few servants were keeping watch at the unusual activity this evening. He had given specific instructions to his guard. They were to bring Jesus to Annas, his father-in-law's house. He would see the torches and hear their arrival. He expected them any moment. He had spun his web, whispered in the ears of those who could expedite his plans. Jesus needed to die. He felt no emotion when this thought filled his heart. He had three years thinking about this man and he was finished. Finally, justice would be his. He would question Malchus upon his return of the events at the time of his arrest to ensure Jesus would have no recourse. *What was taking so long?* His father-in-law was not High Priest anymore, he was! It was only out of respect he directed his guard to bring Jesus there first to appease Annas and make him feel he still had influence, which he regrettably knew he did. He could hear men shouting and he walked quickly out to his courtyard. They were here.

"Malchus, we must return," Elias gently placed his hand on his shoulder.

He had stayed in the garden, partially hidden to wait for his friend. He helped him to his feet and examined the restored ear. It was perfect. Malchus reached up and caressed it again, the two men had no words. They walked slowly at first, Malchus quietly talking to himself.

"Malchus, Caiaphas will be wondering where we are."

He nodded his agreement.

"We need to hurry!" Elias exclaimed.

"Where have they taken him?" Malchus asked.

"To Annas."

"Annas? Why?"

"Politics, family," Elias said dully.

Malchus began to run and didn't stop until he reached the palace.

"Mother," Benjamin laid his hand on her arm and waited. "Mother, I can't sleep."

"Benjamin what is it?" she sat up alarmed.

"I can't go to sleep."

"Did you hear something?" she asked.

"Yes. No. I heard it here, not here."

"Tell me Benjamin."

He never pointed to his heart to say he heard something. She brought him close. He settled against her. He loved her more each day and never wanted to see her hurt or troubled so he was reluctant to tell her what kept him from sleep.

"Was it a bad dream son?"

"Maybe."

She didn't want to press him. "We don't have to talk about it now. Why don't you close your eyes and try to sleep?"

"It's when I close my eyes, I see the man."

"What man Benjamin?"

"I don't know."

She pushed the hair from his forehead. "Do you think you've seen him before?"

"I just saw blood."

"Blood!"

"There was blood around the man's head," he spoke in even tones. She swallowed. Before she could speak, he continued.

"That's when I thought I heard a voice say," he swallowed.

"Go on son."

"Malchus is in trouble."

"Malchus!" Her heart began to race.

"But when I closed my eyes again," and now his lips began to quiver. "Oh Benjamin, what is it?"

"I thought I saw Simon."

"Simon? Are you sure?"

He nodded. "He had blood around his head, but the voice said Malchus."

She didn't know what to say. She hadn't realized she began rocking back and forth.

"But then."

"There's more? Tell me Benjamin!"

"I saw that man Jesus. He had blood around his head too! I don't understand what this means mother. I saw and heard all three names and I'm scared."

She continued to rock her son whispering to him she didn't understand either and they should pray for each one. She didn't allow him to see her tears but as he finally slept, she let them fall. She believed God above had showed the boy something and she prayed all would be well when the new day began. She thought of Simon staring up at the sky, he too sensing something amiss, Malchus out drinking his fears away, and Jesus. She heard rumors all week he might be arrested this time while in Jerusalem. *God, what shall I do?* She cradled her son in her arms. She would go to Simon's as soon as Benjamin awoke.

Jesus was bound as they led him to Caiaphas' house. Elias slipped in with the rest of the guard as Malchus hurried before them. He hoped with all the confusion Caiaphas wouldn't notice his absence. He saw members of the Sanhedrin already gathered. He walked around the perimeter of the courtyard assessing who was there and more importantly who wasn't. He didn't see Nicodemas, but as the shadows formed from the fires, he saw the one who struck him. He was looking for Jesus. He reached up again to the right side of his head. He felt the dried blood matting his hair. *Was he awake? Is this a dream? Is this happening?* Just then a soldier struck Jesus and he winced. He couldn't take this. He was only to be arrested and simply told to leave. They were gathered to put him on trial, in the middle of the night! He looked back for the one called Peter. He had moved closer to the fire. Elias was next to him asking him a question. This Peter and another of Jesus's disciples were brave to have come inside the house, and Jesus, how could he look at him? He was ashamed to have been a part of this betrayal, he knew of Caiaphas' plans, he could have warned him. He felt sick. Voices were becoming louder and the air felt cold but he didn't dare go warm himself by the fire. Peter still had his knife. He was a coward this night in more than one way. He vomited where he stood.

The soldiers were ruthless. They were roughing up Jesus, pushing him, striking him with undue cause. Malchus thought some even spat on him. The sun was up now and he saw the dirt beneath his nails and his own blood that had settled all the way down to the inside of his elbow. Elias was propped up against the wall, his eyes half-closed. He gave a low whistle to alert him to Caiaphas. They were taking Jesus to the Temple. Elias shrugged his shoulders and only followed the other guards. Caiaphas had disappeared but he wouldn't take the chance of running home to let Selah know, know what, that he walked with Judas to the place Jesus had gone for the evening to rest but instead had been forcibly taken and arrested. No, he didn't want to tell her that! *My God in heaven, what do I tell her?* They had entered the Judgement Hall. Nicodemas was there. A few others were assembled. Elias looked to Malchus again, they both understood this was formality. Jesus needed to be tried by the council. He kept his head down. He couldn't bear Jesus looking at him knowing he was associated with this group of men. His whole adult life trained to listen, and now he almost prayed his ear would have been left in the garden, covered with ants by now rather than hearing the accusations against Jesus. He purposed to distract himself but the final words spoken in that hall no man could ignore. He didn't know who asked, "Are you then the Son of God," the five words ringing in his ears were, "You say that I AM".

Selah was numb. Malchus never came home. She would leave soon. She was exhausted. Her mind was made up. Kezi couldn't change it, nor Simon and especially not Malchus! She had no more tears left even when she imagined the worst, the tears didn't fall, only the grinding of her teeth. As she lay there, she began to reminisce over every inch of the small stone walls. She started at the door. *What a fool I was thinking he loved me when he carried me over the threshold.* More grinding. Her jaw hurt. That same door had been slammed shut the past several weeks. It represented anger and abandonment, not love and unity. The curtains had been replaced twice, the dust of the streets and the pleasure of Kezi's hand-me-downs a testimony to the small window. The tiny alcove that Malchus had fashioned for herbs and her pretty little ornaments as he called them, looked sad and lonely. She listened for Balaam's bell forgetting Simon had him. Would Malchus allow her to take him? He was her donkey and she would take him! She looked to her left. One wooden box holding her belongings, the weathered wood beginning to crack in the dry climate. She squinted her eyes. Peeking through was her sea colored scarf. It mocked her now. She hadn't worn it in over a year. It laid buried among the other unfulfilled promises. Her teeth couldn't take anymore gnashing. She began to weep.

Kezi knocked on Simon's door for what seemed an eternity, Benjamin at Balaam's side looking as if he was ready to receive bad news. She did her best to remain calm.

"I think Simon has decided to sleep in today," she yelled over her shoulder hoping Simon would hear. She let out a small scream when he called down to her from his roof.

"What's all this noise first thing in the morning? Can a man sleep in on a holiday?"

"Simon!" They both yelled his name at the same time.

"What are you doing up there? Can I climb up?" Benjamin was on the second rung of the ladder when she stopped him.

"No Benjamin, I want to go see Selah now and see if she needs anything."

He looked at his mother and nodded. His dream. She wanted to check on Malchus.

"Wait, I'll go with you," Simon called down.

"We'll be back. Have yourself some breakfast and we'll have lunch together."

He waved and stretched his legs. Balaam was braying. He was probably hungry too. He came down and went into his house to retrieve some apples. He sat down in the hay next to Balaam and the two old friends had breakfast together.

Avi's mother listened to the sobs of her oldest child and cried silently for her on the other side of the curtain she hung. She heard the crowing of roosters and pulled herself up from the floor to attend to her other children. Avi was sleeping soundly. The girl had tossed and turned all night. She felt helpless. She thought about sending her oldest son to find Joanna. She'd been a good friend to Avi, more like an older sister. Avi always seemed better after speaking with her. She would make the request after breakfast.

When Avi's brother reached Herod's to inquire of Joanna, he was met with a roadblock. He'd never seen so many soldiers. He searched the area for any servants, any familiar face he could get a message to. He argued with his mother about the early hour but she insisted he go to ask Joanna to see Avi. He too heard his sister crying and didn't know what was wrong. He saw movement from the corner of his eye. A girl motioned for him to follow her. She led him to a staircase. She put her fingers to her lips indicating him to be quiet. She pointed. There was Jesus. He had on a robe and branches on his head. Herod was laughing. The boy began to shake and hurried back down the stairs, never looking back to see where the girl might have gone. He ran home as fast as he could.

He was out of breath. His mother wouldn't let him speak until he sat and drank some water. He looked at his oldest sister, her eyes still puffy from a night of sadness and now he would bring more sad news.

"Mother, what is it? Why won't you let Jeremias speak? Where have you been that you're out of breath?"

"The upper city, Herod's."

"Herod's?" She looked at her mother again.

Her brother stood up. He was the man of the house. He would turn fourteen this year.

"Mother had me go and request Joanna to come."

"Mother," Avi said, "Why did you send for her?"

"We heard you Avi, you cried throughout the night," Jeremias answered.

"I'm sorry, I didn't mean to keep you awake. Mother, forgive me, I didn't mean to accuse you."

Avi was tired. No one in the house slept.

"Is Joanna on her way?" she began smoothing her hair.

"No, something's happened."

"To Joanna? Tell me now Jeremias!"

"It's Jesus. He's been arrested. I saw him at Herod's."

"No! Did you see Joanna or Chuza?"

"No sister. When I saw all the people and the soldiers I ran back here."

"Soldiers?" Avi asked.

"They're everywhere," he said. "More than usual."

"I'm going to Kezi's. She probably doesn't know. She was going to rest today."

"Can I go with you?" Jeremias asked.

"Would you stay here with the family? If anyone comes, tell them where I went. I'll come back here before I go anywhere else." Avi put on her outer garment and latched the door before they could protest.

Claudia heard her husband summoned very early this morning. The room was dark. It could only mean trouble. She lay there listening, her skin wet with her own sweat. She hadn't slept, images and dreams invading her rest. Pilate had been gone well over an hour, maybe two. Perhaps there was trouble in Rome. They would have to leave. She was ready. She dressed quickly and followed the voices of the men including her husbands to the hall. When she saw her husband circling Jesus, she fell back against the wall.

Her servant close behind whispered to her, "This is the second time this man has been here."

She began to sweat again. "Get word to my husband! Tell him it's urgent! It has to do with this man!"

She couldn't wait any longer. She saw the women who loved Jesus on their knees pleading, screaming his name. They had no regard for anyone but their Master. She grabbed Pilate's arm as soon as he was close enough for her to do so.

"Have nothing to do with this man! I've had many dreams about him!" She glanced over the guards at Jesus, a crown of thorns had been pushed into his head and a robe given him. He stood motionless, not even the calls of his own mother moved him. She ran back to her room overwhelmed with this injustice.

Joanna couldn't speak. She stood behind Mary and the other women praying she could be of some comfort. Jesus was unrecognizable. They had beaten him severely and she closed her eyes to the insanity of the Romans actions. Her lips bled where she chewed them in absolute horror of the treatment of a man who was only arrested. She had seen other prisoners who never received this brutality. She wanted to curse Herod, Pilate and every filthy, lying leader in her city but she saw love standing in front of her and it overrode the darkness she felt in her heart for the former. The wails and cries were becoming unbearable. Her throat was hoarse. She hadn't realized her own moaning and weeping until she met the eyes of Claudia who also looked upon the One they all loved, and in disgust had ran away. The people were shouting for Barabbas! Joanna's legs were weak and trembling. This can't be happening! It wasn't even the third hour! They had to have arrested Jesus in the middle of the night. His wounds were not fresh. She became angry now. She yelled the name of Jesus as loud as she could but the voices of the men drowned out her cause of mercy.

Simon sat waiting for Kezi to return. He knew when the two women got together, it was hard telling when they might get back. He looked over at Balaam.

"Want to go for a walk Balaam? Maybe go to the Temple and look for Malchus?"

The Temple would be busy. He thought perhaps he would take Balaam to see Joses, thank him again for dinner and take a casual walk before the sun got too hot. He and Joses could talk a little business, perhaps have a cup or two of wine!

"Let's go Balaam, it's just me and you."

Kezi and Benjamin couldn't believe how many people were already lining the streets. They should have been at Selah's already. *Simon was on the roof.*

"What do you think he was doing mother?"

"I think he slept up there looking at his stars."

"His stars?" Benjamin laughed.

"Yes. It's become a favorite thing for him to do. So, our Simon is all right," she breathed a little easier.

Benjamin remained silent. The shrill sound of the woman's voice calling Kezi's name gave her goosebumps all over and Benjamin grabbed her leg, something he hadn't done since she first brought him into her home.

"Mary!" "What's the matter?"

Kezi's friend was white, the color drained from her face, her eyes swollen from crying.

"Jesus! They have taken my Lord!"

"Taken?" Kezi asked.

"Arrested! And Kezi, they've beaten him and..." she burst out crying again.

"Wait, where is he? Where have you come from?"

Benjamin hadn't let go of her and she wanted to comfort her friend.

"Caiaphas had him arrested! Oh Kezi, it's awful. His mother is here. They're saying he is to be put to death!"

Kezi fell to the ground and the women cried on each other's shoulders.

"I can't believe this! This makes no sense! Did you see Malchus Mary?"

"No, and I need to go to his mother. Some of the disciples are there."

"Where Mary? Where is he?" She could hardly breathe. She looked at Benjamin. He was as pale as Mary. He repeated his mother's question.

"Where is he?"

"At Pilate's," she was sobbing.

"Did you see him?" the boy asked.

Mary wiping her face seeing the gentleness of the boy answered as calmly as she could, "Yes."

"Did he have blood on his head?"

She covered her mouth to stifle the sounds of her wailing.

Kezi looked at her son. "Benjamin, oh Benjamin!"

"I have to go to him!" Mary began running towards the Temple.

Kezi didn't know what to do. It was Benjamin who grabbed her hand and squeezed it until she looked at him, the people around them beginning to react to the news.

"Come Benjamin, let us go back to Simon's."

They were both silent as they made their way back. Kezi was visibly upset and the last several blocks she began to run calling for Simon. As they got closer, Benjamin pointed, "Balaam's gone!"

"Simon!" "Simon, its Kezi."

There was no sign of them. Benjamin didn't move. He was trembling.

She bent down, "Simon's alright Benjamin, he probably went to Selah's to look for us and take Balaam home. Let's hurry son!"

Malchus was light-headed. He hadn't eaten. The heat, the animals, the band of soldiers, the buildings, everything was sucking the oxygen from his body. His world was in a whirlwind at this very moment. *Selah.* She must be wondering where he was and her thoughts would be wrong this time. They had shuffled Jesus from Pilate to Herod and back again and he could hardly stand. How Jesus stood only proved to him that he indeed was who he said he was. He could hear the wails and shouting of Jesus' name being called over and over again. He knew then his name would echo in his own mind for many days to come. And then he saw Mary. She was hysterical. Her love and affection for her Rabbi on full display, the Roman guard keeping her at bay which only increased her anguish. He wanted to rip out his hair! He searched the faces of all who cried out. They all shared despair.

He searched for Caiaphas. He was nowhere in sight. He could stop this. This was his doing. They were going to put Jesus to death! This was out of hand. What happened to the plan? He was only to be apprehended and spend some time in prison until he learned his lesson. He thought of Selah again. How could he look at her? He thought he could kill Caiaphas with his bare hands! He had betrayed all of them, for what? Religion? Tradition? Politics? Money? Position? Envy? *Which is it Caiaphas he wanted to shout?* He saw Elias and ran over to him.

"Where's Caiaphas?"

Elias pulled him back so he could speak, "The disciple Judas came to give the money back," he said.

"Money?" Malchus could feel the bile rising in his stomach.

"They paid him for his betrayal."

"How much?" Malchus was sick.

"Malchus, what makes the difference now? They're going to crucify this man and two others and there's nothing we can do."

The procession of people already beginning to move after the guards, some shouting for glee at the release of Barabbas, others continuing their chant of "Crucify him", the sound of the women haunting, but the sound of the wooden stake dragging across the stone of the hall's floor would burn in his memory the rest of his life.

He stayed close to Elias as the people pushed towards Golgotha. Many had died on this hill and now this man Jesus would have his turn. It was a cruel joke he thought. He wanted to wake up! This has been the worst dream of his life. The constant travail of the women seeped in his bones. No words would comfort. Another man now carried the cross. He couldn't look upon him. He never felt so dirty. He was a miserable, wretched man! His life was over. Nothing would ever be the same. Selah would loathe him. He was responsible for this! He was taking part of the death of an innocent man. And not any man, a man who proclaimed he was the Christ. The Pharisees were practically marching in step with the Roman centurions. He thought if there was music they would be dancing. *My God, how could he return to the Temple, to Caiaphas?* Simon, Kezi and even Benjamin, they all would hate him, he might as well cast himself off the nearest cliff. They had brought two men, thieves to be put to death as well. He heard no cries for them. It could have been him. He was convinced he would die alone with not one person concerned. He brought on his own shame. They had reached the final destination. A woman's hand clutched his arm.

"Malchus, oh Malchus, can't you stop this? What can be done? Help us Malchus!"

Joanna's plea hurt his ears. There was nothing that could be done. She knew this to be truth. He understood the desperation. He had to look away from her, and Mary, and the disciple who was with Peter, the young man supporting another Mary, the mother of Jesus. He looked behind him. *Would the fall kill him?* He couldn't take anymore.

Simon was enjoying a leisurely stroll. Joses lived just outside the lower city, preferring to live a more nomadic life he liked to say. The additional tent still stood where they had shared dinner and fellowship. Joses was surprised and delighted to see his friend. They sat under the shade and talked of days gone by. The two men had known each other for many years, more than they would like to admit. The sun was growing hotter and Simon decided he should head back. He and Balaam began their second leg of their journey, Simon whistling at such a beautiful day.

He had no idea what time it was but he was hungry and now as he stopped to wipe his face, he wished he would have accepted the invitation to stay for lunch. It had to be about the sixth hour, the sun directly overhead. He didn't think he had walked a Sabbath's journey. He thought of turning around and heading back. He could spend the night and rise early. He would have plenty of time before the weekly Sabbath. Boy, did he like the holidays. He began whistling again, Balaam's bell a nice accompaniment.

Avi heard the cries and the shouts from several blocks away. She was frantic pushing her way through the crowded streets. She followed the roar of the people, stumbling twice and falling against groups of men who were traveling that held on to her a little too long that she screamed at them. Their laughter rang in her ears and she screamed again at all the people in her city. They had no idea what was taking place! How could they? They were smiling and laughing and celebrating their holiday. They had traveled far, many perhaps the first time in Jerusalem. She could see Herod's palace but the crowds and the soldiers blocked her view. Even if she began calling out Joanna's name, her calls would go unheard within the celebratory fervor of the city's temporary inhabitants. She never felt so frustrated in her life. She was past the walls of Herod's palace when there seemed to be a shift of movement. Many turned towards the Temple but the cries that stirred her were coming from the opposite direction. She followed her heart. She ran alongside the crowds, hidden from the guards as she blended in with the surroundings she had grown up with. The crowd was heading towards the place of the skull. Surely Joanna was here, pleading for Jesus, interceding on his behalf. She ran faster trying to reach her friend, wanting to see for herself if this horrible event truly was taking place. She prayed her brother was wrong! Her strides were long as she willed herself to push on. An open path finally appeared and she gasped as she saw Jesus, bloodied and bruised, under the weight of the crude wooden spike they intended to nail him on. She blacked out.

Chapter Twelve

Selah couldn't sit still any longer. She began to pack. She didn't care about anything. She was hurt! Malchus didn't care either, that was clear. She checked outside. No husband, no donkey, no feeling. The high, holy day would be over tonight and she would have one day to inquire who was traveling to Galilee. She began putting her things in order. God knew she had enough. Perhaps she would go to Kezi's and ask to stay until she could locate a group to travel back home. She didn't want to put her in an uncomfortable position. She could stay at the shop. She just wanted to leave. Her small pile of belongings was pathetic. She and Malchus didn't have much. They hadn't needed much, God always provided. She wouldn't cry anymore. It wouldn't be an easy road for her. She opened the front door and stepped into the courtyard.

She began to sweep. She was breaking the law. And again, she didn't care. Let her husband come and judge her. She would give everyone an earful! It was getting warm; the streets were noisy and the dust thick from the crowds. Dust everywhere! She swept harder. She almost hoped Malchus had too much wine, it would give her an advantage. He could just stumble in and go right to sleep. Her broom sweeping knocked over a small clay pot and she began to pick up the small chards. She heard a collective gasp as she reached down to pick them up. She wanted to shout to all her neighbors, *"Yes, take a good, long look, its Sabbath, I'm cleaning. Well guess what, this will be the last time you see me!"* Just as she was about to recite her courageous statement, she realized they were not looking at her at all, they were staring at Malchus.

"They have hung him on a cross," he finally said.

"What?" she couldn't understand him. His lips were dry and cracked and he hardly opened his mouth to speak. His voice was weak.

"Malchus, are you alright?"

He didn't turn, he didn't move. She stood on his left side. His face was dirty. She looked at his hands resting on the table before him. Even his nails had dirt underneath them.

"Malchus, what did you say?"

"He is hanging on a cross. The Romans have crucified him."

"Who Malchus?"

"Jesus." It took him awhile to speak his name. He sounded out every letter. "J e e s u s s s."

"Malchus, no! You must be mistaken!"

"Not mistaken," he said.

"How could this be? Where have you been Malchus? Does Simon and Kezi know? This can't be true!" The tears wouldn't come. She had to know for herself. She was pacing behind him; he hadn't moved a muscle.

"Malchus, tell me, what happened? Malchus, look at me!" she began to shake him a little. That's when she saw the dried blood on his neck and in his hair.

"Malchus! My God, what's happened? You need to talk to me Malchus! What's happening to us?"

He seemed uninjured, but his eyes were dull and blank and she began to imagine horrible things. She couldn't bring herself to ask him what she was thinking.

"Sit down Selah, please," he pulled the chair close to him. He turned to face her.

"Malchus, let me get you something to drink."

"No. Selah, I need to...you need to listen."

"But Malchus, Jesus, oh poor Mary!"

"Caiaphas had Jesus arrested. I've known for some time his plan."

She began to tremble, her fear of his involvement racing her heart.

"His disciple, a man called Judas betrayed him and was paid off."

"Malchus, were you involved? Does this blood on your neck have anything to do with this? Please tell me you're not involved."

"I was at my tree," he stared at nothing.

"What? Malchus, you're not making any sense."

"Jesus was at my tree," his voice was cracking,

She didn't move. "Your tree?"

"His disciple Judas came to tell Caiaphas Jesus was in the garden and would lead us to where he was," he looked at his wife, "I didn't have a choice. I was commissioned to go." She nodded.

"I only thought they would arrest him, perhaps scare him a little and keep him for a few days. I think he and his disciples were praying and when they realized the betrayal of Judas, things got out of hand. His disciple, Peter they call him, he drew a large knife."

"Malchus! Was anyone hurt?"

He turned; his full body vulnerable to her. His eyes not as dull now, he was attempting to swallow but his mouth was dry. He would not eat or drink anything.

"He, Peter, cut off my right ear."

She looked at her husband with his ear intact and thought he was in shock.

"Malchus, perhaps you should lie down."

"He cut off my ear Selah. The blood in my hair, on my neck is mine. I was in disbelief. It happened so quickly. He struck me in defense of Jesus being arrested. I fell to the ground in agony. All the men were shouting and drawing their swords. You know I carry no weapon. Jesus told Peter to put away his knife and then he," tears began to form in his eyes, he was shaking, "he walked towards me, and laid his hand on mine and restored my ear." Tears were streaming down his face.

"This gentle man was praying in a garden, his friend betrayed him, and he took pity on me? Me, a wretch of a man who joined the soldiers to find him, and he touched me Selah. This man, my God, my Jesus!"

The wail that came from her husband sent shivers down her spine. It was a deep, guttural cry, like a wounded animal. He collapsed in her lap and sobbed like a baby. She was paralyzed. She cradled her husband's blood-stained head. He couldn't be comforted. She began to hum. It wasn't long he fell asleep. She couldn't move. She couldn't think. This was too much to comprehend. She looked at her packed belongings.

Her garment was drenched with sweat from his head and his tears. His hands had clutched the sides of her tunic, a desperate plea to hang onto the present, the unchanging wife who had stood by him. And now she was leaving and he didn't know. He walked into what he thought was his safe haven and wasn't aware of the sadness and confusion inside. He had surrendered, not to her, to God, to Jesus, and now she also had a choice to make. She continued to hum with the same blank stare she had seen on him only an hour ago.

Kezi dragged Benjamin through the streets. They were delayed by the unmoving crowds. She wanted to reach Malchus. He would know the truth. They were living a nightmare. When they finally reached Selah's, Kezi knocked and turned the latch calling out to her. Malchus' bloodied head was the first thing she saw and she fainted.

"Mother!" Benjamin bent down calling to her while gently caressing her face. Selah rose to go to her friend.

"Selah, what happened?" she saw Malchus move a little. She grabbed her heart, she thought him dead with his limp body collapsed in her lap. She looked for Benjamin. He was standing next to Malchus, his small frame rocking back and forth as he hugged himself muttering. Selah helped Kezi to her feet.

"Has the world gone mad today? Benjamin, look, I'm alright son."

"But Malchus," he pointed at his matted hair, the traces of dried blood easy to see. First Jesus, now Malchus," he began to cry. "Simon! Where's Simon? I want Simon! He's hurt, I just know it!"

"Oh Selah, has Simon been here?" Kezi asked.

"No, I haven't seen him today."

"We ran into Mary and," she couldn't repeat the words.

"I know. Malchus has told me all. This is a dark day."

Kezi pointed to the door and she led both Selah and Benjamin outside. Benjamin ran around back in hopes to see Balaam and Simon. The two women sat close together.

"I'm devastated! I don't know where to start Selah."

"I'm hoping we're dreaming Kezi. The day is tragic. Jesus! Oh God, can this be true? Nothing makes sense now. He was our hope."

"When Benjamin and I saw Mary; she was so distraught."

"This is horrible!" Selah was exhausted from today's events, her restless nights, Malchus.

Kezi broke out crying. "My God, what's going on? Simon, where are you? Oh, and my Benjamin."

"Benjamin is fine. He's just around back," Selah tried to comfort her friend.

"No, no it's, he had dreams Selah. He didn't sleep. He saw a man with blood on his head."

"Oh Kezi, no!"

"And he saw three men. Jesus, Malchus and Simon."

"What does this mean? Oh Kezi!"

"When we saw Mary and she told us about Jesus, Benjamin asked if he had blood on his head," she covered her mouth in agony, "and now Malchus. What happened? Did someone strike him? And now we can't find Simon," she was sobbing.

"Benjamin must be scared and confused. We'll find Simon."

Both women now cried openly thinking of Jesus put to death. It was a bad dream they wanted to awaken from. Benjamin was in the house talking softly to Malchus. The women saw him hand Malchus a drink but he wouldn't take a sip.

"Come Kezi, let us go inside. Surely Simon will come here. He has to bring back Balaam."

The women felt beaten. They grieved alone. Selah tried to make everyone comfortable while they waited. She pushed her packed belongings behind a pile of sewing materials hoping Malchus or Kezi didn't notice. They hadn't been inside long when Benjamin said, "It's dark outside", pointing to the small window. "Mother, how can it be dark?"

Avi couldn't begin to comprehend the scene before her. She had gotten sick. She and Joanna had fallen back away from the Romans, the Pharisees, Mary and the crowds.

"I can't look upon him. I'm sorry, I just can't Joanna. I want to go home. What can we do?"

Joanna grabbed her friend's arm, "Let us go."

She looked back one more time. How a mother could watch her son die upon this cross she couldn't fathom. Her heart ached for her and Mary; she didn't know if she would survive this. She gritted her teeth. *Herod! What was his participation?* She would tell her husband upon her return he needed to resign from his position. They began to walk slowly down the hill and Avi shuddered.

"I don't feel the sun. There's no cloud."

While they stood, darkness enveloped them and both women began to shake.

The darkness hadn't lifted and both Kezi and Selah were biting their nails. Benjamin fell asleep. Malchus still hadn't eaten or brought drink to his lips. Selah watched every muscle in his face, his eyes had softened but they held unanswered questions.

"Malchus, can you tell me what happened?" Kezi wanted to know.

He and Selah looked at each other. She knew he didn't have the strength to do so. She told her what he said happened and Kezi's tears flowed again. She went over to him and hugged him.

"This day, all that's taken place and now this darkness! Where's Simon? I can't take anymore!"

Her tears woke up Benjamin but she was able to get him right back to sleep. As she covered him, she saw Selah's packed bag. Selah noticed her discovery and hurriedly looked at Malchus. He wasn't paying attention.

"But he was wounded for our transgressions, he was bruised for our iniquities, the chastisement of our peace was upon him, and with his stripes we are healed," Malchus' voice was strong and both Selah and Kezi drew closer to him.

"Malchus, what are you saying?"

"I remember hearing that from the book of Isaiah. I think it's about Jesus. If you saw him, the soldiers," he put his face in his hands, "I'm thankful you didn't. It was merciless."

"Malchus, I don't understand why Jesus had to die, why some wanted him dead. Everyone thought he would deliver us from the

Romans and their rule over us," Selah spoke calmly, evenly. The table began to shake and then one of her small herb clay pots moved and several fell to the floor.

"Malchus!" she screamed.

Caiaphas stood on holy ground. The Temple was everything to him and today he secured all he held true by ensuring the death of the blasphemous Nazarene. He was in the sanctuary, safe from prying eyes. He ignored the darkness that blanketed the city. There would be a logical explanation. As he contemplated this freedom from Jesus and all his disciples, he began to feel his body sway, the floor was moving! He moved to the side when the largest, loudest splitting of rock was heard outside the doors and then to his horror, the next sound he heard had him collapse, the veil separating him from the Holy of Holies, split from top to bottom. He laid on the floor and trembled long after the earth did.

"It seems the darkness is lifting, I must be on my way," Simon stretched. He had been waiting for the sun to peek back from behind the black curtain of sky.

"Be careful my friend," Joses wasn't comfortable with his friend leaving.

"I know these roads, I've traveled them a thousand times, perhaps more. I'll see you in a few days."

Simon hadn't gone far when he realized it was indeed still very dark. He walked slowly; the familiar path hidden before him. His next footstep would be his last. As his sandal touched the ground, the rocks gave way and he and Balaam began tumbling down the hill, rocks falling on them as they rolled to the bottom, and when they came to rest, both man and donkey were entombed in a rocky grave, the earth quaking its sadness.

The women were huddled together, the wind had picked up making the darkness more palpable. Jesus was dead. They didn't think they would ever see light again. When the earth began to move, they screamed in terror. God was angry. The Romans killed His son. Avi and Joanna were each other's comfort. There was no one else to lean on. Defeat stirred in the air around them. Mary and the mother of Jesus, with one of the disciples never moved from the injustice before them. Where would they go now? All the miracles, all the wonders, everything good hung on a tree, the life taken from cruelty and works of evil men. Everyone's hope had been crushed this day. Avi wanted to go home and tell her family how much she loved them, after that was uncertain.

"Joanna, I'm going home. Where will you go?" she asked.

"Home, I guess. Would you like me to walk with you?"

"I would rather be alone," Avi said.

"I'll stay with Mary. I want to find out where the disciples are, if there are needs."

Avi nodded. She couldn't even smile at this kind gesture, so sad was her heart. Only a few remained on top of this hill, the soldiers would stay until ordered elsewhere. She could barely move her legs. She felt weak. She wished she hadn't been eyewitness to this tragedy. She didn't remember coming home, only waking to hear the voice of Marcus.

Selah and Kezi cleaned up the house while Malchus and Benjamin watched them. No one spoke. It had been a day they would never forget and the day was not over which made Selah shudder. This morning she clearly knew what she was going to do. Now in this small house, her husband, an empty shell of the man that stormed out the prior night, still sat with dirty hands and blood-stained skin. It was almost as if he wore them as a testimony to what he experienced in the early hours.

Kezi kept watch on Benjamin. When he was able to, he ran outside looking for Simon, listening for Balaam's bell. *Where was Simon?* Kezi said he had slept on the roof, "Looking at his stars," she told Selah and they both smiled at their love for him. Selah turned to Malchus. She wanted to wait for him to speak but his blank stare told her he still wasn't ready or unable to do so. She grieved. She groaned inside for everyone. Malchus. Simon. Kezi. Benjamin. Mary. Joanna. None of their lives would be the same. How could they be?

"Selah, Benjamin and I, we're going to go back to Simon's and see if he's there," Kezi came close to give her a hug.

"What if he isn't there?" she regretted this question at Kezi's reaction.

"We'll go home and wait for him."

Kezi shut the door quietly, Malchus not noticing any movement. She never felt more alone.

"Malchus, what shall we do?" She couldn't sit any longer. There must be something they could do to get their minds off the reality of what took place in their city today. "Can I get you something to eat?"

He continued to stare. She went outside. The sky had cleared and the sun was bright. She breathed deeply. She looked at the crowded courtyards and streets, life was going on as if nothing happened. *Had they all been dreaming? Is she still?* She went back in and opened the curtains. The light spilled inside and rested on Malchus. She took water and cloth and gently began washing his face and neck. When she started to wash the dried blood behind his right ear, he grabbed her hand and she stopped. It was only when he nodded and released his grip she continued. She bathed his arms, hands and knelt to wash his feet. Malchus overwhelmed with love, suddenly stood and made her sit at the table where he knelt before her and washed her feet. Soon their tiny home came alive with the fragrance of forgiveness and salvation. He looked up into her eyes and she saw the man she had fallen in love with.

"I am born again." It was the first time the tears that had fallen today were of joy.

"Let's go tell Simon and Kezi."

"Avi," Marcus spoke softly.

Her eyes opened slowly as she tried to focus. "Marcus, it is you. Where am I?"

"You're home. I have traveled to," he stopped speaking. With the tragic events of the day, and all she had seen, perhaps this moment wasn't the right time to declare his intentions.

"What are you doing here? How long have I been sleeping? Oh Marcus, the most terrible thing has happened," her frail body began to shake.

"Yes, I know. I've been told everything. Avi, I've come to tell you I love you. I'm asking you to be my wife, I will live here; nothing matters except you."

"Are you certain Marcus?"

He nodded yes. How he had missed her eyes, the strength he desired, he was overwhelmed with her closeness that he could hardly speak. "Yes Avi, I'm here to stay."

Her mother stepped outside to give her daughter privacy. They were all shocked to see Marcus. He told them his caravan was stopped due to a strange darkness and the earthquake, the two events left everyone shaken. They told him about Jesus. He was stunned. His heart leapt when he discovered she was there, unmarried, her mother confirming her love for him. They told him she was working with Kezi. Now holding her in his arms, both their faces wet with tears of happiness, he genuinely relaxed for the first time since leaving Athens.

They talked in the privacy of her room; the curtains parted so her family could share in this joyous time. They needed this, especially today. They detected the somber tone and knew she was telling him of the awful day. He let her speak without interruption. She needed to release all her emotion.

"Do you know where Joanna is now?" he asked.

"I'm not sure. She's probably with Mary and the mother of Jesus. It must have been torture for her. Oh Marcus, it was so awful. There was nothing we could do. The Romans were preventing us to get close, we couldn't even..." she began to cry again.

"Come, rest your mind. Did you see Malchus?"

"No, I could hardly look at anyone. I thought as I stood there watching what was taking place, that my head would be cast down for the rest of my life and nothing would matter. All joy left my heart.

But now," she looked at his warm eyes, "at this very moment, I feel hope rising."

The two men waited patiently. It was inconceivable they would be standing at the door of Pilate humbly requesting the body of Jesus. He gave them his authority and they hurried from this new alliance of Caiaphas as quickly as they dared before the Prefect could change his mind. Nicodemas hadn't seen Malchus. Now he needed him. Actually, he needed his wife's friend. They had hopes of obtaining linen from the shop of Kezi for Jesus. She would have the finest. They needed to find her quickly. The men wasted no time. Their hearts were heavy. They had conspired to kill Jesus. As much as they told themselves they disagreed with Caiaphas, they were responsible. The three hours of darkness and earthquake confirmed their worst fears and also their hope. Jesus was who He said He was. The two men had sat in the darkness together as they waited for the earth to resume to normal.

Kezi tried to keep a smile on her face for Benjamin's sake when they found Simon still not home. They walked in silence back to their own, Kezi hoping the old man would be there mumbling about her whereabouts all day. The two men saw her and the boy coming towards them. Benjamin began running, calling out Simon's name but stopped abruptly when he realized it wasn't him. Nicodemas stepped forward and uncovered his head. She let out a short gasp, *Nicodemas! What's he doing here?* Joseph stayed back while Nicodemas greeted her. With one look he determined she knew about Jesus.

He kissed both her cheeks and said, "I believed in Him too."

She didn't think she could take anymore today but Nicodemas was sincere and she sighed in relief. Benjamin stood at his mother's side only listening.

"Please pardon us for coming to your home like this, I, well, we have a very important and urgent request. May we come inside?"

It was Benjamin who spoke, "Who are we?"

"Ah, yes, my apologies. My friend Joseph, if we could step inside."

As they approached the door Benjamin stopped again. Joseph now uncovered his head, Benjamin looking intently at him.

"Do you know me son?"

He nodded as they all walked inside.

She lit two small lamps and laid them on her table to see the men clearly, the skies having become gray again.

"Kezi, this is my friend Joseph, of Arimathea. He has gone to Pilate and asked for the body of Jesus."

"Greetings Joseph. This is my son Benjamin."

"I know you," Benjamin leaned across the table. His eyes grew wide as he realized. "Mother! This is the nice man I told you about! The night Simon found me I was looking for him. Remember?"

She could only stare now like Malchus, in shock and disbelief of this day. Benjamin was smiling as Joseph remembered and nodded to her the boy was right.

"Pilate has given his authority to remove Jesus' body and we are here hoping you have linen for His burial," Joseph was brief and to the point.

She knew Sabbath was only a short time away. Her tears began to roll down her face again.

"Have I upset you dear? It's just the merchant I usually buy from hasn't been able to travel and Nicodemas said if anyone would have the quality, it would be you. I have brought money," he laid his coin purse on the table.

She pushed the money back towards Joseph as she rose from the table and disappeared into her adjoining room.

He looked at Nicodemas, "Did I offend her, what shall we do?"

She returned within a minute and laid a neatly tied bundle in front of him. He knew it was the finest linen money could buy and this was her private stock, not to be sold but given. She was overcome with emotion she had the ability and means to provide this cloth for her Lord. It was an offering of her heart.

"Please, take this and hurry. I cannot bear to think of Him on that cross."

They prayed over her and the two men left, the coin purse the only evidence they were here.

"Benjamin! Run after them and return the money. That was a gift. Hurry!"

"Joseph knows it was a gift. He gave this to me and told me to give it to my mother just like the first time he gave me coin. He only wanted to bless us mother as you were able to bless him."

She reached for her son, "Tell me, the day you met him; tell me everything."

Malchus and Selah saw the two men leaving Kezi's house, their heads covered, walking quickly the opposite way.

"Who do you think that was?" Selah was curious.

"I don't know, maybe Joses or...," he stopped.

"Or who Malchus?"

"Or someone with news about Simon," he couldn't hide his thoughts now from her. They had stopped to see if Simon had returned home also. They knocked on Kezi's door and called to her.

"Kezi, who were those men?" Selah called out.

"Nicodemas and..."

"Nicodemas!" Malchus ran back out to the street but the men were nowhere in sight. "What was he doing here? Who was with him?" He was pacing.

"His friend, a man named Joseph. They came to buy linen," Kezi said.

"Linen?" Selah asked, looking at her friend with confusion.

"For Jesus. They went to Pilate and asked for his body."

"Oh Malchus, this is incredible!" she looked at Kezi and back to him. "Do you think we should follow them? Where will they take him? Mary must still be there!"

"Yes, I'm certain she hasn't left. Malchus, where do you think Simon might be?" Kezi wouldn't look Benjamin's way. She didn't want him to see the concern in her eyes.

"I don't know. Who saw him last?" he asked.

"We did!" Benjamin said, "This morning before we came to your house."

"Did he say anything?" he asked Kezi.

"No, I told him I was going to check on Selah," she lowered her eyes. She didn't want him to see the concern she also had for her friend.

"I don't know what to do. It's almost Sabbath, that's why Nicodemas and Joseph left so quickly," Kezi said.

He nodded. He was thinking. "Balaam was gone too so Simon must have come to the house to drop him off."

"No Malchus, he never came by," Selah said. "I was awake early, waiting."

Benjamin just stared trying to figure out where Simon and Balaam could be.

"He's bound to come to one of our houses to look for us," Malchus said.

"Unless something's happened to him," Benjamin whispered.

Malchus had a faint memory of the boy getting upset at the blood in his hair and wanted to ask but the looks of both women prevented him.

"Benjamin, put on your shoes," Kezi said.

"Where are we going?"

"To find Simon."

Joanna met Nicodemas and Joseph and brought spices and perfume for the women to prepare. They followed in silence to the sepulcher where Jesus' wrapped body was placed. Joanna didn't know where Mary and those with her were staying and she wouldn't ask. She didn't want to know. Nothing made sense today. She didn't know if more lives were in danger. No one knew what to say. They all looked like they were preparing for their own burial, the life taken from them, each breath now seemed priceless. She wasn't certain how many were gathered, perhaps fifty or more, a son, a Rabbi, a friend, a promise, the One was still, the linen the only contrast to the darkness in their hearts and minds. When she turned to leave, Avi and Marcus stood before her. Marcus held out his arms and she collapsed within them.

"Marcus, I can't believe you're here!" she tried to sound pleasant but was overwhelmed with the surroundings.

He looked over her at the tomb. He knew not many would be able to say they were here the day this Jesus was placed in a garden tomb and even though he didn't understand this culture and fascination with a messiah, today would never be forgotten and he wanted to support Avi and her friends. Joanna stepped back.

"What are you doing here?"

He simply looked at Avi.

"Oh, I see. Where are you staying?"

"That is yet to be determined. I was hoping with Simon. I only arrived today. The darkness and then the earthquake, it's been an interesting day to say the least. I can't believe what's happened. Several on my caravan believe the darkness and earthquake have something to do with Jesus."

"It is strange Marcus," she said. "I was, well we were there when he died and the earth trembled under our feet, as if even it was saddened by his death."

"Why don't we walk you home Joanna," he said.

"Yes, I'm tired and there's nothing more to be done." They said their farewells to those who would not leave their Rabbi's side even in death and began their walk back.

Malchus, Selah, Kezi and Benjamin headed towards Joses' house. Perhaps Simon was invited back for yet another dinner. He didn't pass up too many meals. Kezi and Selah talked the entire time while Malchus and Benjamin led the way.

"I saw your packed bags."

Selah grabbed Kezi's arm. "I'm not leaving. I was until...oh my, Malchus didn't tell you! This day has been so conflicting," she called for him and he and Benjamin stopped.

"Malchus, tell Kezi what we came to tell her," she was smiling.

"Kezi, I'm born again! I truly know what it means now. I have no doubt Jesus is who he said he was. I told Selah I don't understand everything but I have peace that I will, we all will."

She couldn't believe how confident he sounded and they rejoiced. "Malchus, it's answered prayer to hear you say this," she hoped he could see the genuine love she had for him.

The sun would set soon. They picked up their pace. Malchus stopped and began speaking to Benjamin pointing to the side of the road. Kezi and Selah drew closer.

"Look! That rock has been split right down the middle!" He looked around at the fallen rocks collected in piles at the bottom of the valley floor. It was a strong earthquake.

"Perhaps we should go Malchus. The ground may not be finished," Selah was uneasy. They continued walking but now considered every step. He stopped again.

"What is it Malchus?" Benjamin now asked.

He stared down at his feet and turned to look behind him and then again in front. Selah and Kezi stood not moving. They didn't see or hear anything.

He put up his hand, "Listen."

The women looked at each other, they couldn't hear anything but the rustling of their outer garments in the wind.

"There it is! You don't hear it?" he turned every direction trying to determine what he was hearing and where it was coming from.

"The sound travels Malchus," Kezi said. Are you...?"

"Wait, shhh, I hear something moving."

"Maybe it's an animal!" Benjamin said.

"Malchus let's go!" Selah was getting anxious as the sun would soon not provide adequate light.

"Look Benjamin, see how the road seems to be missing right here?" He watched as he instructed the boy to look before and behind him as he just did. "Can you see the difference?"

"Yes, it's like the rocks gave way right here and all those rocks down there fell from here."

"That's right!" He took several steps beyond the place on firmer ground and peered down at the remnants of the road. Selah watched him carefully. She saw him bend over to get a closer look. The next thing she saw was him clutching his heart and falling to his knees.

"Malchus!" "Malchus!"

They all came running. He looked at them with tears streaming down his face and pointed to the large pile of rocks. There was no mistaking the threadbare blanket of Balaam, only half of it exposed, trapped under the mound of limestone and debris, the visible half flying like a flag to mark the accident. He turned to Kezi.

"Stop! Don't come near here!" He didn't want Benjamin to see. He jumped up and moved away from the edge.

"Selah, Kezi, listen! You need to run to Joses' house. Have him bring men, rope, a cart, two, if he has them, blankets, food and drink and you need to run as fast as you can!"

Benjamin held by Kezi, didn't have to look, he knew it was Simon. And Balaam. When he heard Malchus shouting to run to Joses', he took off and Kezi ran after him.

"Oh Malchus, my God, Simon! And my poor Balaam!" Selah was sobbing.

"Selah, you need to go. Hurry!"

"Malchus, what...," she didn't finish as he grabbed both her shoulders.

"Look at me Selah, look!"

It was hard for her not to gaze down hoping to see a sign of life. He shook her a little.

"Don't tarry Selah. I'll put a pile of rocks here to mark the spot for when you return."

"Where are you going? Malchus!"

"I'm going down there to see...to begin removing whatever rocks I can. Have faith Selah. Pray. Now run!"

She took off calling after Kezi and he began carrying and building a good pile of rocks that would be visible from a distance and Joses would know man-made. He let his tears flow easily now, and didn't realize he was sobbing calling out to the Lord in such anguish until he heard that voice again. *Be still and know that I am God.* His wails filled the cavern. *"How can you love me? I'm not worthy!"* Oh God, help me to know all! Help us now! He was spent. His makeshift altar started as a marker. The sun was low in the sky and he began his descent down. He carefully placed each step hoping he wouldn't disturb any loose rocks that would cause further burial. He could see his rock pile and hoped the daylight would last until help arrived. He skidded down the rest of the way, only a small number of broken pieces under his feet. He was overwhelmed, but focused as he studied how the rocks fell, their placement and which ones to remove first. There was a calm and stillness and he inhaled deeply as he removed the top stones that covered his friend.

He threw them as far as he could, a strength building inside of him. He began muttering prayers, prayers he heard as a young boy tossing the rocks now like small pebbles. *Simon.* He whispered his name. *Simon.* He called a little louder. He told Selah to have faith and now as he dug, he wasn't sure if he would get a response.

"Simon, can you hear me?" he shouted.

"Yes, Malchus I can. What took you so long?" Simon's voice was as strong as his stubbornness.

"You old man! What is the meaning of this, dragging us all over Israel to find you underneath this pile of rocks?"

"I love you too son. Now get us out of here!"

"Balaam?" he asked timidly thinking of Selah and Benjamin.

"Well the ol' donkey is as stubborn as me and I think asleep at the moment. We're both beat up a little."

"Don't move," Malchus chided him.

"Like I could," Simon answered.

"I've sent for help to your friend Joses. Is that where you were all day?"

"Yes. Waiting on the women, I would have been waiting all day! So, I took Balaam and went to his place."

Malchus kept removing what he could and finally was able to see all of Simon's face. The toothless grin made him burst out laughing and crying again.

"Do you feel any pain Simon?"

"Well, I can't feel my legs but they don't hurt. Balaam broke my fall."

He tried to raise up and Malchus scolded him. A large rock had pinned both Simon and Balaam. The sun seemed to linger in the sky and he continued to pray under his breath.

"Simon, if I got behind you and tried to pull, do you think the rock would give or would it shift on Balaam?"

"I don't know Malchus, but I'm fine. I can wait for Joses. It might be better if you all lifted the rock to release both of us. What do you say donkey?"

There was no sound. Malchus dug with his hands around Simon's body to get underneath him as much as he could.

"How long do you think you've been here?" Malchus asked.

"I don't know. We left Joses' after a long lunch, and Malchus it was dark! I know these roads and it seemed the darkness was fading and I hadn't been walking too long when the ground began to move and my next step, well the road gave way and down we came! It was perhaps the ninth hour."

Simon's breathing sounded shallow, Malchus knew it was the ninth hour. Simon had been here close to four hours. He heard other rocks falling and stopped moving, glancing all around him. The dull clang of Balaam's bell brought a fresh round of tears. Balaam was moving.

"Relax Balaam, help is on the way!" Simon called to him.

Malchus, drenched with sweat and tears dug as fast as he could. In the distance they heard the shouts of men. It wasn't long they saw the lanterns. He thought he heard music and singing. A small army of men soon emerged. He heard Joses giving orders to his sons and their sons. Several yards away, bundles of rope and supplies begin resting on the earthen floor. A steady stream of light began to appear and the singing became louder.

"I feel like a bride," Simon said and the bridegroom is coming to fetch me!"

Malchus shook his head overwhelmed at what he saw. As soon as some of the men reached the bottom and could illuminate Simon's position, Benjamin got his first glimpse and before anyone could stop him, he was halfway down the hill.

"Simon!" "Simon!" Benjamin only stopped when Malchus grabbed for him.

"Not too close Benjamin. We need to get these larger rocks off. Stand back a little," he spoke gently but firmly to the boy.

He got behind Simon again ready to pull him loose. He could see Balaam's head resting on Simon's legs and to his amazement, saw space between Balaam and the rock that had trapped them. This air pocket was probably what saved them.

"The whole family is here Simon," Joses stood by his side and then crouched down to help Malchus pull him out. Benjamin could see the red in Simon's beard, the same dull, dried blood from scrapes on his face and head. He never wanted to have a dream like this again. The men had torches stuck in the ground and rope tied around the largest stone and waited for Joses to tell them when to pull and lift. Within minutes he was free.

"Hallelujah!" Simon shouted.

Kezi and Selah were being helped down the hill, and with bandages and water they rushed to him. Malchus took charge once again.

"Hold on Selah." He looked at Simon's legs, they didn't seem broken or crushed and he asked him if he could move them.

"Well, if your donkey wasn't laying on top of them perhaps."

"Don't ever do this again!" Kezi told him.

She bent down and showered him with kisses and tears. The women gave him drink and began to fuss over him wiping his face trying to make him comfortable. Benjamin was at Balaam's side speaking softly to him while the men moved the last of the rocks covering him. Malchus was amazed that both his friend and this donkey had no broken bones and suffered no damage. It was a miracle he thought. He looked up into the sky, the stars still hidden and thanked God for their lives. Selah joined Malchus.

"Look around Malchus." Tents had been erected, there were several small fires, and Joses' family were still streaming down the hill with food and blankets.

"When we told Joses what happened, Malchus, I've never seen anything like it. Within a few moments this lovely family began packing and...well it's just wonderful!"

"Simon will see his stars tonight," he said. "He has no idea what's happened today."

"Malchus, this day, what does it mean?"

He already told her he didn't understand, she hoped to make sense of everything. He looked back at Simon, Kezi, Benjamin and Balaam. They all were alright. It had been the most stressful, emotional day of his life. How could anyone make sense of anything today? It was Sabbath and yet with the actions of Joses and his family, Simon was the focus. It was a man, not a law they celebrated. Everyone was thankful to God. He was convinced this is what God wanted, our thanks.

The music and singing began and Malchus took Selah's hand to lead her back to the group. They sang hymns of praise and Joses led everyone in prayer thanking God for Simon's safety and Balaam too. Benjamin never left Simon's side, Kezi either while she made sure he had soup and bread. They decided they would stay until he had strength to climb back up the hill. His legs were swollen and his back hurt. He had scrapes and bruises but everyone knew it could have been much worse. Balaam had bandages too. He had cuts from the jagged rocks on his front legs and seemed quite content listening to the music. The breeze picked up and stirred the cook fires shooting embers high into the sky. The younger children were soon asleep and Benjamin nodding, not wanting to join them until Kezi took him by the hand. He hugged Simon's neck for a long time. Malchus, Selah, Simon and Kezi found themselves around a small fire, the stars winking as they took their place in the heavens.

"Simon, how are you feeling?" Malchus came close to see his full face.

"Malchus, I promise, I feel good."

"No trouble breathing? Nothing hurts inside?"

"Well my side is sore, but I know I have no broken bones, I think just some bruised ribs. I feel so foolish! I should have waited until it was completely light outside."

"But it was the earthquake!" Selah said.

"Yes! Did you see that big rock split right in two?" Simon looked at all of them.

"We saw it, yes," Malchus answered.

"Where were all of you when the darkness came?" Simon asked.

Malchus looked at Selah and Kezi and they seemed to say "You tell him" with their eyes. Simon didn't miss the exchange.

"What are you not telling me?"

"We were at my house Simon. We...it was...I had been up all night," Malchus didn't want to alarm Simon. *How do you tell a man that had been buried under a rock that another man now was buried in one?*

"Jesus was crucified this morning. Caiaphas had him arrested last night. One of his disciples betrayed him. While he hung on the cross, I think God must have closed His eyes and blanketed the earth in sadness and when He died, the earth rebelled."

Selah and Kezi began to weep again as Simon folded his hands over his heart in shock.

"Nicodemas and a man called Joseph came to my house to buy linen. They went to Pilate to ask for His body," Kezi's voice broke. "Oh Simon, it's awful. Mary of course is here and even the mother of Jesus. It's been a difficult, hard day and then when we couldn't find you," she began crying out loud.

"Shhh, there, there now, you found me. I have no words." He turned to Malchus, "Were you there?"

Malchus was tired. He was mentally wiped out. He couldn't repeat to Simon the events at Jesus arrest.

"May we speak tomorrow? I think we should all try and get some rest."

Simon was propped up and Kezi like a mother hen, fluttered about him. He was tucked in a corner, no one could disturb him and she would sleep close by to ensure no one accidentally ran into his legs. She checked his bandages again and said goodnight to Malchus and Selah as they disappeared behind another section of the large tent. Benjamin lay awake. He didn't feel tired and closing his eyes he would most likely fall asleep and dream, and he didn't want that to happen. He crawled over to the side of the tent to peek around the dividing curtain, his mother's body placed in a strategic location. He wanted to sneak over and speak to Simon. So, he waited, checking every few minutes at the children scattered on mats behind him. No one was awake. Except him and Simon. He stayed on his knees and made his way over.

"I heard you Benjamin when you opened the curtain. Come and tell me what you have come to say in this late hour," Simon was smiling.

"I was as quiet as a field mouse; how did you hear me?" Benjamin covered his mouth to not laugh out loud. He began whispering.

"I had a dream."

"Just now?" Simon asked.

"No, the night before."

"Go on my boy, tell me."

"I saw a man with blood on his head," Benjamin said.

Simon waited for him to continue. He had stopped. He looked over and, in the darkness, he could see his furrowed brow, his hesitation.

"Was it me Benjamin?" he finally asked.

"Yes. You were one of them," he said.

"Them?" Simon was curious.

"First, the man I saw, I think it was Jesus. But then somehow the man was Malchus and then it was you."

Simon was thinking and before he could respond Benjamin continued.

"When mother and I ran into Mary, she told us about Jesus and when I asked her if he had blood on his head she began crying and ran."

"So, the man in your dream was Jesus."

"He was the first man. Malchus was next."

"Malchus?" Simon turned and tried to prop himself up on one elbow.

"Yes, when we went looking for you at his house," Benjamin stopped, maybe he shouldn't tell Simon this part. "Simon," he whispered.

"I'm listening Benjamin."

"I won't get in trouble will I if I tell you something, will I?" Benjamin kept his eye on his sleeping mother.

"I don't think so Benjamin. Were you told not to tell me?"

"No," he said.

"Then I think it's all right. You're telling me about your dream."

"But, the dream, it has all come true."

"It has?" Simon asked.

"Jesus had blood on his head and Malchus did too when we saw him."

"Well now Benjamin, Malchus is fine. I don't know what blood you saw."

"He got his ear cut off! He had blood all on his neck and in his hair," the boy's voice was becoming excited.

"Malchus' ear has not been cut off Benjamin. Are you telling me your dream now?"

"No Simon! A man called Peter cut off his ear when they arrested Jesus and Jesus put his ear back on!"

"It's true Simon," Kezi said. She sat up and Benjamin went to her. "Benjamin awakened me with his dream and as he said, when we saw Mary and heard Jesus had been crucified, I feared the worst. When we reached Selah's house, Malchus was sitting at the table, and when Benjamin saw the blood on his head, I fainted. You can imagine how I, how we all felt when we couldn't find you and had no idea where you were."

"And I had blood on my head from the fall," Simon could hardly speak.

"Let Malchus tell you Simon what took place. Benjamin, you need to go back to your mat."

"Have you been awake all this time?" he asked her.

"Of course, I'm your mother. And even field mice make noise."

"May I stay here with you and Simon?" he rested his head on her shoulder.

"Yes, but you'll need to sleep on this side of me," she reached out to touch Simon's legs. The swelling had begun to go down.

"I think this dark day, somehow I knew it was coming," Simon finally said.

"When you were staring at the sky?" Benjamin asked.

"What? Staring at the sky?" Simon repeated.

"The day you hid in the alleyway. You kept looking at the sky," Benjamin said.

"We both saw you," Kezi said.

"Well can an old man go anywhere without your prying eyes?" he was smiling, his heart was smiling.

"Yes, that day, I was watching for storm clouds. I could feel something in the air; that a storm was coming and indeed it has."

Chapter Thirteen

Marcus wondered where everyone was. When he found Simon not at home, he went to Kezi's. He stopped to pat Gray and walked completely around her house. He then went to Malchus and Selah's and found the small house vacant. He went back to Simon's and decided to wait. He climbed the ladder to the roof, it looked like Simon had been up there recently. He settled in for the night. He was so tired his thoughts of all that happened didn't elude him from sleep.

The morning sun beckoned him to rise, the stone warm beneath him. He couldn't wait to see Avi, they had much to discuss. He stood and stretched and examined his surroundings. He liked the rooftop advantage. He didn't like Jerusalem. He loved Avi, had great affection for Joanna and of course Simon and other friends, but this wasn't his home. It seemed backward. Culture and society were progressing but not here. And now with this horrible event of this innocent man Jesus being put to death, he couldn't imagine why anyone would want to live here.

He gave Avi false hope by telling her of his willingness to stay and he would if she truly objected, but he could leave tomorrow and not look back. He didn't understand this city. They were divided in their thinking. He supposed every city was but Jerusalem seemed deep-rooted in their faith to this one god and the one some said was this god's son, who was now dead. He was trying for Avi's sake to reason things out. All their hope was placed on one man's shoulders and now they were wrapped in linen lying in a tomb. He overheard the women; they would prepare the body after their Sabbath with spices and perfume. Avi would join them. Surely Selah and Kezi would be there. He didn't want to go to their Temple and inquire of Malchus. He would be restricted there. Yes, nothing made sense here. Except Avi.

Simon was snoring. He had an audience. Kezi kept watch as the children kept their distance. They giggled behind their hands. Benjamin taught them to count between each outburst. They put up their tiny fingers while some stomped their feet, one, two, three, four, and on five, Simon would snort like an old bull. While they all laughed bent over, he opened one eye and winked at Kezi. On the next count to five he sat up and growled like a bear sending them all screaming and running in every direction.

"That was mean," Kezi said.

"No, that was funny!" he replied.

"How are your legs this morning?" she walked over to see for herself.

"Look, I can bring this one up," he grabbed onto his knee to help make his case.

"Am I the only one that has slept in today?"

"You and Balaam," she laughed.

"How is my old friend?" he asked.

"Benjamin had him up walking today, but you both need another day of rest."

He nodded. She was right. He would try and get up to walk around later with assistance of course.

"Joses and his family have been a blessing to all of us once again. We have all we need. Some of his family left this morning but they're returning tomorrow to help carry everything back."

She handed him some broth. "Eat," she said.

"Where's Malchus?" he asked.

"He's just outside. He's not going anywhere," she drew closer. "Simon, Malchus won't be going back."

"What do you mean?"

"To Caiaphas, to the Temple, to his position," she said.

"You know this for certain?" he held his cup out for more broth.

"How could he Simon? Caiaphas, he planned Jesus' arrest. He was waiting for the right time."

"I want to speak with him about the arrest, what happened last night," he finished his broth and needed to get up. "Kezi, can you go find him for me?"

The two men spent the next few hours talking. No one interrupted them. Selah and Kezi sat outside the tent with the other women and watched the children play. Selah got up quickly and began running, Kezi followed. She looked for some privacy and Kezi stopped until she heard her getting sick.

"Selah are you ill? Shall I get Malchus?"

"No, I'm fine. My stomach has been upset for a few weeks. It's my nerves Kezi, Malchus not coming home, his drinking and now, she looked around, all of this! It's everything."

"How long have you been getting sick like this?" she asked, a smile beginning to form on her lips.

"Like I said, a few weeks, maybe four, ever since Malchus started staying away. Kezi, I was going to leave him! I didn't care about any consequences. I planned to go home," she was leaning back on the rocky wall hoping she was finished vomiting.

"And did you think about the obvious?" Kezi asked.

"What are you talking about?" Selah had no idea why her friend was grinning.

"Selah, I think you're with child."

Her face went white. Kezi saw her eyes searching her mind, calculating and then slowly the color came back and she grabbed Kezi's hands.

"Oh Kezi, I might be," she pulled her closer out of view from the other women. "How will I know?" she asked.

"You will know. Soon, you'll be certain," she saw alarm in Selah's eyes. She made her sit down.

"When you know for certain, you'll tell Malchus. He'll be thrilled! I won't breathe a word and I will do my very best not to look at you any differently until he knows. You're not going home to Tiberias, not now anyway and between me and Simon we'll figure things out for Malchus."

"Caiaphas," Selah whispered.

"Yes, Malchus may need to disappear for a while, perhaps even here among Joses and his family."

Selah shook her head yes, "Thank you Kezi, I don't know what I would do without you."

Avi was singing this morning. Given the last twenty-four hours she shouldn't be, but her heart was glad. Marcus was here. She felt like a young girl. Her family seemed happy for her. She expected him any moment. She wanted to go by Kezi's and Selah's to let them know he returned. Most shops would be closed today. This would be a good day to visit everyone and of course talk about what happened. Her heart grew heavy. She suddenly thought of Claudia. She was married to the man who gave authority for Jesus' death. *Is she singing this morning?* Joanna told her Jesus had been sent to Herod also and that yesterday a new alliance formed between the two men. *These men were irrational! Who would want to live here with this unstable leadership?* She would tell Marcus today she will go to Athens with him if that's what he truly wished. She sat for the longest time at the realization she was prepared to leave her home. She didn't sing the rest of the morning.

Joses and Malchus had Simon up and walking, a few steps at first, only his ankles swollen now and he needed to move. They would stay the night and go home tomorrow. Everyone agreed. Even if Simon had to ride in a cart home, he was determined to leave this ravine. Malchus' pile of rocks was a clever idea to mark this temporary camp.

"Stop staring at my ear," Malchus turned to Simon.

"It's quite remarkable Malchus, almost wish I could have been there! Sliced it right off, did he?"

"Simon!"

"You're right, this is not something to speak lightly about. I can't believe it happened to you. I can't believe the past two days. It doesn't seem real Malchus. Nothing seems real. All you told me, Caiaphas, that night, Jesus, oh my God Malchus, Jesus!"

"My life will never be the same Simon. I can't go back to Caiaphas. I don't know what I'm going to do. I'm questioning everything now. I don't know what Caiaphas is capable of. I don't want to return to my home."

"Would you like me to speak to Joses? Perhaps you and Selah could stay here among his family," Simon wasn't thinking about how that might affect Kezi with Selah not there to help her.

"I'm not a farmer Simon. I'm worried about Selah. It's not fair for her to give up what she loves to do and what, hide out in the desert? I can't do that to her," his voice sounded defeated.

"Are you afraid for your life Malchus? Do you think Caiaphas would seek to harm you?" Simon was concerned hearing him speak about not returning home.

He looked away. All the years of serving Caiaphas, the risk he took, the people he deceived, all for Caiaphas and the pain hit him behind his eyes. He knew Caiaphas wouldn't hesitate to dismiss him, even arrest him if he thought he could somehow jeopardize his position.

"I need to speak to Nicodemas," Malchus said.

"Come, help me to walk some more. Tomorrow we'll return to my house. You and Selah can stay there and we'll find Nicodemas," Simon pushed himself up and Malchus embraced him.

"I'm sorry for the heartache I've brought you," he spoke in Simon's ear. "I'm going to be a better man."

Simon hugged him tighter. "A father will always love his son. Now, let us walk, I have a hill to climb."

Joanna felt lonely. She hadn't slept. Images of Jesus and his suffering made her weak in spirit. All he had done for her and in his time of need, they were helpless to do anything. She grieved for her Lord. She would meet the women to prepare the spices, to help, she couldn't bear it! She would never see the eyes of him who looked at her with such love and compassion, the hands that held her deliverance from every infirmity, the peace she felt in his presence. She buried her face in her hands and wept again. Chuza knocked softly on her door.

"Joanna, you must eat a little, you need your strength," he brought her some broth and she sipped it slowly. He would wait until she finished. She looked at her husband. He looked as tired as she felt.

"Chuza, I can't return to Herod's."

"I understand," he said.

"I want to go with Mary to take the spices...," her lips began to tremble again.

"Pilate has set guards at his tomb," he informed her.

"Guards? Why?" she asked.

"The Pharisees have convinced Pilate Jesus' disciples may try to take his body. Don't concern yourself with this. Please, finish your soup, get some rest. The women will not go until after Sabbath." There was nothing to do but wait.

Marcus couldn't believe Simon never returned and Kezi's house still empty, also Malchus and Selah's. Avi would be wondering where he was. Hardly anyone was out, as if the whole city was in hiding. Avi waited for him at the door. He thought she looked refreshed, there was no doubt she genuinely missed him and was happy he was here.

"Where did you stay? Were you able to see Simon?" she held his hand as they moved to sit down.

"No, he never came home. I slept on his roof! And Kezi's not home or Malchus and Selah. I have gone to each house."

"Marcus, I've been doing a lot of thinking, and I'll go with you to Athens," she said it so matter-of-factly he asked her to repeat it.

"I will live in Athens."

He couldn't contain his excitement. "Avi! Are you sure? What about your mother, your family?" he looked towards the small windows wondering if they were all gathered listening, watching.

"My mother will be fine. My brothers and sisters are older now. They can take care of things."

He drew her close, "It will be very different Avi," he said.

"I'm ready," she assured him.

They walked the quiet neighborhood, he chatted away about his studies, the city, his family and friends. She knew he was relieved. Deep down she knew staying here would have been a sacrifice. Now she would sacrifice all she knew and loved for this one man. She was both excited and anxious. She would have to rely on him for everything. She wasn't used to depending on another. She didn't think she would like it. Kezi wasn't home, her mother wouldn't understand and Joanna, she didn't want to disturb her today as she didn't have any words of comfort.

Joses was pleased to see Simon walking more as the day came to a close. He told his friend he would climb the hill on his own and not be pulled up like a stranded ox. Malchus said it would probably take a couple of oxen to pull him up and the laughter of the men filled the camp. It was a beautiful sunset. It was calm here. Selah felt protected within the clutches of the high rock walls. When no one was watching she ran her hand over her belly. *Was a child growing within?* She didn't want to get her hopes up. Kezi said she would know but she didn't. She trusted she would and wanted to take precautions. She missed her mother now. She would know. She pictured her packed bag at the house. She was prepared to leave and now enclosed in this temporary fortress, it reminded her of home somehow. It was the safe feeling. She heard Malchus laughing. It brought a smile to her lips. She overheard him speaking to Simon about Caiaphas. If he didn't serve Caiaphas, what would he do? If she was pregnant, her work with Kezi would subside. Her heart began to race and then she heard the clang of Balaam's bell. She looked at the donkey with his bandaged legs, and he shook his head at her as if to say, 'I will climb the hill and we'll all be alright,' she began to laugh herself and went inside the tent for a good night's sleep.

The faint tremor awoke Benjamin. Not again. He laid there holding his breath. Everyone was sound asleep. *Maybe he was dreaming.* He closed his eyes. It was dark outside. There were no fires burning, no lanterns lit, complete darkness. He was near the outside of the tent, and on his elbows, he backed up until he was able to exit. The stars were bright but didn't light his way. He carefully stepped to the place they had sat around the fire. He could see Malchus' pile of rocks and leaned back fixing his eyes on the marker. He put his hands on the ground, palms down, the earth was still. He closed his eyes and just listened. He heard nothing. He didn't even hear the snoring of Simon. He had no idea how long he had been sleeping. It had to be close to morning.

The sound of falling pebbles had him sit straight up! He wasn't imagining anything! He was wide awake! He looked at Malchus' pile. The rocks were moving! With a blast, Benjamin watched them fall, the earth shifting underneath him. He sat there unable to move, scared to move without seeing if he too may take a tumble down another hidden chasm. There was no movement from the tents. He looked up to where the rocks had marked their location and the sun began to rise as he saw light filter through the darkness, but it wasn't the sun. The sun rose behind their tent. The brightest light filled the sky. He thought it was a comet. Malchus told him he saw one when he was young but the light wasn't above in the sky, it was filling space. He thought he could touch it; he could feel it on his skin. It was as if it was inside him, warm and flowing. He saw a man standing on the road where the rock pile had fallen. He waved at him and then he was gone. *Jesus. It was Jesus.* Somehow, he knew it was him. But he died. How could this be? He wasn't dreaming.

"No one is going to believe me."

"I do Benjamin."

He looked behind him to see Simon on his knees pointing to where the Light stood.

The city shook once again. It was a strong earthquake. It was early morning, the sun not risen. Caiaphas wouldn't know if there was new damage to the Temple until daylight. His nerves were as shaken as his home. The timing of these earthquakes and the odd darkness was a coincidence. He would accept no other explanation. Nicodemas didn't know about the torn curtain and other damage. Caiaphas hadn't seen him. He hadn't seen Malchus either but given the events of the last three days and the incident with Malchus losing his ear if that were really true, he would not reprimand him. The fact was however, he did think it true. There were too many witnesses. But Jesus was lying in a tomb now and he would never hear of another miracle or healing, raising the dead or other nonsense. It was over. He had accomplished his biggest hurdle and Pilate had played right into his hand. The rumbling had stopped. Caiaphas went back to bed.

Marcus couldn't believe there was another earthquake. He didn't know if he should attempt to leave his rooftop sleeping quarters or take a chance Simon's house would withstand the shaking. He actually felt the earth move and had it been daylight, he was certain he would see the shifting ground. He hoped Avi would be ready to depart soon. The city had been fickle since his arrival. He wanted to tell Joanna goodbye and of course Simon and the others. Avi would tell Kezi today she would be leaving. He knew she had reservations, but there was a new chapter for just the two of them to write. He agreed to an intimate wedding ceremony before leaving. This would be their first challenge. He could barely see the top of the ladder poking the roof line. He was glad the shaking didn't move it from its place.

Balaam trotted up the rocky hill and stood waiting for everyone else to follow. The morning had been one they wouldn't forget. Most of the children slept through the earthquake but Malchus, Selah and Kezi all ran outside of the tent, especially when neither Simon or Benjamin were seen. They packed quickly, all anxious to return to their homes. Selah felt nauseous but this morning she blamed it on her nerves again. Kezi noticed the blank look on both Simon and Benjamin's faces and decided there was enough going on to question them. Malchus stood behind Simon as they helped him up and noticed his altar lay broken in pieces. He looked back down to where they had slept and was thankful no one else would need to mark their location. He and Selah would stay with Simon. They would keep an eye on him until they were certain of his full recovery. They walked in silence, studying the road before them. They stopped several times for Simon's behalf. He refused to be pulled in a cart or carried. The walk home wasn't far. Kezi again caught the exchange between Simon and Benjamin but didn't ask. It was between them.

Marcus heard them before he saw them. He hurried down the ladder and waited for their approach.

"Marcus!" Kezi was the first to see him. "What are you doing here?"

After several greetings and hugs he turned to Simon. "I've been sleeping on your roof for two nights!"

"And you're welcome to stay as long as you like!" Simon answered.

"Where have all of you been?" he looked at each one. Malchus looked different but he couldn't put his finger on it. He saw the bandages on Balaam's legs and the scrapes on Simon's face and arms. "What's happened? You and Balaam having more donkey races?"

"Well that's a story I could tell," Simon laughed. It was Malchus who spoke next.

"When did you arrive Marcus?"

"Right after the earthquake on Friday."

"So, you know all that has taken place?" he asked.

"Yes, unfortunately I do," he said. "It's awful. I've been with Avi and Joanna, and naturally everyone is very distraught. But Simon, did you have an accident?"

"Yes, Balaam and I took a tumble. It was the earthquake, the road we were on just gave way under us. I was with Joses. His family set up camp for us until I could walk."

"How are you feeling now?" Marcus asked.

"Oh, I'm fine. Good to be home. Malchus and Selah will stay with me a few days."

"Marcus, you haven't told us why you're here?" Selah said, but I think we probably know."

"Avi and I, well I came to ask her."

"You're getting married?" Kezi asked.

"Yes, I don't know when but soon," he was smiling.

"And you'll live here in Jerusalem?" she asked. She knew the answer by the look on his face. And Marcus knew she knew. She nodded, "I see."

"See what?" Selah turned to Kezi. "What did I miss?"

"I was just on my way to Avi's. Why don't I bring her back here?" He took the opportunity to leave. He wanted Avi to be the one to tell Selah and Kezi of their plans. He saw the disappointment in Kezi's eyes. He knew he would see it in Joanna's also.

"Kezi, was Marcus saying that he and Avi are leaving?" Selah was confused.

"I'm sure he would rather stay in Athens," Kezi said. "Avi has probably agreed to go this time. We'll be back. We need to go check on Gray and we'll come back."

Malchus and Selah helped Simon inside and she began to open windows to allow fresh air inside. Joses sent ample supplies of food and drink so they didn't need to purchase anything. She started unpacking. She bent down to pick up the rug and became dizzy and she knew. *She was carrying a child.* Kezi said she would know and now she was certain. It was a strange feeling to know. She would tell Malchus when they had privacy. How things changed in a few days was perplexing to her. She was convinced going home was her only answer which meant leaving her husband and now, this life, his seed growing within her, she looked at him with a new, deeper love she didn't think she was capable of until this very moment.

Marcus promised he would walk back to the place they laid Jesus. Avi hoped to see Mary and Joanna. He knew the women would be emotional and as much as he wanted to see Joanna, he didn't relish her poignant questions when Avi confirmed their home would be in Athens. They walked briskly.

"I told Simon we would come back to his house for a proper visit."

"Yes Marcus, I want to see Selah and Kezi and of course tell them our plans."

When they reached Herod's, they sensed something was wrong. There were many soldiers, more than usual and some he recognized from late night dice games. They looked frightened. Avi didn't stop, she pressed through and headed towards the garden. They saw more soldiers. He strained to see beyond them and stopped short. The large stone that had been rolled over the tomb was on the ground. He thought it looked cracked. He didn't know how close they could get. The women were not there. The tomb was empty. Avi let out a small scream. There was confusion here. He saw Pharisees and soldiers speaking in agitated tones.

"Avi, would they have moved the body to another place?" he asked.

She was staring at the large stone.

"Avi, is this a custom?"

She only continued to stare and turned to him.

"Marcus, the soldiers who were placed here to guard this tomb will probably be put to death."

"What?"

"Look, the seal has been broken. Roman law. They may have fallen asleep or perhaps the earthquake caused the stone to fall, but where's Jesus?" He thought immediately of the frightened faces of the soldiers.

"Marcus, this is very strange. Oh, I wish I knew where Mary was."

She was hesitant to leave. *Would the disciples take the body?* She didn't think so. There were laws. *My God, who has Jesus? Why would they remove his body?* She looked again at those gathered. Standing to the side of the group of Pharisees was Nicodemas. He and another man seemed to be smiling. The blood was rushing to her head.

"Marcus, let's leave. Nothing makes sense here anymore."

"I know," Selah whispered to Kezi. She put her finger to her lips and continued, "I'll wait to tell Malchus when we're alone."

Kezi squeezed her hand and nodded her joy for her friend. Marcus and Avi arrived and after everyone greeted each other, it was Marcus who spoke for all of them.

"We went to the place where they laid Jesus," his voice was somber and they nodded thinking it was out of respect. "He's not there."

"Not there?" Malchus rose up. "I don't understand."

"The stone was on the ground. It looked like it was first rolled away and then fell and split in two," Avi said.

"We thought maybe it was from the earthquake earlier," Marcus said.

"But where or why would they take the body?" Kezi asked.

"Were soldiers there?" Malchus wanted to know.

"Yes, there were many and we saw many at Herod's too," Marcus told them.

"Anyone else?" Malchus knew the answer but asked anyway.

"Pharisees, Avi said. Oh, and Nicodemus!"

Simon exchanged looks with Malchus. "What does this mean Malchus?" He didn't look at Benjamin. They would keep to themselves the strange sight of the early morning.

Avi was nervous. She needed to let Kezi know she would be leaving. "I have some news," she finally said. "Marcus and I will be married and then depart for Athens."

"To live?" Simon asked.

"Yes, Avi said softly, she looked at Kezi, "I guess this is my notice to you Kezi."

Kezi reached out to grab her hand, "I'm so happy for you, and you too Marcus! I know we'll miss you terribly."

The friends filled the afternoon with stories, the past few day's events and the impact each one thought it would have. Marcus was surprised when Malchus announced he would not be returning to Caiaphas.

"What will you do?" he asked.

"I haven't thought that through yet." He tried to change the subject. "Meanwhile we will stay with Simon until we know he's able to walk to the market without assistance."

Simon grumbled but knew he wasn't ready. The walk today took twice as long and he was short of breath. Marcus turned to Simon, "Do you have room for me as well?"

"Yes, of course if you like my rooftop!"

"I do like it. It's seldom I sleep outside," he said.

"I may join you tonight," Simon lifted up his cup as if to toast to the idea.

"You're not climbing that ladder old man!" Malchus and Kezi said together.

Simon looked at Benjamin and winked. Kezi and Benjamin rose to go home.

"Simon, I plan to work tomorrow, but we'll stop by here on our way," Kezi said. "If anyone is looking for you, what should we tell them?"

He scratched his beard thinking of some spectacular tale he could relay. He looked at Benjamin, "Do you think you can handle the cart?"

"Yes!" the boy jumped to his feet.

"Oh, Simon I don't know," Kezi said.

"You'll be right there. Benjamin has learned a lot. The people love him and no one would try to fool him."

"Please mother, I'll do a good job," Benjamin was shifting his feet, practically dancing.

"How about we decide in the morning," she said. "I need to sleep on it. That's my final word."

Both Simon and Benjamin nodded their agreement. They talked another hour before Marcus bid them goodnight. Malchus and Selah were tired and it wasn't long they were both sound asleep. Simon waited until he was certain any movement from him wouldn't wake them. He grabbed two cups and a skin of wine and flung the bag over his shoulder. He was halfway up the ladder when Marcus approached the side of the house.

"Simon, do you need help?" he laughed at his persistence.

"No, I've been climbing this ladder for years. We'll have a cup of wine and enjoy the stars tonight!" he said as he handed Marcus the bag. Simon poured them a small cup of wine.

He lifted his cup, "To your impending marriage," they drank together.

Marcus then raised his, "To your hospitality," they drank again.

"To the stars!" Simon cheered.

"To the stars," Marcus repeated. After more cheers to Balaam, friends and no rain, the skin was empty and Marcus yawned ready for sleep. "Must be this night air," he said.

"Yes, that's it!" Simon laughed.

"Goodnight Simon, thank you for a nice evening."

"My pleasure. Don't ever take for granted God's beauty and this wonderful blanket of stars he covers us with every night."

Marcus looked up. It was beautiful. "I won't Simon, goodnight."

Simon wasn't sleepy. He stared up at the stars, happy, content and marveled at all God had showed him the past year. He finally let sleep overtake him and closed his eyes.

Marcus smiled at the old man still sleeping. He quietly went down the ladder and joined Malchus and Selah at the table.

"Simon is still asleep," he said casually.

"Yes, he's quiet this morning," Selah looked over at his mat.

"Selah!" Marcus laughed, "Simon is on the roof!"

Malchus looked over at the pile of clothes and began to laugh. "That crazy old man snuck out!"

"We had a great time looking at his stars," Marcus told them.

"Did he bring up wine?" Malchus asked.

"He did," Marcus answered. "I slept well."

"He's like a kid sometimes," Selah couldn't be mad at him.

"Good morning," Kezi called as she entered the house. "How's our patient today?"

"Sleeping on the roof!" Malchus pointed up enjoying Kezi's surprised look.

"I can't believe he went up there!" she would give him a good scolding when he woke up.

"Can I go wake him up?" Benjamin asked his mother.

"Alright, but be careful and take your time on that ladder," she gave him the look he had grown to love. It said I love you more than life itself. She sat down and asked Marcus if he had heard from Chuza, did he find out anything?

"He wasn't home so...," the scream from Benjamin gave him goosebumps. Kezi sat paralyzed in fear.

"He has fallen! Malchus!"

The men ran outside. Benjamin was nowhere to be seen. Malchus shouted his name. Marcus was halfway up the ladder when he yelled down to Malchus.

"Up here!"

Benjamin was draped over Simon's body sobbing, his words incoherent. Marcus rushed to Simon's side. He was gone. His body temperature already changing, Marcus thought he probably died several hours ago. He looked at Malchus and shook his head.

"No, oh God no!" Malchus sat back while Marcus continued to confirm what they all knew, Benjamin wailing, "Wake up Simon! Please wake up!"

Selah was standing at the bottom of the ladder, the tears flowing freely down her face, the men's voices and Benjamin's cries heard plainly. She vomited right there, not from her pregnancy, but from sheer sorrow. Kezi somehow managed to get up and by the time she rounded the corner of the house, Malchus was bringing Benjamin down, the boy limp in his arms. Without saying a word, he walked past the women and laid the boy down to let him grieve alone. Marcus was comforting Kezi when he returned and took Selah in his arms.

"My God what's happening? We found him! We brought him home."

Their tears were one. Both their cheeks wet with grief for their dear friend, Kezi sobbing on Marcus. A few neighbors began walking over, they knew they needed to get Simon off the roof. Marcus volunteered for anything they might need. He was touched by the love they had for their friend. Malchus told Selah to take Kezi inside. She was inconsolable.

"What do you think he died from Marcus?" Malchus knew he had medical knowledge.

"Given that he fell, he may have had internal bleeding that shut down his organs or heart failure."

It was difficult to see Malchus upset. He was trying hard to stay strong for Selah and Kezi and the young boy who had been like Simon's own grandson. Marcus put his arm around his shoulder.

"He was a good man, he loved you and Selah, Kezi and the boy, all his friends were family."

Malchus nodded and sniffled.

Marcus continued, "He had a beautiful night Malchus, he loved his stars!"

Malchus burst into sobs again at this fond remembrance.

"I believe he had a peaceful rest," Marcus wasn't sure what else to say. Peaceful rest he said. You were born and then you died. He wasn't certain of anything else.

"Malchus, what needs to be done? Shall I inform anyone else? Is there something I can do?"

"I can't think. Maybe you should go tell Avi and Joanna. We need, we bury our people right away. I can't believe he's gone."

Just then he heard Balaam's bell and the donkey began braying. It was too much for him. He sank to the ground and bawled like a baby. Selah came back out and Marcus left him in her hands and said he would be back within the hour. He would tell Avi and Joanna, they would know what to do. The last four days in this city had been a whirlwind. No one would believe it unless they experienced it themselves. He ran all the way to Avi's.

Kezi kept a close eye on Benjamin. He had curled himself up and sank into the deepest corner he could find. He was sleeping from pure anguish. Kezi and Selah were attended to by Simon's neighbors and one had gone to tell Joses.

"Our lives have turned completely upside down the past few days and I've ran out of words." Selah had not been able to eat, drink, think or speak until it was only she and Kezi in the house. Malchus helped bring Simon down and they had him covered next door.

"Selah, I'm not sure I want to stay here," Kezi's voice was weak.

"Do you wish to go back to your house?"

"No, I mean I don't know if I want to stay in Jerusalem," Kezi said.

"Where would you go? What would you do?"

"Where were you going?" she looked up and saw Selah's face was as drained as hers.

"I was going home," she said.

"Maybe I should too," Kezi looked over at her son. He hadn't moved. "I don't know how this will affect him."

"Malchus doesn't want to return to our home," Selah said quietly. She got up and shut the door, and sat next to Kezi. "Perhaps we all should go to Galilee, start fresh up there."

"I could open a shop. I would be closer to the trade routes," Kezi said.

"I don't know what Malchus will do," Selah said.

"We'll figure it out," Kezi had the first hint of a smile.

"We'll?" Selah countered.

"Yes, it's settled. I, we, will go home," Kezi said firmly.

The two women sat in the silence of grief and promise of a new beginning. Strength and hope became their banner and as much as they mourned for Simon, they knew he would have joined them and encouraged them the entire way.

"Selah," Kezi looked at her friend.

"Yes, what is it Kezi?"

"It's going to be fine, isn't it?"

"Yes, it is."

Avi wept on Marcus' chest. She couldn't believe it.

"Everyone loved Simon, he will be greatly missed. I need to go to Joanna's and I want to return quickly to help."

He didn't need her to finish, they knew Simon would be buried today. When Joanna answered the door, she knew by the expressions on their faces something else happened. She gathered spices and money and told them to hurry, they needed to find out where Simon could be laid. She was willing to purchase a place if no other preparations were made. Chuza was coming in as they were going out.

"Where are you going?" he could see they were all distressed.

"We have sad news Chuza," Marcus said. "Simon died in his sleep last night."

"Were you leaving to go to his house?" Chuza stood next to his wife.

"Yes, everyone's there," Marcus said.

"I'll come with you."

When they arrived back at Simon's, a fresh set of tears could be heard as the women comforted one another. Benjamin rested his head on Malchus' arm holding it with both hands. Malchus nodded his greeting not disturbing the boy's hold. They were all in shock again. Joses was next door with his family preparing Simon as they knew it would be too emotional for them, especially Kezi and the boy. He would be carried to the land by his house and placed in a cave that had been in his family for decades. It was an honor he told them to do this for his friend. They talked in low tones and decided they would stay there and let Joses bid farewell to his longtime friend. Chuza had news. He waited until Benjamin went out to check on the donkeys.

"Gather around everyone," he motioned for them to come away from the door. "The confusion you saw yesterday by Herod's and at the tomb where they put Jesus was indeed because the body was gone. I've heard, there is rumor the Roman guards have been paid to give a false statement that the disciples of Jesus came and stole his body."

"That can't be," it was Avi who spoke. "I told Marcus how they put a seal on the tomb and it would be certain death if a Roman guard slept on the job or disobeyed."

"Yes, the guards that were there, they're very afraid because," he leaned in, "they say the stone was rolled away by angels and Jesus is alive! Mary has seen him!" Chuza kept his voice low, Joanna remained silent. Marcus was having a difficult time processing this and the women had their hands on their heart or over their mouth.

"The disciples fear for their arrest and are in hiding," Chuza continued. He looked at each of them, "This is hard to believe but throughout the city those who have died were seen walking in the streets."

Malchus hadn't breathed. Marcus couldn't remain seated. Avi was nervous, she saw his disbelief. He was ready to leave this city and all these fables he heard. Kezi and Selah were whispering to each other. There was a hush that commanded the room.

Joanna grabbed her husband's hands. "He said in three days I will rise."

"I believe," Malchus was smiling. "I believe He has risen," his voice was a little stronger. "I believe!" he was almost laughing. "My God, I believe Jesus has risen and He is... He is God!"

No one noticed Benjamin at the door.

"I believe too Malchus, me and Simon saw him yesterday." He ran into his arms and the next few hours Simon's small home was filled with dancing, laughter, rejoicing, love and his family.

"Tiberias? You want to go home?" Malchus was staring at Selah with an open mouth.

"Yes Malchus, it's time. We haven't been home. We can't hide here at Simon's house."

"We're not hiding," he said. She looked at him until he thought about what he said.

"Alright, we haven't left here for a week. You're right Selah, we need to go somewhere, but Tiberias?"

"I would like to raise our family where I grew up," she sat down to be eye level with him.

"Yes, I guess that would be nice eventually," he nodded.

"That's why I want to go now," she smiled.

"Now, today?" he laughed.

"Well the first member of our family will be here soon and with the travel and finding a place and of course I want to get settled," she was rambling.

"Selah. Wait a minute. What did you say?" he missed something.

"I said I'll want to get settled," her smile was bigger.

"Selah!"

"Yes?"

"Are you saying what I think you're saying?" he was on his knees in front of her.

She grabbed his hand and brought it over her stomach. He laid his head in her lap. He had never been so completely happy and full of joy. "We can leave tomorrow," he said.

"Malchus, not tomorrow but soon," she stroked his hair. "Malchus if it's a boy..."

"It will be a boy and we will name him Simon."

She exhaled. Her breath was warm on his face. They stayed there a long time enjoying the quiet and peace of Simon's house. She heard the ladder put up again. She walked over to the window and listened. Malchus was praying on the roof. His voice was strong and confident. She laid back down reflecting on all that had changed in their lives in one very short week. She smiled to herself. She had her husband back. She was going to have his baby. She was going home. They needed to plan. He came back in and settled once again by her.

"I want to find the disciple they call Peter."

"Malchus, why?" she was alarmed.

"I just know I'm supposed to," he brought her close. "He can teach us Selah. I want to know more about Jesus, what He said, and this Peter can tell me."

"How will we find him?" she asked.

"Joanna," he smiled.

Kezi watched Benjamin attend to both Balaam and Gray, spending more time with Balaam. The donkey still wore a bandage. She was amazed at her son. He shared with her the morning of the last earthquake when he felt the earth move under his hands and then the miraculous light, the man Jesus and how this moment, this wonder was one of the last memories he shared with Simon and how happy he was to have that in his heart, and he was sure if Jesus was alive after dying, then Simon was too and that's all he needed to know. It had given him great comfort. She talked to him about leaving.

"Where shall we go mother?"

"Galilee. Actually, a city called Tiberias. They have a huge market."

He listened as she told him about the sea and Malchus and Selah would be going too.

"So, we would all be together," he said.

"Yes."

"When would we go mother?"

"Soon."

Chuza and Joanna needed to travel back to Herod's home and their own. His palace in Jerusalem had served them well but they both missed their home, the sea, the place where Jesus started his ministry. Their hearts were full. He is who He said He was. Joanna would speak to Marcus. Perhaps she could convince him to come to Tiberias for a year. Avi wouldn't be far from home, Marcus may be surprised at the city and feel quite at home himself. Most of those she had come to know who followed Jesus had already headed back. She would continue to aid the disciples in whatever means she could. She would see Malchus and Selah today to inform them of her departure.

Selah heard the familiar bell and she thought of Simon and all the moments they shared over this donkey. She ran out to greet him. She hugged him while he nuzzled her neck. "Did you miss me Balaam?"

"He did Selah," Benjamin said. He knew she was thinking of Simon. "He misses him too," he added.

"I think we're all agreed to go to Tiberias," Kezi said. Malchus and Selah nodded yes.

"I'm going to learn to fish," Benjamin said.

"Me too!" Malchus gave him a wink.

"This all seems so final doesn't it? Will we return to live here? Selah, shall we go to your house and collect the things you want to bring?" Kezi asked. She wondered even now if Caiaphas had the Temple guard watching their home. "Benjamin and I can manage quite a bit. We can take Gray and Simon's cart."

"I'll go with you," Selah said. "There isn't too much."

"When shall we leave?" Kezi asked Malchus.

"I can't go to the upper city. How will I see Joanna? When are Marcus and Avi leaving?" he asked the women.

"They didn't say," Selah said. "Should we go now Kezi?"

"Yes, let's not delay. Now that we've made decisions, I'm ready to leave. I'm having a hard time standing here in Simon's house and I can't imagine going to the market without him by my side. I'm ready to leave Jerusalem. I didn't think I would ever leave, but with all that's happened, I am," she had her hand on the door. She was startled when someone knocked on it. It was Joanna.

"Joanna, we're all going to Tiberias. We need help," Malchus said.

"Wait! Why are you traveling to Tiberias?" she looked at each one.

"We're leaving Jerusalem. We're moving there," Kezi said.

"All of you?" Joanna asked.

"Yes. We plan to leave right away," Malchus told her.

Joanna was smiling, "We're heading back. We'll also leave in the next few days. It would be wise if we all travel together. We will be escorted however," she looked at Malchus, "Are they looking for you Malchus?"

"I don't know. I just know I can't return to Caiaphas. Whatever God has planned for me, I'm ready to accept."

"Herod's guards are from the Galilee region. They travel with us between Tiberias and Jerusalem. They don't know who you are. It's settled! We'll go together."

Balaam and Gray were loaded with two carts full of their belongings. Joanna assured them they didn't need to worry about anything else, *it had been provided* she simply said. Selah grew emotional as she gathered her hidden bag and other personal items they would bring. She was thankful Kezi was with her.

"Your child will be born in your hometown. It's exciting, is it not? We'll start again. I'm sad too Selah, but I'm anxious to see what lies ahead."

"Yes, I am too. Kezi. I don't have any more words. It's as if all our lives were waiting to come to this time, that all we've experienced, the people that have been closest to us, it's this moment that somehow has been waiting for us," she fumbled at her words and could tell by Kezi's expression she wasn't making her point.

"It's the unknown," Kezi said. "We don't know what tomorrow will bring, but we're moving forward with faith and hope that there's purpose in this new challenge and I think more importantly, we're going together, as family. There's a bond between us and our dear Simon was instrumental in our lives being woven together. It doesn't seem fair he's not embarking on this journey with us."

"In a way he is," Selah smiled and patted her stomach. "Malchus has told me we're having a boy and he will be called Simon."

"So, Simon is going with us!" Kezi clapped her hands. "And when we see that toothless grin for the first time," both women didn't know to laugh or cry.

Joanna knocked on Avi's door. Marcus answered it.

"Perfect! You're just the man I wanted to see," Joanna felt energized today. She was going home, and friends were coming with her. Like Malchus, she didn't waste time.

"Sit! I have something to say."

"Joanna, please tell us its good news," Avi said.

"Yes, Avi it is! We're going to Tiberias, and Malchus, Selah, Kezi and Benjamin are coming too," Joanna started.

"They're escorting you home?" Avi asked.

"They're moving back! Remember both Selah and Kezi are from the area and Kezi's very excited to open a shop, which you Avi can work and Marcus, have you ever been to Tiberias?" Joanna hardly took a breath. He nodded no.

"Well I think you two should come with us. Give it a year. Marcus, you can study there and we will make our trips back here for the feasts, Avi would be closer to her family, and our custom is a one-year honeymoon so, think of it as a honeymoon at sea," she exhaled.

Marcus saw the look in Avi's eyes which said everything.

"We will honeymoon in Tiberias," he said, "if we marry tonight!"

They stood outside the Fortress of Antonia, Jerusalem behind them; the empty tomb in front. Joanna would tell them all she hid in her heart and promised Malchus he would meet Peter. Kezi and Benjamin never looked back, their eyes on a new beginning that awaited them. Marcus and Avi would stay in the back of the small caravan for privacy as their journey began as one.

Selah glowed in the warm sunlight, her joy reached the banks of the sea she soon would walk, the familiar sounds calling to her, beckoning her return. Malchus had written two letters. She watched as he relinquished them to Elias to hand deliver to Caiaphas and Nicodemas. She didn't ask about the contents; she knew they held truth. Jesus changed everything.

CPSIA information can be obtained
at www.ICGtesting.com
Printed in the USA
BVHW041748131120
R11460100001B/R114601PG593172BVX17B/8